# Diamond Hands

**GME GO BRRR. TLDR: Its literally just 150 pages of GME GO BRRR. You've been warned.**

David Adams

Copyright © 2021 David Adams
All rights reserved.
ISBN:  9798734108604

# <u>Chapter 1</u>

## The Final and Only Chapter

**GME GO BRRRRRRRRRRRRRRRRRRRRRRRRRRRRRRRRR
RRRRRRRRRRRRRRRRRRRRRRRRRRRRRRRRRRRRR
RRRRRRRRRRRRRRRRRRRRRRRRRRRRRRRRRRRRR
RRRRRRRRRRRRRRRRRRRRRRRRRRRRRRRRRRRRR
RRRRRRRRRRRRRRRRRRRRRRRRRRRRRRRRRRRRR
RRRRRRRRRRRRRRRRRRRRRRRRRRRRRRRRRRRRR
RRRRRRRRRRRRRRRRRRRRRRRRRRRRRRRRRRRRR
RRRRRRRRRRRRRRRRRRRRRRRRRRRRRRRRRRRRR
RRRRRRRRRRRRRRRRRRRRRRRRRRRRRRRRRRRRR
RRRRRRRRRRRRRRRRRRRRRRRRRRRRRRRRRRRRR
RRRRRRRRRRRRRRRRRRRRRRRRRRRRRRRRRRRRR
RRRRRRRRRRRRRRRRRRRRRRRRRRRRRRRRRRRRR
RRRRRRRRRRRRRRRRRRRRRRRRRRRRRRRRRRRRR
RRRRRRRRRRRRRRRRRRRRRRRRRRRRRRRRRRRRR
RRRRRRRRRRRRRRRRRRRRRRRRRRRRRRRRRRRRR
RRRRRRRRRRRRRRRRRRRRRRRRRRRRRRRRRRRRR
RRRRRRRRRRRRRRRRRRRRRRRRRRRRRRRRRRRRR
RRRRRRRRRRRRRRRRRRRRRRRRRRRRRRRRRRRRR**

RRRRRRRRRRRRRRRRRRRRRRRRRRRRRRRRRRRRRRRRRRRRRRRRRRRR
RRRRRRRRRRRRRRRRRRRRRRRRRRRRRRRRRRRRRRRRRRRRRRRRRRRR
RRRRRRRRRRRRRRRRRRRRRRRRRRRRRRRRRRRRRRRRRRRRRRRRRRRR
RRRRRRRRRRRRRRRRRRRRRRRRRRRRRRRRRRRRRRRRRRRRRRRRRRRR
RRRRRRRRRRRRRRRRRRRRRRRRRRRRRRRRRRRRRRRRRRRRRRRRRRRR
RRRRRRRRRRRRRRRRRRRRRRRRRRRRRRRRRRRRRRRRRRRRRRRRRRRR
RRRRRRRRRRRRRRRRRRRRRRRRRRRRRRRRRRRRRRRRRRRRRRRRRRRR
RRRRRRRRRRRRRRRRRRRRRRRRRRRRRRRRRRRRRRRRRRRRRRRRRRRR
RRRRRRRRRRRRRRRRRRRRRRRRRRRRRRRRRRRRRRRRRRRRRRRRRRRR
RRRRRRRRRRRRRRRRRRRRRRRRRRRRRRRRRRRRRRRRRRRRRRRRRRRR
RRRRRRRRRRRRRRRRRRRRRRRRRRRRRRRRRRRRRRRRRRRRRRRRRRRR
RRRRRRRRRRRRRRRRRRRRRRRRRRRRRRRRRRRRRRRRRRRRRRRRRRRR
RRRRRRRRRRRRRRRRRRRRRRRRRRRRRRRRRRRRRRRRRRRRRRRRRRRR
RRRRRRRRRRRRRRRRRRRRRRRRRRRRRRRRRRRRRRRRRRRRRRRRRRRR
RRRRRRRRRRRRRRRRRRRRRRRRRRRRRRRRRRRRRRRRRRRRRRRRRRRR
RRRRRRRRRRRRRRRRRRRRRRRRRRRRRRRRRRRRRRRRRRRRRRRRRRRR
RRRRRRRRRRRRRRRRRRRRRRRRRRRRRRRRRRRRRRRRRRRRRRRRRRRR
RRRRRRRRRRRRRRRRRRRRRRRRRRRRRRRRRRRRRRRRRRRRRRRRRRRR
RRRRRRRRRRRRRRRRRRRRRRRRRRRRRRRRRRRRRRRRRRRRRRRRRRRR
RRRRRRRRRRRRRRRRRRRRRRRRRRRRRRRRRRRRRRRRRRRRRRRRRRRR
RRRRRRRRRRRRRRRRRRRRRRRRRRRRRRRRRRRRRRRRRRRRRRRRRRRR
RRRRRRRRRRRRRRRRRRRRRRRRRRRRRRRRRRRRRRRRRRRRRRRRRRRR
RRRRRRRRRRRRRRRRRRRRRRRRRRRRRRRRRRRRRRRRRRRRRRRRRRRR
RRRRRRRRRRRRRRRRRRRRRRRRRRRRRRRRRRRRRRRRRRRRRRRRRRRR
RRRRRRRRRRRRRRRRRRRRRRRRRRRRRRRRRRRRRRRRRRRRRRRRRRRR
RRRRRRRRRRRRRRRRRRRRRRRRRRRRRRRRRRRRRRRRRRRRRRRRRRRR
RRRRRRRRRRRRRRRRRRRRRRRRRRRRRRRRRRRRRRRRRRRRRRRRRRRR
RRRRRRRRRRRRRRRRRRRRRRRRRRRRRRRRRRRRRRRRRRRRRRRRRRRR
RRRRRRRRRRRRRRRRRRRRRRRRRRRRRRRRRRRRRRRRRRRRRRRRRRRR

RRRRRRRRRRRRRRRRRRRRRRRRRRRRRRRRRRRRRRRRRRRR
RRRRRRRRRRRRRRRRRRRRRRRRRRRRRRRRRRRRRRRRRRRR
RRRRRRRRRRRRRRRRRRRRRRRRRRRRRRRRRRRRRRRRRRRR
RRRRRRRRRRRRRRRRRRRRRRRRRRRRRRRRRRRRRRRRRRRR
RRRRRRRRRRRRRRRRRRRRRRRRRRRRRRRRRRRRRRRRRRRR
RRRRRRRRRRRRRRRRRRRRRRRRRRRRRRRRRRRRRRRRRRRR
RRRRRRRRRRRRRRRRRRRRRRRRRRRRRRRRRRRRRRRRRRRR
RRRRRRRRRRRRRRRRRRRRRRRRRRRRRRRRRRRRRRRRRRRR
RRRRRRRRRRRRRRRRRRRRRRRRRRRRRRRRRRRRRRRRRRRR
RRRRRRRRRRRRRRRRRRRRRRRRRRRRRRRRRRRRRRRRRRRR
RRRRRRRRRRRRRRRRRRRRRRRRRRRRRRRRRRRRRRRRRRRR
RRRRRRRRRRRRRRRRRRRRRRRRRRRRRRRRRRRRRRRRRRRR
RRRRRRRRRRRRRRRRRRRRRRRRRRRRRRRRRRRRRRRRRRRR
RRRRRRRRRRRRRRRRRRRRRRRRRRRRRRRRRRRRRRRRRRRR
RRRRRRRRRRRRRRRRRRRRRRRRRRRRRRRRRRRRRRRRRRRR
RRRRRRRRRRRRRRRRRRRRRRRRRRRRRRRRRRRRRRRRRRRR
RRRRRRRRRRRRRRRRRRRRRRRRRRRRRRRRRRRRRRRRRRRR
RRRRRRRRRRRRRRRRRRRRRRRRRRRRRRRRRRRRRRRRRRRR
RRRRRRRRRRRRRRRRRRRRRRRRRRRRRRRRRRRRRRRRRRRR
RRRRRRRRRRRRRRRRRRRRRRRRRRRRRRRRRRRRRRRRRRRR
RRRRRRRRRRRRRRRRRRRRRRRRRRRRRRRRRRRRRRRRRRRR
RRRRRRRRRRRRRRRRRRRRRRRRRRRRRRRRRRRRRRRRRRRR
RRRRRRRRRRRRRRRRRRRRRRRRRRRRRRRRRRRRRRRRRRRR
RRRRRRRRRRRRRRRRRRRRRRRRRRRRRRRRRRRRRRRRRRRR
RRRRRRRRRRRRRRRRRRRRRRRRRRRRRRRRRRRRRRRRRRRR

RRRRRRRRRRRRRRRRRRRRRRRRRRRRRRRRRRRRRRRRRRRR
RRRRRRRRRRRRRRRRRRRRRRRRRRRRRRRRRRRRRRRRRRRR
RRRRRRRRRRRRRRRRRRRRRRRRRRRRRRRRRRRRRRRRRRRR
RRRRRRRRRRRRRRRRRRRRRRRRRRRRRRRRRRRRRRRRRRRR
RRRRRRRRRRRRRRRRRRRRRRRRRRRRRRRRRRRRRRRRRRRR
RRRRRRRRRRRRRRRRRRRRRRRRRRRRRRRRRRRRRRRRRRRR
RRRRRRRRRRRRRRRRRRRRRRRRRRRRRRRRRRRRRRRRRRRR
RRRRRRRRRRRRRRRRRRRRRRRRRRRRRRRRRRRRRRRRRRRR
RRRRRRRRRRRRRRRRRRRRRRRRRRRRRRRRRRRRRRRRRRRR
RRRRRRRRRRRRRRRRRRRRRRRRRRRRRRRRRRRRRRRRRRRR
RRRRRRRRRRRRRRRRRRRRRRRRRRRRRRRRRRRRRRRRRRRR
RRRRRRRRRRRRRRRRRRRRRRRRRRRRRRRRRRRRRRRRRRRR
RRRRRRRRRRRRRRRRRRRRRRRRRRRRRRRRRRRRRRRRRRRR
RRRRRRRRRRRRRRRRRRRRRRRRRRRRRRRRRRRRRRRRRRRR
RRRRRRRRRRRRRRRRRRRRRRRRRRRRRRRRRRRRRRRRRRRR
RRRRRRRRRRRRRRRRRRRRRRRRRRRRRRRRRRRRRRRRRRRR
RRRRRRRRRRRRRRRRRRRRRRRRRRRRRRRRRRRRRRRRRRRR
RRRRRRRRRRRRRRRRRRRRRRRRRRRRRRRRRRRRRRRRRRRR
RRRRRRRRRRRRRRRRRRRRRRRRRRRRRRRRRRRRRRRRRRRR
RRRRRRRRRRRRRRRRRRRRRRRRRRRRRRRRRRRRRRRRRRRR
RRRRRRRRRRRRRRRRRRRRRRRRRRRRRRRRRRRRRRRRRRRR
RRRRRRRRRRRRRRRRRRRRRRRRRRRRRRRRRRRRRRRRRRRR
RRRRRRRRRRRRRRRRRRRRRRRRRRRRRRRRRRRRRRRRRRRR
RRRRRRRRRRRRRRRRRRRRRRRRRRRRRRRRRRRRRRRRRRRR
RRRRRRRRRRRRRRRRRRRRRRRRRRRRRRRRRRRRRRRRRRRR
RRRRRRRRRRRRRRRRRRRRRRRRRRRRRRRRRRRRRRRRRRRR
RRRRRRRRRRRRRRRRRRRRRRRRRRRRRRRRRRRRRRRRRRRR
RRRRRRRRRRRRRRRRRRRRRRRRRRRRRRRRRRRRRRRRRRRR

RRRRRRRRRRRRRRRRRRRRRRRRRRRRRRRRRRRRRRRRRRRRRRRR
RRRRRRRRRRRRRRRRRRRRRRRRRRRRRRRRRRRRRRRRRRRRRRRR
RRRRRRRRRRRRRRRRRRRRRRRRRRRRRRRRRRRRRRRRRRRRRRRR
RRRRRRRRRRRRRRRRRRRRRRRRRRRRRRRRRRRRRRRRRRRRRRRR
RRRRRRRRRRRRRRRRRRRRRRRRRRRRRRRRRRRRRRRRRRRRRRRR
RRRRRRRRRRRRRRRRRRRRRRRRRRRRRRRRRRRRRRRRRRRRRRRR
RRRRRRRRRRRRRRRRRRRRRRRRRRRRRRRRRRRRRRRRRRRRRRRR
RRRRRRRRRRRRRRRRRRRRRRRRRRRRRRRRRRRRRRRRRRRRRRRR
RRRRRRRRRRRRRRRRRRRRRRRRRRRRRRRRRRRRRRRRRRRRRRRR
RRRRRRRRRRRRRRRRRRRRRRRRRRRRRRRRRRRRRRRRRRRRRRRR
RRRRRRRRRRRRRRRRRRRRRRRRRRRRRRRRRRRRRRRRRRRRRRRR
RRRRRRRRRRRRRRRRRRRRRRRRRRRRRRRRRRRRRRRRRRRRRRRR
RRRRRRRRRRRRRRRRRRRRRRRRRRRRRRRRRRRRRRRRRRRRRRRR
RRRRRRRRRRRRRRRRRRRRRRRRRRRRRRRRRRRRRRRRRRRRRRRR
RRRRRRRRRRRRRRRRRRRRRRRRRRRRRRRRRRRRRRRRRRRRRRRR
RRRRRRRRRRRRRRRRRRRRRRRRRRRRRRRRRRRRRRRRRRRRRRRR
RRRRRRRRRRRRRRRRRRRRRRRRRRRRRRRRRRRRRRRRRRRRRRRR
RRRRRRRRRRRRRRRRRRRRRRRRRRRRRRRRRRRRRRRRRRRRRRRR
RRRRRRRRRRRRRRRRRRRRRRRRRRRRRRRRRRRRRRRRRRRRRRRR
RRRRRRRRRRRRRRRRRRRRRRRRRRRRRRRRRRRRRRRRRRRRRRRR
RRRRRRRRRRRRRRRRRRRRRRRRRRRRRRRRRRRRRRRRRRRRRRRR
RRRRRRRRRRRRRRRRRRRRRRRRRRRRRRRRRRRRRRRRRRRRRRRR
RRRRRRRRRRRRRRRRRRRRRRRRRRRRRRRRRRRRRRRRRRRRRRRR
RRRRRRRRRRRRRRRRRRRRRRRRRRRRRRRRRRRRRRRRRRRRRRRR
RRRRRRRRRRRRRRRRRRRRRRRRRRRRRRRRRRRRRRRRRRRRRRRR
RRRRRRRRRRRRRRRRRRRRRRRRRRRRRRRRRRRRRRRRRRRRRRRR

RRRRRRRRRRRRRRRRRRRRRRRRRRRRRRRRRRRRRRRRRRRR
RRRRRRRRRRRRRRRRRRRRRRRRRRRRRRRRRRRRRRRRRRRR
RRRRRRRRRRRRRRRRRRRRRRRRRRRRRRRRRRRRRRRRRRRR
RRRRRRRRRRRRRRRRRRRRRRRRRRRRRRRRRRRRRRRRRRRR
RRRRRRRRRRRRRRRRRRRRRRRRRRRRRRRRRRRRRRRRRRRR
RRRRRRRRRRRRRRRRRRRRRRRRRRRRRRRRRRRRRRRRRRRR
RRRRRRRRRRRRRRRRRRRRRRRRRRRRRRRRRRRRRRRRRRRR
RRRRRRRRRRRRRRRRRRRRRRRRRRRRRRRRRRRRRRRRRRRR
RRRRRRRRRRRRRRRRRRRRRRRRRRRRRRRRRRRRRRRRRRRR
RRRRRRRRRRRRRRRRRRRRRRRRRRRRRRRRRRRRRRRRRRRR
RRRRRRRRRRRRRRRRRRRRRRRRRRRRRRRRRRRRRRRRRRRR
RRRRRRRRRRRRRRRRRRRRRRRRRRRRRRRRRRRRRRRRRRRR
RRRRRRRRRRRRRRRRRRRRRRRRRRRRRRRRRRRRRRRRRRRR
RRRRRRRRRRRRRRRRRRRRRRRRRRRRRRRRRRRRRRRRRRRR
RRRRRRRRRRRRRRRRRRRRRRRRRRRRRRRRRRRRRRRRRRRR
RRRRRRRRRRRRRRRRRRRRRRRRRRRRRRRRRRRRRRRRRRRR
RRRRRRRRRRRRRRRRRRRRRRRRRRRRRRRRRRRRRRRRRRRR
RRRRRRRRRRRRRRRRRRRRRRRRRRRRRRRRRRRRRRRRRRRR
RRRRRRRRRRRRRRRRRRRRRRRRRRRRRRRRRRRRRRRRRRRR
RRRRRRRRRRRRRRRRRRRRRRRRRRRRRRRRRRRRRRRRRRRR
RRRRRRRRRRRRRRRRRRRRRRRRRRRRRRRRRRRRRRRRRRRR
RRRRRRRRRRRRRRRRRRRRRRRRRRRRRRRRRRRRRRRRRRRR
RRRRRRRRRRRRRRRRRRRRRRRRRRRRRRRRRRRRRRRRRRRR
RRRRRRRRRRRRRRRRRRRRRRRRRRRRRRRRRRRRRRRRRRRR
RRRRRRRRRRRRRRRRRRRRRRRRRRRRRRRRRRRRRRRRRRRR
RRRRRRRRRRRRRRRRRRRRRRRRRRRRRRRRRRRRRRRRRRRR
RRRRRRRRRRRRRRRRRRRRRRRRRRRRRRRRRRRRRRRRRRRR
RRRRRRRRRRRRRRRRRRRRRRRRRRRRRRRRRRRRRRRRRRRR
RRRRRRRRRRRRRRRRRRRRRRRRRRRRRRRRRRRRRRRRRRRR
RRRRRRRRRRRRRRRRRRRRRRRRRRRRRRRRRRRRRRRRRRRR

RRRRRRRRRRRRRRRRRRRRRRRRRRRRRRRRRRRRR
RRRRRRRRRRRRRRRRRRRRRRRRRRRRRRRRRRRRR
RRRRRRRRRRRRRRRRRRRRRRRRRRRRRRRRRRRRR
RRRRRRRRRRRRRRRRRRRRRRRRRRRRRRRRRRRRR
RRRRRRRRRRRRRRRRRRRRRRRRRRRRRRRRRRRRR
RRRRRRRRRRRRRRRRRRRRRRRRRRRRRRRRRRRRR
RRRRRRRRRRRRRRRRRRRRRRRRRRRRRRRRRRRRR
RRRRRRRRRRRRRRRRRRRRRRRRRRRRRRRRRRRRR
RRRRRRRRRRRRRRRRRRRRRRRRRRRRRRRRRRRRR
RRRRRRRRRRRRRRRRRRRRRRRRRRRRRRRRRRRRR
RRRRRRRRRRRRRRRRRRRRRRRRRRRRRRRRRRRRR
RRRRRRRRRRRRRRRRRRRRRRRRRRRRRRRRRRRRR
RRRRRRRRRRRRRRRRRRRRRRRRRRRRRRRRRRRRR
RRRRRRRRRRRRRRRRRRRRRRRRRRRRRRRRRRRRR
RRRRRRRRRRRRRRRRRRRRRRRRRRRRRRRRRRRRR
RRRRRRRRRRRRRRRRRRRRRRRRRRRRRRRRRRRRR
RRRRRRRRRRRRRRRRRRRRRRRRRRRRRRRRRRRRR
RRRRRRRRRRRRRRRRRRRRRRRRRRRRRRRRRRRRR
RRRRRRRRRRRRRRRRRRRRRRRRRRRRRRRRRRRRR
RRRRRRRRRRRRRRRRRRRRRRRRRRRRRRRRRRRRR
RRRRRRRRRRRRRRRRRRRRRRRRRRRRRRRRRRRRR
RRRRRRRRRRRRRRRRRRRRRRRRRRRRRRRRRRRRR
RRRRRRRRRRRRRRRRRRRRRRRRRRRRRRRRRRRRR
RRRRRRRRRRRRRRRRRRRRRRRRRRRRRRRRRRRRR
RRRRRRRRRRRRRRRRRRRRRRRRRRRRRRRRRRRRR
RRRRRRRRRRRRRRRRRRRRRRRRRRRRRRRRRRRRR
RRRRRRRRRRRRRRRRRRRRRRRRRRRRRRRRRRRRR
RRRRRRRRRRRRRRRRRRRRRRRRRRRRRRRRRRRRR

RRRRRRRRRRRRRRRRRRRRRRRRRRRRRRRRRRRRRRRRRRR
RRRRRRRRRRRRRRRRRRRRRRRRRRRRRRRRRRRRRRRRRRR
RRRRRRRRRRRRRRRRRRRRRRRRRRRRRRRRRRRRRRRRRRR
RRRRRRRRRRRRRRRRRRRRRRRRRRRRRRRRRRRRRRRRRRR
RRRRRRRRRRRRRRRRRRRRRRRRRRRRRRRRRRRRRRRRRRR
RRRRRRRRRRRRRRRRRRRRRRRRRRRRRRRRRRRRRRRRRRR
RRRRRRRRRRRRRRRRRRRRRRRRRRRRRRRRRRRRRRRRRRR
RRRRRRRRRRRRRRRRRRRRRRRRRRRRRRRRRRRRRRRRRRR
RRRRRRRRRRRRRRRRRRRRRRRRRRRRRRRRRRRRRRRRRRR
RRRRRRRRRRRRRRRRRRRRRRRRRRRRRRRRRRRRRRRRRRR
RRRRRRRRRRRRRRRRRRRRRRRRRRRRRRRRRRRRRRRRRRR
RRRRRRRRRRRRRRRRRRRRRRRRRRRRRRRRRRRRRRRRRRR
RRRRRRRRRRRRRRRRRRRRRRRRRRRRRRRRRRRRRRRRRRR
RRRRRRRRRRRRRRRRRRRRRRRRRRRRRRRRRRRRRRRRRRR
RRRRRRRRRRRRRRRRRRRRRRRRRRRRRRRRRRRRRRRRRRR
RRRRRRRRRRRRRRRRRRRRRRRRRRRRRRRRRRRRRRRRRRR
RRRRRRRRRRRRRRRRRRRRRRRRRRRRRRRRRRRRRRRRRRR
RRRRRRRRRRRRRRRRRRRRRRRRRRRRRRRRRRRRRRRRRRR
RRRRRRRRRRRRRRRRRRRRRRRRRRRRRRRRRRRRRRRRRRR
RRRRRRRRRRRRRRRRRRRRRRRRRRRRRRRRRRRRRRRRRRR
RRRRRRRRRRRRRRRRRRRRRRRRRRRRRRRRRRRRRRRRRRR
RRRRRRRRRRRRRRRRRRRRRRRRRRRRRRRRRRRRRRRRRRR
RRRRRRRRRRRRRRRRRRRRRRRRRRRRRRRRRRRRRRRRRRR
RRRRRRRRRRRRRRRRRRRRRRRRRRRRRRRRRRRRRRRRRRR
RRRRRRRRRRRRRRRRRRRRRRRRRRRRRRRRRRRRRRRRRRR
RRRRRRRRRRRRRRRRRRRRRRRRRRRRRRRRRRRRRRRRRRR

RRRRRRRRRRRRRRRRRRRRRRRRRRRRRRRRRRRRRRRRRRRR
RRRRRRRRRRRRRRRRRRRRRRRRRRRRRRRRRRRRRRRRRRRR
RRRRRRRRRRRRRRRRRRRRRRRRRRRRRRRRRRRRRRRRRRRR
RRRRRRRRRRRRRRRRRRRRRRRRRRRRRRRRRRRRRRRRRRRR
RRRRRRRRRRRRRRRRRRRRRRRRRRRRRRRRRRRRRRRRRRRR
RRRRRRRRRRRRRRRRRRRRRRRRRRRRRRRRRRRRRRRRRRRR
RRRRRRRRRRRRRRRRRRRRRRRRRRRRRRRRRRRRRRRRRRRR
RRRRRRRRRRRRRRRRRRRRRRRRRRRRRRRRRRRRRRRRRRRR
RRRRRRRRRRRRRRRRRRRRRRRRRRRRRRRRRRRRRRRRRRRR
RRRRRRRRRRRRRRRRRRRRRRRRRRRRRRRRRRRRRRRRRRRR
RRRRRRRRRRRRRRRRRRRRRRRRRRRRRRRRRRRRRRRRRRRR
RRRRRRRRRRRRRRRRRRRRRRRRRRRRRRRRRRRRRRRRRRRR
RRRRRRRRRRRRRRRRRRRRRRRRRRRRRRRRRRRRRRRRRRRR
RRRRRRRRRRRRRRRRRRRRRRRRRRRRRRRRRRRRRRRRRRRR
RRRRRRRRRRRRRRRRRRRRRRRRRRRRRRRRRRRRRRRRRRRR
RRRRRRRRRRRRRRRRRRRRRRRRRRRRRRRRRRRRRRRRRRRR
RRRRRRRRRRRRRRRRRRRRRRRRRRRRRRRRRRRRRRRRRRRR
RRRRRRRRRRRRRRRRRRRRRRRRRRRRRRRRRRRRRRRRRRRR
RRRRRRRRRRRRRRRRRRRRRRRRRRRRRRRRRRRRRRRRRRRR
RRRRRRRRRRRRRRRRRRRRRRRRRRRRRRRRRRRRRRRRRRRR
RRRRRRRRRRRRRRRRRRRRRRRRRRRRRRRRRRRRRRRRRRRR
RRRRRRRRRRRRRRRRRRRRRRRRRRRRRRRRRRRRRRRRRRRR
RRRRRRRRRRRRRRRRRRRRRRRRRRRRRRRRRRRRRRRRRRRR
RRRRRRRRRRRRRRRRRRRRRRRRRRRRRRRRRRRRRRRRRRRR
RRRRRRRRRRRRRRRRRRRRRRRRRRRRRRRRRRRRRRRRRRRR
RRRRRRRRRRRRRRRRRRRRRRRRRRRRRRRRRRRRRRRRRRRR

RRRRRRRRRRRRRRRRRRRRRRRRRRRRRRRRRRRRRRRRRR
RRRRRRRRRRRRRRRRRRRRRRRRRRRRRRRRRRRRRRRRRR
RRRRRRRRRRRRRRRRRRRRRRRRRRRRRRRRRRRRRRRRRR
RRRRRRRRRRRRRRRRRRRRRRRRRRRRRRRRRRRRRRRRRR
RRRRRRRRRRRRRRRRRRRRRRRRRRRRRRRRRRRRRRRRRR
RRRRRRRRRRRRRRRRRRRRRRRRRRRRRRRRRRRRRRRRRR
RRRRRRRRRRRRRRRRRRRRRRRRRRRRRRRRRRRRRRRRRR
RRRRRRRRRRRRRRRRRRRRRRRRRRRRRRRRRRRRRRRRRR
RRRRRRRRRRRRRRRRRRRRRRRRRRRRRRRRRRRRRRRRRR
RRRRRRRRRRRRRRRRRRRRRRRRRRRRRRRRRRRRRRRRRR
RRRRRRRRRRRRRRRRRRRRRRRRRRRRRRRRRRRRRRRRRR
RRRRRRRRRRRRRRRRRRRRRRRRRRRRRRRRRRRRRRRRRR
RRRRRRRRRRRRRRRRRRRRRRRRRRRRRRRRRRRRRRRRRR
RRRRRRRRRRRRRRRRRRRRRRRRRRRRRRRRRRRRRRRRRR
RRRRRRRRRRRRRRRRRRRRRRRRRRRRRRRRRRRRRRRRRR
RRRRRRRRRRRRRRRRRRRRRRRRRRRRRRRRRRRRRRRRRR
RRRRRRRRRRRRRRRRRRRRRRRRRRRRRRRRRRRRRRRRRR
RRRRRRRRRRRRRRRRRRRRRRRRRRRRRRRRRRRRRRRRRR
RRRRRRRRRRRRRRRRRRRRRRRRRRRRRRRRRRRRRRRRRR
RRRRRRRRRRRRRRRRRRRRRRRRRRRRRRRRRRRRRRRRRR
RRRRRRRRRRRRRRRRRRRRRRRRRRRRRRRRRRRRRRRRRR
RRRRRRRRRRRRRRRRRRRRRRRRRRRRRRRRRRRRRRRRRR
RRRRRRRRRRRRRRRRRRRRRRRRRRRRRRRRRRRRRRRRRR
RRRRRRRRRRRRRRRRRRRRRRRRRRRRRRRRRRRRRRRRRR
RRRRRRRRRRRRRRRRRRRRRRRRRRRRRRRRRRRRRRRRRR
RRRRRRRRRRRRRRRRRRRRRRRRRRRRRRRRRRRRRRRRRR
RRRRRRRRRRRRRRRRRRRRRRRRRRRRRRRRRRRRRRRRRR
RRRRRRRRRRRRRRRRRRRRRRRRRRRRRRRRRRRRRRRRRR

RRRRRRRRRRRRRRRRRRRRRRRRRRRRRRRRRRRRRRRRR
RRRRRRRRRRRRRRRRRRRRRRRRRRRRRRRRRRRRRRRRR
RRRRRRRRRRRRRRRRRRRRRRRRRRRRRRRRRRRRRRRRR
RRRRRRRRRRRRRRRRRRRRRRRRRRRRRRRRRRRRRRRRR
RRRRRRRRRRRRRRRRRRRRRRRRRRRRRRRRRRRRRRRRR
RRRRRRRRRRRRRRRRRRRRRRRRRRRRRRRRRRRRRRRRR
RRRRRRRRRRRRRRRRRRRRRRRRRRRRRRRRRRRRRRRRR
RRRRRRRRRRRRRRRRRRRRRRRRRRRRRRRRRRRRRRRRR
RRRRRRRRRRRRRRRRRRRRRRRRRRRRRRRRRRRRRRRRR
RRRRRRRRRRRRRRRRRRRRRRRRRRRRRRRRRRRRRRRRR
RRRRRRRRRRRRRRRRRRRRRRRRRRRRRRRRRRRRRRRRR
RRRRRRRRRRRRRRRRRRRRRRRRRRRRRRRRRRRRRRRRR
RRRRRRRRRRRRRRRRRRRRRRRRRRRRRRRRRRRRRRRRR
RRRRRRRRRRRRRRRRRRRRRRRRRRRRRRRRRRRRRRRRR
RRRRRRRRRRRRRRRRRRRRRRRRRRRRRRRRRRRRRRRRR
RRRRRRRRRRRRRRRRRRRRRRRRRRRRRRRRRRRRRRRRR
RRRRRRRRRRRRRRRRRRRRRRRRRRRRRRRRRRRRRRRRR
RRRRRRRRRRRRRRRRRRRRRRRRRRRRRRRRRRRRRRRRR
RRRRRRRRRRRRRRRRRRRRRRRRRRRRRRRRRRRRRRRRR
RRRRRRRRRRRRRRRRRRRRRRRRRRRRRRRRRRRRRRRRR
RRRRRRRRRRRRRRRRRRRRRRRRRRRRRRRRRRRRRRRRR
RRRRRRRRRRRRRRRRRRRRRRRRRRRRRRRRRRRRRRRRR
RRRRRRRRRRRRRRRRRRRRRRRRRRRRRRRRRRRRRRRRR
RRRRRRRRRRRRRRRRRRRRRRRRRRRRRRRRRRRRRRRRR
RRRRRRRRRRRRRRRRRRRRRRRRRRRRRRRRRRRRRRRRR
RRRRRRRRRRRRRRRRRRRRRRRRRRRRRRRRRRRRRRRRR
RRRRRRRRRRRRRRRRRRRRRRRRRRRRRRRRRRRRRRRRR

RRRRRRRRRRRRRRRRRRRRRRRRRRRRRRRRRRRRRRRRRRRRRRR
RRRRRRRRRRRRRRRRRRRRRRRRRRRRRRRRRRRRRRRRRRRRRRR
RRRRRRRRRRRRRRRRRRRRRRRRRRRRRRRRRRRRRRRRRRRRRRR
RRRRRRRRRRRRRRRRRRRRRRRRRRRRRRRRRRRRRRRRRRRRRRR
RRRRRRRRRRRRRRRRRRRRRRRRRRRRRRRRRRRRRRRRRRRRRRR
RRRRRRRRRRRRRRRRRRRRRRRRRRRRRRRRRRRRRRRRRRRRRRR
RRRRRRRRRRRRRRRRRRRRRRRRRRRRRRRRRRRRRRRRRRRRRRR
RRRRRRRRRRRRRRRRRRRRRRRRRRRRRRRRRRRRRRRRRRRRRRR
RRRRRRRRRRRRRRRRRRRRRRRRRRRRRRRRRRRRRRRRRRRRRRR
RRRRRRRRRRRRRRRRRRRRRRRRRRRRRRRRRRRRRRRRRRRRRRR
RRRRRRRRRRRRRRRRRRRRRRRRRRRRRRRRRRRRRRRRRRRRRRR
RRRRRRRRRRRRRRRRRRRRRRRRRRRRRRRRRRRRRRRRRRRRRRR
RRRRRRRRRRRRRRRRRRRRRRRRRRRRRRRRRRRRRRRRRRRRRRR
RRRRRRRRRRRRRRRRRRRRRRRRRRRRRRRRRRRRRRRRRRRRRRR
RRRRRRRRRRRRRRRRRRRRRRRRRRRRRRRRRRRRRRRRRRRRRRR
RRRRRRRRRRRRRRRRRRRRRRRRRRRRRRRRRRRRRRRRRRRRRRR
RRRRRRRRRRRRRRRRRRRRRRRRRRRRRRRRRRRRRRRRRRRRRRR
RRRRRRRRRRRRRRRRRRRRRRRRRRRRRRRRRRRRRRRRRRRRRRR
RRRRRRRRRRRRRRRRRRRRRRRRRRRRRRRRRRRRRRRRRRRRRRR
RRRRRRRRRRRRRRRRRRRRRRRRRRRRRRRRRRRRRRRRRRRRRRR
RRRRRRRRRRRRRRRRRRRRRRRRRRRRRRRRRRRRRRRRRRRRRRR
RRRRRRRRRRRRRRRRRRRRRRRRRRRRRRRRRRRRRRRRRRRRRRR
RRRRRRRRRRRRRRRRRRRRRRRRRRRRRRRRRRRRRRRRRRRRRRR
RRRRRRRRRRRRRRRRRRRRRRRRRRRRRRRRRRRRRRRRRRRRRRR
RRRRRRRRRRRRRRRRRRRRRRRRRRRRRRRRRRRRRRRRRRRRRRR
RRRRRRRRRRRRRRRRRRRRRRRRRRRRRRRRRRRRRRRRRRRRRRR
RRRRRRRRRRRRRRRRRRRRRRRRRRRRRRRRRRRRRRRRRRRRRRR
RRRRRRRRRRRRRRRRRRRRRRRRRRRRRRRRRRRRRRRRRRRRRRR

RRRRRRRRRRRRRRRRRRRRRRRRRRRRRRRRRRRRRRRRRRRRRRRRR
RRRRRRRRRRRRRRRRRRRRRRRRRRRRRRRRRRRRRRRRRRRRRRRRR
RRRRRRRRRRRRRRRRRRRRRRRRRRRRRRRRRRRRRRRRRRRRRRRRR
RRRRRRRRRRRRRRRRRRRRRRRRRRRRRRRRRRRRRRRRRRRRRRRRR
RRRRRRRRRRRRRRRRRRRRRRRRRRRRRRRRRRRRRRRRRRRRRRRRR
RRRRRRRRRRRRRRRRRRRRRRRRRRRRRRRRRRRRRRRRRRRRRRRRR
RRRRRRRRRRRRRRRRRRRRRRRRRRRRRRRRRRRRRRRRRRRRRRRRR
RRRRRRRRRRRRRRRRRRRRRRRRRRRRRRRRRRRRRRRRRRRRRRRRR
RRRRRRRRRRRRRRRRRRRRRRRRRRRRRRRRRRRRRRRRRRRRRRRRR
RRRRRRRRRRRRRRRRRRRRRRRRRRRRRRRRRRRRRRRRRRRRRRRRR
RRRRRRRRRRRRRRRRRRRRRRRRRRRRRRRRRRRRRRRRRRRRRRRRR
RRRRRRRRRRRRRRRRRRRRRRRRRRRRRRRRRRRRRRRRRRRRRRRRR
RRRRRRRRRRRRRRRRRRRRRRRRRRRRRRRRRRRRRRRRRRRRRRRRR
RRRRRRRRRRRRRRRRRRRRRRRRRRRRRRRRRRRRRRRRRRRRRRRRR
RRRRRRRRRRRRRRRRRRRRRRRRRRRRRRRRRRRRRRRRRRRRRRRRR
RRRRRRRRRRRRRRRRRRRRRRRRRRRRRRRRRRRRRRRRRRRRRRRRR
RRRRRRRRRRRRRRRRRRRRRRRRRRRRRRRRRRRRRRRRRRRRRRRRR
RRRRRRRRRRRRRRRRRRRRRRRRRRRRRRRRRRRRRRRRRRRRRRRRR
RRRRRRRRRRRRRRRRRRRRRRRRRRRRRRRRRRRRRRRRRRRRRRRRR
RRRRRRRRRRRRRRRRRRRRRRRRRRRRRRRRRRRRRRRRRRRRRRRRR
RRRRRRRRRRRRRRRRRRRRRRRRRRRRRRRRRRRRRRRRRRRRRRRRR
RRRRRRRRRRRRRRRRRRRRRRRRRRRRRRRRRRRRRRRRRRRRRRRRR
RRRRRRRRRRRRRRRRRRRRRRRRRRRRRRRRRRRRRRRRRRRRRRRRR
RRRRRRRRRRRRRRRRRRRRRRRRRRRRRRRRRRRRRRRRRRRRRRRRR
RRRRRRRRRRRRRRRRRRRRRRRRRRRRRRRRRRRRRRRRRRRRRRRRR

RRRRRRRRRRRRRRRRRRRRRRRRRRRRRRRRRRRRRRRRRRRRRRRRRR
RRRRRRRRRRRRRRRRRRRRRRRRRRRRRRRRRRRRRRRRRRRRRRRRRR
RRRRRRRRRRRRRRRRRRRRRRRRRRRRRRRRRRRRRRRRRRRRRRRRRR
RRRRRRRRRRRRRRRRRRRRRRRRRRRRRRRRRRRRRRRRRRRRRRRRRR
RRRRRRRRRRRRRRRRRRRRRRRRRRRRRRRRRRRRRRRRRRRRRRRRRR
RRRRRRRRRRRRRRRRRRRRRRRRRRRRRRRRRRRRRRRRRRRRRRRRRR
RRRRRRRRRRRRRRRRRRRRRRRRRRRRRRRRRRRRRRRRRRRRRRRRRR
RRRRRRRRRRRRRRRRRRRRRRRRRRRRRRRRRRRRRRRRRRRRRRRRRR
RRRRRRRRRRRRRRRRRRRRRRRRRRRRRRRRRRRRRRRRRRRRRRRRRR
RRRRRRRRRRRRRRRRRRRRRRRRRRRRRRRRRRRRRRRRRRRRRRRRRR
RRRRRRRRRRRRRRRRRRRRRRRRRRRRRRRRRRRRRRRRRRRRRRRRRR
RRRRRRRRRRRRRRRRRRRRRRRRRRRRRRRRRRRRRRRRRRRRRRRRRR
RRRRRRRRRRRRRRRRRRRRRRRRRRRRRRRRRRRRRRRRRRRRRRRRRR
RRRRRRRRRRRRRRRRRRRRRRRRRRRRRRRRRRRRRRRRRRRRRRRRRR
RRRRRRRRRRRRRRRRRRRRRRRRRRRRRRRRRRRRRRRRRRRRRRRRRR
RRRRRRRRRRRRRRRRRRRRRRRRRRRRRRRRRRRRRRRRRRRRRRRRRR
RRRRRRRRRRRRRRRRRRRRRRRRRRRRRRRRRRRRRRRRRRRRRRRRRR
RRRRRRRRRRRRRRRRRRRRRRRRRRRRRRRRRRRRRRRRRRRRRRRRRR
RRRRRRRRRRRRRRRRRRRRRRRRRRRRRRRRRRRRRRRRRRRRRRRRRR
RRRRRRRRRRRRRRRRRRRRRRRRRRRRRRRRRRRRRRRRRRRRRRRRRR
RRRRRRRRRRRRRRRRRRRRRRRRRRRRRRRRRRRRRRRRRRRRRRRRRR
RRRRRRRRRRRRRRRRRRRRRRRRRRRRRRRRRRRRRRRRRRRRRRRRRR
RRRRRRRRRRRRRRRRRRRRRRRRRRRRRRRRRRRRRRRRRRRRRRRRRR
RRRRRRRRRRRRRRRRRRRRRRRRRRRRRRRRRRRRRRRRRRRRRRRRRR
RRRRRRRRRRRRRRRRRRRRRRRRRRRRRRRRRRRRRRRRRRRRRRRRRR

RRRRRRRRRRRRRRRRRRRRRRRRRRRRRRRRRRRRRRRRRRRRRR
RRRRRRRRRRRRRRRRRRRRRRRRRRRRRRRRRRRRRRRRRRRRRR
RRRRRRRRRRRRRRRRRRRRRRRRRRRRRRRRRRRRRRRRRRRRRR
RRRRRRRRRRRRRRRRRRRRRRRRRRRRRRRRRRRRRRRRRRRRRR
RRRRRRRRRRRRRRRRRRRRRRRRRRRRRRRRRRRRRRRRRRRRRR
RRRRRRRRRRRRRRRRRRRRRRRRRRRRRRRRRRRRRRRRRRRRRR
RRRRRRRRRRRRRRRRRRRRRRRRRRRRRRRRRRRRRRRRRRRRRR
RRRRRRRRRRRRRRRRRRRRRRRRRRRRRRRRRRRRRRRRRRRRRR
RRRRRRRRRRRRRRRRRRRRRRRRRRRRRRRRRRRRRRRRRRRRRR
RRRRRRRRRRRRRRRRRRRRRRRRRRRRRRRRRRRRRRRRRRRRRR
RRRRRRRRRRRRRRRRRRRRRRRRRRRRRRRRRRRRRRRRRRRRRR
RRRRRRRRRRRRRRRRRRRRRRRRRRRRRRRRRRRRRRRRRRRRRR
RRRRRRRRRRRRRRRRRRRRRRRRRRRRRRRRRRRRRRRRRRRRRR
RRRRRRRRRRRRRRRRRRRRRRRRRRRRRRRRRRRRRRRRRRRRRR
RRRRRRRRRRRRRRRRRRRRRRRRRRRRRRRRRRRRRRRRRRRRRR
RRRRRRRRRRRRRRRRRRRRRRRRRRRRRRRRRRRRRRRRRRRRRR
RRRRRRRRRRRRRRRRRRRRRRRRRRRRRRRRRRRRRRRRRRRRRR
RRRRRRRRRRRRRRRRRRRRRRRRRRRRRRRRRRRRRRRRRRRRRR
RRRRRRRRRRRRRRRRRRRRRRRRRRRRRRRRRRRRRRRRRRRRRR
RRRRRRRRRRRRRRRRRRRRRRRRRRRRRRRRRRRRRRRRRRRRRR
RRRRRRRRRRRRRRRRRRRRRRRRRRRRRRRRRRRRRRRRRRRRRR
RRRRRRRRRRRRRRRRRRRRRRRRRRRRRRRRRRRRRRRRRRRRRR
RRRRRRRRRRRRRRRRRRRRRRRRRRRRRRRRRRRRRRRRRRRRRR
RRRRRRRRRRRRRRRRRRRRRRRRRRRRRRRRRRRRRRRRRRRRRR
RRRRRRRRRRRRRRRRRRRRRRRRRRRRRRRRRRRRRRRRRRRRRR

RRRRRRRRRRRRRRRRRRRRRRRRRRRRRRRRRRRRRRRRRR
RRRRRRRRRRRRRRRRRRRRRRRRRRRRRRRRRRRRRRRRRR
RRRRRRRRRRRRRRRRRRRRRRRRRRRRRRRRRRRRRRRRRR
RRRRRRRRRRRRRRRRRRRRRRRRRRRRRRRRRRRRRRRRRR
RRRRRRRRRRRRRRRRRRRRRRRRRRRRRRRRRRRRRRRRRR
RRRRRRRRRRRRRRRRRRRRRRRRRRRRRRRRRRRRRRRRRR
RRRRRRRRRRRRRRRRRRRRRRRRRRRRRRRRRRRRRRRRRR
RRRRRRRRRRRRRRRRRRRRRRRRRRRRRRRRRRRRRRRRRR
RRRRRRRRRRRRRRRRRRRRRRRRRRRRRRRRRRRRRRRRRR
RRRRRRRRRRRRRRRRRRRRRRRRRRRRRRRRRRRRRRRRRR
RRRRRRRRRRRRRRRRRRRRRRRRRRRRRRRRRRRRRRRRRR
RRRRRRRRRRRRRRRRRRRRRRRRRRRRRRRRRRRRRRRRRR
RRRRRRRRRRRRRRRRRRRRRRRRRRRRRRRRRRRRRRRRRR
RRRRRRRRRRRRRRRRRRRRRRRRRRRRRRRRRRRRRRRRRR
RRRRRRRRRRRRRRRRRRRRRRRRRRRRRRRRRRRRRRRRRR
RRRRRRRRRRRRRRRRRRRRRRRRRRRRRRRRRRRRRRRRRR
RRRRRRRRRRRRRRRRRRRRRRRRRRRRRRRRRRRRRRRRRR
RRRRRRRRRRRRRRRRRRRRRRRRRRRRRRRRRRRRRRRRRR
RRRRRRRRRRRRRRRRRRRRRRRRRRRRRRRRRRRRRRRRRR
RRRRRRRRRRRRRRRRRRRRRRRRRRRRRRRRRRRRRRRRRR
RRRRRRRRRRRRRRRRRRRRRRRRRRRRRRRRRRRRRRRRRR
RRRRRRRRRRRRRRRRRRRRRRRRRRRRRRRRRRRRRRRRRR
RRRRRRRRRRRRRRRRRRRRRRRRRRRRRRRRRRRRRRRRRR
RRRRRRRRRRRRRRRRRRRRRRRRRRRRRRRRRRRRRRRRRR
RRRRRRRRRRRRRRRRRRRRRRRRRRRRRRRRRRRRRRRRRR
RRRRRRRRRRRRRRRRRRRRRRRRRRRRRRRRRRRRRRRRRR
RRRRRRRRRRRRRRRRRRRRRRRRRRRRRRRRRRRRRRRRRR
RRRRRRRRRRRRRRRRRRRRRRRRRRRRRRRRRRRRRRRRRR

RRRRRRRRRRRRRRRRRRRRRRRRRRRRRRRRRRRRRRRRRRRRRRRRRR
RRRRRRRRRRRRRRRRRRRRRRRRRRRRRRRRRRRRRRRRRRRRRRRRRR
RRRRRRRRRRRRRRRRRRRRRRRRRRRRRRRRRRRRRRRRRRRRRRRRRR
RRRRRRRRRRRRRRRRRRRRRRRRRRRRRRRRRRRRRRRRRRRRRRRRRR
RRRRRRRRRRRRRRRRRRRRRRRRRRRRRRRRRRRRRRRRRRRRRRRRRR
RRRRRRRRRRRRRRRRRRRRRRRRRRRRRRRRRRRRRRRRRRRRRRRRRR
RRRRRRRRRRRRRRRRRRRRRRRRRRRRRRRRRRRRRRRRRRRRRRRRRR
RRRRRRRRRRRRRRRRRRRRRRRRRRRRRRRRRRRRRRRRRRRRRRRRRR
RRRRRRRRRRRRRRRRRRRRRRRRRRRRRRRRRRRRRRRRRRRRRRRRRR
RRRRRRRRRRRRRRRRRRRRRRRRRRRRRRRRRRRRRRRRRRRRRRRRRR
RRRRRRRRRRRRRRRRRRRRRRRRRRRRRRRRRRRRRRRRRRRRRRRRRR
RRRRRRRRRRRRRRRRRRRRRRRRRRRRRRRRRRRRRRRRRRRRRRRRRR
RRRRRRRRRRRRRRRRRRRRRRRRRRRRRRRRRRRRRRRRRRRRRRRRRR
RRRRRRRRRRRRRRRRRRRRRRRRRRRRRRRRRRRRRRRRRRRRRRRRRR
RRRRRRRRRRRRRRRRRRRRRRRRRRRRRRRRRRRRRRRRRRRRRRRRRR
RRRRRRRRRRRRRRRRRRRRRRRRRRRRRRRRRRRRRRRRRRRRRRRRRR
RRRRRRRRRRRRRRRRRRRRRRRRRRRRRRRRRRRRRRRRRRRRRRRRRR
RRRRRRRRRRRRRRRRRRRRRRRRRRRRRRRRRRRRRRRRRRRRRRRRRR
RRRRRRRRRRRRRRRRRRRRRRRRRRRRRRRRRRRRRRRRRRRRRRRRRR
RRRRRRRRRRRRRRRRRRRRRRRRRRRRRRRRRRRRRRRRRRRRRRRRRR
RRRRRRRRRRRRRRRRRRRRRRRRRRRRRRRRRRRRRRRRRRRRRRRRRR
RRRRRRRRRRRRRRRRRRRRRRRRRRRRRRRRRRRRRRRRRRRRRRRRRR
RRRRRRRRRRRRRRRRRRRRRRRRRRRRRRRRRRRRRRRRRRRRRRRRRR
RRRRRRRRRRRRRRRRRRRRRRRRRRRRRRRRRRRRRRRRRRRRRRRRRR
RRRRRRRRRRRRRRRRRRRRRRRRRRRRRRRRRRRRRRRRRRRRRRRRRR
RRRRRRRRRRRRRRRRRRRRRRRRRRRRRRRRRRRRRRRRRRRRRRRRRR

RRRRRRRRRRRRRRRRRRRRRRRRRRRRRRRRRRRRRRRRRRRRRRRRRRRR
RRRRRRRRRRRRRRRRRRRRRRRRRRRRRRRRRRRRRRRRRRRRRRRRRRRR
RRRRRRRRRRRRRRRRRRRRRRRRRRRRRRRRRRRRRRRRRRRRRRRRRRRR
RRRRRRRRRRRRRRRRRRRRRRRRRRRRRRRRRRRRRRRRRRRRRRRRRRRR
RRRRRRRRRRRRRRRRRRRRRRRRRRRRRRRRRRRRRRRRRRRRRRRRRRRR
RRRRRRRRRRRRRRRRRRRRRRRRRRRRRRRRRRRRRRRRRRRRRRRRRRRR
RRRRRRRRRRRRRRRRRRRRRRRRRRRRRRRRRRRRRRRRRRRRRRRRRRRR
RRRRRRRRRRRRRRRRRRRRRRRRRRRRRRRRRRRRRRRRRRRRRRRRRRRR
RRRRRRRRRRRRRRRRRRRRRRRRRRRRRRRRRRRRRRRRRRRRRRRRRRRR
RRRRRRRRRRRRRRRRRRRRRRRRRRRRRRRRRRRRRRRRRRRRRRRRRRRR
RRRRRRRRRRRRRRRRRRRRRRRRRRRRRRRRRRRRRRRRRRRRRRRRRRRR
RRRRRRRRRRRRRRRRRRRRRRRRRRRRRRRRRRRRRRRRRRRRRRRRRRRR
RRRRRRRRRRRRRRRRRRRRRRRRRRRRRRRRRRRRRRRRRRRRRRRRRRRR
RRRRRRRRRRRRRRRRRRRRRRRRRRRRRRRRRRRRRRRRRRRRRRRRRRRR
RRRRRRRRRRRRRRRRRRRRRRRRRRRRRRRRRRRRRRRRRRRRRRRRRRRR
RRRRRRRRRRRRRRRRRRRRRRRRRRRRRRRRRRRRRRRRRRRRRRRRRRRR
RRRRRRRRRRRRRRRRRRRRRRRRRRRRRRRRRRRRRRRRRRRRRRRRRRRR
RRRRRRRRRRRRRRRRRRRRRRRRRRRRRRRRRRRRRRRRRRRRRRRRRRRR
RRRRRRRRRRRRRRRRRRRRRRRRRRRRRRRRRRRRRRRRRRRRRRRRRRRR
RRRRRRRRRRRRRRRRRRRRRRRRRRRRRRRRRRRRRRRRRRRRRRRRRRRR
RRRRRRRRRRRRRRRRRRRRRRRRRRRRRRRRRRRRRRRRRRRRRRRRRRRR
RRRRRRRRRRRRRRRRRRRRRRRRRRRRRRRRRRRRRRRRRRRRRRRRRRRR
RRRRRRRRRRRRRRRRRRRRRRRRRRRRRRRRRRRRRRRRRRRRRRRRRRRR
RRRRRRRRRRRRRRRRRRRRRRRRRRRRRRRRRRRRRRRRRRRRRRRRRRRR
RRRRRRRRRRRRRRRRRRRRRRRRRRRRRRRRRRRRRRRRRRRRRRRRRRRR
RRRRRRRRRRRRRRRRRRRRRRRRRRRRRRRRRRRRRRRRRRRRRRRRRRRR
RRRRRRRRRRRRRRRRRRRRRRRRRRRRRRRRRRRRRRRRRRRRRRRRRRRR

RRRRRRRRRRRRRRRRRRRRRRRRRRRRRRRRRRRRRRRRRRRR
RRRRRRRRRRRRRRRRRRRRRRRRRRRRRRRRRRRRRRRRRRRR
RRRRRRRRRRRRRRRRRRRRRRRRRRRRRRRRRRRRRRRRRRRR
RRRRRRRRRRRRRRRRRRRRRRRRRRRRRRRRRRRRRRRRRRRR
RRRRRRRRRRRRRRRRRRRRRRRRRRRRRRRRRRRRRRRRRRRR
RRRRRRRRRRRRRRRRRRRRRRRRRRRRRRRRRRRRRRRRRRRR
RRRRRRRRRRRRRRRRRRRRRRRRRRRRRRRRRRRRRRRRRRRR
RRRRRRRRRRRRRRRRRRRRRRRRRRRRRRRRRRRRRRRRRRRR
RRRRRRRRRRRRRRRRRRRRRRRRRRRRRRRRRRRRRRRRRRRR
RRRRRRRRRRRRRRRRRRRRRRRRRRRRRRRRRRRRRRRRRRRR
RRRRRRRRRRRRRRRRRRRRRRRRRRRRRRRRRRRRRRRRRRRR
RRRRRRRRRRRRRRRRRRRRRRRRRRRRRRRRRRRRRRRRRRRR
RRRRRRRRRRRRRRRRRRRRRRRRRRRRRRRRRRRRRRRRRRRR
RRRRRRRRRRRRRRRRRRRRRRRRRRRRRRRRRRRRRRRRRRRR
RRRRRRRRRRRRRRRRRRRRRRRRRRRRRRRRRRRRRRRRRRRR
RRRRRRRRRRRRRRRRRRRRRRRRRRRRRRRRRRRRRRRRRRRR
RRRRRRRRRRRRRRRRRRRRRRRRRRRRRRRRRRRRRRRRRRRR
RRRRRRRRRRRRRRRRRRRRRRRRRRRRRRRRRRRRRRRRRRRR
RRRRRRRRRRRRRRRRRRRRRRRRRRRRRRRRRRRRRRRRRRRR
RRRRRRRRRRRRRRRRRRRRRRRRRRRRRRRRRRRRRRRRRRRR
RRRRRRRRRRRRRRRRRRRRRRRRRRRRRRRRRRRRRRRRRRRR
RRRRRRRRRRRRRRRRRRRRRRRRRRRRRRRRRRRRRRRRRRRR
RRRRRRRRRRRRRRRRRRRRRRRRRRRRRRRRRRRRRRRRRRRR
RRRRRRRRRRRRRRRRRRRRRRRRRRRRRRRRRRRRRRRRRRRR
RRRRRRRRRRRRRRRRRRRRRRRRRRRRRRRRRRRRRRRRRRRR
RRRRRRRRRRRRRRRRRRRRRRRRRRRRRRRRRRRRRRRRRRRR
RRRRRRRRRRRRRRRRRRRRRRRRRRRRRRRRRRRRRRRRRRRR

RRRRRRRRRRRRRRRRRRRRRRRRRRRRRRRRRRRRRRRRRRRRRRRRRR
RRRRRRRRRRRRRRRRRRRRRRRRRRRRRRRRRRRRRRRRRRRRRRRRRR
RRRRRRRRRRRRRRRRRRRRRRRRRRRRRRRRRRRRRRRRRRRRRRRRRR
RRRRRRRRRRRRRRRRRRRRRRRRRRRRRRRRRRRRRRRRRRRRRRRRRR
RRRRRRRRRRRRRRRRRRRRRRRRRRRRRRRRRRRRRRRRRRRRRRRRRR
RRRRRRRRRRRRRRRRRRRRRRRRRRRRRRRRRRRRRRRRRRRRRRRRRR
RRRRRRRRRRRRRRRRRRRRRRRRRRRRRRRRRRRRRRRRRRRRRRRRRR
RRRRRRRRRRRRRRRRRRRRRRRRRRRRRRRRRRRRRRRRRRRRRRRRRR
RRRRRRRRRRRRRRRRRRRRRRRRRRRRRRRRRRRRRRRRRRRRRRRRRR
RRRRRRRRRRRRRRRRRRRRRRRRRRRRRRRRRRRRRRRRRRRRRRRRRR
RRRRRRRRRRRRRRRRRRRRRRRRRRRRRRRRRRRRRRRRRRRRRRRRRR
RRRRRRRRRRRRRRRRRRRRRRRRRRRRRRRRRRRRRRRRRRRRRRRRRR
RRRRRRRRRRRRRRRRRRRRRRRRRRRRRRRRRRRRRRRRRRRRRRRRRR
RRRRRRRRRRRRRRRRRRRRRRRRRRRRRRRRRRRRRRRRRRRRRRRRRR
RRRRRRRRRRRRRRRRRRRRRRRRRRRRRRRRRRRRRRRRRRRRRRRRRR
RRRRRRRRRRRRRRRRRRRRRRRRRRRRRRRRRRRRRRRRRRRRRRRRRR
RRRRRRRRRRRRRRRRRRRRRRRRRRRRRRRRRRRRRRRRRRRRRRRRRR
RRRRRRRRRRRRRRRRRRRRRRRRRRRRRRRRRRRRRRRRRRRRRRRRRR
RRRRRRRRRRRRRRRRRRRRRRRRRRRRRRRRRRRRRRRRRRRRRRRRRR
RRRRRRRRRRRRRRRRRRRRRRRRRRRRRRRRRRRRRRRRRRRRRRRRRR
RRRRRRRRRRRRRRRRRRRRRRRRRRRRRRRRRRRRRRRRRRRRRRRRRR
RRRRRRRRRRRRRRRRRRRRRRRRRRRRRRRRRRRRRRRRRRRRRRRRRR
RRRRRRRRRRRRRRRRRRRRRRRRRRRRRRRRRRRRRRRRRRRRRRRRRR
RRRRRRRRRRRRRRRRRRRRRRRRRRRRRRRRRRRRRRRRRRRRRRRRRR
RRRRRRRRRRRRRRRRRRRRRRRRRRRRRRRRRRRRRRRRRRRRRRRRRR
RRRRRRRRRRRRRRRRRRRRRRRRRRRRRRRRRRRRRRRRRRRRRRRRRR

RRRRRRRRRRRRRRRRRRRRRRRRRRRRRRRRRRRRRRRRRRRRRR
RRRRRRRRRRRRRRRRRRRRRRRRRRRRRRRRRRRRRRRRRRRRRR
RRRRRRRRRRRRRRRRRRRRRRRRRRRRRRRRRRRRRRRRRRRRRR
RRRRRRRRRRRRRRRRRRRRRRRRRRRRRRRRRRRRRRRRRRRRRR
RRRRRRRRRRRRRRRRRRRRRRRRRRRRRRRRRRRRRRRRRRRRRR
RRRRRRRRRRRRRRRRRRRRRRRRRRRRRRRRRRRRRRRRRRRRRR
RRRRRRRRRRRRRRRRRRRRRRRRRRRRRRRRRRRRRRRRRRRRRR
RRRRRRRRRRRRRRRRRRRRRRRRRRRRRRRRRRRRRRRRRRRRRR
RRRRRRRRRRRRRRRRRRRRRRRRRRRRRRRRRRRRRRRRRRRRRR
RRRRRRRRRRRRRRRRRRRRRRRRRRRRRRRRRRRRRRRRRRRRRR
RRRRRRRRRRRRRRRRRRRRRRRRRRRRRRRRRRRRRRRRRRRRRR
RRRRRRRRRRRRRRRRRRRRRRRRRRRRRRRRRRRRRRRRRRRRRR
RRRRRRRRRRRRRRRRRRRRRRRRRRRRRRRRRRRRRRRRRRRRRR
RRRRRRRRRRRRRRRRRRRRRRRRRRRRRRRRRRRRRRRRRRRRRR
RRRRRRRRRRRRRRRRRRRRRRRRRRRRRRRRRRRRRRRRRRRRRR
RRRRRRRRRRRRRRRRRRRRRRRRRRRRRRRRRRRRRRRRRRRRRR
RRRRRRRRRRRRRRRRRRRRRRRRRRRRRRRRRRRRRRRRRRRRRR
RRRRRRRRRRRRRRRRRRRRRRRRRRRRRRRRRRRRRRRRRRRRRR
RRRRRRRRRRRRRRRRRRRRRRRRRRRRRRRRRRRRRRRRRRRRRR
RRRRRRRRRRRRRRRRRRRRRRRRRRRRRRRRRRRRRRRRRRRRRR
RRRRRRRRRRRRRRRRRRRRRRRRRRRRRRRRRRRRRRRRRRRRRR
RRRRRRRRRRRRRRRRRRRRRRRRRRRRRRRRRRRRRRRRRRRRRR
RRRRRRRRRRRRRRRRRRRRRRRRRRRRRRRRRRRRRRRRRRRRRR
RRRRRRRRRRRRRRRRRRRRRRRRRRRRRRRRRRRRRRRRRRRRRR
RRRRRRRRRRRRRRRRRRRRRRRRRRRRRRRRRRRRRRRRRRRRRR
RRRRRRRRRRRRRRRRRRRRRRRRRRRRRRRRRRRRRRRRRRRRRR
RRRRRRRRRRRRRRRRRRRRRRRRRRRRRRRRRRRRRRRRRRRRRR
RRRRRRRRRRRRRRRRRRRRRRRRRRRRRRRRRRRRRRRRRRRRRR

RRRRRRRRRRRRRRRRRRRRRRRRRRRRRRRRRRRRRRRRRRRRRRR
RRRRRRRRRRRRRRRRRRRRRRRRRRRRRRRRRRRRRRRRRRRRRRR
RRRRRRRRRRRRRRRRRRRRRRRRRRRRRRRRRRRRRRRRRRRRRRR
RRRRRRRRRRRRRRRRRRRRRRRRRRRRRRRRRRRRRRRRRRRRRRR
RRRRRRRRRRRRRRRRRRRRRRRRRRRRRRRRRRRRRRRRRRRRRRR
RRRRRRRRRRRRRRRRRRRRRRRRRRRRRRRRRRRRRRRRRRRRRRR
RRRRRRRRRRRRRRRRRRRRRRRRRRRRRRRRRRRRRRRRRRRRRRR
RRRRRRRRRRRRRRRRRRRRRRRRRRRRRRRRRRRRRRRRRRRRRRR
RRRRRRRRRRRRRRRRRRRRRRRRRRRRRRRRRRRRRRRRRRRRRRR
RRRRRRRRRRRRRRRRRRRRRRRRRRRRRRRRRRRRRRRRRRRRRRR
RRRRRRRRRRRRRRRRRRRRRRRRRRRRRRRRRRRRRRRRRRRRRRR
RRRRRRRRRRRRRRRRRRRRRRRRRRRRRRRRRRRRRRRRRRRRRRR
RRRRRRRRRRRRRRRRRRRRRRRRRRRRRRRRRRRRRRRRRRRRRRR
RRRRRRRRRRRRRRRRRRRRRRRRRRRRRRRRRRRRRRRRRRRRRRR
RRRRRRRRRRRRRRRRRRRRRRRRRRRRRRRRRRRRRRRRRRRRRRR
RRRRRRRRRRRRRRRRRRRRRRRRRRRRRRRRRRRRRRRRRRRRRRR
RRRRRRRRRRRRRRRRRRRRRRRRRRRRRRRRRRRRRRRRRRRRRRR
RRRRRRRRRRRRRRRRRRRRRRRRRRRRRRRRRRRRRRRRRRRRRRR
RRRRRRRRRRRRRRRRRRRRRRRRRRRRRRRRRRRRRRRRRRRRRRR
RRRRRRRRRRRRRRRRRRRRRRRRRRRRRRRRRRRRRRRRRRRRRRR
RRRRRRRRRRRRRRRRRRRRRRRRRRRRRRRRRRRRRRRRRRRRRRR
RRRRRRRRRRRRRRRRRRRRRRRRRRRRRRRRRRRRRRRRRRRRRRR
RRRRRRRRRRRRRRRRRRRRRRRRRRRRRRRRRRRRRRRRRRRRRRR
RRRRRRRRRRRRRRRRRRRRRRRRRRRRRRRRRRRRRRRRRRRRRRR
RRRRRRRRRRRRRRRRRRRRRRRRRRRRRRRRRRRRRRRRRRRRRRR
RRRRRRRRRRRRRRRRRRRRRRRRRRRRRRRRRRRRRRRRRRRRRRR
RRRRRRRRRRRRRRRRRRRRRRRRRRRRRRRRRRRRRRRRRRRRRRR
RRRRRRRRRRRRRRRRRRRRRRRRRRRRRRRRRRRRRRRRRRRRRRR
RRRRRRRRRRRRRRRRRRRRRRRRRRRRRRRRRRRRRRRRRRRRRRR

RRRRRRRRRRRRRRRRRRRRRRRRRRRRRRRRRRRRRRRRRRRRRR
RRRRRRRRRRRRRRRRRRRRRRRRRRRRRRRRRRRRRRRRRRRRRR
RRRRRRRRRRRRRRRRRRRRRRRRRRRRRRRRRRRRRRRRRRRRRR
RRRRRRRRRRRRRRRRRRRRRRRRRRRRRRRRRRRRRRRRRRRRRR
RRRRRRRRRRRRRRRRRRRRRRRRRRRRRRRRRRRRRRRRRRRRRR
RRRRRRRRRRRRRRRRRRRRRRRRRRRRRRRRRRRRRRRRRRRRRR
RRRRRRRRRRRRRRRRRRRRRRRRRRRRRRRRRRRRRRRRRRRRRR
RRRRRRRRRRRRRRRRRRRRRRRRRRRRRRRRRRRRRRRRRRRRRR
RRRRRRRRRRRRRRRRRRRRRRRRRRRRRRRRRRRRRRRRRRRRRR
RRRRRRRRRRRRRRRRRRRRRRRRRRRRRRRRRRRRRRRRRRRRRR
RRRRRRRRRRRRRRRRRRRRRRRRRRRRRRRRRRRRRRRRRRRRRR
RRRRRRRRRRRRRRRRRRRRRRRRRRRRRRRRRRRRRRRRRRRRRR
RRRRRRRRRRRRRRRRRRRRRRRRRRRRRRRRRRRRRRRRRRRRRR
RRRRRRRRRRRRRRRRRRRRRRRRRRRRRRRRRRRRRRRRRRRRRR
RRRRRRRRRRRRRRRRRRRRRRRRRRRRRRRRRRRRRRRRRRRRRR
RRRRRRRRRRRRRRRRRRRRRRRRRRRRRRRRRRRRRRRRRRRRRR
RRRRRRRRRRRRRRRRRRRRRRRRRRRRRRRRRRRRRRRRRRRRRR
RRRRRRRRRRRRRRRRRRRRRRRRRRRRRRRRRRRRRRRRRRRRRR
RRRRRRRRRRRRRRRRRRRRRRRRRRRRRRRRRRRRRRRRRRRRRR
RRRRRRRRRRRRRRRRRRRRRRRRRRRRRRRRRRRRRRRRRRRRRR
RRRRRRRRRRRRRRRRRRRRRRRRRRRRRRRRRRRRRRRRRRRRRR
RRRRRRRRRRRRRRRRRRRRRRRRRRRRRRRRRRRRRRRRRRRRRR
RRRRRRRRRRRRRRRRRRRRRRRRRRRRRRRRRRRRRRRRRRRRRR
RRRRRRRRRRRRRRRRRRRRRRRRRRRRRRRRRRRRRRRRRRRRRR
RRRRRRRRRRRRRRRRRRRRRRRRRRRRRRRRRRRRRRRRRRRRRR
RRRRRRRRRRRRRRRRRRRRRRRRRRRRRRRRRRRRRRRRRRRRRR
RRRRRRRRRRRRRRRRRRRRRRRRRRRRRRRRRRRRRRRRRRRRRR
RRRRRRRRRRRRRRRRRRRRRRRRRRRRRRRRRRRRRRRRRRRRRR
RRRRRRRRRRRRRRRRRRRRRRRRRRRRRRRRRRRRRRRRRRRRRR

RRRRRRRRRRRRRRRRRRRRRRRRRRRRRRRRRRRRRRRRRRRRRRR
RRRRRRRRRRRRRRRRRRRRRRRRRRRRRRRRRRRRRRRRRRRRRRR
RRRRRRRRRRRRRRRRRRRRRRRRRRRRRRRRRRRRRRRRRRRRRRR
RRRRRRRRRRRRRRRRRRRRRRRRRRRRRRRRRRRRRRRRRRRRRRR
RRRRRRRRRRRRRRRRRRRRRRRRRRRRRRRRRRRRRRRRRRRRRRR
RRRRRRRRRRRRRRRRRRRRRRRRRRRRRRRRRRRRRRRRRRRRRRR
RRRRRRRRRRRRRRRRRRRRRRRRRRRRRRRRRRRRRRRRRRRRRRR
RRRRRRRRRRRRRRRRRRRRRRRRRRRRRRRRRRRRRRRRRRRRRRR
RRRRRRRRRRRRRRRRRRRRRRRRRRRRRRRRRRRRRRRRRRRRRRR
RRRRRRRRRRRRRRRRRRRRRRRRRRRRRRRRRRRRRRRRRRRRRRR
RRRRRRRRRRRRRRRRRRRRRRRRRRRRRRRRRRRRRRRRRRRRRRR
RRRRRRRRRRRRRRRRRRRRRRRRRRRRRRRRRRRRRRRRRRRRRRR
RRRRRRRRRRRRRRRRRRRRRRRRRRRRRRRRRRRRRRRRRRRRRRR
RRRRRRRRRRRRRRRRRRRRRRRRRRRRRRRRRRRRRRRRRRRRRRR
RRRRRRRRRRRRRRRRRRRRRRRRRRRRRRRRRRRRRRRRRRRRRRR
RRRRRRRRRRRRRRRRRRRRRRRRRRRRRRRRRRRRRRRRRRRRRRR
RRRRRRRRRRRRRRRRRRRRRRRRRRRRRRRRRRRRRRRRRRRRRRR
RRRRRRRRRRRRRRRRRRRRRRRRRRRRRRRRRRRRRRRRRRRRRRR
RRRRRRRRRRRRRRRRRRRRRRRRRRRRRRRRRRRRRRRRRRRRRRR
RRRRRRRRRRRRRRRRRRRRRRRRRRRRRRRRRRRRRRRRRRRRRRR
RRRRRRRRRRRRRRRRRRRRRRRRRRRRRRRRRRRRRRRRRRRRRRR
RRRRRRRRRRRRRRRRRRRRRRRRRRRRRRRRRRRRRRRRRRRRRRR
RRRRRRRRRRRRRRRRRRRRRRRRRRRRRRRRRRRRRRRRRRRRRRR
RRRRRRRRRRRRRRRRRRRRRRRRRRRRRRRRRRRRRRRRRRRRRRR
RRRRRRRRRRRRRRRRRRRRRRRRRRRRRRRRRRRRRRRRRRRRRRR
RRRRRRRRRRRRRRRRRRRRRRRRRRRRRRRRRRRRRRRRRRRRRRR

RRRRRRRRRRRRRRRRRRRRRRRRRRRRRRRRRRRRRRRRRRRRRR
RRRRRRRRRRRRRRRRRRRRRRRRRRRRRRRRRRRRRRRRRRRRRR
RRRRRRRRRRRRRRRRRRRRRRRRRRRRRRRRRRRRRRRRRRRRRR
RRRRRRRRRRRRRRRRRRRRRRRRRRRRRRRRRRRRRRRRRRRRRR
RRRRRRRRRRRRRRRRRRRRRRRRRRRRRRRRRRRRRRRRRRRRRR
RRRRRRRRRRRRRRRRRRRRRRRRRRRRRRRRRRRRRRRRRRRRRR
RRRRRRRRRRRRRRRRRRRRRRRRRRRRRRRRRRRRRRRRRRRRRR
RRRRRRRRRRRRRRRRRRRRRRRRRRRRRRRRRRRRRRRRRRRRRR
RRRRRRRRRRRRRRRRRRRRRRRRRRRRRRRRRRRRRRRRRRRRRR
RRRRRRRRRRRRRRRRRRRRRRRRRRRRRRRRRRRRRRRRRRRRRR
RRRRRRRRRRRRRRRRRRRRRRRRRRRRRRRRRRRRRRRRRRRRRR
RRRRRRRRRRRRRRRRRRRRRRRRRRRRRRRRRRRRRRRRRRRRRR
RRRRRRRRRRRRRRRRRRRRRRRRRRRRRRRRRRRRRRRRRRRRRR
RRRRRRRRRRRRRRRRRRRRRRRRRRRRRRRRRRRRRRRRRRRRRR
RRRRRRRRRRRRRRRRRRRRRRRRRRRRRRRRRRRRRRRRRRRRRR
RRRRRRRRRRRRRRRRRRRRRRRRRRRRRRRRRRRRRRRRRRRRRR
RRRRRRRRRRRRRRRRRRRRRRRRRRRRRRRRRRRRRRRRRRRRRR
RRRRRRRRRRRRRRRRRRRRRRRRRRRRRRRRRRRRRRRRRRRRRR
RRRRRRRRRRRRRRRRRRRRRRRRRRRRRRRRRRRRRRRRRRRRRR
RRRRRRRRRRRRRRRRRRRRRRRRRRRRRRRRRRRRRRRRRRRRRR
RRRRRRRRRRRRRRRRRRRRRRRRRRRRRRRRRRRRRRRRRRRRRR
RRRRRRRRRRRRRRRRRRRRRRRRRRRRRRRRRRRRRRRRRRRRRR
RRRRRRRRRRRRRRRRRRRRRRRRRRRRRRRRRRRRRRRRRRRRRR
RRRRRRRRRRRRRRRRRRRRRRRRRRRRRRRRRRRRRRRRRRRRRR
RRRRRRRRRRRRRRRRRRRRRRRRRRRRRRRRRRRRRRRRRRRRRR
RRRRRRRRRRRRRRRRRRRRRRRRRRRRRRRRRRRRRRRRRRRRRR

RRRRRRRRRRRRRRRRRRRRRRRRRRRRRRRRRRRRRRRRRRRRRRRRRR
RRRRRRRRRRRRRRRRRRRRRRRRRRRRRRRRRRRRRRRRRRRRRRRRRR
RRRRRRRRRRRRRRRRRRRRRRRRRRRRRRRRRRRRRRRRRRRRRRRRRR
RRRRRRRRRRRRRRRRRRRRRRRRRRRRRRRRRRRRRRRRRRRRRRRRRR
RRRRRRRRRRRRRRRRRRRRRRRRRRRRRRRRRRRRRRRRRRRRRRRRRR
RRRRRRRRRRRRRRRRRRRRRRRRRRRRRRRRRRRRRRRRRRRRRRRRRR
RRRRRRRRRRRRRRRRRRRRRRRRRRRRRRRRRRRRRRRRRRRRRRRRRR
RRRRRRRRRRRRRRRRRRRRRRRRRRRRRRRRRRRRRRRRRRRRRRRRRR
RRRRRRRRRRRRRRRRRRRRRRRRRRRRRRRRRRRRRRRRRRRRRRRRRR
RRRRRRRRRRRRRRRRRRRRRRRRRRRRRRRRRRRRRRRRRRRRRRRRRR
RRRRRRRRRRRRRRRRRRRRRRRRRRRRRRRRRRRRRRRRRRRRRRRRRR
RRRRRRRRRRRRRRRRRRRRRRRRRRRRRRRRRRRRRRRRRRRRRRRRRR
RRRRRRRRRRRRRRRRRRRRRRRRRRRRRRRRRRRRRRRRRRRRRRRRRR
RRRRRRRRRRRRRRRRRRRRRRRRRRRRRRRRRRRRRRRRRRRRRRRRRR
RRRRRRRRRRRRRRRRRRRRRRRRRRRRRRRRRRRRRRRRRRRRRRRRRR
RRRRRRRRRRRRRRRRRRRRRRRRRRRRRRRRRRRRRRRRRRRRRRRRRR
RRRRRRRRRRRRRRRRRRRRRRRRRRRRRRRRRRRRRRRRRRRRRRRRRR
RRRRRRRRRRRRRRRRRRRRRRRRRRRRRRRRRRRRRRRRRRRRRRRRRR
RRRRRRRRRRRRRRRRRRRRRRRRRRRRRRRRRRRRRRRRRRRRRRRRRR
RRRRRRRRRRRRRRRRRRRRRRRRRRRRRRRRRRRRRRRRRRRRRRRRRR
RRRRRRRRRRRRRRRRRRRRRRRRRRRRRRRRRRRRRRRRRRRRRRRRRR
RRRRRRRRRRRRRRRRRRRRRRRRRRRRRRRRRRRRRRRRRRRRRRRRRR
RRRRRRRRRRRRRRRRRRRRRRRRRRRRRRRRRRRRRRRRRRRRRRRRRR
RRRRRRRRRRRRRRRRRRRRRRRRRRRRRRRRRRRRRRRRRRRRRRRRRR
RRRRRRRRRRRRRRRRRRRRRRRRRRRRRRRRRRRRRRRRRRRRRRRRRR
RRRRRRRRRRRRRRRRRRRRRRRRRRRRRRRRRRRRRRRRRRRRRRRRRR
RRRRRRRRRRRRRRRRRRRRRRRRRRRRRRRRRRRRRRRRRRRRRRRRRR
RRRRRRRRRRRRRRRRRRRRRRRRRRRRRRRRRRRRRRRRRRRRRRRRRR
RRRRRRRRRRRRRRRRRRRRRRRRRRRRRRRRRRRRRRRRRRRRRRRRRR

RRRRRRRRRRRRRRRRRRRRRRRRRRRRRRRRRRRRRRRRRRRR
RRRRRRRRRRRRRRRRRRRRRRRRRRRRRRRRRRRRRRRRRRRR
RRRRRRRRRRRRRRRRRRRRRRRRRRRRRRRRRRRRRRRRRRRR
RRRRRRRRRRRRRRRRRRRRRRRRRRRRRRRRRRRRRRRRRRRR
RRRRRRRRRRRRRRRRRRRRRRRRRRRRRRRRRRRRRRRRRRRR
RRRRRRRRRRRRRRRRRRRRRRRRRRRRRRRRRRRRRRRRRRRR
RRRRRRRRRRRRRRRRRRRRRRRRRRRRRRRRRRRRRRRRRRRR
RRRRRRRRRRRRRRRRRRRRRRRRRRRRRRRRRRRRRRRRRRRR
RRRRRRRRRRRRRRRRRRRRRRRRRRRRRRRRRRRRRRRRRRRR
RRRRRRRRRRRRRRRRRRRRRRRRRRRRRRRRRRRRRRRRRRRR
RRRRRRRRRRRRRRRRRRRRRRRRRRRRRRRRRRRRRRRRRRRR
RRRRRRRRRRRRRRRRRRRRRRRRRRRRRRRRRRRRRRRRRRRR
RRRRRRRRRRRRRRRRRRRRRRRRRRRRRRRRRRRRRRRRRRRR
RRRRRRRRRRRRRRRRRRRRRRRRRRRRRRRRRRRRRRRRRRRR
RRRRRRRRRRRRRRRRRRRRRRRRRRRRRRRRRRRRRRRRRRRR
RRRRRRRRRRRRRRRRRRRRRRRRRRRRRRRRRRRRRRRRRRRR
RRRRRRRRRRRRRRRRRRRRRRRRRRRRRRRRRRRRRRRRRRRR
RRRRRRRRRRRRRRRRRRRRRRRRRRRRRRRRRRRRRRRRRRRR
RRRRRRRRRRRRRRRRRRRRRRRRRRRRRRRRRRRRRRRRRRRR
RRRRRRRRRRRRRRRRRRRRRRRRRRRRRRRRRRRRRRRRRRRR
RRRRRRRRRRRRRRRRRRRRRRRRRRRRRRRRRRRRRRRRRRRR
RRRRRRRRRRRRRRRRRRRRRRRRRRRRRRRRRRRRRRRRRRRR
RRRRRRRRRRRRRRRRRRRRRRRRRRRRRRRRRRRRRRRRRRRR
RRRRRRRRRRRRRRRRRRRRRRRRRRRRRRRRRRRRRRRRRRRR
RRRRRRRRRRRRRRRRRRRRRRRRRRRRRRRRRRRRRRRRRRRR
RRRRRRRRRRRRRRRRRRRRRRRRRRRRRRRRRRRRRRRRRRRR

RRRRRRRRRRRRRRRRRRRRRRRRRRRRRRRRRRRRRRRRRRRRRR
RRRRRRRRRRRRRRRRRRRRRRRRRRRRRRRRRRRRRRRRRRRRRR
RRRRRRRRRRRRRRRRRRRRRRRRRRRRRRRRRRRRRRRRRRRRRR
RRRRRRRRRRRRRRRRRRRRRRRRRRRRRRRRRRRRRRRRRRRRRR
RRRRRRRRRRRRRRRRRRRRRRRRRRRRRRRRRRRRRRRRRRRRRR
RRRRRRRRRRRRRRRRRRRRRRRRRRRRRRRRRRRRRRRRRRRRRR
RRRRRRRRRRRRRRRRRRRRRRRRRRRRRRRRRRRRRRRRRRRRRR
RRRRRRRRRRRRRRRRRRRRRRRRRRRRRRRRRRRRRRRRRRRRRR
RRRRRRRRRRRRRRRRRRRRRRRRRRRRRRRRRRRRRRRRRRRRRR
RRRRRRRRRRRRRRRRRRRRRRRRRRRRRRRRRRRRRRRRRRRRRR
RRRRRRRRRRRRRRRRRRRRRRRRRRRRRRRRRRRRRRRRRRRRRR
RRRRRRRRRRRRRRRRRRRRRRRRRRRRRRRRRRRRRRRRRRRRRR
RRRRRRRRRRRRRRRRRRRRRRRRRRRRRRRRRRRRRRRRRRRRRR
RRRRRRRRRRRRRRRRRRRRRRRRRRRRRRRRRRRRRRRRRRRRRR
RRRRRRRRRRRRRRRRRRRRRRRRRRRRRRRRRRRRRRRRRRRRRR
RRRRRRRRRRRRRRRRRRRRRRRRRRRRRRRRRRRRRRRRRRRRRR
RRRRRRRRRRRRRRRRRRRRRRRRRRRRRRRRRRRRRRRRRRRRRR
RRRRRRRRRRRRRRRRRRRRRRRRRRRRRRRRRRRRRRRRRRRRRR
RRRRRRRRRRRRRRRRRRRRRRRRRRRRRRRRRRRRRRRRRRRRRR
RRRRRRRRRRRRRRRRRRRRRRRRRRRRRRRRRRRRRRRRRRRRRR
RRRRRRRRRRRRRRRRRRRRRRRRRRRRRRRRRRRRRRRRRRRRRR
RRRRRRRRRRRRRRRRRRRRRRRRRRRRRRRRRRRRRRRRRRRRRR
RRRRRRRRRRRRRRRRRRRRRRRRRRRRRRRRRRRRRRRRRRRRRR
RRRRRRRRRRRRRRRRRRRRRRRRRRRRRRRRRRRRRRRRRRRRRR

RRRRRRRRRRRRRRRRRRRRRRRRRRRRRRRRRRRRRRRRRRRR
RRRRRRRRRRRRRRRRRRRRRRRRRRRRRRRRRRRRRRRRRRRR
RRRRRRRRRRRRRRRRRRRRRRRRRRRRRRRRRRRRRRRRRRRR
RRRRRRRRRRRRRRRRRRRRRRRRRRRRRRRRRRRRRRRRRRRR
RRRRRRRRRRRRRRRRRRRRRRRRRRRRRRRRRRRRRRRRRRRR
RRRRRRRRRRRRRRRRRRRRRRRRRRRRRRRRRRRRRRRRRRRR
RRRRRRRRRRRRRRRRRRRRRRRRRRRRRRRRRRRRRRRRRRRR
RRRRRRRRRRRRRRRRRRRRRRRRRRRRRRRRRRRRRRRRRRRR
RRRRRRRRRRRRRRRRRRRRRRRRRRRRRRRRRRRRRRRRRRRR
RRRRRRRRRRRRRRRRRRRRRRRRRRRRRRRRRRRRRRRRRRRR
RRRRRRRRRRRRRRRRRRRRRRRRRRRRRRRRRRRRRRRRRRRR
RRRRRRRRRRRRRRRRRRRRRRRRRRRRRRRRRRRRRRRRRRRR
RRRRRRRRRRRRRRRRRRRRRRRRRRRRRRRRRRRRRRRRRRRR
RRRRRRRRRRRRRRRRRRRRRRRRRRRRRRRRRRRRRRRRRRRR
RRRRRRRRRRRRRRRRRRRRRRRRRRRRRRRRRRRRRRRRRRRR
RRRRRRRRRRRRRRRRRRRRRRRRRRRRRRRRRRRRRRRRRRRR
RRRRRRRRRRRRRRRRRRRRRRRRRRRRRRRRRRRRRRRRRRRR
RRRRRRRRRRRRRRRRRRRRRRRRRRRRRRRRRRRRRRRRRRRR
RRRRRRRRRRRRRRRRRRRRRRRRRRRRRRRRRRRRRRRRRRRR
RRRRRRRRRRRRRRRRRRRRRRRRRRRRRRRRRRRRRRRRRRRR
RRRRRRRRRRRRRRRRRRRRRRRRRRRRRRRRRRRRRRRRRRRR
RRRRRRRRRRRRRRRRRRRRRRRRRRRRRRRRRRRRRRRRRRRR
RRRRRRRRRRRRRRRRRRRRRRRRRRRRRRRRRRRRRRRRRRRR
RRRRRRRRRRRRRRRRRRRRRRRRRRRRRRRRRRRRRRRRRRRR
RRRRRRRRRRRRRRRRRRRRRRRRRRRRRRRRRRRRRRRRRRRR
RRRRRRRRRRRRRRRRRRRRRRRRRRRRRRRRRRRRRRRRRRRR
RRRRRRRRRRRRRRRRRRRRRRRRRRRRRRRRRRRRRRRRRRRR
RRRRRRRRRRRRRRRRRRRRRRRRRRRRRRRRRRRRRRRRRRRR
RRRRRRRRRRRRRRRRRRRRRRRRRRRRRRRRRRRRRRRRRRRR

RRRRRRRRRRRRRRRRRRRRRRRRRRRRRRRRRRRRRRRRRRRRRRRR
RRRRRRRRRRRRRRRRRRRRRRRRRRRRRRRRRRRRRRRRRRRRRRRR
RRRRRRRRRRRRRRRRRRRRRRRRRRRRRRRRRRRRRRRRRRRRRRRR
RRRRRRRRRRRRRRRRRRRRRRRRRRRRRRRRRRRRRRRRRRRRRRRR
RRRRRRRRRRRRRRRRRRRRRRRRRRRRRRRRRRRRRRRRRRRRRRRR
RRRRRRRRRRRRRRRRRRRRRRRRRRRRRRRRRRRRRRRRRRRRRRRR
RRRRRRRRRRRRRRRRRRRRRRRRRRRRRRRRRRRRRRRRRRRRRRRR
RRRRRRRRRRRRRRRRRRRRRRRRRRRRRRRRRRRRRRRRRRRRRRRR
RRRRRRRRRRRRRRRRRRRRRRRRRRRRRRRRRRRRRRRRRRRRRRRR
RRRRRRRRRRRRRRRRRRRRRRRRRRRRRRRRRRRRRRRRRRRRRRRR
RRRRRRRRRRRRRRRRRRRRRRRRRRRRRRRRRRRRRRRRRRRRRRRR
RRRRRRRRRRRRRRRRRRRRRRRRRRRRRRRRRRRRRRRRRRRRRRRR
RRRRRRRRRRRRRRRRRRRRRRRRRRRRRRRRRRRRRRRRRRRRRRRR
RRRRRRRRRRRRRRRRRRRRRRRRRRRRRRRRRRRRRRRRRRRRRRRR
RRRRRRRRRRRRRRRRRRRRRRRRRRRRRRRRRRRRRRRRRRRRRRRR
RRRRRRRRRRRRRRRRRRRRRRRRRRRRRRRRRRRRRRRRRRRRRRRR
RRRRRRRRRRRRRRRRRRRRRRRRRRRRRRRRRRRRRRRRRRRRRRRR
RRRRRRRRRRRRRRRRRRRRRRRRRRRRRRRRRRRRRRRRRRRRRRRR
RRRRRRRRRRRRRRRRRRRRRRRRRRRRRRRRRRRRRRRRRRRRRRRR
RRRRRRRRRRRRRRRRRRRRRRRRRRRRRRRRRRRRRRRRRRRRRRRR
RRRRRRRRRRRRRRRRRRRRRRRRRRRRRRRRRRRRRRRRRRRRRRRR
RRRRRRRRRRRRRRRRRRRRRRRRRRRRRRRRRRRRRRRRRRRRRRRR
RRRRRRRRRRRRRRRRRRRRRRRRRRRRRRRRRRRRRRRRRRRRRRRR
RRRRRRRRRRRRRRRRRRRRRRRRRRRRRRRRRRRRRRRRRRRRRRRR
RRRRRRRRRRRRRRRRRRRRRRRRRRRRRRRRRRRRRRRRRRRRRRRR
RRRRRRRRRRRRRRRRRRRRRRRRRRRRRRRRRRRRRRRRRRRRRRRR
RRRRRRRRRRRRRRRRRRRRRRRRRRRRRRRRRRRRRRRRRRRRRRRR
RRRRRRRRRRRRRRRRRRRRRRRRRRRRRRRRRRRRRRRRRRRRRRRR
RRRRRRRRRRRRRRRRRRRRRRRRRRRRRRRRRRRRRRRRRRRRRRRR
RRRRRRRRRRRRRRRRRRRRRRRRRRRRRRRRRRRRRRRRRRRRRRRR

RRRRRRRRRRRRRRRRRRRRRRRRRRRRRRRRRRRRRRRRRR
RRRRRRRRRRRRRRRRRRRRRRRRRRRRRRRRRRRRRRRRRR
RRRRRRRRRRRRRRRRRRRRRRRRRRRRRRRRRRRRRRRRRR
RRRRRRRRRRRRRRRRRRRRRRRRRRRRRRRRRRRRRRRRRR
RRRRRRRRRRRRRRRRRRRRRRRRRRRRRRRRRRRRRRRRRR
RRRRRRRRRRRRRRRRRRRRRRRRRRRRRRRRRRRRRRRRRR
RRRRRRRRRRRRRRRRRRRRRRRRRRRRRRRRRRRRRRRRRR
RRRRRRRRRRRRRRRRRRRRRRRRRRRRRRRRRRRRRRRRRR
RRRRRRRRRRRRRRRRRRRRRRRRRRRRRRRRRRRRRRRRRR
RRRRRRRRRRRRRRRRRRRRRRRRRRRRRRRRRRRRRRRRRR
RRRRRRRRRRRRRRRRRRRRRRRRRRRRRRRRRRRRRRRRRR
RRRRRRRRRRRRRRRRRRRRRRRRRRRRRRRRRRRRRRRRRR
RRRRRRRRRRRRRRRRRRRRRRRRRRRRRRRRRRRRRRRRRR
RRRRRRRRRRRRRRRRRRRRRRRRRRRRRRRRRRRRRRRRRR
RRRRRRRRRRRRRRRRRRRRRRRRRRRRRRRRRRRRRRRRRR
RRRRRRRRRRRRRRRRRRRRRRRRRRRRRRRRRRRRRRRRRR
RRRRRRRRRRRRRRRRRRRRRRRRRRRRRRRRRRRRRRRRRR
RRRRRRRRRRRRRRRRRRRRRRRRRRRRRRRRRRRRRRRRRR
RRRRRRRRRRRRRRRRRRRRRRRRRRRRRRRRRRRRRRRRRR
RRRRRRRRRRRRRRRRRRRRRRRRRRRRRRRRRRRRRRRRRR
RRRRRRRRRRRRRRRRRRRRRRRRRRRRRRRRRRRRRRRRRR
RRRRRRRRRRRRRRRRRRRRRRRRRRRRRRRRRRRRRRRRRR
RRRRRRRRRRRRRRRRRRRRRRRRRRRRRRRRRRRRRRRRRR
RRRRRRRRRRRRRRRRRRRRRRRRRRRRRRRRRRRRRRRRRR
RRRRRRRRRRRRRRRRRRRRRRRRRRRRRRRRRRRRRRRRRR
RRRRRRRRRRRRRRRRRRRRRRRRRRRRRRRRRRRRRRRRRR
RRRRRRRRRRRRRRRRRRRRRRRRRRRRRRRRRRRRRRRRRR
RRRRRRRRRRRRRRRRRRRRRRRRRRRRRRRRRRRRRRRRRR
RRRRRRRRRRRRRRRRRRRRRRRRRRRRRRRRRRRRRRRRRR

RRRRRRRRRRRRRRRRRRRRRRRRRRRRRRRRRRRRRRRRRRRR
RRRRRRRRRRRRRRRRRRRRRRRRRRRRRRRRRRRRRRRRRRRR
RRRRRRRRRRRRRRRRRRRRRRRRRRRRRRRRRRRRRRRRRRRR
RRRRRRRRRRRRRRRRRRRRRRRRRRRRRRRRRRRRRRRRRRRR
RRRRRRRRRRRRRRRRRRRRRRRRRRRRRRRRRRRRRRRRRRRR
RRRRRRRRRRRRRRRRRRRRRRRRRRRRRRRRRRRRRRRRRRRR
RRRRRRRRRRRRRRRRRRRRRRRRRRRRRRRRRRRRRRRRRRRR
RRRRRRRRRRRRRRRRRRRRRRRRRRRRRRRRRRRRRRRRRRRR
RRRRRRRRRRRRRRRRRRRRRRRRRRRRRRRRRRRRRRRRRRRR
RRRRRRRRRRRRRRRRRRRRRRRRRRRRRRRRRRRRRRRRRRRR
RRRRRRRRRRRRRRRRRRRRRRRRRRRRRRRRRRRRRRRRRRRR
RRRRRRRRRRRRRRRRRRRRRRRRRRRRRRRRRRRRRRRRRRRR
RRRRRRRRRRRRRRRRRRRRRRRRRRRRRRRRRRRRRRRRRRRR
RRRRRRRRRRRRRRRRRRRRRRRRRRRRRRRRRRRRRRRRRRRR
RRRRRRRRRRRRRRRRRRRRRRRRRRRRRRRRRRRRRRRRRRRR
RRRRRRRRRRRRRRRRRRRRRRRRRRRRRRRRRRRRRRRRRRRR
RRRRRRRRRRRRRRRRRRRRRRRRRRRRRRRRRRRRRRRRRRRR
RRRRRRRRRRRRRRRRRRRRRRRRRRRRRRRRRRRRRRRRRRRR
RRRRRRRRRRRRRRRRRRRRRRRRRRRRRRRRRRRRRRRRRRRR
RRRRRRRRRRRRRRRRRRRRRRRRRRRRRRRRRRRRRRRRRRRR
RRRRRRRRRRRRRRRRRRRRRRRRRRRRRRRRRRRRRRRRRRRR
RRRRRRRRRRRRRRRRRRRRRRRRRRRRRRRRRRRRRRRRRRRR
RRRRRRRRRRRRRRRRRRRRRRRRRRRRRRRRRRRRRRRRRRRR
RRRRRRRRRRRRRRRRRRRRRRRRRRRRRRRRRRRRRRRRRRRR
RRRRRRRRRRRRRRRRRRRRRRRRRRRRRRRRRRRRRRRRRRRR
RRRRRRRRRRRRRRRRRRRRRRRRRRRRRRRRRRRRRRRRRRRR
RRRRRRRRRRRRRRRRRRRRRRRRRRRRRRRRRRRRRRRRRRRR
RRRRRRRRRRRRRRRRRRRRRRRRRRRRRRRRRRRRRRRRRRRR
RRRRRRRRRRRRRRRRRRRRRRRRRRRRRRRRRRRRRRRRRRRR

RRRRRRRRRRRRRRRRRRRRRRRRRRRRRRRRRRRRRRRRRR
RRRRRRRRRRRRRRRRRRRRRRRRRRRRRRRRRRRRRRRRRR
RRRRRRRRRRRRRRRRRRRRRRRRRRRRRRRRRRRRRRRRRR
RRRRRRRRRRRRRRRRRRRRRRRRRRRRRRRRRRRRRRRRRR
RRRRRRRRRRRRRRRRRRRRRRRRRRRRRRRRRRRRRRRRRR
RRRRRRRRRRRRRRRRRRRRRRRRRRRRRRRRRRRRRRRRRR
RRRRRRRRRRRRRRRRRRRRRRRRRRRRRRRRRRRRRRRRRR
RRRRRRRRRRRRRRRRRRRRRRRRRRRRRRRRRRRRRRRRRR
RRRRRRRRRRRRRRRRRRRRRRRRRRRRRRRRRRRRRRRRRR
RRRRRRRRRRRRRRRRRRRRRRRRRRRRRRRRRRRRRRRRRR
RRRRRRRRRRRRRRRRRRRRRRRRRRRRRRRRRRRRRRRRRR
RRRRRRRRRRRRRRRRRRRRRRRRRRRRRRRRRRRRRRRRRR
RRRRRRRRRRRRRRRRRRRRRRRRRRRRRRRRRRRRRRRRRR
RRRRRRRRRRRRRRRRRRRRRRRRRRRRRRRRRRRRRRRRRR
RRRRRRRRRRRRRRRRRRRRRRRRRRRRRRRRRRRRRRRRRR
RRRRRRRRRRRRRRRRRRRRRRRRRRRRRRRRRRRRRRRRRR
RRRRRRRRRRRRRRRRRRRRRRRRRRRRRRRRRRRRRRRRRR
RRRRRRRRRRRRRRRRRRRRRRRRRRRRRRRRRRRRRRRRRR
RRRRRRRRRRRRRRRRRRRRRRRRRRRRRRRRRRRRRRRRRR
RRRRRRRRRRRRRRRRRRRRRRRRRRRRRRRRRRRRRRRRRR
RRRRRRRRRRRRRRRRRRRRRRRRRRRRRRRRRRRRRRRRRR
RRRRRRRRRRRRRRRRRRRRRRRRRRRRRRRRRRRRRRRRRR
RRRRRRRRRRRRRRRRRRRRRRRRRRRRRRRRRRRRRRRRRR
RRRRRRRRRRRRRRRRRRRRRRRRRRRRRRRRRRRRRRRRRR
RRRRRRRRRRRRRRRRRRRRRRRRRRRRRRRRRRRRRRRRRR
RRRRRRRRRRRRRRRRRRRRRRRRRRRRRRRRRRRRRRRRRR
RRRRRRRRRRRRRRRRRRRRRRRRRRRRRRRRRRRRRRRRRR
RRRRRRRRRRRRRRRRRRRRRRRRRRRRRRRRRRRRRRRRRR

RRRRRRRRRRRRRRRRRRRRRRRRRRRRRRRRRRRRRRRRRRRRR
RRRRRRRRRRRRRRRRRRRRRRRRRRRRRRRRRRRRRRRRRRRRR
RRRRRRRRRRRRRRRRRRRRRRRRRRRRRRRRRRRRRRRRRRRRR
RRRRRRRRRRRRRRRRRRRRRRRRRRRRRRRRRRRRRRRRRRRRR
RRRRRRRRRRRRRRRRRRRRRRRRRRRRRRRRRRRRRRRRRRRRR
RRRRRRRRRRRRRRRRRRRRRRRRRRRRRRRRRRRRRRRRRRRRR
RRRRRRRRRRRRRRRRRRRRRRRRRRRRRRRRRRRRRRRRRRRRR
RRRRRRRRRRRRRRRRRRRRRRRRRRRRRRRRRRRRRRRRRRRRR
RRRRRRRRRRRRRRRRRRRRRRRRRRRRRRRRRRRRRRRRRRRRR
RRRRRRRRRRRRRRRRRRRRRRRRRRRRRRRRRRRRRRRRRRRRR
RRRRRRRRRRRRRRRRRRRRRRRRRRRRRRRRRRRRRRRRRRRRR
RRRRRRRRRRRRRRRRRRRRRRRRRRRRRRRRRRRRRRRRRRRRR
RRRRRRRRRRRRRRRRRRRRRRRRRRRRRRRRRRRRRRRRRRRRR
RRRRRRRRRRRRRRRRRRRRRRRRRRRRRRRRRRRRRRRRRRRRR
RRRRRRRRRRRRRRRRRRRRRRRRRRRRRRRRRRRRRRRRRRRRR
RRRRRRRRRRRRRRRRRRRRRRRRRRRRRRRRRRRRRRRRRRRRR
RRRRRRRRRRRRRRRRRRRRRRRRRRRRRRRRRRRRRRRRRRRRR
RRRRRRRRRRRRRRRRRRRRRRRRRRRRRRRRRRRRRRRRRRRRR
RRRRRRRRRRRRRRRRRRRRRRRRRRRRRRRRRRRRRRRRRRRRR
RRRRRRRRRRRRRRRRRRRRRRRRRRRRRRRRRRRRRRRRRRRRR
RRRRRRRRRRRRRRRRRRRRRRRRRRRRRRRRRRRRRRRRRRRRR
RRRRRRRRRRRRRRRRRRRRRRRRRRRRRRRRRRRRRRRRRRRRR
RRRRRRRRRRRRRRRRRRRRRRRRRRRRRRRRRRRRRRRRRRRRR
RRRRRRRRRRRRRRRRRRRRRRRRRRRRRRRRRRRRRRRRRRRRR
RRRRRRRRRRRRRRRRRRRRRRRRRRRRRRRRRRRRRRRRRRRRR
RRRRRRRRRRRRRRRRRRRRRRRRRRRRRRRRRRRRRRRRRRRRR
RRRRRRRRRRRRRRRRRRRRRRRRRRRRRRRRRRRRRRRRRRRRR

RRRRRRRRRRRRRRRRRRRRRRRRRRRRRRRRRRRRR
RRRRRRRRRRRRRRRRRRRRRRRRRRRRRRRRRRRRR
RRRRRRRRRRRRRRRRRRRRRRRRRRRRRRRRRRRRR
RRRRRRRRRRRRRRRRRRRRRRRRRRRRRRRRRRRRR
RRRRRRRRRRRRRRRRRRRRRRRRRRRRRRRRRRRRR
RRRRRRRRRRRRRRRRRRRRRRRRRRRRRRRRRRRRR
RRRRRRRRRRRRRRRRRRRRRRRRRRRRRRRRRRRRR
RRRRRRRRRRRRRRRRRRRRRRRRRRRRRRRRRRRRR
RRRRRRRRRRRRRRRRRRRRRRRRRRRRRRRRRRRRR
RRRRRRRRRRRRRRRRRRRRRRRRRRRRRRRRRRRRR
RRRRRRRRRRRRRRRRRRRRRRRRRRRRRRRRRRRRR
RRRRRRRRRRRRRRRRRRRRRRRRRRRRRRRRRRRRR
RRRRRRRRRRRRRRRRRRRRRRRRRRRRRRRRRRRRR
RRRRRRRRRRRRRRRRRRRRRRRRRRRRRRRRRRRRR
RRRRRRRRRRRRRRRRRRRRRRRRRRRRRRRRRRRRR
RRRRRRRRRRRRRRRRRRRRRRRRRRRRRRRRRRRRR
RRRRRRRRRRRRRRRRRRRRRRRRRRRRRRRRRRRRR
RRRRRRRRRRRRRRRRRRRRRRRRRRRRRRRRRRRRR
RRRRRRRRRRRRRRRRRRRRRRRRRRRRRRRRRRRRR
RRRRRRRRRRRRRRRRRRRRRRRRRRRRRRRRRRRRR
RRRRRRRRRRRRRRRRRRRRRRRRRRRRRRRRRRRRR
RRRRRRRRRRRRRRRRRRRRRRRRRRRRRRRRRRRRR
RRRRRRRRRRRRRRRRRRRRRRRRRRRRRRRRRRRRR
RRRRRRRRRRRRRRRRRRRRRRRRRRRRRRRRRRRRR
RRRRRRRRRRRRRRRRRRRRRRRRRRRRRRRRRRRRR
RRRRRRRRRRRRRRRRRRRRRRRRRRRRRRRRRRRRR
RRRRRRRRRRRRRRRRRRRRRRRRRRRRRRRRRRRRR
RRRRRRRRRRRRRRRRRRRRRRRRRRRRRRRRRRRRR

RRRRRRRRRRRRRRRRRRRRRRRRRRRRRRRRRRRRRRRRRRRRRRR
RRRRRRRRRRRRRRRRRRRRRRRRRRRRRRRRRRRRRRRRRRRRRRR
RRRRRRRRRRRRRRRRRRRRRRRRRRRRRRRRRRRRRRRRRRRRRRR
RRRRRRRRRRRRRRRRRRRRRRRRRRRRRRRRRRRRRRRRRRRRRRR
RRRRRRRRRRRRRRRRRRRRRRRRRRRRRRRRRRRRRRRRRRRRRRR
RRRRRRRRRRRRRRRRRRRRRRRRRRRRRRRRRRRRRRRRRRRRRRR
RRRRRRRRRRRRRRRRRRRRRRRRRRRRRRRRRRRRRRRRRRRRRRR
RRRRRRRRRRRRRRRRRRRRRRRRRRRRRRRRRRRRRRRRRRRRRRR
RRRRRRRRRRRRRRRRRRRRRRRRRRRRRRRRRRRRRRRRRRRRRRR
RRRRRRRRRRRRRRRRRRRRRRRRRRRRRRRRRRRRRRRRRRRRRRR
RRRRRRRRRRRRRRRRRRRRRRRRRRRRRRRRRRRRRRRRRRRRRRR
RRRRRRRRRRRRRRRRRRRRRRRRRRRRRRRRRRRRRRRRRRRRRRR
RRRRRRRRRRRRRRRRRRRRRRRRRRRRRRRRRRRRRRRRRRRRRRR
RRRRRRRRRRRRRRRRRRRRRRRRRRRRRRRRRRRRRRRRRRRRRRR
RRRRRRRRRRRRRRRRRRRRRRRRRRRRRRRRRRRRRRRRRRRRRRR
RRRRRRRRRRRRRRRRRRRRRRRRRRRRRRRRRRRRRRRRRRRRRRR
RRRRRRRRRRRRRRRRRRRRRRRRRRRRRRRRRRRRRRRRRRRRRRR
RRRRRRRRRRRRRRRRRRRRRRRRRRRRRRRRRRRRRRRRRRRRRRR
RRRRRRRRRRRRRRRRRRRRRRRRRRRRRRRRRRRRRRRRRRRRRRR
RRRRRRRRRRRRRRRRRRRRRRRRRRRRRRRRRRRRRRRRRRRRRRR
RRRRRRRRRRRRRRRRRRRRRRRRRRRRRRRRRRRRRRRRRRRRRRR
RRRRRRRRRRRRRRRRRRRRRRRRRRRRRRRRRRRRRRRRRRRRRRR
RRRRRRRRRRRRRRRRRRRRRRRRRRRRRRRRRRRRRRRRRRRRRRR
RRRRRRRRRRRRRRRRRRRRRRRRRRRRRRRRRRRRRRRRRRRRRRR
RRRRRRRRRRRRRRRRRRRRRRRRRRRRRRRRRRRRRRRRRRRRRRR
RRRRRRRRRRRRRRRRRRRRRRRRRRRRRRRRRRRRRRRRRRRRRRR

RRRRRRRRRRRRRRRRRRRRRRRRRRRRRRRRRRRRRRRRRRRRR
RRRRRRRRRRRRRRRRRRRRRRRRRRRRRRRRRRRRRRRRRRRRR
RRRRRRRRRRRRRRRRRRRRRRRRRRRRRRRRRRRRRRRRRRRRR
RRRRRRRRRRRRRRRRRRRRRRRRRRRRRRRRRRRRRRRRRRRRR
RRRRRRRRRRRRRRRRRRRRRRRRRRRRRRRRRRRRRRRRRRRRR
RRRRRRRRRRRRRRRRRRRRRRRRRRRRRRRRRRRRRRRRRRRRR
RRRRRRRRRRRRRRRRRRRRRRRRRRRRRRRRRRRRRRRRRRRRR
RRRRRRRRRRRRRRRRRRRRRRRRRRRRRRRRRRRRRRRRRRRRR
RRRRRRRRRRRRRRRRRRRRRRRRRRRRRRRRRRRRRRRRRRRRR
RRRRRRRRRRRRRRRRRRRRRRRRRRRRRRRRRRRRRRRRRRRRR
RRRRRRRRRRRRRRRRRRRRRRRRRRRRRRRRRRRRRRRRRRRRR
RRRRRRRRRRRRRRRRRRRRRRRRRRRRRRRRRRRRRRRRRRRRR
RRRRRRRRRRRRRRRRRRRRRRRRRRRRRRRRRRRRRRRRRRRRR
RRRRRRRRRRRRRRRRRRRRRRRRRRRRRRRRRRRRRRRRRRRRR
RRRRRRRRRRRRRRRRRRRRRRRRRRRRRRRRRRRRRRRRRRRRR
RRRRRRRRRRRRRRRRRRRRRRRRRRRRRRRRRRRRRRRRRRRRR
RRRRRRRRRRRRRRRRRRRRRRRRRRRRRRRRRRRRRRRRRRRRR
RRRRRRRRRRRRRRRRRRRRRRRRRRRRRRRRRRRRRRRRRRRRR
RRRRRRRRRRRRRRRRRRRRRRRRRRRRRRRRRRRRRRRRRRRRR
RRRRRRRRRRRRRRRRRRRRRRRRRRRRRRRRRRRRRRRRRRRRR
RRRRRRRRRRRRRRRRRRRRRRRRRRRRRRRRRRRRRRRRRRRRR
RRRRRRRRRRRRRRRRRRRRRRRRRRRRRRRRRRRRRRRRRRRRR
RRRRRRRRRRRRRRRRRRRRRRRRRRRRRRRRRRRRRRRRRRRRR
RRRRRRRRRRRRRRRRRRRRRRRRRRRRRRRRRRRRRRRRRRRRR
RRRRRRRRRRRRRRRRRRRRRRRRRRRRRRRRRRRRRRRRRRRRR
RRRRRRRRRRRRRRRRRRRRRRRRRRRRRRRRRRRRRRRRRRRRR

RRRRRRRRRRRRRRRRRRRRRRRRRRRRRRRRRRRRRRRRRRR
RRRRRRRRRRRRRRRRRRRRRRRRRRRRRRRRRRRRRRRRRRR
RRRRRRRRRRRRRRRRRRRRRRRRRRRRRRRRRRRRRRRRRRR
RRRRRRRRRRRRRRRRRRRRRRRRRRRRRRRRRRRRRRRRRRR
RRRRRRRRRRRRRRRRRRRRRRRRRRRRRRRRRRRRRRRRRRR
RRRRRRRRRRRRRRRRRRRRRRRRRRRRRRRRRRRRRRRRRRR
RRRRRRRRRRRRRRRRRRRRRRRRRRRRRRRRRRRRRRRRRRR
RRRRRRRRRRRRRRRRRRRRRRRRRRRRRRRRRRRRRRRRRRR
RRRRRRRRRRRRRRRRRRRRRRRRRRRRRRRRRRRRRRRRRRR
RRRRRRRRRRRRRRRRRRRRRRRRRRRRRRRRRRRRRRRRRRR
RRRRRRRRRRRRRRRRRRRRRRRRRRRRRRRRRRRRRRRRRRR
RRRRRRRRRRRRRRRRRRRRRRRRRRRRRRRRRRRRRRRRRRR
RRRRRRRRRRRRRRRRRRRRRRRRRRRRRRRRRRRRRRRRRRR
RRRRRRRRRRRRRRRRRRRRRRRRRRRRRRRRRRRRRRRRRRR
RRRRRRRRRRRRRRRRRRRRRRRRRRRRRRRRRRRRRRRRRRR
RRRRRRRRRRRRRRRRRRRRRRRRRRRRRRRRRRRRRRRRRRR
RRRRRRRRRRRRRRRRRRRRRRRRRRRRRRRRRRRRRRRRRRR
RRRRRRRRRRRRRRRRRRRRRRRRRRRRRRRRRRRRRRRRRRR
RRRRRRRRRRRRRRRRRRRRRRRRRRRRRRRRRRRRRRRRRRR
RRRRRRRRRRRRRRRRRRRRRRRRRRRRRRRRRRRRRRRRRRR
RRRRRRRRRRRRRRRRRRRRRRRRRRRRRRRRRRRRRRRRRRR
RRRRRRRRRRRRRRRRRRRRRRRRRRRRRRRRRRRRRRRRRRR
RRRRRRRRRRRRRRRRRRRRRRRRRRRRRRRRRRRRRRRRRRR
RRRRRRRRRRRRRRRRRRRRRRRRRRRRRRRRRRRRRRRRRRR
RRRRRRRRRRRRRRRRRRRRRRRRRRRRRRRRRRRRRRRRRRR
RRRRRRRRRRRRRRRRRRRRRRRRRRRRRRRRRRRRRRRRRRR
RRRRRRRRRRRRRRRRRRRRRRRRRRRRRRRRRRRRRRRRRRR
RRRRRRRRRRRRRRRRRRRRRRRRRRRRRRRRRRRRRRRRRRR

RRRRRRRRRRRRRRRRRRRRRRRRRRRRRRRRRRRRRRRRRRRRR
RRRRRRRRRRRRRRRRRRRRRRRRRRRRRRRRRRRRRRRRRRRRR
RRRRRRRRRRRRRRRRRRRRRRRRRRRRRRRRRRRRRRRRRRRRR
RRRRRRRRRRRRRRRRRRRRRRRRRRRRRRRRRRRRRRRRRRRRR
RRRRRRRRRRRRRRRRRRRRRRRRRRRRRRRRRRRRRRRRRRRRR
RRRRRRRRRRRRRRRRRRRRRRRRRRRRRRRRRRRRRRRRRRRRR
RRRRRRRRRRRRRRRRRRRRRRRRRRRRRRRRRRRRRRRRRRRRR
RRRRRRRRRRRRRRRRRRRRRRRRRRRRRRRRRRRRRRRRRRRRR
RRRRRRRRRRRRRRRRRRRRRRRRRRRRRRRRRRRRRRRRRRRRR
RRRRRRRRRRRRRRRRRRRRRRRRRRRRRRRRRRRRRRRRRRRRR
RRRRRRRRRRRRRRRRRRRRRRRRRRRRRRRRRRRRRRRRRRRRR
RRRRRRRRRRRRRRRRRRRRRRRRRRRRRRRRRRRRRRRRRRRRR
RRRRRRRRRRRRRRRRRRRRRRRRRRRRRRRRRRRRRRRRRRRRR
RRRRRRRRRRRRRRRRRRRRRRRRRRRRRRRRRRRRRRRRRRRRR
RRRRRRRRRRRRRRRRRRRRRRRRRRRRRRRRRRRRRRRRRRRRR
RRRRRRRRRRRRRRRRRRRRRRRRRRRRRRRRRRRRRRRRRRRRR
RRRRRRRRRRRRRRRRRRRRRRRRRRRRRRRRRRRRRRRRRRRRR
RRRRRRRRRRRRRRRRRRRRRRRRRRRRRRRRRRRRRRRRRRRRR
RRRRRRRRRRRRRRRRRRRRRRRRRRRRRRRRRRRRRRRRRRRRR
RRRRRRRRRRRRRRRRRRRRRRRRRRRRRRRRRRRRRRRRRRRRR
RRRRRRRRRRRRRRRRRRRRRRRRRRRRRRRRRRRRRRRRRRRRR
RRRRRRRRRRRRRRRRRRRRRRRRRRRRRRRRRRRRRRRRRRRRR
RRRRRRRRRRRRRRRRRRRRRRRRRRRRRRRRRRRRRRRRRRRRR
RRRRRRRRRRRRRRRRRRRRRRRRRRRRRRRRRRRRRRRRRRRRR
RRRRRRRRRRRRRRRRRRRRRRRRRRRRRRRRRRRRRRRRRRRRR
RRRRRRRRRRRRRRRRRRRRRRRRRRRRRRRRRRRRRRRRRRRRR
RRRRRRRRRRRRRRRRRRRRRRRRRRRRRRRRRRRRRRRRRRRRR
RRRRRRRRRRRRRRRRRRRRRRRRRRRRRRRRRRRRRRRRRRRRR
RRRRRRRRRRRRRRRRRRRRRRRRRRRRRRRRRRRRRRRRRRRRR

RRRRRRRRRRRRRRRRRRRRRRRRRRRRRRRRRRRRRRRRRRRRRRR
RRRRRRRRRRRRRRRRRRRRRRRRRRRRRRRRRRRRRRRRRRRRRRR
RRRRRRRRRRRRRRRRRRRRRRRRRRRRRRRRRRRRRRRRRRRRRRR
RRRRRRRRRRRRRRRRRRRRRRRRRRRRRRRRRRRRRRRRRRRRRRR
RRRRRRRRRRRRRRRRRRRRRRRRRRRRRRRRRRRRRRRRRRRRRRR
RRRRRRRRRRRRRRRRRRRRRRRRRRRRRRRRRRRRRRRRRRRRRRR
RRRRRRRRRRRRRRRRRRRRRRRRRRRRRRRRRRRRRRRRRRRRRRR
RRRRRRRRRRRRRRRRRRRRRRRRRRRRRRRRRRRRRRRRRRRRRRR
RRRRRRRRRRRRRRRRRRRRRRRRRRRRRRRRRRRRRRRRRRRRRRR
RRRRRRRRRRRRRRRRRRRRRRRRRRRRRRRRRRRRRRRRRRRRRRR
RRRRRRRRRRRRRRRRRRRRRRRRRRRRRRRRRRRRRRRRRRRRRRR
RRRRRRRRRRRRRRRRRRRRRRRRRRRRRRRRRRRRRRRRRRRRRRR
RRRRRRRRRRRRRRRRRRRRRRRRRRRRRRRRRRRRRRRRRRRRRRR
RRRRRRRRRRRRRRRRRRRRRRRRRRRRRRRRRRRRRRRRRRRRRRR
RRRRRRRRRRRRRRRRRRRRRRRRRRRRRRRRRRRRRRRRRRRRRRR
RRRRRRRRRRRRRRRRRRRRRRRRRRRRRRRRRRRRRRRRRRRRRRR
RRRRRRRRRRRRRRRRRRRRRRRRRRRRRRRRRRRRRRRRRRRRRRR
RRRRRRRRRRRRRRRRRRRRRRRRRRRRRRRRRRRRRRRRRRRRRRR
RRRRRRRRRRRRRRRRRRRRRRRRRRRRRRRRRRRRRRRRRRRRRRR
RRRRRRRRRRRRRRRRRRRRRRRRRRRRRRRRRRRRRRRRRRRRRRR
RRRRRRRRRRRRRRRRRRRRRRRRRRRRRRRRRRRRRRRRRRRRRRR
RRRRRRRRRRRRRRRRRRRRRRRRRRRRRRRRRRRRRRRRRRRRRRR
RRRRRRRRRRRRRRRRRRRRRRRRRRRRRRRRRRRRRRRRRRRRRRR
RRRRRRRRRRRRRRRRRRRRRRRRRRRRRRRRRRRRRRRRRRRRRRR
RRRRRRRRRRRRRRRRRRRRRRRRRRRRRRRRRRRRRRRRRRRRRRR
RRRRRRRRRRRRRRRRRRRRRRRRRRRRRRRRRRRRRRRRRRRRRRR
RRRRRRRRRRRRRRRRRRRRRRRRRRRRRRRRRRRRRRRRRRRRRRR

RRRRRRRRRRRRRRRRRRRRRRRRRRRRRRRRRRRRRRRRRRRR
RRRRRRRRRRRRRRRRRRRRRRRRRRRRRRRRRRRRRRRRRRRR
RRRRRRRRRRRRRRRRRRRRRRRRRRRRRRRRRRRRRRRRRRRR
RRRRRRRRRRRRRRRRRRRRRRRRRRRRRRRRRRRRRRRRRRRR
RRRRRRRRRRRRRRRRRRRRRRRRRRRRRRRRRRRRRRRRRRRR
RRRRRRRRRRRRRRRRRRRRRRRRRRRRRRRRRRRRRRRRRRRR
RRRRRRRRRRRRRRRRRRRRRRRRRRRRRRRRRRRRRRRRRRRR
RRRRRRRRRRRRRRRRRRRRRRRRRRRRRRRRRRRRRRRRRRRR
RRRRRRRRRRRRRRRRRRRRRRRRRRRRRRRRRRRRRRRRRRRR
RRRRRRRRRRRRRRRRRRRRRRRRRRRRRRRRRRRRRRRRRRRR
RRRRRRRRRRRRRRRRRRRRRRRRRRRRRRRRRRRRRRRRRRRR
RRRRRRRRRRRRRRRRRRRRRRRRRRRRRRRRRRRRRRRRRRRR
RRRRRRRRRRRRRRRRRRRRRRRRRRRRRRRRRRRRRRRRRRRR
RRRRRRRRRRRRRRRRRRRRRRRRRRRRRRRRRRRRRRRRRRRR
RRRRRRRRRRRRRRRRRRRRRRRRRRRRRRRRRRRRRRRRRRRR
RRRRRRRRRRRRRRRRRRRRRRRRRRRRRRRRRRRRRRRRRRRR
RRRRRRRRRRRRRRRRRRRRRRRRRRRRRRRRRRRRRRRRRRRR
RRRRRRRRRRRRRRRRRRRRRRRRRRRRRRRRRRRRRRRRRRRR
RRRRRRRRRRRRRRRRRRRRRRRRRRRRRRRRRRRRRRRRRRRR
RRRRRRRRRRRRRRRRRRRRRRRRRRRRRRRRRRRRRRRRRRRR
RRRRRRRRRRRRRRRRRRRRRRRRRRRRRRRRRRRRRRRRRRRR
RRRRRRRRRRRRRRRRRRRRRRRRRRRRRRRRRRRRRRRRRRRR
RRRRRRRRRRRRRRRRRRRRRRRRRRRRRRRRRRRRRRRRRRRR
RRRRRRRRRRRRRRRRRRRRRRRRRRRRRRRRRRRRRRRRRRRR
RRRRRRRRRRRRRRRRRRRRRRRRRRRRRRRRRRRRRRRRRRRR
RRRRRRRRRRRRRRRRRRRRRRRRRRRRRRRRRRRRRRRRRRRR
RRRRRRRRRRRRRRRRRRRRRRRRRRRRRRRRRRRRRRRRRRRR
RRRRRRRRRRRRRRRRRRRRRRRRRRRRRRRRRRRRRRRRRRRR

RRRRRRRRRRRRRRRRRRRRRRRRRRRRRRRRRRRRRRRRRRRR
RRRRRRRRRRRRRRRRRRRRRRRRRRRRRRRRRRRRRRRRRRRR
RRRRRRRRRRRRRRRRRRRRRRRRRRRRRRRRRRRRRRRRRRRR
RRRRRRRRRRRRRRRRRRRRRRRRRRRRRRRRRRRRRRRRRRRR
RRRRRRRRRRRRRRRRRRRRRRRRRRRRRRRRRRRRRRRRRRRR
RRRRRRRRRRRRRRRRRRRRRRRRRRRRRRRRRRRRRRRRRRRR
RRRRRRRRRRRRRRRRRRRRRRRRRRRRRRRRRRRRRRRRRRRR
RRRRRRRRRRRRRRRRRRRRRRRRRRRRRRRRRRRRRRRRRRRR
RRRRRRRRRRRRRRRRRRRRRRRRRRRRRRRRRRRRRRRRRRRR
RRRRRRRRRRRRRRRRRRRRRRRRRRRRRRRRRRRRRRRRRRRR
RRRRRRRRRRRRRRRRRRRRRRRRRRRRRRRRRRRRRRRRRRRR
RRRRRRRRRRRRRRRRRRRRRRRRRRRRRRRRRRRRRRRRRRRR
RRRRRRRRRRRRRRRRRRRRRRRRRRRRRRRRRRRRRRRRRRRR
RRRRRRRRRRRRRRRRRRRRRRRRRRRRRRRRRRRRRRRRRRRR
RRRRRRRRRRRRRRRRRRRRRRRRRRRRRRRRRRRRRRRRRRRR
RRRRRRRRRRRRRRRRRRRRRRRRRRRRRRRRRRRRRRRRRRRR
RRRRRRRRRRRRRRRRRRRRRRRRRRRRRRRRRRRRRRRRRRRR
RRRRRRRRRRRRRRRRRRRRRRRRRRRRRRRRRRRRRRRRRRRR
RRRRRRRRRRRRRRRRRRRRRRRRRRRRRRRRRRRRRRRRRRRR
RRRRRRRRRRRRRRRRRRRRRRRRRRRRRRRRRRRRRRRRRRRR
RRRRRRRRRRRRRRRRRRRRRRRRRRRRRRRRRRRRRRRRRRRR
RRRRRRRRRRRRRRRRRRRRRRRRRRRRRRRRRRRRRRRRRRRR
RRRRRRRRRRRRRRRRRRRRRRRRRRRRRRRRRRRRRRRRRRRR
RRRRRRRRRRRRRRRRRRRRRRRRRRRRRRRRRRRRRRRRRRRR
RRRRRRRRRRRRRRRRRRRRRRRRRRRRRRRRRRRRRRRRRRRR

RRRRRRRRRRRRRRRRRRRRRRRRRRRRRRRRRRRRRRRRRRRRR
RRRRRRRRRRRRRRRRRRRRRRRRRRRRRRRRRRRRRRRRRRRRR
RRRRRRRRRRRRRRRRRRRRRRRRRRRRRRRRRRRRRRRRRRRRR
RRRRRRRRRRRRRRRRRRRRRRRRRRRRRRRRRRRRRRRRRRRRR
RRRRRRRRRRRRRRRRRRRRRRRRRRRRRRRRRRRRRRRRRRRRR
RRRRRRRRRRRRRRRRRRRRRRRRRRRRRRRRRRRRRRRRRRRRR
RRRRRRRRRRRRRRRRRRRRRRRRRRRRRRRRRRRRRRRRRRRRR
RRRRRRRRRRRRRRRRRRRRRRRRRRRRRRRRRRRRRRRRRRRRR
RRRRRRRRRRRRRRRRRRRRRRRRRRRRRRRRRRRRRRRRRRRRR
RRRRRRRRRRRRRRRRRRRRRRRRRRRRRRRRRRRRRRRRRRRRR
RRRRRRRRRRRRRRRRRRRRRRRRRRRRRRRRRRRRRRRRRRRRR
RRRRRRRRRRRRRRRRRRRRRRRRRRRRRRRRRRRRRRRRRRRRR
RRRRRRRRRRRRRRRRRRRRRRRRRRRRRRRRRRRRRRRRRRRRR
RRRRRRRRRRRRRRRRRRRRRRRRRRRRRRRRRRRRRRRRRRRRR
RRRRRRRRRRRRRRRRRRRRRRRRRRRRRRRRRRRRRRRRRRRRR
RRRRRRRRRRRRRRRRRRRRRRRRRRRRRRRRRRRRRRRRRRRRR
RRRRRRRRRRRRRRRRRRRRRRRRRRRRRRRRRRRRRRRRRRRRR
RRRRRRRRRRRRRRRRRRRRRRRRRRRRRRRRRRRRRRRRRRRRR
RRRRRRRRRRRRRRRRRRRRRRRRRRRRRRRRRRRRRRRRRRRRR
RRRRRRRRRRRRRRRRRRRRRRRRRRRRRRRRRRRRRRRRRRRRR
RRRRRRRRRRRRRRRRRRRRRRRRRRRRRRRRRRRRRRRRRRRRR
RRRRRRRRRRRRRRRRRRRRRRRRRRRRRRRRRRRRRRRRRRRRR
RRRRRRRRRRRRRRRRRRRRRRRRRRRRRRRRRRRRRRRRRRRRR
RRRRRRRRRRRRRRRRRRRRRRRRRRRRRRRRRRRRRRRRRRRRR
RRRRRRRRRRRRRRRRRRRRRRRRRRRRRRRRRRRRRRRRRRRRR
RRRRRRRRRRRRRRRRRRRRRRRRRRRRRRRRRRRRRRRRRRRRR
RRRRRRRRRRRRRRRRRRRRRRRRRRRRRRRRRRRRRRRRRRRRR
RRRRRRRRRRRRRRRRRRRRRRRRRRRRRRRRRRRRRRRRRRRRR
RRRRRRRRRRRRRRRRRRRRRRRRRRRRRRRRRRRRRRRRRRRRR
RRRRRRRRRRRRRRRRRRRRRRRRRRRRRRRRRRRRRRRRRRRRR

RRRRRRRRRRRRRRRRRRRRRRRRRRRRRRRRRRRR
RRRRRRRRRRRRRRRRRRRRRRRRRRRRRRRRRRRR
RRRRRRRRRRRRRRRRRRRRRRRRRRRRRRRRRRRR
RRRRRRRRRRRRRRRRRRRRRRRRRRRRRRRRRRRR
RRRRRRRRRRRRRRRRRRRRRRRRRRRRRRRRRRRR
RRRRRRRRRRRRRRRRRRRRRRRRRRRRRRRRRRRR
RRRRRRRRRRRRRRRRRRRRRRRRRRRRRRRRRRRR
RRRRRRRRRRRRRRRRRRRRRRRRRRRRRRRRRRRR
RRRRRRRRRRRRRRRRRRRRRRRRRRRRRRRRRRRR
RRRRRRRRRRRRRRRRRRRRRRRRRRRRRRRRRRRR
RRRRRRRRRRRRRRRRRRRRRRRRRRRRRRRRRRRR
RRRRRRRRRRRRRRRRRRRRRRRRRRRRRRRRRRRR
RRRRRRRRRRRRRRRRRRRRRRRRRRRRRRRRRRRR
RRRRRRRRRRRRRRRRRRRRRRRRRRRRRRRRRRRR
RRRRRRRRRRRRRRRRRRRRRRRRRRRRRRRRRRRR
RRRRRRRRRRRRRRRRRRRRRRRRRRRRRRRRRRRR
RRRRRRRRRRRRRRRRRRRRRRRRRRRRRRRRRRRR
RRRRRRRRRRRRRRRRRRRRRRRRRRRRRRRRRRRR
RRRRRRRRRRRRRRRRRRRRRRRRRRRRRRRRRRRR
RRRRRRRRRRRRRRRRRRRRRRRRRRRRRRRRRRRR
RRRRRRRRRRRRRRRRRRRRRRRRRRRRRRRRRRRR
RRRRRRRRRRRRRRRRRRRRRRRRRRRRRRRRRRRR
RRRRRRRRRRRRRRRRRRRRRRRRRRRRRRRRRRRR
RRRRRRRRRRRRRRRRRRRRRRRRRRRRRRRRRRRR
RRRRRRRRRRRRRRRRRRRRRRRRRRRRRRRRRRRR
RRRRRRRRRRRRRRRRRRRRRRRRRRRRRRRRRRRR

RRRRRRRRRRRRRRRRRRRRRRRRRRRRRRRRRRRRRRRRRRRR
RRRRRRRRRRRRRRRRRRRRRRRRRRRRRRRRRRRRRRRRRRRR
RRRRRRRRRRRRRRRRRRRRRRRRRRRRRRRRRRRRRRRRRRRR
RRRRRRRRRRRRRRRRRRRRRRRRRRRRRRRRRRRRRRRRRRRR
RRRRRRRRRRRRRRRRRRRRRRRRRRRRRRRRRRRRRRRRRRRR
RRRRRRRRRRRRRRRRRRRRRRRRRRRRRRRRRRRRRRRRRRRR
RRRRRRRRRRRRRRRRRRRRRRRRRRRRRRRRRRRRRRRRRRRR
RRRRRRRRRRRRRRRRRRRRRRRRRRRRRRRRRRRRRRRRRRRR
RRRRRRRRRRRRRRRRRRRRRRRRRRRRRRRRRRRRRRRRRRRR
RRRRRRRRRRRRRRRRRRRRRRRRRRRRRRRRRRRRRRRRRRRR
RRRRRRRRRRRRRRRRRRRRRRRRRRRRRRRRRRRRRRRRRRRR
RRRRRRRRRRRRRRRRRRRRRRRRRRRRRRRRRRRRRRRRRRRR
RRRRRRRRRRRRRRRRRRRRRRRRRRRRRRRRRRRRRRRRRRRR
RRRRRRRRRRRRRRRRRRRRRRRRRRRRRRRRRRRRRRRRRRRR
RRRRRRRRRRRRRRRRRRRRRRRRRRRRRRRRRRRRRRRRRRRR
RRRRRRRRRRRRRRRRRRRRRRRRRRRRRRRRRRRRRRRRRRRR
RRRRRRRRRRRRRRRRRRRRRRRRRRRRRRRRRRRRRRRRRRRR
RRRRRRRRRRRRRRRRRRRRRRRRRRRRRRRRRRRRRRRRRRRR
RRRRRRRRRRRRRRRRRRRRRRRRRRRRRRRRRRRRRRRRRRRR
RRRRRRRRRRRRRRRRRRRRRRRRRRRRRRRRRRRRRRRRRRRR
RRRRRRRRRRRRRRRRRRRRRRRRRRRRRRRRRRRRRRRRRRRR
RRRRRRRRRRRRRRRRRRRRRRRRRRRRRRRRRRRRRRRRRRRR
RRRRRRRRRRRRRRRRRRRRRRRRRRRRRRRRRRRRRRRRRRRR
RRRRRRRRRRRRRRRRRRRRRRRRRRRRRRRRRRRRRRRRRRRR
RRRRRRRRRRRRRRRRRRRRRRRRRRRRRRRRRRRRRRRRRRRR
RRRRRRRRRRRRRRRRRRRRRRRRRRRRRRRRRRRRRRRRRRRR

RRRRRRRRRRRRRRRRRRRRRRRRRRRRRRRRRRRRRRRRRRRRRR
RRRRRRRRRRRRRRRRRRRRRRRRRRRRRRRRRRRRRRRRRRRRRR
RRRRRRRRRRRRRRRRRRRRRRRRRRRRRRRRRRRRRRRRRRRRRR
RRRRRRRRRRRRRRRRRRRRRRRRRRRRRRRRRRRRRRRRRRRRRR
RRRRRRRRRRRRRRRRRRRRRRRRRRRRRRRRRRRRRRRRRRRRRR
RRRRRRRRRRRRRRRRRRRRRRRRRRRRRRRRRRRRRRRRRRRRRR
RRRRRRRRRRRRRRRRRRRRRRRRRRRRRRRRRRRRRRRRRRRRRR
RRRRRRRRRRRRRRRRRRRRRRRRRRRRRRRRRRRRRRRRRRRRRR
RRRRRRRRRRRRRRRRRRRRRRRRRRRRRRRRRRRRRRRRRRRRRR
RRRRRRRRRRRRRRRRRRRRRRRRRRRRRRRRRRRRRRRRRRRRRR
RRRRRRRRRRRRRRRRRRRRRRRRRRRRRRRRRRRRRRRRRRRRRR
RRRRRRRRRRRRRRRRRRRRRRRRRRRRRRRRRRRRRRRRRRRRRR
RRRRRRRRRRRRRRRRRRRRRRRRRRRRRRRRRRRRRRRRRRRRRR
RRRRRRRRRRRRRRRRRRRRRRRRRRRRRRRRRRRRRRRRRRRRRR
RRRRRRRRRRRRRRRRRRRRRRRRRRRRRRRRRRRRRRRRRRRRRR
RRRRRRRRRRRRRRRRRRRRRRRRRRRRRRRRRRRRRRRRRRRRRR
RRRRRRRRRRRRRRRRRRRRRRRRRRRRRRRRRRRRRRRRRRRRRR
RRRRRRRRRRRRRRRRRRRRRRRRRRRRRRRRRRRRRRRRRRRRRR
RRRRRRRRRRRRRRRRRRRRRRRRRRRRRRRRRRRRRRRRRRRRRR
RRRRRRRRRRRRRRRRRRRRRRRRRRRRRRRRRRRRRRRRRRRRRR
RRRRRRRRRRRRRRRRRRRRRRRRRRRRRRRRRRRRRRRRRRRRRR
RRRRRRRRRRRRRRRRRRRRRRRRRRRRRRRRRRRRRRRRRRRRRR
RRRRRRRRRRRRRRRRRRRRRRRRRRRRRRRRRRRRRRRRRRRRRR
RRRRRRRRRRRRRRRRRRRRRRRRRRRRRRRRRRRRRRRRRRRRRR
RRRRRRRRRRRRRRRRRRRRRRRRRRRRRRRRRRRRRRRRRRRRRR
RRRRRRRRRRRRRRRRRRRRRRRRRRRRRRRRRRRRRRRRRRRRRR
RRRRRRRRRRRRRRRRRRRRRRRRRRRRRRRRRRRRRRRRRRRRRR
RRRRRRRRRRRRRRRRRRRRRRRRRRRRRRRRRRRRRRRRRRRRRR

RRRRRRRRRRRRRRRRRRRRRRRRRRRRRRRRRRRRRRRRRRRRR
RRRRRRRRRRRRRRRRRRRRRRRRRRRRRRRRRRRRRRRRRRRRR
RRRRRRRRRRRRRRRRRRRRRRRRRRRRRRRRRRRRRRRRRRRRR
RRRRRRRRRRRRRRRRRRRRRRRRRRRRRRRRRRRRRRRRRRRRR
RRRRRRRRRRRRRRRRRRRRRRRRRRRRRRRRRRRRRRRRRRRRR
RRRRRRRRRRRRRRRRRRRRRRRRRRRRRRRRRRRRRRRRRRRRR
RRRRRRRRRRRRRRRRRRRRRRRRRRRRRRRRRRRRRRRRRRRRR
RRRRRRRRRRRRRRRRRRRRRRRRRRRRRRRRRRRRRRRRRRRRR
RRRRRRRRRRRRRRRRRRRRRRRRRRRRRRRRRRRRRRRRRRRRR
RRRRRRRRRRRRRRRRRRRRRRRRRRRRRRRRRRRRRRRRRRRRR
RRRRRRRRRRRRRRRRRRRRRRRRRRRRRRRRRRRRRRRRRRRRR
RRRRRRRRRRRRRRRRRRRRRRRRRRRRRRRRRRRRRRRRRRRRR
RRRRRRRRRRRRRRRRRRRRRRRRRRRRRRRRRRRRRRRRRRRRR
RRRRRRRRRRRRRRRRRRRRRRRRRRRRRRRRRRRRRRRRRRRRR
RRRRRRRRRRRRRRRRRRRRRRRRRRRRRRRRRRRRRRRRRRRRR
RRRRRRRRRRRRRRRRRRRRRRRRRRRRRRRRRRRRRRRRRRRRR
RRRRRRRRRRRRRRRRRRRRRRRRRRRRRRRRRRRRRRRRRRRRR
RRRRRRRRRRRRRRRRRRRRRRRRRRRRRRRRRRRRRRRRRRRRR
RRRRRRRRRRRRRRRRRRRRRRRRRRRRRRRRRRRRRRRRRRRRR
RRRRRRRRRRRRRRRRRRRRRRRRRRRRRRRRRRRRRRRRRRRRR
RRRRRRRRRRRRRRRRRRRRRRRRRRRRRRRRRRRRRRRRRRRRR
RRRRRRRRRRRRRRRRRRRRRRRRRRRRRRRRRRRRRRRRRRRRR
RRRRRRRRRRRRRRRRRRRRRRRRRRRRRRRRRRRRRRRRRRRRR
RRRRRRRRRRRRRRRRRRRRRRRRRRRRRRRRRRRRRRRRRRRRR
RRRRRRRRRRRRRRRRRRRRRRRRRRRRRRRRRRRRRRRRRRRRR
RRRRRRRRRRRRRRRRRRRRRRRRRRRRRRRRRRRRRRRRRRRRR

RRRRRRRRRRRRRRRRRRRRRRRRRRRRRRRRRRRRRRRRRRRRRR
RRRRRRRRRRRRRRRRRRRRRRRRRRRRRRRRRRRRRRRRRRRRRR
RRRRRRRRRRRRRRRRRRRRRRRRRRRRRRRRRRRRRRRRRRRRRR
RRRRRRRRRRRRRRRRRRRRRRRRRRRRRRRRRRRRRRRRRRRRRR
RRRRRRRRRRRRRRRRRRRRRRRRRRRRRRRRRRRRRRRRRRRRRR
RRRRRRRRRRRRRRRRRRRRRRRRRRRRRRRRRRRRRRRRRRRRRR
RRRRRRRRRRRRRRRRRRRRRRRRRRRRRRRRRRRRRRRRRRRRRR
RRRRRRRRRRRRRRRRRRRRRRRRRRRRRRRRRRRRRRRRRRRRRR
RRRRRRRRRRRRRRRRRRRRRRRRRRRRRRRRRRRRRRRRRRRRRR
RRRRRRRRRRRRRRRRRRRRRRRRRRRRRRRRRRRRRRRRRRRRRR
RRRRRRRRRRRRRRRRRRRRRRRRRRRRRRRRRRRRRRRRRRRRRR
RRRRRRRRRRRRRRRRRRRRRRRRRRRRRRRRRRRRRRRRRRRRRR
RRRRRRRRRRRRRRRRRRRRRRRRRRRRRRRRRRRRRRRRRRRRRR
RRRRRRRRRRRRRRRRRRRRRRRRRRRRRRRRRRRRRRRRRRRRRR
RRRRRRRRRRRRRRRRRRRRRRRRRRRRRRRRRRRRRRRRRRRRRR
RRRRRRRRRRRRRRRRRRRRRRRRRRRRRRRRRRRRRRRRRRRRRR
RRRRRRRRRRRRRRRRRRRRRRRRRRRRRRRRRRRRRRRRRRRRRR
RRRRRRRRRRRRRRRRRRRRRRRRRRRRRRRRRRRRRRRRRRRRRR
RRRRRRRRRRRRRRRRRRRRRRRRRRRRRRRRRRRRRRRRRRRRRR
RRRRRRRRRRRRRRRRRRRRRRRRRRRRRRRRRRRRRRRRRRRRRR
RRRRRRRRRRRRRRRRRRRRRRRRRRRRRRRRRRRRRRRRRRRRRR
RRRRRRRRRRRRRRRRRRRRRRRRRRRRRRRRRRRRRRRRRRRRRR
RRRRRRRRRRRRRRRRRRRRRRRRRRRRRRRRRRRRRRRRRRRRRR
RRRRRRRRRRRRRRRRRRRRRRRRRRRRRRRRRRRRRRRRRRRRRR
RRRRRRRRRRRRRRRRRRRRRRRRRRRRRRRRRRRRRRRRRRRRRR
RRRRRRRRRRRRRRRRRRRRRRRRRRRRRRRRRRRRRRRRRRRRRR
RRRRRRRRRRRRRRRRRRRRRRRRRRRRRRRRRRRRRRRRRRRRRR

RRRRRRRRRRRRRRRRRRRRRRRRRRRRRRRRRRRRRRRRRR
RRRRRRRRRRRRRRRRRRRRRRRRRRRRRRRRRRRRRRRRRR
RRRRRRRRRRRRRRRRRRRRRRRRRRRRRRRRRRRRRRRRRR
RRRRRRRRRRRRRRRRRRRRRRRRRRRRRRRRRRRRRRRRRR
RRRRRRRRRRRRRRRRRRRRRRRRRRRRRRRRRRRRRRRRRR
RRRRRRRRRRRRRRRRRRRRRRRRRRRRRRRRRRRRRRRRRR
RRRRRRRRRRRRRRRRRRRRRRRRRRRRRRRRRRRRRRRRRR
RRRRRRRRRRRRRRRRRRRRRRRRRRRRRRRRRRRRRRRRRR
RRRRRRRRRRRRRRRRRRRRRRRRRRRRRRRRRRRRRRRRRR
RRRRRRRRRRRRRRRRRRRRRRRRRRRRRRRRRRRRRRRRRR
RRRRRRRRRRRRRRRRRRRRRRRRRRRRRRRRRRRRRRRRRR
RRRRRRRRRRRRRRRRRRRRRRRRRRRRRRRRRRRRRRRRRR
RRRRRRRRRRRRRRRRRRRRRRRRRRRRRRRRRRRRRRRRRR
RRRRRRRRRRRRRRRRRRRRRRRRRRRRRRRRRRRRRRRRRR
RRRRRRRRRRRRRRRRRRRRRRRRRRRRRRRRRRRRRRRRRR
RRRRRRRRRRRRRRRRRRRRRRRRRRRRRRRRRRRRRRRRRR
RRRRRRRRRRRRRRRRRRRRRRRRRRRRRRRRRRRRRRRRRR
RRRRRRRRRRRRRRRRRRRRRRRRRRRRRRRRRRRRRRRRRR
RRRRRRRRRRRRRRRRRRRRRRRRRRRRRRRRRRRRRRRRRR
RRRRRRRRRRRRRRRRRRRRRRRRRRRRRRRRRRRRRRRRRR
RRRRRRRRRRRRRRRRRRRRRRRRRRRRRRRRRRRRRRRRRR
RRRRRRRRRRRRRRRRRRRRRRRRRRRRRRRRRRRRRRRRRR
RRRRRRRRRRRRRRRRRRRRRRRRRRRRRRRRRRRRRRRRRR
RRRRRRRRRRRRRRRRRRRRRRRRRRRRRRRRRRRRRRRRRR
RRRRRRRRRRRRRRRRRRRRRRRRRRRRRRRRRRRRRRRRRR
RRRRRRRRRRRRRRRRRRRRRRRRRRRRRRRRRRRRRRRRRR
RRRRRRRRRRRRRRRRRRRRRRRRRRRRRRRRRRRRRRRRRR

RRRRRRRRRRRRRRRRRRRRRRRRRRRRRRRRRRRRRRRRRRRRRRR
RRRRRRRRRRRRRRRRRRRRRRRRRRRRRRRRRRRRRRRRRRRRRRR
RRRRRRRRRRRRRRRRRRRRRRRRRRRRRRRRRRRRRRRRRRRRRRR
RRRRRRRRRRRRRRRRRRRRRRRRRRRRRRRRRRRRRRRRRRRRRRR
RRRRRRRRRRRRRRRRRRRRRRRRRRRRRRRRRRRRRRRRRRRRRRR
RRRRRRRRRRRRRRRRRRRRRRRRRRRRRRRRRRRRRRRRRRRRRRR
RRRRRRRRRRRRRRRRRRRRRRRRRRRRRRRRRRRRRRRRRRRRRRR
RRRRRRRRRRRRRRRRRRRRRRRRRRRRRRRRRRRRRRRRRRRRRRR
RRRRRRRRRRRRRRRRRRRRRRRRRRRRRRRRRRRRRRRRRRRRRRR
RRRRRRRRRRRRRRRRRRRRRRRRRRRRRRRRRRRRRRRRRRRRRRR
RRRRRRRRRRRRRRRRRRRRRRRRRRRRRRRRRRRRRRRRRRRRRRR
RRRRRRRRRRRRRRRRRRRRRRRRRRRRRRRRRRRRRRRRRRRRRRR
RRRRRRRRRRRRRRRRRRRRRRRRRRRRRRRRRRRRRRRRRRRRRRR
RRRRRRRRRRRRRRRRRRRRRRRRRRRRRRRRRRRRRRRRRRRRRRR
RRRRRRRRRRRRRRRRRRRRRRRRRRRRRRRRRRRRRRRRRRRRRRR
RRRRRRRRRRRRRRRRRRRRRRRRRRRRRRRRRRRRRRRRRRRRRRR
RRRRRRRRRRRRRRRRRRRRRRRRRRRRRRRRRRRRRRRRRRRRRRR
RRRRRRRRRRRRRRRRRRRRRRRRRRRRRRRRRRRRRRRRRRRRRRR
RRRRRRRRRRRRRRRRRRRRRRRRRRRRRRRRRRRRRRRRRRRRRRR
RRRRRRRRRRRRRRRRRRRRRRRRRRRRRRRRRRRRRRRRRRRRRRR
RRRRRRRRRRRRRRRRRRRRRRRRRRRRRRRRRRRRRRRRRRRRRRR
RRRRRRRRRRRRRRRRRRRRRRRRRRRRRRRRRRRRRRRRRRRRRRR
RRRRRRRRRRRRRRRRRRRRRRRRRRRRRRRRRRRRRRRRRRRRRRR
RRRRRRRRRRRRRRRRRRRRRRRRRRRRRRRRRRRRRRRRRRRRRRR
RRRRRRRRRRRRRRRRRRRRRRRRRRRRRRRRRRRRRRRRRRRRRRR

RRRRRRRRRRRRRRRRRRRRRRRRRRRRRRRRRRRRRRRRRRRR
RRRRRRRRRRRRRRRRRRRRRRRRRRRRRRRRRRRRRRRRRRRR
RRRRRRRRRRRRRRRRRRRRRRRRRRRRRRRRRRRRRRRRRRRR
RRRRRRRRRRRRRRRRRRRRRRRRRRRRRRRRRRRRRRRRRRRR
RRRRRRRRRRRRRRRRRRRRRRRRRRRRRRRRRRRRRRRRRRRR
RRRRRRRRRRRRRRRRRRRRRRRRRRRRRRRRRRRRRRRRRRRR
RRRRRRRRRRRRRRRRRRRRRRRRRRRRRRRRRRRRRRRRRRRR
RRRRRRRRRRRRRRRRRRRRRRRRRRRRRRRRRRRRRRRRRRRR
RRRRRRRRRRRRRRRRRRRRRRRRRRRRRRRRRRRRRRRRRRRR
RRRRRRRRRRRRRRRRRRRRRRRRRRRRRRRRRRRRRRRRRRRR
RRRRRRRRRRRRRRRRRRRRRRRRRRRRRRRRRRRRRRRRRRRR
RRRRRRRRRRRRRRRRRRRRRRRRRRRRRRRRRRRRRRRRRRRR
RRRRRRRRRRRRRRRRRRRRRRRRRRRRRRRRRRRRRRRRRRRR
RRRRRRRRRRRRRRRRRRRRRRRRRRRRRRRRRRRRRRRRRRRR
RRRRRRRRRRRRRRRRRRRRRRRRRRRRRRRRRRRRRRRRRRRR
RRRRRRRRRRRRRRRRRRRRRRRRRRRRRRRRRRRRRRRRRRRR
RRRRRRRRRRRRRRRRRRRRRRRRRRRRRRRRRRRRRRRRRRRR
RRRRRRRRRRRRRRRRRRRRRRRRRRRRRRRRRRRRRRRRRRRR
RRRRRRRRRRRRRRRRRRRRRRRRRRRRRRRRRRRRRRRRRRRR
RRRRRRRRRRRRRRRRRRRRRRRRRRRRRRRRRRRRRRRRRRRR
RRRRRRRRRRRRRRRRRRRRRRRRRRRRRRRRRRRRRRRRRRRR
RRRRRRRRRRRRRRRRRRRRRRRRRRRRRRRRRRRRRRRRRRRR
RRRRRRRRRRRRRRRRRRRRRRRRRRRRRRRRRRRRRRRRRRRR
RRRRRRRRRRRRRRRRRRRRRRRRRRRRRRRRRRRRRRRRRRRR
RRRRRRRRRRRRRRRRRRRRRRRRRRRRRRRRRRRRRRRRRRRR
RRRRRRRRRRRRRRRRRRRRRRRRRRRRRRRRRRRRRRRRRRRR
RRRRRRRRRRRRRRRRRRRRRRRRRRRRRRRRRRRRRRRRRRRR
RRRRRRRRRRRRRRRRRRRRRRRRRRRRRRRRRRRRRRRRRRRR
RRRRRRRRRRRRRRRRRRRRRRRRRRRRRRRRRRRRRRRRRRRR
RRRRRRRRRRRRRRRRRRRRRRRRRRRRRRRRRRRRRRRRRRRR

RRRRRRRRRRRRRRRRRRRRRRRRRRRRRRRRRRRRRRRRRRRRRR
RRRRRRRRRRRRRRRRRRRRRRRRRRRRRRRRRRRRRRRRRRRRRR
RRRRRRRRRRRRRRRRRRRRRRRRRRRRRRRRRRRRRRRRRRRRRR
RRRRRRRRRRRRRRRRRRRRRRRRRRRRRRRRRRRRRRRRRRRRRR
RRRRRRRRRRRRRRRRRRRRRRRRRRRRRRRRRRRRRRRRRRRRRR
RRRRRRRRRRRRRRRRRRRRRRRRRRRRRRRRRRRRRRRRRRRRRR
RRRRRRRRRRRRRRRRRRRRRRRRRRRRRRRRRRRRRRRRRRRRRR
RRRRRRRRRRRRRRRRRRRRRRRRRRRRRRRRRRRRRRRRRRRRRR
RRRRRRRRRRRRRRRRRRRRRRRRRRRRRRRRRRRRRRRRRRRRRR
RRRRRRRRRRRRRRRRRRRRRRRRRRRRRRRRRRRRRRRRRRRRRR
RRRRRRRRRRRRRRRRRRRRRRRRRRRRRRRRRRRRRRRRRRRRRR
RRRRRRRRRRRRRRRRRRRRRRRRRRRRRRRRRRRRRRRRRRRRRR
RRRRRRRRRRRRRRRRRRRRRRRRRRRRRRRRRRRRRRRRRRRRRR
RRRRRRRRRRRRRRRRRRRRRRRRRRRRRRRRRRRRRRRRRRRRRR
RRRRRRRRRRRRRRRRRRRRRRRRRRRRRRRRRRRRRRRRRRRRRR
RRRRRRRRRRRRRRRRRRRRRRRRRRRRRRRRRRRRRRRRRRRRRR
RRRRRRRRRRRRRRRRRRRRRRRRRRRRRRRRRRRRRRRRRRRRRR
RRRRRRRRRRRRRRRRRRRRRRRRRRRRRRRRRRRRRRRRRRRRRR
RRRRRRRRRRRRRRRRRRRRRRRRRRRRRRRRRRRRRRRRRRRRRR
RRRRRRRRRRRRRRRRRRRRRRRRRRRRRRRRRRRRRRRRRRRRRR
RRRRRRRRRRRRRRRRRRRRRRRRRRRRRRRRRRRRRRRRRRRRRR
RRRRRRRRRRRRRRRRRRRRRRRRRRRRRRRRRRRRRRRRRRRRRR
RRRRRRRRRRRRRRRRRRRRRRRRRRRRRRRRRRRRRRRRRRRRRR
RRRRRRRRRRRRRRRRRRRRRRRRRRRRRRRRRRRRRRRRRRRRRR
RRRRRRRRRRRRRRRRRRRRRRRRRRRRRRRRRRRRRRRRRRRRRR
RRRRRRRRRRRRRRRRRRRRRRRRRRRRRRRRRRRRRRRRRRRRRR
RRRRRRRRRRRRRRRRRRRRRRRRRRRRRRRRRRRRRRRRRRRRRR
RRRRRRRRRRRRRRRRRRRRRRRRRRRRRRRRRRRRRRRRRRRRRR

RRRRRRRRRRRRRRRRRRRRRRRRRRRRRRRRRRRRRRRRRRRRRRR
RRRRRRRRRRRRRRRRRRRRRRRRRRRRRRRRRRRRRRRRRRRRRRR
RRRRRRRRRRRRRRRRRRRRRRRRRRRRRRRRRRRRRRRRRRRRRRR
RRRRRRRRRRRRRRRRRRRRRRRRRRRRRRRRRRRRRRRRRRRRRRR
RRRRRRRRRRRRRRRRRRRRRRRRRRRRRRRRRRRRRRRRRRRRRRR
RRRRRRRRRRRRRRRRRRRRRRRRRRRRRRRRRRRRRRRRRRRRRRR
RRRRRRRRRRRRRRRRRRRRRRRRRRRRRRRRRRRRRRRRRRRRRRR
RRRRRRRRRRRRRRRRRRRRRRRRRRRRRRRRRRRRRRRRRRRRRRR
RRRRRRRRRRRRRRRRRRRRRRRRRRRRRRRRRRRRRRRRRRRRRRR
RRRRRRRRRRRRRRRRRRRRRRRRRRRRRRRRRRRRRRRRRRRRRRR
RRRRRRRRRRRRRRRRRRRRRRRRRRRRRRRRRRRRRRRRRRRRRRR
RRRRRRRRRRRRRRRRRRRRRRRRRRRRRRRRRRRRRRRRRRRRRRR
RRRRRRRRRRRRRRRRRRRRRRRRRRRRRRRRRRRRRRRRRRRRRRR
RRRRRRRRRRRRRRRRRRRRRRRRRRRRRRRRRRRRRRRRRRRRRRR
RRRRRRRRRRRRRRRRRRRRRRRRRRRRRRRRRRRRRRRRRRRRRRR
RRRRRRRRRRRRRRRRRRRRRRRRRRRRRRRRRRRRRRRRRRRRRRR
RRRRRRRRRRRRRRRRRRRRRRRRRRRRRRRRRRRRRRRRRRRRRRR
RRRRRRRRRRRRRRRRRRRRRRRRRRRRRRRRRRRRRRRRRRRRRRR
RRRRRRRRRRRRRRRRRRRRRRRRRRRRRRRRRRRRRRRRRRRRRRR
RRRRRRRRRRRRRRRRRRRRRRRRRRRRRRRRRRRRRRRRRRRRRRR
RRRRRRRRRRRRRRRRRRRRRRRRRRRRRRRRRRRRRRRRRRRRRRR
RRRRRRRRRRRRRRRRRRRRRRRRRRRRRRRRRRRRRRRRRRRRRRR
RRRRRRRRRRRRRRRRRRRRRRRRRRRRRRRRRRRRRRRRRRRRRRR
RRRRRRRRRRRRRRRRRRRRRRRRRRRRRRRRRRRRRRRRRRRRRRR
RRRRRRRRRRRRRRRRRRRRRRRRRRRRRRRRRRRRRRRRRRRRRRR

RRRRRRRRRRRRRRRRRRRRRRRRRRRRRRRRRRRRRRRRRRRRRRR
RRRRRRRRRRRRRRRRRRRRRRRRRRRRRRRRRRRRRRRRRRRRRRR
RRRRRRRRRRRRRRRRRRRRRRRRRRRRRRRRRRRRRRRRRRRRRRR
RRRRRRRRRRRRRRRRRRRRRRRRRRRRRRRRRRRRRRRRRRRRRRR
RRRRRRRRRRRRRRRRRRRRRRRRRRRRRRRRRRRRRRRRRRRRRRR
RRRRRRRRRRRRRRRRRRRRRRRRRRRRRRRRRRRRRRRRRRRRRRR
RRRRRRRRRRRRRRRRRRRRRRRRRRRRRRRRRRRRRRRRRRRRRRR
RRRRRRRRRRRRRRRRRRRRRRRRRRRRRRRRRRRRRRRRRRRRRRR
RRRRRRRRRRRRRRRRRRRRRRRRRRRRRRRRRRRRRRRRRRRRRRR
RRRRRRRRRRRRRRRRRRRRRRRRRRRRRRRRRRRRRRRRRRRRRRR
RRRRRRRRRRRRRRRRRRRRRRRRRRRRRRRRRRRRRRRRRRRRRRR
RRRRRRRRRRRRRRRRRRRRRRRRRRRRRRRRRRRRRRRRRRRRRRR
RRRRRRRRRRRRRRRRRRRRRRRRRRRRRRRRRRRRRRRRRRRRRRR
RRRRRRRRRRRRRRRRRRRRRRRRRRRRRRRRRRRRRRRRRRRRRRR
RRRRRRRRRRRRRRRRRRRRRRRRRRRRRRRRRRRRRRRRRRRRRRR
RRRRRRRRRRRRRRRRRRRRRRRRRRRRRRRRRRRRRRRRRRRRRRR
RRRRRRRRRRRRRRRRRRRRRRRRRRRRRRRRRRRRRRRRRRRRRRR
RRRRRRRRRRRRRRRRRRRRRRRRRRRRRRRRRRRRRRRRRRRRRRR
RRRRRRRRRRRRRRRRRRRRRRRRRRRRRRRRRRRRRRRRRRRRRRR
RRRRRRRRRRRRRRRRRRRRRRRRRRRRRRRRRRRRRRRRRRRRRRR
RRRRRRRRRRRRRRRRRRRRRRRRRRRRRRRRRRRRRRRRRRRRRRR
RRRRRRRRRRRRRRRRRRRRRRRRRRRRRRRRRRRRRRRRRRRRRRR
RRRRRRRRRRRRRRRRRRRRRRRRRRRRRRRRRRRRRRRRRRRRRRR
RRRRRRRRRRRRRRRRRRRRRRRRRRRRRRRRRRRRRRRRRRRRRRR
RRRRRRRRRRRRRRRRRRRRRRRRRRRRRRRRRRRRRRRRRRRRRRR
RRRRRRRRRRRRRRRRRRRRRRRRRRRRRRRRRRRRRRRRRRRRRRR

RRRRRRRRRRRRRRRRRRRRRRRRRRRRRRRRRRRRRRRRRRRRRRRRR
RRRRRRRRRRRRRRRRRRRRRRRRRRRRRRRRRRRRRRRRRRRRRRRRR
RRRRRRRRRRRRRRRRRRRRRRRRRRRRRRRRRRRRRRRRRRRRRRRRR
RRRRRRRRRRRRRRRRRRRRRRRRRRRRRRRRRRRRRRRRRRRRRRRRR
RRRRRRRRRRRRRRRRRRRRRRRRRRRRRRRRRRRRRRRRRRRRRRRRR
RRRRRRRRRRRRRRRRRRRRRRRRRRRRRRRRRRRRRRRRRRRRRRRRR
RRRRRRRRRRRRRRRRRRRRRRRRRRRRRRRRRRRRRRRRRRRRRRRRR
RRRRRRRRRRRRRRRRRRRRRRRRRRRRRRRRRRRRRRRRRRRRRRRRR
RRRRRRRRRRRRRRRRRRRRRRRRRRRRRRRRRRRRRRRRRRRRRRRRR
RRRRRRRRRRRRRRRRRRRRRRRRRRRRRRRRRRRRRRRRRRRRRRRRR
RRRRRRRRRRRRRRRRRRRRRRRRRRRRRRRRRRRRRRRRRRRRRRRRR
RRRRRRRRRRRRRRRRRRRRRRRRRRRRRRRRRRRRRRRRRRRRRRRRR
RRRRRRRRRRRRRRRRRRRRRRRRRRRRRRRRRRRRRRRRRRRRRRRRR
RRRRRRRRRRRRRRRRRRRRRRRRRRRRRRRRRRRRRRRRRRRRRRRRR
RRRRRRRRRRRRRRRRRRRRRRRRRRRRRRRRRRRRRRRRRRRRRRRRR
RRRRRRRRRRRRRRRRRRRRRRRRRRRRRRRRRRRRRRRRRRRRRRRRR
RRRRRRRRRRRRRRRRRRRRRRRRRRRRRRRRRRRRRRRRRRRRRRRRR
RRRRRRRRRRRRRRRRRRRRRRRRRRRRRRRRRRRRRRRRRRRRRRRRR
RRRRRRRRRRRRRRRRRRRRRRRRRRRRRRRRRRRRRRRRRRRRRRRRR
RRRRRRRRRRRRRRRRRRRRRRRRRRRRRRRRRRRRRRRRRRRRRRRRR
RRRRRRRRRRRRRRRRRRRRRRRRRRRRRRRRRRRRRRRRRRRRRRRRR
RRRRRRRRRRRRRRRRRRRRRRRRRRRRRRRRRRRRRRRRRRRRRRRRR
RRRRRRRRRRRRRRRRRRRRRRRRRRRRRRRRRRRRRRRRRRRRRRRRR
RRRRRRRRRRRRRRRRRRRRRRRRRRRRRRRRRRRRRRRRRRRRRRRRR
RRRRRRRRRRRRRRRRRRRRRRRRRRRRRRRRRRRRRRRRRRRRRRRRR
RRRRRRRRRRRRRRRRRRRRRRRRRRRRRRRRRRRRRRRRRRRRRRRRR

RRRRRRRRRRRRRRRRRRRRRRRRRRRRRRRRRRRRRRRRRRRRRR
RRRRRRRRRRRRRRRRRRRRRRRRRRRRRRRRRRRRRRRRRRRRRR
RRRRRRRRRRRRRRRRRRRRRRRRRRRRRRRRRRRRRRRRRRRRRR
RRRRRRRRRRRRRRRRRRRRRRRRRRRRRRRRRRRRRRRRRRRRRR
RRRRRRRRRRRRRRRRRRRRRRRRRRRRRRRRRRRRRRRRRRRRRR
RRRRRRRRRRRRRRRRRRRRRRRRRRRRRRRRRRRRRRRRRRRRRR
RRRRRRRRRRRRRRRRRRRRRRRRRRRRRRRRRRRRRRRRRRRRRR
RRRRRRRRRRRRRRRRRRRRRRRRRRRRRRRRRRRRRRRRRRRRRR
RRRRRRRRRRRRRRRRRRRRRRRRRRRRRRRRRRRRRRRRRRRRRR
RRRRRRRRRRRRRRRRRRRRRRRRRRRRRRRRRRRRRRRRRRRRRR
RRRRRRRRRRRRRRRRRRRRRRRRRRRRRRRRRRRRRRRRRRRRRR
RRRRRRRRRRRRRRRRRRRRRRRRRRRRRRRRRRRRRRRRRRRRRR
RRRRRRRRRRRRRRRRRRRRRRRRRRRRRRRRRRRRRRRRRRRRRR
RRRRRRRRRRRRRRRRRRRRRRRRRRRRRRRRRRRRRRRRRRRRRR
RRRRRRRRRRRRRRRRRRRRRRRRRRRRRRRRRRRRRRRRRRRRRR
RRRRRRRRRRRRRRRRRRRRRRRRRRRRRRRRRRRRRRRRRRRRRR
RRRRRRRRRRRRRRRRRRRRRRRRRRRRRRRRRRRRRRRRRRRRRR
RRRRRRRRRRRRRRRRRRRRRRRRRRRRRRRRRRRRRRRRRRRRRR
RRRRRRRRRRRRRRRRRRRRRRRRRRRRRRRRRRRRRRRRRRRRRR
RRRRRRRRRRRRRRRRRRRRRRRRRRRRRRRRRRRRRRRRRRRRRR
RRRRRRRRRRRRRRRRRRRRRRRRRRRRRRRRRRRRRRRRRRRRRR
RRRRRRRRRRRRRRRRRRRRRRRRRRRRRRRRRRRRRRRRRRRRRR
RRRRRRRRRRRRRRRRRRRRRRRRRRRRRRRRRRRRRRRRRRRRRR
RRRRRRRRRRRRRRRRRRRRRRRRRRRRRRRRRRRRRRRRRRRRRR
RRRRRRRRRRRRRRRRRRRRRRRRRRRRRRRRRRRRRRRRRRRRRR

RRRRRRRRRRRRRRRRRRRRRRRRRRRRRRRRRRRRRRRR
RRRRRRRRRRRRRRRRRRRRRRRRRRRRRRRRRRRRRRRR
RRRRRRRRRRRRRRRRRRRRRRRRRRRRRRRRRRRRRRRR
RRRRRRRRRRRRRRRRRRRRRRRRRRRRRRRRRRRRRRRR
RRRRRRRRRRRRRRRRRRRRRRRRRRRRRRRRRRRRRRRR
RRRRRRRRRRRRRRRRRRRRRRRRRRRRRRRRRRRRRRRR
RRRRRRRRRRRRRRRRRRRRRRRRRRRRRRRRRRRRRRRR
RRRRRRRRRRRRRRRRRRRRRRRRRRRRRRRRRRRRRRRR
RRRRRRRRRRRRRRRRRRRRRRRRRRRRRRRRRRRRRRRR
RRRRRRRRRRRRRRRRRRRRRRRRRRRRRRRRRRRRRRRR
RRRRRRRRRRRRRRRRRRRRRRRRRRRRRRRRRRRRRRRR
RRRRRRRRRRRRRRRRRRRRRRRRRRRRRRRRRRRRRRRR
RRRRRRRRRRRRRRRRRRRRRRRRRRRRRRRRRRRRRRRR
RRRRRRRRRRRRRRRRRRRRRRRRRRRRRRRRRRRRRRRR
RRRRRRRRRRRRRRRRRRRRRRRRRRRRRRRRRRRRRRRR
RRRRRRRRRRRRRRRRRRRRRRRRRRRRRRRRRRRRRRRR
RRRRRRRRRRRRRRRRRRRRRRRRRRRRRRRRRRRRRRRR
RRRRRRRRRRRRRRRRRRRRRRRRRRRRRRRRRRRRRRRR
RRRRRRRRRRRRRRRRRRRRRRRRRRRRRRRRRRRRRRRR
RRRRRRRRRRRRRRRRRRRRRRRRRRRRRRRRRRRRRRRR
RRRRRRRRRRRRRRRRRRRRRRRRRRRRRRRRRRRRRRRR
RRRRRRRRRRRRRRRRRRRRRRRRRRRRRRRRRRRRRRRR
RRRRRRRRRRRRRRRRRRRRRRRRRRRRRRRRRRRRRRRR
RRRRRRRRRRRRRRRRRRRRRRRRRRRRRRRRRRRRRRRR
RRRRRRRRRRRRRRRRRRRRRRRRRRRRRRRRRRRRRRRR
RRRRRRRRRRRRRRRRRRRRRRRRRRRRRRRRRRRRRRRR
RRRRRRRRRRRRRRRRRRRRRRRRRRRRRRRRRRRRRRRR

RRRRRRRRRRRRRRRRRRRRRRRRRRRRRRRRRRRRRRRR
RRRRRRRRRRRRRRRRRRRRRRRRRRRRRRRRRRRRRRRR
RRRRRRRRRRRRRRRRRRRRRRRRRRRRRRRRRRRRRRRR
RRRRRRRRRRRRRRRRRRRRRRRRRRRRRRRRRRRRRRRR
RRRRRRRRRRRRRRRRRRRRRRRRRRRRRRRRRRRRRRRR
RRRRRRRRRRRRRRRRRRRRRRRRRRRRRRRRRRRRRRRR
RRRRRRRRRRRRRRRRRRRRRRRRRRRRRRRRRRRRRRRR
RRRRRRRRRRRRRRRRRRRRRRRRRRRRRRRRRRRRRRRR
RRRRRRRRRRRRRRRRRRRRRRRRRRRRRRRRRRRRRRRR
RRRRRRRRRRRRRRRRRRRRRRRRRRRRRRRRRRRRRRRR
RRRRRRRRRRRRRRRRRRRRRRRRRRRRRRRRRRRRRRRR
RRRRRRRRRRRRRRRRRRRRRRRRRRRRRRRRRRRRRRRR
RRRRRRRRRRRRRRRRRRRRRRRRRRRRRRRRRRRRRRRR
RRRRRRRRRRRRRRRRRRRRRRRRRRRRRRRRRRRRRRRR
RRRRRRRRRRRRRRRRRRRRRRRRRRRRRRRRRRRRRRRR
RRRRRRRRRRRRRRRRRRRRRRRRRRRRRRRRRRRRRRRR
RRRRRRRRRRRRRRRRRRRRRRRRRRRRRRRRRRRRRRRR
RRRRRRRRRRRRRRRRRRRRRRRRRRRRRRRRRRRRRRRR
RRRRRRRRRRRRRRRRRRRRRRRRRRRRRRRRRRRRRRRR
RRRRRRRRRRRRRRRRRRRRRRRRRRRRRRRRRRRRRRRR
RRRRRRRRRRRRRRRRRRRRRRRRRRRRRRRRRRRRRRRR
RRRRRRRRRRRRRRRRRRRRRRRRRRRRRRRRRRRRRRRR
RRRRRRRRRRRRRRRRRRRRRRRRRRRRRRRRRRRRRRRR
RRRRRRRRRRRRRRRRRRRRRRRRRRRRRRRRRRRRRRRR
RRRRRRRRRRRRRRRRRRRRRRRRRRRRRRRRRRRRRRRR
RRRRRRRRRRRRRRRRRRRRRRRRRRRRRRRRRRRRRRRR
RRRRRRRRRRRRRRRRRRRRRRRRRRRRRRRRRRRRRRRR
RRRRRRRRRRRRRRRRRRRRRRRRRRRRRRRRRRRRRRRR
RRRRRRRRRRRRRRRRRRRRRRRRRRRRRRRRRRRRRRRR
RRRRRRRRRRRRRRRRRRRRRRRRRRRRRRRRRRRRRRRR

RRRRRRRRRRRRRRRRRRRRRRRRRRRRRRRRRRRRRRRRRRRRRRR
RRRRRRRRRRRRRRRRRRRRRRRRRRRRRRRRRRRRRRRRRRRRRRR
RRRRRRRRRRRRRRRRRRRRRRRRRRRRRRRRRRRRRRRRRRRRRRR
RRRRRRRRRRRRRRRRRRRRRRRRRRRRRRRRRRRRRRRRRRRRRRR
RRRRRRRRRRRRRRRRRRRRRRRRRRRRRRRRRRRRRRRRRRRRRRR
RRRRRRRRRRRRRRRRRRRRRRRRRRRRRRRRRRRRRRRRRRRRRRR
RRRRRRRRRRRRRRRRRRRRRRRRRRRRRRRRRRRRRRRRRRRRRRR
RRRRRRRRRRRRRRRRRRRRRRRRRRRRRRRRRRRRRRRRRRRRRRR
RRRRRRRRRRRRRRRRRRRRRRRRRRRRRRRRRRRRRRRRRRRRRRR
RRRRRRRRRRRRRRRRRRRRRRRRRRRRRRRRRRRRRRRRRRRRRRR
RRRRRRRRRRRRRRRRRRRRRRRRRRRRRRRRRRRRRRRRRRRRRRR
RRRRRRRRRRRRRRRRRRRRRRRRRRRRRRRRRRRRRRRRRRRRRRR
RRRRRRRRRRRRRRRRRRRRRRRRRRRRRRRRRRRRRRRRRRRRRRR
RRRRRRRRRRRRRRRRRRRRRRRRRRRRRRRRRRRRRRRRRRRRRRR
RRRRRRRRRRRRRRRRRRRRRRRRRRRRRRRRRRRRRRRRRRRRRRR
RRRRRRRRRRRRRRRRRRRRRRRRRRRRRRRRRRRRRRRRRRRRRRR
RRRRRRRRRRRRRRRRRRRRRRRRRRRRRRRRRRRRRRRRRRRRRRR
RRRRRRRRRRRRRRRRRRRRRRRRRRRRRRRRRRRRRRRRRRRRRRR
RRRRRRRRRRRRRRRRRRRRRRRRRRRRRRRRRRRRRRRRRRRRRRR
RRRRRRRRRRRRRRRRRRRRRRRRRRRRRRRRRRRRRRRRRRRRRRR
RRRRRRRRRRRRRRRRRRRRRRRRRRRRRRRRRRRRRRRRRRRRRRR
RRRRRRRRRRRRRRRRRRRRRRRRRRRRRRRRRRRRRRRRRRRRRRR
RRRRRRRRRRRRRRRRRRRRRRRRRRRRRRRRRRRRRRRRRRRRRRR
RRRRRRRRRRRRRRRRRRRRRRRRRRRRRRRRRRRRRRRRRRRRRRR

RRRRRRRRRRRRRRRRRRRRRRRRRRRRRRRRRRRRRRRRR
RRRRRRRRRRRRRRRRRRRRRRRRRRRRRRRRRRRRRRRRR
RRRRRRRRRRRRRRRRRRRRRRRRRRRRRRRRRRRRRRRRR
RRRRRRRRRRRRRRRRRRRRRRRRRRRRRRRRRRRRRRRRR
RRRRRRRRRRRRRRRRRRRRRRRRRRRRRRRRRRRRRRRRR
RRRRRRRRRRRRRRRRRRRRRRRRRRRRRRRRRRRRRRRRR
RRRRRRRRRRRRRRRRRRRRRRRRRRRRRRRRRRRRRRRRR
RRRRRRRRRRRRRRRRRRRRRRRRRRRRRRRRRRRRRRRRR
RRRRRRRRRRRRRRRRRRRRRRRRRRRRRRRRRRRRRRRRR
RRRRRRRRRRRRRRRRRRRRRRRRRRRRRRRRRRRRRRRRR
RRRRRRRRRRRRRRRRRRRRRRRRRRRRRRRRRRRRRRRRR
RRRRRRRRRRRRRRRRRRRRRRRRRRRRRRRRRRRRRRRRR
RRRRRRRRRRRRRRRRRRRRRRRRRRRRRRRRRRRRRRRRR
RRRRRRRRRRRRRRRRRRRRRRRRRRRRRRRRRRRRRRRRR
RRRRRRRRRRRRRRRRRRRRRRRRRRRRRRRRRRRRRRRRR
RRRRRRRRRRRRRRRRRRRRRRRRRRRRRRRRRRRRRRRRR
RRRRRRRRRRRRRRRRRRRRRRRRRRRRRRRRRRRRRRRRR
RRRRRRRRRRRRRRRRRRRRRRRRRRRRRRRRRRRRRRRRR
RRRRRRRRRRRRRRRRRRRRRRRRRRRRRRRRRRRRRRRRR
RRRRRRRRRRRRRRRRRRRRRRRRRRRRRRRRRRRRRRRRR
RRRRRRRRRRRRRRRRRRRRRRRRRRRRRRRRRRRRRRRRR
RRRRRRRRRRRRRRRRRRRRRRRRRRRRRRRRRRRRRRRRR
RRRRRRRRRRRRRRRRRRRRRRRRRRRRRRRRRRRRRRRRR
RRRRRRRRRRRRRRRRRRRRRRRRRRRRRRRRRRRRRRRRR
RRRRRRRRRRRRRRRRRRRRRRRRRRRRRRRRRRRRRRRRR
RRRRRRRRRRRRRRRRRRRRRRRRRRRRRRRRRRRRRRRRR
RRRRRRRRRRRRRRRRRRRRRRRRRRRRRRRRRRRRRRRRR
RRRRRRRRRRRRRRRRRRRRRRRRRRRRRRRRRRRRRRRRR

RRRRRRRRRRRRRRRRRRRRRRRRRRRRRRRRRRRRRRRRR
RRRRRRRRRRRRRRRRRRRRRRRRRRRRRRRRRRRRRRRRR
RRRRRRRRRRRRRRRRRRRRRRRRRRRRRRRRRRRRRRRRR
RRRRRRRRRRRRRRRRRRRRRRRRRRRRRRRRRRRRRRRRR
RRRRRRRRRRRRRRRRRRRRRRRRRRRRRRRRRRRRRRRRR
RRRRRRRRRRRRRRRRRRRRRRRRRRRRRRRRRRRRRRRRR
RRRRRRRRRRRRRRRRRRRRRRRRRRRRRRRRRRRRRRRRR
RRRRRRRRRRRRRRRRRRRRRRRRRRRRRRRRRRRRRRRRR
RRRRRRRRRRRRRRRRRRRRRRRRRRRRRRRRRRRRRRRRR
RRRRRRRRRRRRRRRRRRRRRRRRRRRRRRRRRRRRRRRRR
RRRRRRRRRRRRRRRRRRRRRRRRRRRRRRRRRRRRRRRRR
RRRRRRRRRRRRRRRRRRRRRRRRRRRRRRRRRRRRRRRRR
RRRRRRRRRRRRRRRRRRRRRRRRRRRRRRRRRRRRRRRRR
RRRRRRRRRRRRRRRRRRRRRRRRRRRRRRRRRRRRRRRRR
RRRRRRRRRRRRRRRRRRRRRRRRRRRRRRRRRRRRRRRRR
RRRRRRRRRRRRRRRRRRRRRRRRRRRRRRRRRRRRRRRRR
RRRRRRRRRRRRRRRRRRRRRRRRRRRRRRRRRRRRRRRRR
RRRRRRRRRRRRRRRRRRRRRRRRRRRRRRRRRRRRRRRRR
RRRRRRRRRRRRRRRRRRRRRRRRRRRRRRRRRRRRRRRRR
RRRRRRRRRRRRRRRRRRRRRRRRRRRRRRRRRRRRRRRRR
RRRRRRRRRRRRRRRRRRRRRRRRRRRRRRRRRRRRRRRRR
RRRRRRRRRRRRRRRRRRRRRRRRRRRRRRRRRRRRRRRRR
RRRRRRRRRRRRRRRRRRRRRRRRRRRRRRRRRRRRRRRRR
RRRRRRRRRRRRRRRRRRRRRRRRRRRRRRRRRRRRRRRRR
RRRRRRRRRRRRRRRRRRRRRRRRRRRRRRRRRRRRRRRRR
RRRRRRRRRRRRRRRRRRRRRRRRRRRRRRRRRRRRRRRRR
RRRRRRRRRRRRRRRRRRRRRRRRRRRRRRRRRRRRRRRRR

RRRRRRRRRRRRRRRRRRRRRRRRRRRRRRRRRRRRRRRRRRRR
RRRRRRRRRRRRRRRRRRRRRRRRRRRRRRRRRRRRRRRRRRRR
RRRRRRRRRRRRRRRRRRRRRRRRRRRRRRRRRRRRRRRRRRRR
RRRRRRRRRRRRRRRRRRRRRRRRRRRRRRRRRRRRRRRRRRRR
RRRRRRRRRRRRRRRRRRRRRRRRRRRRRRRRRRRRRRRRRRRR
RRRRRRRRRRRRRRRRRRRRRRRRRRRRRRRRRRRRRRRRRRRR
RRRRRRRRRRRRRRRRRRRRRRRRRRRRRRRRRRRRRRRRRRRR
RRRRRRRRRRRRRRRRRRRRRRRRRRRRRRRRRRRRRRRRRRRR
RRRRRRRRRRRRRRRRRRRRRRRRRRRRRRRRRRRRRRRRRRRR
RRRRRRRRRRRRRRRRRRRRRRRRRRRRRRRRRRRRRRRRRRRR
RRRRRRRRRRRRRRRRRRRRRRRRRRRRRRRRRRRRRRRRRRRR
RRRRRRRRRRRRRRRRRRRRRRRRRRRRRRRRRRRRRRRRRRRR
RRRRRRRRRRRRRRRRRRRRRRRRRRRRRRRRRRRRRRRRRRRR
RRRRRRRRRRRRRRRRRRRRRRRRRRRRRRRRRRRRRRRRRRRR
RRRRRRRRRRRRRRRRRRRRRRRRRRRRRRRRRRRRRRRRRRRR
RRRRRRRRRRRRRRRRRRRRRRRRRRRRRRRRRRRRRRRRRRRR
RRRRRRRRRRRRRRRRRRRRRRRRRRRRRRRRRRRRRRRRRRRR
RRRRRRRRRRRRRRRRRRRRRRRRRRRRRRRRRRRRRRRRRRRR
RRRRRRRRRRRRRRRRRRRRRRRRRRRRRRRRRRRRRRRRRRRR
RRRRRRRRRRRRRRRRRRRRRRRRRRRRRRRRRRRRRRRRRRRR
RRRRRRRRRRRRRRRRRRRRRRRRRRRRRRRRRRRRRRRRRRRR
RRRRRRRRRRRRRRRRRRRRRRRRRRRRRRRRRRRRRRRRRRRR
RRRRRRRRRRRRRRRRRRRRRRRRRRRRRRRRRRRRRRRRRRRR
RRRRRRRRRRRRRRRRRRRRRRRRRRRRRRRRRRRRRRRRRRRR
RRRRRRRRRRRRRRRRRRRRRRRRRRRRRRRRRRRRRRRRRRRR

RRRRRRRRRRRRRRRRRRRRRRRRRRRRRRRRRRRRRRRRRRRRR
RRRRRRRRRRRRRRRRRRRRRRRRRRRRRRRRRRRRRRRRRRRRR
RRRRRRRRRRRRRRRRRRRRRRRRRRRRRRRRRRRRRRRRRRRRR
RRRRRRRRRRRRRRRRRRRRRRRRRRRRRRRRRRRRRRRRRRRRR
RRRRRRRRRRRRRRRRRRRRRRRRRRRRRRRRRRRRRRRRRRRRR
RRRRRRRRRRRRRRRRRRRRRRRRRRRRRRRRRRRRRRRRRRRRR
RRRRRRRRRRRRRRRRRRRRRRRRRRRRRRRRRRRRRRRRRRRRR
RRRRRRRRRRRRRRRRRRRRRRRRRRRRRRRRRRRRRRRRRRRRR
RRRRRRRRRRRRRRRRRRRRRRRRRRRRRRRRRRRRRRRRRRRRR
RRRRRRRRRRRRRRRRRRRRRRRRRRRRRRRRRRRRRRRRRRRRR
RRRRRRRRRRRRRRRRRRRRRRRRRRRRRRRRRRRRRRRRRRRRR
RRRRRRRRRRRRRRRRRRRRRRRRRRRRRRRRRRRRRRRRRRRRR
RRRRRRRRRRRRRRRRRRRRRRRRRRRRRRRRRRRRRRRRRRRRR
RRRRRRRRRRRRRRRRRRRRRRRRRRRRRRRRRRRRRRRRRRRRR
RRRRRRRRRRRRRRRRRRRRRRRRRRRRRRRRRRRRRRRRRRRRR
RRRRRRRRRRRRRRRRRRRRRRRRRRRRRRRRRRRRRRRRRRRRR
RRRRRRRRRRRRRRRRRRRRRRRRRRRRRRRRRRRRRRRRRRRRR
RRRRRRRRRRRRRRRRRRRRRRRRRRRRRRRRRRRRRRRRRRRRR
RRRRRRRRRRRRRRRRRRRRRRRRRRRRRRRRRRRRRRRRRRRRR
RRRRRRRRRRRRRRRRRRRRRRRRRRRRRRRRRRRRRRRRRRRRR
RRRRRRRRRRRRRRRRRRRRRRRRRRRRRRRRRRRRRRRRRRRRR
RRRRRRRRRRRRRRRRRRRRRRRRRRRRRRRRRRRRRRRRRRRRR
RRRRRRRRRRRRRRRRRRRRRRRRRRRRRRRRRRRRRRRRRRRRR
RRRRRRRRRRRRRRRRRRRRRRRRRRRRRRRRRRRRRRRRRRRRR
RRRRRRRRRRRRRRRRRRRRRRRRRRRRRRRRRRRRRRRRRRRRR

RRRRRRRRRRRRRRRRRRRRRRRRRRRRRRRRRRRRRRRRRRRRRRRR
RRRRRRRRRRRRRRRRRRRRRRRRRRRRRRRRRRRRRRRRRRRRRRRR
RRRRRRRRRRRRRRRRRRRRRRRRRRRRRRRRRRRRRRRRRRRRRRRR
RRRRRRRRRRRRRRRRRRRRRRRRRRRRRRRRRRRRRRRRRRRRRRRR
RRRRRRRRRRRRRRRRRRRRRRRRRRRRRRRRRRRRRRRRRRRRRRRR
RRRRRRRRRRRRRRRRRRRRRRRRRRRRRRRRRRRRRRRRRRRRRRRR
RRRRRRRRRRRRRRRRRRRRRRRRRRRRRRRRRRRRRRRRRRRRRRRR
RRRRRRRRRRRRRRRRRRRRRRRRRRRRRRRRRRRRRRRRRRRRRRRR
RRRRRRRRRRRRRRRRRRRRRRRRRRRRRRRRRRRRRRRRRRRRRRRR
RRRRRRRRRRRRRRRRRRRRRRRRRRRRRRRRRRRRRRRRRRRRRRRR
RRRRRRRRRRRRRRRRRRRRRRRRRRRRRRRRRRRRRRRRRRRRRRRR
RRRRRRRRRRRRRRRRRRRRRRRRRRRRRRRRRRRRRRRRRRRRRRRR
RRRRRRRRRRRRRRRRRRRRRRRRRRRRRRRRRRRRRRRRRRRRRRRR
RRRRRRRRRRRRRRRRRRRRRRRRRRRRRRRRRRRRRRRRRRRRRRRR
RRRRRRRRRRRRRRRRRRRRRRRRRRRRRRRRRRRRRRRRRRRRRRRR
RRRRRRRRRRRRRRRRRRRRRRRRRRRRRRRRRRRRRRRRRRRRRRRR
RRRRRRRRRRRRRRRRRRRRRRRRRRRRRRRRRRRRRRRRRRRRRRRR
RRRRRRRRRRRRRRRRRRRRRRRRRRRRRRRRRRRRRRRRRRRRRRRR
RRRRRRRRRRRRRRRRRRRRRRRRRRRRRRRRRRRRRRRRRRRRRRRR
RRRRRRRRRRRRRRRRRRRRRRRRRRRRRRRRRRRRRRRRRRRRRRRR
RRRRRRRRRRRRRRRRRRRRRRRRRRRRRRRRRRRRRRRRRRRRRRRR
RRRRRRRRRRRRRRRRRRRRRRRRRRRRRRRRRRRRRRRRRRRRRRRR
RRRRRRRRRRRRRRRRRRRRRRRRRRRRRRRRRRRRRRRRRRRRRRRR
RRRRRRRRRRRRRRRRRRRRRRRRRRRRRRRRRRRRRRRRRRRRRRRR
RRRRRRRRRRRRRRRRRRRRRRRRRRRRRRRRRRRRRRRRRRRRRRRR

RRRRRRRRRRRRRRRRRRRRRRRRRRRRRRRRRRRRRRRRRR
RRRRRRRRRRRRRRRRRRRRRRRRRRRRRRRRRRRRRRRRRR
RRRRRRRRRRRRRRRRRRRRRRRRRRRRRRRRRRRRRRRRRR
RRRRRRRRRRRRRRRRRRRRRRRRRRRRRRRRRRRRRRRRRR
RRRRRRRRRRRRRRRRRRRRRRRRRRRRRRRRRRRRRRRRRR
RRRRRRRRRRRRRRRRRRRRRRRRRRRRRRRRRRRRRRRRRR
RRRRRRRRRRRRRRRRRRRRRRRRRRRRRRRRRRRRRRRRRR
RRRRRRRRRRRRRRRRRRRRRRRRRRRRRRRRRRRRRRRRRR
RRRRRRRRRRRRRRRRRRRRRRRRRRRRRRRRRRRRRRRRRR
RRRRRRRRRRRRRRRRRRRRRRRRRRRRRRRRRRRRRRRRRR
RRRRRRRRRRRRRRRRRRRRRRRRRRRRRRRRRRRRRRRRRR
RRRRRRRRRRRRRRRRRRRRRRRRRRRRRRRRRRRRRRRRRR
RRRRRRRRRRRRRRRRRRRRRRRRRRRRRRRRRRRRRRRRRR
RRRRRRRRRRRRRRRRRRRRRRRRRRRRRRRRRRRRRRRRRR
RRRRRRRRRRRRRRRRRRRRRRRRRRRRRRRRRRRRRRRRRR
RRRRRRRRRRRRRRRRRRRRRRRRRRRRRRRRRRRRRRRRRR
RRRRRRRRRRRRRRRRRRRRRRRRRRRRRRRRRRRRRRRRRR
RRRRRRRRRRRRRRRRRRRRRRRRRRRRRRRRRRRRRRRRRR
RRRRRRRRRRRRRRRRRRRRRRRRRRRRRRRRRRRRRRRRRR
RRRRRRRRRRRRRRRRRRRRRRRRRRRRRRRRRRRRRRRRRR
RRRRRRRRRRRRRRRRRRRRRRRRRRRRRRRRRRRRRRRRRR
RRRRRRRRRRRRRRRRRRRRRRRRRRRRRRRRRRRRRRRRRR
RRRRRRRRRRRRRRRRRRRRRRRRRRRRRRRRRRRRRRRRRR
RRRRRRRRRRRRRRRRRRRRRRRRRRRRRRRRRRRRRRRRRR
RRRRRRRRRRRRRRRRRRRRRRRRRRRRRRRRRRRRRRRRRR
RRRRRRRRRRRRRRRRRRRRRRRRRRRRRRRRRRRRRRRRRR
RRRRRRRRRRRRRRRRRRRRRRRRRRRRRRRRRRRRRRRRRR
RRRRRRRRRRRRRRRRRRRRRRRRRRRRRRRRRRRRRRRRRR

RRRRRRRRRRRRRRRRRRRRRRRRRRRRRRRRRRRRRRRRRRRR
RRRRRRRRRRRRRRRRRRRRRRRRRRRRRRRRRRRRRRRRRRRR
RRRRRRRRRRRRRRRRRRRRRRRRRRRRRRRRRRRRRRRRRRRR
RRRRRRRRRRRRRRRRRRRRRRRRRRRRRRRRRRRRRRRRRRRR
RRRRRRRRRRRRRRRRRRRRRRRRRRRRRRRRRRRRRRRRRRRR
RRRRRRRRRRRRRRRRRRRRRRRRRRRRRRRRRRRRRRRRRRRR
RRRRRRRRRRRRRRRRRRRRRRRRRRRRRRRRRRRRRRRRRRRR
RRRRRRRRRRRRRRRRRRRRRRRRRRRRRRRRRRRRRRRRRRRR
RRRRRRRRRRRRRRRRRRRRRRRRRRRRRRRRRRRRRRRRRRRR
RRRRRRRRRRRRRRRRRRRRRRRRRRRRRRRRRRRRRRRRRRRR
RRRRRRRRRRRRRRRRRRRRRRRRRRRRRRRRRRRRRRRRRRRR
RRRRRRRRRRRRRRRRRRRRRRRRRRRRRRRRRRRRRRRRRRRR
RRRRRRRRRRRRRRRRRRRRRRRRRRRRRRRRRRRRRRRRRRRR
RRRRRRRRRRRRRRRRRRRRRRRRRRRRRRRRRRRRRRRRRRRR
RRRRRRRRRRRRRRRRRRRRRRRRRRRRRRRRRRRRRRRRRRRR
RRRRRRRRRRRRRRRRRRRRRRRRRRRRRRRRRRRRRRRRRRRR
RRRRRRRRRRRRRRRRRRRRRRRRRRRRRRRRRRRRRRRRRRRR
RRRRRRRRRRRRRRRRRRRRRRRRRRRRRRRRRRRRRRRRRRRR
RRRRRRRRRRRRRRRRRRRRRRRRRRRRRRRRRRRRRRRRRRRR
RRRRRRRRRRRRRRRRRRRRRRRRRRRRRRRRRRRRRRRRRRRR
RRRRRRRRRRRRRRRRRRRRRRRRRRRRRRRRRRRRRRRRRRRR
RRRRRRRRRRRRRRRRRRRRRRRRRRRRRRRRRRRRRRRRRRRR
RRRRRRRRRRRRRRRRRRRRRRRRRRRRRRRRRRRRRRRRRRRR
RRRRRRRRRRRRRRRRRRRRRRRRRRRRRRRRRRRRRRRRRRRR
RRRRRRRRRRRRRRRRRRRRRRRRRRRRRRRRRRRRRRRRRRRR
RRRRRRRRRRRRRRRRRRRRRRRRRRRRRRRRRRRRRRRRRRRR
RRRRRRRRRRRRRRRRRRRRRRRRRRRRRRRRRRRRRRRRRRRR

RRRRRRRRRRRRRRRRRRRRRRRRRRRRRRRRRRRRRRRRRRRR
RRRRRRRRRRRRRRRRRRRRRRRRRRRRRRRRRRRRRRRRRRRR
RRRRRRRRRRRRRRRRRRRRRRRRRRRRRRRRRRRRRRRRRRRR
RRRRRRRRRRRRRRRRRRRRRRRRRRRRRRRRRRRRRRRRRRRR
RRRRRRRRRRRRRRRRRRRRRRRRRRRRRRRRRRRRRRRRRRRR
RRRRRRRRRRRRRRRRRRRRRRRRRRRRRRRRRRRRRRRRRRRR
RRRRRRRRRRRRRRRRRRRRRRRRRRRRRRRRRRRRRRRRRRRR
RRRRRRRRRRRRRRRRRRRRRRRRRRRRRRRRRRRRRRRRRRRR
RRRRRRRRRRRRRRRRRRRRRRRRRRRRRRRRRRRRRRRRRRRR
RRRRRRRRRRRRRRRRRRRRRRRRRRRRRRRRRRRRRRRRRRRR
RRRRRRRRRRRRRRRRRRRRRRRRRRRRRRRRRRRRRRRRRRRR
RRRRRRRRRRRRRRRRRRRRRRRRRRRRRRRRRRRRRRRRRRRR
RRRRRRRRRRRRRRRRRRRRRRRRRRRRRRRRRRRRRRRRRRRR
RRRRRRRRRRRRRRRRRRRRRRRRRRRRRRRRRRRRRRRRRRRR
RRRRRRRRRRRRRRRRRRRRRRRRRRRRRRRRRRRRRRRRRRRR
RRRRRRRRRRRRRRRRRRRRRRRRRRRRRRRRRRRRRRRRRRRR
RRRRRRRRRRRRRRRRRRRRRRRRRRRRRRRRRRRRRRRRRRRR
RRRRRRRRRRRRRRRRRRRRRRRRRRRRRRRRRRRRRRRRRRRR
RRRRRRRRRRRRRRRRRRRRRRRRRRRRRRRRRRRRRRRRRRRR
RRRRRRRRRRRRRRRRRRRRRRRRRRRRRRRRRRRRRRRRRRRR
RRRRRRRRRRRRRRRRRRRRRRRRRRRRRRRRRRRRRRRRRRRR
RRRRRRRRRRRRRRRRRRRRRRRRRRRRRRRRRRRRRRRRRRRR
RRRRRRRRRRRRRRRRRRRRRRRRRRRRRRRRRRRRRRRRRRRR
RRRRRRRRRRRRRRRRRRRRRRRRRRRRRRRRRRRRRRRRRRRR
RRRRRRRRRRRRRRRRRRRRRRRRRRRRRRRRRRRRRRRRRRRR

RRRRRRRRRRRRRRRRRRRRRRRRRRRRRRRRRRRRRRRRRRRR
RRRRRRRRRRRRRRRRRRRRRRRRRRRRRRRRRRRRRRRRRRRR
RRRRRRRRRRRRRRRRRRRRRRRRRRRRRRRRRRRRRRRRRRRR
RRRRRRRRRRRRRRRRRRRRRRRRRRRRRRRRRRRRRRRRRRRR
RRRRRRRRRRRRRRRRRRRRRRRRRRRRRRRRRRRRRRRRRRRR
RRRRRRRRRRRRRRRRRRRRRRRRRRRRRRRRRRRRRRRRRRRR
RRRRRRRRRRRRRRRRRRRRRRRRRRRRRRRRRRRRRRRRRRRR
RRRRRRRRRRRRRRRRRRRRRRRRRRRRRRRRRRRRRRRRRRRR
RRRRRRRRRRRRRRRRRRRRRRRRRRRRRRRRRRRRRRRRRRRR
RRRRRRRRRRRRRRRRRRRRRRRRRRRRRRRRRRRRRRRRRRRR
RRRRRRRRRRRRRRRRRRRRRRRRRRRRRRRRRRRRRRRRRRRR
RRRRRRRRRRRRRRRRRRRRRRRRRRRRRRRRRRRRRRRRRRRR
RRRRRRRRRRRRRRRRRRRRRRRRRRRRRRRRRRRRRRRRRRRR
RRRRRRRRRRRRRRRRRRRRRRRRRRRRRRRRRRRRRRRRRRRR
RRRRRRRRRRRRRRRRRRRRRRRRRRRRRRRRRRRRRRRRRRRR
RRRRRRRRRRRRRRRRRRRRRRRRRRRRRRRRRRRRRRRRRRRR
RRRRRRRRRRRRRRRRRRRRRRRRRRRRRRRRRRRRRRRRRRRR
RRRRRRRRRRRRRRRRRRRRRRRRRRRRRRRRRRRRRRRRRRRR
RRRRRRRRRRRRRRRRRRRRRRRRRRRRRRRRRRRRRRRRRRRR
RRRRRRRRRRRRRRRRRRRRRRRRRRRRRRRRRRRRRRRRRRRR
RRRRRRRRRRRRRRRRRRRRRRRRRRRRRRRRRRRRRRRRRRRR
RRRRRRRRRRRRRRRRRRRRRRRRRRRRRRRRRRRRRRRRRRRR
RRRRRRRRRRRRRRRRRRRRRRRRRRRRRRRRRRRRRRRRRRRR
RRRRRRRRRRRRRRRRRRRRRRRRRRRRRRRRRRRRRRRRRRRR
RRRRRRRRRRRRRRRRRRRRRRRRRRRRRRRRRRRRRRRRRRRR
RRRRRRRRRRRRRRRRRRRRRRRRRRRRRRRRRRRRRRRRRRRR

RRRRRRRRRRRRRRRRRRRRRRRRRRRRRRRRRRRRRRRRRRRRRR
RRRRRRRRRRRRRRRRRRRRRRRRRRRRRRRRRRRRRRRRRRRRRR
RRRRRRRRRRRRRRRRRRRRRRRRRRRRRRRRRRRRRRRRRRRRRR
RRRRRRRRRRRRRRRRRRRRRRRRRRRRRRRRRRRRRRRRRRRRRR
RRRRRRRRRRRRRRRRRRRRRRRRRRRRRRRRRRRRRRRRRRRRRR
RRRRRRRRRRRRRRRRRRRRRRRRRRRRRRRRRRRRRRRRRRRRRR
RRRRRRRRRRRRRRRRRRRRRRRRRRRRRRRRRRRRRRRRRRRRRR
RRRRRRRRRRRRRRRRRRRRRRRRRRRRRRRRRRRRRRRRRRRRRR
RRRRRRRRRRRRRRRRRRRRRRRRRRRRRRRRRRRRRRRRRRRRRR
RRRRRRRRRRRRRRRRRRRRRRRRRRRRRRRRRRRRRRRRRRRRRR
RRRRRRRRRRRRRRRRRRRRRRRRRRRRRRRRRRRRRRRRRRRRRR
RRRRRRRRRRRRRRRRRRRRRRRRRRRRRRRRRRRRRRRRRRRRRR
RRRRRRRRRRRRRRRRRRRRRRRRRRRRRRRRRRRRRRRRRRRRRR
RRRRRRRRRRRRRRRRRRRRRRRRRRRRRRRRRRRRRRRRRRRRRR
RRRRRRRRRRRRRRRRRRRRRRRRRRRRRRRRRRRRRRRRRRRRRR
RRRRRRRRRRRRRRRRRRRRRRRRRRRRRRRRRRRRRRRRRRRRRR
RRRRRRRRRRRRRRRRRRRRRRRRRRRRRRRRRRRRRRRRRRRRRR
RRRRRRRRRRRRRRRRRRRRRRRRRRRRRRRRRRRRRRRRRRRRRR
RRRRRRRRRRRRRRRRRRRRRRRRRRRRRRRRRRRRRRRRRRRRRR
RRRRRRRRRRRRRRRRRRRRRRRRRRRRRRRRRRRRRRRRRRRRRR
RRRRRRRRRRRRRRRRRRRRRRRRRRRRRRRRRRRRRRRRRRRRRR
RRRRRRRRRRRRRRRRRRRRRRRRRRRRRRRRRRRRRRRRRRRRRR
RRRRRRRRRRRRRRRRRRRRRRRRRRRRRRRRRRRRRRRRRRRRRR
RRRRRRRRRRRRRRRRRRRRRRRRRRRRRRRRRRRRRRRRRRRRRR
RRRRRRRRRRRRRRRRRRRRRRRRRRRRRRRRRRRRRRRRRRRRRR

RRRRRRRRRRRRRRRRRRRRRRRRRRRRRRRRRRRRRRR
RRRRRRRRRRRRRRRRRRRRRRRRRRRRRRRRRRRRRRR
RRRRRRRRRRRRRRRRRRRRRRRRRRRRRRRRRRRRRRR
RRRRRRRRRRRRRRRRRRRRRRRRRRRRRRRRRRRRRRR
RRRRRRRRRRRRRRRRRRRRRRRRRRRRRRRRRRRRRRR
RRRRRRRRRRRRRRRRRRRRRRRRRRRRRRRRRRRRRRR
RRRRRRRRRRRRRRRRRRRRRRRRRRRRRRRRRRRRRRR
RRRRRRRRRRRRRRRRRRRRRRRRRRRRRRRRRRRRRRR
RRRRRRRRRRRRRRRRRRRRRRRRRRRRRRRRRRRRRRR
RRRRRRRRRRRRRRRRRRRRRRRRRRRRRRRRRRRRRRR
RRRRRRRRRRRRRRRRRRRRRRRRRRRRRRRRRRRRRRR
RRRRRRRRRRRRRRRRRRRRRRRRRRRRRRRRRRRRRRR
RRRRRRRRRRRRRRRRRRRRRRRRRRRRRRRRRRRRRRR
RRRRRRRRRRRRRRRRRRRRRRRRRRRRRRRRRRRRRRR
RRRRRRRRRRRRRRRRRRRRRRRRRRRRRRRRRRRRRRR
RRRRRRRRRRRRRRRRRRRRRRRRRRRRRRRRRRRRRRR
RRRRRRRRRRRRRRRRRRRRRRRRRRRRRRRRRRRRRRR
RRRRRRRRRRRRRRRRRRRRRRRRRRRRRRRRRRRRRRR
RRRRRRRRRRRRRRRRRRRRRRRRRRRRRRRRRRRRRRR
RRRRRRRRRRRRRRRRRRRRRRRRRRRRRRRRRRRRRRR
RRRRRRRRRRRRRRRRRRRRRRRRRRRRRRRRRRRRRRR
RRRRRRRRRRRRRRRRRRRRRRRRRRRRRRRRRRRRRRR
RRRRRRRRRRRRRRRRRRRRRRRRRRRRRRRRRRRRRRR
RRRRRRRRRRRRRRRRRRRRRRRRRRRRRRRRRRRRRRR
RRRRRRRRRRRRRRRRRRRRRRRRRRRRRRRRRRRRRRR
RRRRRRRRRRRRRRRRRRRRRRRRRRRRRRRRRRRRRRR
RRRRRRRRRRRRRRRRRRRRRRRRRRRRRRRRRRRRRRR
RRRRRRRRRRRRRRRRRRRRRRRRRRRRRRRRRRRRRRR

RRRRRRRRRRRRRRRRRRRRRRRRRRRRRRRRRRRRRRRRRRR
RRRRRRRRRRRRRRRRRRRRRRRRRRRRRRRRRRRRRRRRRRR
RRRRRRRRRRRRRRRRRRRRRRRRRRRRRRRRRRRRRRRRRRR
RRRRRRRRRRRRRRRRRRRRRRRRRRRRRRRRRRRRRRRRRRR
RRRRRRRRRRRRRRRRRRRRRRRRRRRRRRRRRRRRRRRRRRR
RRRRRRRRRRRRRRRRRRRRRRRRRRRRRRRRRRRRRRRRRRR
RRRRRRRRRRRRRRRRRRRRRRRRRRRRRRRRRRRRRRRRRRR
RRRRRRRRRRRRRRRRRRRRRRRRRRRRRRRRRRRRRRRRRRR
RRRRRRRRRRRRRRRRRRRRRRRRRRRRRRRRRRRRRRRRRRR
RRRRRRRRRRRRRRRRRRRRRRRRRRRRRRRRRRRRRRRRRRR
RRRRRRRRRRRRRRRRRRRRRRRRRRRRRRRRRRRRRRRRRRR
RRRRRRRRRRRRRRRRRRRRRRRRRRRRRRRRRRRRRRRRRRR
RRRRRRRRRRRRRRRRRRRRRRRRRRRRRRRRRRRRRRRRRRR
RRRRRRRRRRRRRRRRRRRRRRRRRRRRRRRRRRRRRRRRRRR
RRRRRRRRRRRRRRRRRRRRRRRRRRRRRRRRRRRRRRRRRRR
RRRRRRRRRRRRRRRRRRRRRRRRRRRRRRRRRRRRRRRRRRR
RRRRRRRRRRRRRRRRRRRRRRRRRRRRRRRRRRRRRRRRRRR
RRRRRRRRRRRRRRRRRRRRRRRRRRRRRRRRRRRRRRRRRRR
RRRRRRRRRRRRRRRRRRRRRRRRRRRRRRRRRRRRRRRRRRR
RRRRRRRRRRRRRRRRRRRRRRRRRRRRRRRRRRRRRRRRRRR
RRRRRRRRRRRRRRRRRRRRRRRRRRRRRRRRRRRRRRRRRRR
RRRRRRRRRRRRRRRRRRRRRRRRRRRRRRRRRRRRRRRRRRR
RRRRRRRRRRRRRRRRRRRRRRRRRRRRRRRRRRRRRRRRRRR
RRRRRRRRRRRRRRRRRRRRRRRRRRRRRRRRRRRRRRRRRRR
RRRRRRRRRRRRRRRRRRRRRRRRRRRRRRRRRRRRRRRRRRR
RRRRRRRRRRRRRRRRRRRRRRRRRRRRRRRRRRRRRRRRRRR

RRRRRRRRRRRRRRRRRRRRRRRRRRRRRRRRRRRRRRRRRRR
RRRRRRRRRRRRRRRRRRRRRRRRRRRRRRRRRRRRRRRRRRR
RRRRRRRRRRRRRRRRRRRRRRRRRRRRRRRRRRRRRRRRRRR
RRRRRRRRRRRRRRRRRRRRRRRRRRRRRRRRRRRRRRRRRRR
RRRRRRRRRRRRRRRRRRRRRRRRRRRRRRRRRRRRRRRRRRR
RRRRRRRRRRRRRRRRRRRRRRRRRRRRRRRRRRRRRRRRRRR
RRRRRRRRRRRRRRRRRRRRRRRRRRRRRRRRRRRRRRRRRRR
RRRRRRRRRRRRRRRRRRRRRRRRRRRRRRRRRRRRRRRRRRR
RRRRRRRRRRRRRRRRRRRRRRRRRRRRRRRRRRRRRRRRRRR
RRRRRRRRRRRRRRRRRRRRRRRRRRRRRRRRRRRRRRRRRRR
RRRRRRRRRRRRRRRRRRRRRRRRRRRRRRRRRRRRRRRRRRR
RRRRRRRRRRRRRRRRRRRRRRRRRRRRRRRRRRRRRRRRRRR
RRRRRRRRRRRRRRRRRRRRRRRRRRRRRRRRRRRRRRRRRRR
RRRRRRRRRRRRRRRRRRRRRRRRRRRRRRRRRRRRRRRRRRR
RRRRRRRRRRRRRRRRRRRRRRRRRRRRRRRRRRRRRRRRRRR
RRRRRRRRRRRRRRRRRRRRRRRRRRRRRRRRRRRRRRRRRRR
RRRRRRRRRRRRRRRRRRRRRRRRRRRRRRRRRRRRRRRRRRR
RRRRRRRRRRRRRRRRRRRRRRRRRRRRRRRRRRRRRRRRRRR
RRRRRRRRRRRRRRRRRRRRRRRRRRRRRRRRRRRRRRRRRRR
RRRRRRRRRRRRRRRRRRRRRRRRRRRRRRRRRRRRRRRRRRR
RRRRRRRRRRRRRRRRRRRRRRRRRRRRRRRRRRRRRRRRRRR
RRRRRRRRRRRRRRRRRRRRRRRRRRRRRRRRRRRRRRRRRRR
RRRRRRRRRRRRRRRRRRRRRRRRRRRRRRRRRRRRRRRRRRR
RRRRRRRRRRRRRRRRRRRRRRRRRRRRRRRRRRRRRRRRRRR
RRRRRRRRRRRRRRRRRRRRRRRRRRRRRRRRRRRRRRRRRRR
RRRRRRRRRRRRRRRRRRRRRRRRRRRRRRRRRRRRRRRRRRR
RRRRRRRRRRRRRRRRRRRRRRRRRRRRRRRRRRRRRRRRRRR

RRRRRRRRRRRRRRRRRRRRRRRRRRRRRRRRRRRRRRRRRRRRRR
RRRRRRRRRRRRRRRRRRRRRRRRRRRRRRRRRRRRRRRRRRRRRR
RRRRRRRRRRRRRRRRRRRRRRRRRRRRRRRRRRRRRRRRRRRRRR
RRRRRRRRRRRRRRRRRRRRRRRRRRRRRRRRRRRRRRRRRRRRRR
RRRRRRRRRRRRRRRRRRRRRRRRRRRRRRRRRRRRRRRRRRRRRR
RRRRRRRRRRRRRRRRRRRRRRRRRRRRRRRRRRRRRRRRRRRRRR
RRRRRRRRRRRRRRRRRRRRRRRRRRRRRRRRRRRRRRRRRRRRRR
RRRRRRRRRRRRRRRRRRRRRRRRRRRRRRRRRRRRRRRRRRRRRR
RRRRRRRRRRRRRRRRRRRRRRRRRRRRRRRRRRRRRRRRRRRRRR
RRRRRRRRRRRRRRRRRRRRRRRRRRRRRRRRRRRRRRRRRRRRRR
RRRRRRRRRRRRRRRRRRRRRRRRRRRRRRRRRRRRRRRRRRRRRR
RRRRRRRRRRRRRRRRRRRRRRRRRRRRRRRRRRRRRRRRRRRRRR
RRRRRRRRRRRRRRRRRRRRRRRRRRRRRRRRRRRRRRRRRRRRRR
RRRRRRRRRRRRRRRRRRRRRRRRRRRRRRRRRRRRRRRRRRRRRR
RRRRRRRRRRRRRRRRRRRRRRRRRRRRRRRRRRRRRRRRRRRRRR
RRRRRRRRRRRRRRRRRRRRRRRRRRRRRRRRRRRRRRRRRRRRRR
RRRRRRRRRRRRRRRRRRRRRRRRRRRRRRRRRRRRRRRRRRRRRR
RRRRRRRRRRRRRRRRRRRRRRRRRRRRRRRRRRRRRRRRRRRRRR
RRRRRRRRRRRRRRRRRRRRRRRRRRRRRRRRRRRRRRRRRRRRRR
RRRRRRRRRRRRRRRRRRRRRRRRRRRRRRRRRRRRRRRRRRRRRR
RRRRRRRRRRRRRRRRRRRRRRRRRRRRRRRRRRRRRRRRRRRRRR
RRRRRRRRRRRRRRRRRRRRRRRRRRRRRRRRRRRRRRRRRRRRRR
RRRRRRRRRRRRRRRRRRRRRRRRRRRRRRRRRRRRRRRRRRRRRR
RRRRRRRRRRRRRRRRRRRRRRRRRRRRRRRRRRRRRRRRRRRRRR
RRRRRRRRRRRRRRRRRRRRRRRRRRRRRRRRRRRRRRRRRRRRRR
RRRRRRRRRRRRRRRRRRRRRRRRRRRRRRRRRRRRRRRRRRRRRR

RRRRRRRRRRRRRRRRRRRRRRRRRRRRRRRRRRRRRRRRRRRRRRRRR
RRRRRRRRRRRRRRRRRRRRRRRRRRRRRRRRRRRRRRRRRRRRRRRRR
RRRRRRRRRRRRRRRRRRRRRRRRRRRRRRRRRRRRRRRRRRRRRRRRR
RRRRRRRRRRRRRRRRRRRRRRRRRRRRRRRRRRRRRRRRRRRRRRRRR
RRRRRRRRRRRRRRRRRRRRRRRRRRRRRRRRRRRRRRRRRRRRRRRRR
RRRRRRRRRRRRRRRRRRRRRRRRRRRRRRRRRRRRRRRRRRRRRRRRR
RRRRRRRRRRRRRRRRRRRRRRRRRRRRRRRRRRRRRRRRRRRRRRRRR
RRRRRRRRRRRRRRRRRRRRRRRRRRRRRRRRRRRRRRRRRRRRRRRRR
RRRRRRRRRRRRRRRRRRRRRRRRRRRRRRRRRRRRRRRRRRRRRRRRR
RRRRRRRRRRRRRRRRRRRRRRRRRRRRRRRRRRRRRRRRRRRRRRRRR
RRRRRRRRRRRRRRRRRRRRRRRRRRRRRRRRRRRRRRRRRRRRRRRRR
RRRRRRRRRRRRRRRRRRRRRRRRRRRRRRRRRRRRRRRRRRRRRRRRR
RRRRRRRRRRRRRRRRRRRRRRRRRRRRRRRRRRRRRRRRRRRRRRRRR
RRRRRRRRRRRRRRRRRRRRRRRRRRRRRRRRRRRRRRRRRRRRRRRRR
RRRRRRRRRRRRRRRRRRRRRRRRRRRRRRRRRRRRRRRRRRRRRRRRR
RRRRRRRRRRRRRRRRRRRRRRRRRRRRRRRRRRRRRRRRRRRRRRRRR
RRRRRRRRRRRRRRRRRRRRRRRRRRRRRRRRRRRRRRRRRRRRRRRRR
RRRRRRRRRRRRRRRRRRRRRRRRRRRRRRRRRRRRRRRRRRRRRRRRR
RRRRRRRRRRRRRRRRRRRRRRRRRRRRRRRRRRRRRRRRRRRRRRRRR
RRRRRRRRRRRRRRRRRRRRRRRRRRRRRRRRRRRRRRRRRRRRRRRRR
RRRRRRRRRRRRRRRRRRRRRRRRRRRRRRRRRRRRRRRRRRRRRRRRR
RRRRRRRRRRRRRRRRRRRRRRRRRRRRRRRRRRRRRRRRRRRRRRRRR
RRRRRRRRRRRRRRRRRRRRRRRRRRRRRRRRRRRRRRRRRRRRRRRRR
RRRRRRRRRRRRRRRRRRRRRRRRRRRRRRRRRRRRRRRRRRRRRRRRR
RRRRRRRRRRRRRRRRRRRRRRRRRRRRRRRRRRRRRRRRRRRRRRRRR
RRRRRRRRRRRRRRRRRRRRRRRRRRRRRRRRRRRRRRRRRRRRRRRRR
RRRRRRRRRRRRRRRRRRRRRRRRRRRRRRRRRRRRRRRRRRRRRRRRR
RRRRRRRRRRRRRRRRRRRRRRRRRRRRRRRRRRRRRRRRRRRRRRRRR
RRRRRRRRRRRRRRRRRRRRRRRRRRRRRRRRRRRRRRRRRRRRRRRRR
RRRRRRRRRRRRRRRRRRRRRRRRRRRRRRRRRRRRRRRRRRRRRRRRR

RRRRRRRRRRRRRRRRRRRRRRRRRRRRRRRRRRRRRRRRRRRR
RRRRRRRRRRRRRRRRRRRRRRRRRRRRRRRRRRRRRRRRRRRR
RRRRRRRRRRRRRRRRRRRRRRRRRRRRRRRRRRRRRRRRRRRR
RRRRRRRRRRRRRRRRRRRRRRRRRRRRRRRRRRRRRRRRRRRR
RRRRRRRRRRRRRRRRRRRRRRRRRRRRRRRRRRRRRRRRRRRR
RRRRRRRRRRRRRRRRRRRRRRRRRRRRRRRRRRRRRRRRRRRR
RRRRRRRRRRRRRRRRRRRRRRRRRRRRRRRRRRRRRRRRRRRR
RRRRRRRRRRRRRRRRRRRRRRRRRRRRRRRRRRRRRRRRRRRR
RRRRRRRRRRRRRRRRRRRRRRRRRRRRRRRRRRRRRRRRRRRR
RRRRRRRRRRRRRRRRRRRRRRRRRRRRRRRRRRRRRRRRRRRR
RRRRRRRRRRRRRRRRRRRRRRRRRRRRRRRRRRRRRRRRRRRR
RRRRRRRRRRRRRRRRRRRRRRRRRRRRRRRRRRRRRRRRRRRR
RRRRRRRRRRRRRRRRRRRRRRRRRRRRRRRRRRRRRRRRRRRR
RRRRRRRRRRRRRRRRRRRRRRRRRRRRRRRRRRRRRRRRRRRR
RRRRRRRRRRRRRRRRRRRRRRRRRRRRRRRRRRRRRRRRRRRR
RRRRRRRRRRRRRRRRRRRRRRRRRRRRRRRRRRRRRRRRRRRR
RRRRRRRRRRRRRRRRRRRRRRRRRRRRRRRRRRRRRRRRRRRR
RRRRRRRRRRRRRRRRRRRRRRRRRRRRRRRRRRRRRRRRRRRR
RRRRRRRRRRRRRRRRRRRRRRRRRRRRRRRRRRRRRRRRRRRR
RRRRRRRRRRRRRRRRRRRRRRRRRRRRRRRRRRRRRRRRRRRR
RRRRRRRRRRRRRRRRRRRRRRRRRRRRRRRRRRRRRRRRRRRR
RRRRRRRRRRRRRRRRRRRRRRRRRRRRRRRRRRRRRRRRRRRR
RRRRRRRRRRRRRRRRRRRRRRRRRRRRRRRRRRRRRRRRRRRR
RRRRRRRRRRRRRRRRRRRRRRRRRRRRRRRRRRRRRRRRRRRR
RRRRRRRRRRRRRRRRRRRRRRRRRRRRRRRRRRRRRRRRRRRR
RRRRRRRRRRRRRRRRRRRRRRRRRRRRRRRRRRRRRRRRRRRR
RRRRRRRRRRRRRRRRRRRRRRRRRRRRRRRRRRRRRRRRRRRR
RRRRRRRRRRRRRRRRRRRRRRRRRRRRRRRRRRRRRRRRRRRR

RRRRRRRRRRRRRRRRRRRRRRRRRRRRRRRRRRRRRRRRRRRRRRR
RRRRRRRRRRRRRRRRRRRRRRRRRRRRRRRRRRRRRRRRRRRRRRR
RRRRRRRRRRRRRRRRRRRRRRRRRRRRRRRRRRRRRRRRRRRRRRR
RRRRRRRRRRRRRRRRRRRRRRRRRRRRRRRRRRRRRRRRRRRRRRR
RRRRRRRRRRRRRRRRRRRRRRRRRRRRRRRRRRRRRRRRRRRRRRR
RRRRRRRRRRRRRRRRRRRRRRRRRRRRRRRRRRRRRRRRRRRRRRR
RRRRRRRRRRRRRRRRRRRRRRRRRRRRRRRRRRRRRRRRRRRRRRR
RRRRRRRRRRRRRRRRRRRRRRRRRRRRRRRRRRRRRRRRRRRRRRR
RRRRRRRRRRRRRRRRRRRRRRRRRRRRRRRRRRRRRRRRRRRRRRR
RRRRRRRRRRRRRRRRRRRRRRRRRRRRRRRRRRRRRRRRRRRRRRR
RRRRRRRRRRRRRRRRRRRRRRRRRRRRRRRRRRRRRRRRRRRRRRR
RRRRRRRRRRRRRRRRRRRRRRRRRRRRRRRRRRRRRRRRRRRRRRR
RRRRRRRRRRRRRRRRRRRRRRRRRRRRRRRRRRRRRRRRRRRRRRR
RRRRRRRRRRRRRRRRRRRRRRRRRRRRRRRRRRRRRRRRRRRRRRR
RRRRRRRRRRRRRRRRRRRRRRRRRRRRRRRRRRRRRRRRRRRRRRR
RRRRRRRRRRRRRRRRRRRRRRRRRRRRRRRRRRRRRRRRRRRRRRR
RRRRRRRRRRRRRRRRRRRRRRRRRRRRRRRRRRRRRRRRRRRRRRR
RRRRRRRRRRRRRRRRRRRRRRRRRRRRRRRRRRRRRRRRRRRRRRR
RRRRRRRRRRRRRRRRRRRRRRRRRRRRRRRRRRRRRRRRRRRRRRR
RRRRRRRRRRRRRRRRRRRRRRRRRRRRRRRRRRRRRRRRRRRRRRR
RRRRRRRRRRRRRRRRRRRRRRRRRRRRRRRRRRRRRRRRRRRRRRR
RRRRRRRRRRRRRRRRRRRRRRRRRRRRRRRRRRRRRRRRRRRRRRR
RRRRRRRRRRRRRRRRRRRRRRRRRRRRRRRRRRRRRRRRRRRRRRR
RRRRRRRRRRRRRRRRRRRRRRRRRRRRRRRRRRRRRRRRRRRRRRR
RRRRRRRRRRRRRRRRRRRRRRRRRRRRRRRRRRRRRRRRRRRRRRR
RRRRRRRRRRRRRRRRRRRRRRRRRRRRRRRRRRRRRRRRRRRRRRR

RRRRRRRRRRRRRRRRRRRRRRRRRRRRRRRRRRRRRRRRRRR
RRRRRRRRRRRRRRRRRRRRRRRRRRRRRRRRRRRRRRRRRRR
RRRRRRRRRRRRRRRRRRRRRRRRRRRRRRRRRRRRRRRRRRR
RRRRRRRRRRRRRRRRRRRRRRRRRRRRRRRRRRRRRRRRRRR
RRRRRRRRRRRRRRRRRRRRRRRRRRRRRRRRRRRRRRRRRRR
RRRRRRRRRRRRRRRRRRRRRRRRRRRRRRRRRRRRRRRRRRR
RRRRRRRRRRRRRRRRRRRRRRRRRRRRRRRRRRRRRRRRRRR
RRRRRRRRRRRRRRRRRRRRRRRRRRRRRRRRRRRRRRRRRRR
RRRRRRRRRRRRRRRRRRRRRRRRRRRRRRRRRRRRRRRRRRR
RRRRRRRRRRRRRRRRRRRRRRRRRRRRRRRRRRRRRRRRRRR
RRRRRRRRRRRRRRRRRRRRRRRRRRRRRRRRRRRRRRRRRRR
RRRRRRRRRRRRRRRRRRRRRRRRRRRRRRRRRRRRRRRRRRR
RRRRRRRRRRRRRRRRRRRRRRRRRRRRRRRRRRRRRRRRRRR
RRRRRRRRRRRRRRRRRRRRRRRRRRRRRRRRRRRRRRRRRRR
RRRRRRRRRRRRRRRRRRRRRRRRRRRRRRRRRRRRRRRRRRR
RRRRRRRRRRRRRRRRRRRRRRRRRRRRRRRRRRRRRRRRRRR
RRRRRRRRRRRRRRRRRRRRRRRRRRRRRRRRRRRRRRRRRRR
RRRRRRRRRRRRRRRRRRRRRRRRRRRRRRRRRRRRRRRRRRR
RRRRRRRRRRRRRRRRRRRRRRRRRRRRRRRRRRRRRRRRRRR
RRRRRRRRRRRRRRRRRRRRRRRRRRRRRRRRRRRRRRRRRRR
RRRRRRRRRRRRRRRRRRRRRRRRRRRRRRRRRRRRRRRRRRR
RRRRRRRRRRRRRRRRRRRRRRRRRRRRRRRRRRRRRRRRRRR
RRRRRRRRRRRRRRRRRRRRRRRRRRRRRRRRRRRRRRRRRRR
RRRRRRRRRRRRRRRRRRRRRRRRRRRRRRRRRRRRRRRRRRR
RRRRRRRRRRRRRRRRRRRRRRRRRRRRRRRRRRRRRRRRRRR

RRRRRRRRRRRRRRRRRRRRRRRRRRRRRRRRRRRRRRRRRRRRR
RRRRRRRRRRRRRRRRRRRRRRRRRRRRRRRRRRRRRRRRRRRRR
RRRRRRRRRRRRRRRRRRRRRRRRRRRRRRRRRRRRRRRRRRRRR
RRRRRRRRRRRRRRRRRRRRRRRRRRRRRRRRRRRRRRRRRRRRR
RRRRRRRRRRRRRRRRRRRRRRRRRRRRRRRRRRRRRRRRRRRRR
RRRRRRRRRRRRRRRRRRRRRRRRRRRRRRRRRRRRRRRRRRRRR
RRRRRRRRRRRRRRRRRRRRRRRRRRRRRRRRRRRRRRRRRRRRR
RRRRRRRRRRRRRRRRRRRRRRRRRRRRRRRRRRRRRRRRRRRRR
RRRRRRRRRRRRRRRRRRRRRRRRRRRRRRRRRRRRRRRRRRRRR
RRRRRRRRRRRRRRRRRRRRRRRRRRRRRRRRRRRRRRRRRRRRR
RRRRRRRRRRRRRRRRRRRRRRRRRRRRRRRRRRRRRRRRRRRRR
RRRRRRRRRRRRRRRRRRRRRRRRRRRRRRRRRRRRRRRRRRRRR
RRRRRRRRRRRRRRRRRRRRRRRRRRRRRRRRRRRRRRRRRRRRR
RRRRRRRRRRRRRRRRRRRRRRRRRRRRRRRRRRRRRRRRRRRRR
RRRRRRRRRRRRRRRRRRRRRRRRRRRRRRRRRRRRRRRRRRRRR
RRRRRRRRRRRRRRRRRRRRRRRRRRRRRRRRRRRRRRRRRRRRR
RRRRRRRRRRRRRRRRRRRRRRRRRRRRRRRRRRRRRRRRRRRRR
RRRRRRRRRRRRRRRRRRRRRRRRRRRRRRRRRRRRRRRRRRRRR
RRRRRRRRRRRRRRRRRRRRRRRRRRRRRRRRRRRRRRRRRRRRR
RRRRRRRRRRRRRRRRRRRRRRRRRRRRRRRRRRRRRRRRRRRRR
RRRRRRRRRRRRRRRRRRRRRRRRRRRRRRRRRRRRRRRRRRRRR
RRRRRRRRRRRRRRRRRRRRRRRRRRRRRRRRRRRRRRRRRRRRR
RRRRRRRRRRRRRRRRRRRRRRRRRRRRRRRRRRRRRRRRRRRRR
RRRRRRRRRRRRRRRRRRRRRRRRRRRRRRRRRRRRRRRRRRRRR
RRRRRRRRRRRRRRRRRRRRRRRRRRRRRRRRRRRRRRRRRRRRR
RRRRRRRRRRRRRRRRRRRRRRRRRRRRRRRRRRRRRRRRRRRRR
RRRRRRRRRRRRRRRRRRRRRRRRRRRRRRRRRRRRRRRRRRRRR

RRRRRRRRRRRRRRRRRRRRRRRRRRRRRRRRRRRRRRRRRR
RRRRRRRRRRRRRRRRRRRRRRRRRRRRRRRRRRRRRRRRRR
RRRRRRRRRRRRRRRRRRRRRRRRRRRRRRRRRRRRRRRRRR
RRRRRRRRRRRRRRRRRRRRRRRRRRRRRRRRRRRRRRRRRR
RRRRRRRRRRRRRRRRRRRRRRRRRRRRRRRRRRRRRRRRRR
RRRRRRRRRRRRRRRRRRRRRRRRRRRRRRRRRRRRRRRRRR
RRRRRRRRRRRRRRRRRRRRRRRRRRRRRRRRRRRRRRRRRR
RRRRRRRRRRRRRRRRRRRRRRRRRRRRRRRRRRRRRRRRRR
RRRRRRRRRRRRRRRRRRRRRRRRRRRRRRRRRRRRRRRRRR
RRRRRRRRRRRRRRRRRRRRRRRRRRRRRRRRRRRRRRRRRR
RRRRRRRRRRRRRRRRRRRRRRRRRRRRRRRRRRRRRRRRRR
RRRRRRRRRRRRRRRRRRRRRRRRRRRRRRRRRRRRRRRRRR
RRRRRRRRRRRRRRRRRRRRRRRRRRRRRRRRRRRRRRRRRR
RRRRRRRRRRRRRRRRRRRRRRRRRRRRRRRRRRRRRRRRRR
RRRRRRRRRRRRRRRRRRRRRRRRRRRRRRRRRRRRRRRRRR
RRRRRRRRRRRRRRRRRRRRRRRRRRRRRRRRRRRRRRRRRR
RRRRRRRRRRRRRRRRRRRRRRRRRRRRRRRRRRRRRRRRRR
RRRRRRRRRRRRRRRRRRRRRRRRRRRRRRRRRRRRRRRRRR
RRRRRRRRRRRRRRRRRRRRRRRRRRRRRRRRRRRRRRRRRR
RRRRRRRRRRRRRRRRRRRRRRRRRRRRRRRRRRRRRRRRRR
RRRRRRRRRRRRRRRRRRRRRRRRRRRRRRRRRRRRRRRRRR
RRRRRRRRRRRRRRRRRRRRRRRRRRRRRRRRRRRRRRRRRR
RRRRRRRRRRRRRRRRRRRRRRRRRRRRRRRRRRRRRRRRRR
RRRRRRRRRRRRRRRRRRRRRRRRRRRRRRRRRRRRRRRRRR
RRRRRRRRRRRRRRRRRRRRRRRRRRRRRRRRRRRRRRRRRR
RRRRRRRRRRRRRRRRRRRRRRRRRRRRRRRRRRRRRRRRRR
RRRRRRRRRRRRRRRRRRRRRRRRRRRRRRRRRRRRRRRRRR

RRRRRRRRRRRRRRRRRRRRRRRRRRRRRRRRRRRRRRRRRRRR
RRRRRRRRRRRRRRRRRRRRRRRRRRRRRRRRRRRRRRRRRRRR
RRRRRRRRRRRRRRRRRRRRRRRRRRRRRRRRRRRRRRRRRRRR
RRRRRRRRRRRRRRRRRRRRRRRRRRRRRRRRRRRRRRRRRRRR
RRRRRRRRRRRRRRRRRRRRRRRRRRRRRRRRRRRRRRRRRRRR
RRRRRRRRRRRRRRRRRRRRRRRRRRRRRRRRRRRRRRRRRRRR
RRRRRRRRRRRRRRRRRRRRRRRRRRRRRRRRRRRRRRRRRRRR
RRRRRRRRRRRRRRRRRRRRRRRRRRRRRRRRRRRRRRRRRRRR
RRRRRRRRRRRRRRRRRRRRRRRRRRRRRRRRRRRRRRRRRRRR
RRRRRRRRRRRRRRRRRRRRRRRRRRRRRRRRRRRRRRRRRRRR
RRRRRRRRRRRRRRRRRRRRRRRRRRRRRRRRRRRRRRRRRRRR
RRRRRRRRRRRRRRRRRRRRRRRRRRRRRRRRRRRRRRRRRRRR
RRRRRRRRRRRRRRRRRRRRRRRRRRRRRRRRRRRRRRRRRRRR
RRRRRRRRRRRRRRRRRRRRRRRRRRRRRRRRRRRRRRRRRRRR
RRRRRRRRRRRRRRRRRRRRRRRRRRRRRRRRRRRRRRRRRRRR
RRRRRRRRRRRRRRRRRRRRRRRRRRRRRRRRRRRRRRRRRRRR
RRRRRRRRRRRRRRRRRRRRRRRRRRRRRRRRRRRRRRRRRRRR
RRRRRRRRRRRRRRRRRRRRRRRRRRRRRRRRRRRRRRRRRRRR
RRRRRRRRRRRRRRRRRRRRRRRRRRRRRRRRRRRRRRRRRRRR
RRRRRRRRRRRRRRRRRRRRRRRRRRRRRRRRRRRRRRRRRRRR
RRRRRRRRRRRRRRRRRRRRRRRRRRRRRRRRRRRRRRRRRRRR
RRRRRRRRRRRRRRRRRRRRRRRRRRRRRRRRRRRRRRRRRRRR
RRRRRRRRRRRRRRRRRRRRRRRRRRRRRRRRRRRRRRRRRRRR
RRRRRRRRRRRRRRRRRRRRRRRRRRRRRRRRRRRRRRRRRRRR
RRRRRRRRRRRRRRRRRRRRRRRRRRRRRRRRRRRRRRRRRRRR

RRRRRRRRRRRRRRRRRRRRRRRRRRRRRRRRRRRRRRRRRRRRRRRRR
RRRRRRRRRRRRRRRRRRRRRRRRRRRRRRRRRRRRRRRRRRRRRRRRR
RRRRRRRRRRRRRRRRRRRRRRRRRRRRRRRRRRRRRRRRRRRRRRRRR
RRRRRRRRRRRRRRRRRRRRRRRRRRRRRRRRRRRRRRRRRRRRRRRRR
RRRRRRRRRRRRRRRRRRRRRRRRRRRRRRRRRRRRRRRRRRRRRRRRR
RRRRRRRRRRRRRRRRRRRRRRRRRRRRRRRRRRRRRRRRRRRRRRRRR
RRRRRRRRRRRRRRRRRRRRRRRRRRRRRRRRRRRRRRRRRRRRRRRRR
RRRRRRRRRRRRRRRRRRRRRRRRRRRRRRRRRRRRRRRRRRRRRRRRR
RRRRRRRRRRRRRRRRRRRRRRRRRRRRRRRRRRRRRRRRRRRRRRRRR
RRRRRRRRRRRRRRRRRRRRRRRRRRRRRRRRRRRRRRRRRRRRRRRRR
RRRRRRRRRRRRRRRRRRRRRRRRRRRRRRRRRRRRRRRRRRRRRRRRR
RRRRRRRRRRRRRRRRRRRRRRRRRRRRRRRRRRRRRRRRRRRRRRRRR
RRRRRRRRRRRRRRRRRRRRRRRRRRRRRRRRRRRRRRRRRRRRRRRRR
RRRRRRRRRRRRRRRRRRRRRRRRRRRRRRRRRRRRRRRRRRRRRRRRR
RRRRRRRRRRRRRRRRRRRRRRRRRRRRRRRRRRRRRRRRRRRRRRRRR
RRRRRRRRRRRRRRRRRRRRRRRRRRRRRRRRRRRRRRRRRRRRRRRRR
RRRRRRRRRRRRRRRRRRRRRRRRRRRRRRRRRRRRRRRRRRRRRRRRR
RRRRRRRRRRRRRRRRRRRRRRRRRRRRRRRRRRRRRRRRRRRRRRRRR
RRRRRRRRRRRRRRRRRRRRRRRRRRRRRRRRRRRRRRRRRRRRRRRRR
RRRRRRRRRRRRRRRRRRRRRRRRRRRRRRRRRRRRRRRRRRRRRRRRR
RRRRRRRRRRRRRRRRRRRRRRRRRRRRRRRRRRRRRRRRRRRRRRRRR
RRRRRRRRRRRRRRRRRRRRRRRRRRRRRRRRRRRRRRRRRRRRRRRRR
RRRRRRRRRRRRRRRRRRRRRRRRRRRRRRRRRRRRRRRRRRRRRRRRR
RRRRRRRRRRRRRRRRRRRRRRRRRRRRRRRRRRRRRRRRRRRRRRRRR
RRRRRRRRRRRRRRRRRRRRRRRRRRRRRRRRRRRRRRRRRRRRRRRRR

RRRRRRRRRRRRRRRRRRRRRRRRRRRRRRRRRRRRRRRRR
RRRRRRRRRRRRRRRRRRRRRRRRRRRRRRRRRRRRRRRRR
RRRRRRRRRRRRRRRRRRRRRRRRRRRRRRRRRRRRRRRRR
RRRRRRRRRRRRRRRRRRRRRRRRRRRRRRRRRRRRRRRRR
RRRRRRRRRRRRRRRRRRRRRRRRRRRRRRRRRRRRRRRRR
RRRRRRRRRRRRRRRRRRRRRRRRRRRRRRRRRRRRRRRRR
RRRRRRRRRRRRRRRRRRRRRRRRRRRRRRRRRRRRRRRRR
RRRRRRRRRRRRRRRRRRRRRRRRRRRRRRRRRRRRRRRRR
RRRRRRRRRRRRRRRRRRRRRRRRRRRRRRRRRRRRRRRRR
RRRRRRRRRRRRRRRRRRRRRRRRRRRRRRRRRRRRRRRRR
RRRRRRRRRRRRRRRRRRRRRRRRRRRRRRRRRRRRRRRRR
RRRRRRRRRRRRRRRRRRRRRRRRRRRRRRRRRRRRRRRRR
RRRRRRRRRRRRRRRRRRRRRRRRRRRRRRRRRRRRRRRRR
RRRRRRRRRRRRRRRRRRRRRRRRRRRRRRRRRRRRRRRRR
RRRRRRRRRRRRRRRRRRRRRRRRRRRRRRRRRRRRRRRRR
RRRRRRRRRRRRRRRRRRRRRRRRRRRRRRRRRRRRRRRRR
RRRRRRRRRRRRRRRRRRRRRRRRRRRRRRRRRRRRRRRRR
RRRRRRRRRRRRRRRRRRRRRRRRRRRRRRRRRRRRRRRRR
RRRRRRRRRRRRRRRRRRRRRRRRRRRRRRRRRRRRRRRRR
RRRRRRRRRRRRRRRRRRRRRRRRRRRRRRRRRRRRRRRRR
RRRRRRRRRRRRRRRRRRRRRRRRRRRRRRRRRRRRRRRRR
RRRRRRRRRRRRRRRRRRRRRRRRRRRRRRRRRRRRRRRRR
RRRRRRRRRRRRRRRRRRRRRRRRRRRRRRRRRRRRRRRRR
RRRRRRRRRRRRRRRRRRRRRRRRRRRRRRRRRRRRRRRRR
RRRRRRRRRRRRRRRRRRRRRRRRRRRRRRRRRRRRRRRRR
RRRRRRRRRRRRRRRRRRRRRRRRRRRRRRRRRRRRRRRRR
RRRRRRRRRRRRRRRRRRRRRRRRRRRRRRRRRRRRRRRRR
RRRRRRRRRRRRRRRRRRRRRRRRRRRRRRRRRRRRRRRRR

RRRRRRRRRRRRRRRRRRRRRRRRRRRRRRRRRRRRRRRRRRRRRRRR
RRRRRRRRRRRRRRRRRRRRRRRRRRRRRRRRRRRRRRRRRRRRRRRR
RRRRRRRRRRRRRRRRRRRRRRRRRRRRRRRRRRRRRRRRRRRRRRRR
RRRRRRRRRRRRRRRRRRRRRRRRRRRRRRRRRRRRRRRRRRRRRRRR
RRRRRRRRRRRRRRRRRRRRRRRRRRRRRRRRRRRRRRRRRRRRRRRR
RRRRRRRRRRRRRRRRRRRRRRRRRRRRRRRRRRRRRRRRRRRRRRRR
RRRRRRRRRRRRRRRRRRRRRRRRRRRRRRRRRRRRRRRRRRRRRRRR
RRRRRRRRRRRRRRRRRRRRRRRRRRRRRRRRRRRRRRRRRRRRRRRR
RRRRRRRRRRRRRRRRRRRRRRRRRRRRRRRRRRRRRRRRRRRRRRRR
RRRRRRRRRRRRRRRRRRRRRRRRRRRRRRRRRRRRRRRRRRRRRRRR
RRRRRRRRRRRRRRRRRRRRRRRRRRRRRRRRRRRRRRRRRRRRRRRR
RRRRRRRRRRRRRRRRRRRRRRRRRRRRRRRRRRRRRRRRRRRRRRRR
RRRRRRRRRRRRRRRRRRRRRRRRRRRRRRRRRRRRRRRRRRRRRRRR
RRRRRRRRRRRRRRRRRRRRRRRRRRRRRRRRRRRRRRRRRRRRRRRR
RRRRRRRRRRRRRRRRRRRRRRRRRRRRRRRRRRRRRRRRRRRRRRRR
RRRRRRRRRRRRRRRRRRRRRRRRRRRRRRRRRRRRRRRRRRRRRRRR
RRRRRRRRRRRRRRRRRRRRRRRRRRRRRRRRRRRRRRRRRRRRRRRR
RRRRRRRRRRRRRRRRRRRRRRRRRRRRRRRRRRRRRRRRRRRRRRRR
RRRRRRRRRRRRRRRRRRRRRRRRRRRRRRRRRRRRRRRRRRRRRRRR
RRRRRRRRRRRRRRRRRRRRRRRRRRRRRRRRRRRRRRRRRRRRRRRR
RRRRRRRRRRRRRRRRRRRRRRRRRRRRRRRRRRRRRRRRRRRRRRRR
RRRRRRRRRRRRRRRRRRRRRRRRRRRRRRRRRRRRRRRRRRRRRRRR
RRRRRRRRRRRRRRRRRRRRRRRRRRRRRRRRRRRRRRRRRRRRRRRR
RRRRRRRRRRRRRRRRRRRRRRRRRRRRRRRRRRRRRRRRRRRRRRRR
RRRRRRRRRRRRRRRRRRRRRRRRRRRRRRRRRRRRRRRRRRRRRRRR
RRRRRRRRRRRRRRRRRRRRRRRRRRRRRRRRRRRRRRRRRRRRRRRR
RRRRRRRRRRRRRRRRRRRRRRRRRRRRRRRRRRRRRRRRRRRRRRRR
RRRRRRRRRRRRRRRRRRRRRRRRRRRRRRRRRRRRRRRRRRRRRRRR
RRRRRRRRRRRRRRRRRRRRRRRRRRRRRRRRRRRRRRRRRRRRRRRR
RRRRRRRRRRRRRRRRRRRRRRRRRRRRRRRRRRRRRRRRRRRRRRRR

RRRRRRRRRRRRRRRRRRRRRRRRRRRRRRRRRRRRRRRRRRRRR
RRRRRRRRRRRRRRRRRRRRRRRRRRRRRRRRRRRRRRRRRRRRR
RRRRRRRRRRRRRRRRRRRRRRRRRRRRRRRRRRRRRRRRRRRRR
RRRRRRRRRRRRRRRRRRRRRRRRRRRRRRRRRRRRRRRRRRRRR
RRRRRRRRRRRRRRRRRRRRRRRRRRRRRRRRRRRRRRRRRRRRR
RRRRRRRRRRRRRRRRRRRRRRRRRRRRRRRRRRRRRRRRRRRRR
RRRRRRRRRRRRRRRRRRRRRRRRRRRRRRRRRRRRRRRRRRRRR
RRRRRRRRRRRRRRRRRRRRRRRRRRRRRRRRRRRRRRRRRRRRR
RRRRRRRRRRRRRRRRRRRRRRRRRRRRRRRRRRRRRRRRRRRRR
RRRRRRRRRRRRRRRRRRRRRRRRRRRRRRRRRRRRRRRRRRRRR
RRRRRRRRRRRRRRRRRRRRRRRRRRRRRRRRRRRRRRRRRRRRR
RRRRRRRRRRRRRRRRRRRRRRRRRRRRRRRRRRRRRRRRRRRRR
RRRRRRRRRRRRRRRRRRRRRRRRRRRRRRRRRRRRRRRRRRRRR
RRRRRRRRRRRRRRRRRRRRRRRRRRRRRRRRRRRRRRRRRRRRR
RRRRRRRRRRRRRRRRRRRRRRRRRRRRRRRRRRRRRRRRRRRRR
RRRRRRRRRRRRRRRRRRRRRRRRRRRRRRRRRRRRRRRRRRRRR
RRRRRRRRRRRRRRRRRRRRRRRRRRRRRRRRRRRRRRRRRRRRR
RRRRRRRRRRRRRRRRRRRRRRRRRRRRRRRRRRRRRRRRRRRRR
RRRRRRRRRRRRRRRRRRRRRRRRRRRRRRRRRRRRRRRRRRRRR
RRRRRRRRRRRRRRRRRRRRRRRRRRRRRRRRRRRRRRRRRRRRR
RRRRRRRRRRRRRRRRRRRRRRRRRRRRRRRRRRRRRRRRRRRRR
RRRRRRRRRRRRRRRRRRRRRRRRRRRRRRRRRRRRRRRRRRRRR
RRRRRRRRRRRRRRRRRRRRRRRRRRRRRRRRRRRRRRRRRRRRR
RRRRRRRRRRRRRRRRRRRRRRRRRRRRRRRRRRRRRRRRRRRRR
RRRRRRRRRRRRRRRRRRRRRRRRRRRRRRRRRRRRRRRRRRRRR
RRRRRRRRRRRRRRRRRRRRRRRRRRRRRRRRRRRRRRRRRRRRR

RRRRRRRRRRRRRRRRRRRRRRRRRRRRRRRRRRRRRRRR
RRRRRRRRRRRRRRRRRRRRRRRRRRRRRRRRRRRRRRRR
RRRRRRRRRRRRRRRRRRRRRRRRRRRRRRRRRRRRRRRR
RRRRRRRRRRRRRRRRRRRRRRRRRRRRRRRRRRRRRRRR
RRRRRRRRRRRRRRRRRRRRRRRRRRRRRRRRRRRRRRRR
RRRRRRRRRRRRRRRRRRRRRRRRRRRRRRRRRRRRRRRR
RRRRRRRRRRRRRRRRRRRRRRRRRRRRRRRRRRRRRRRR
RRRRRRRRRRRRRRRRRRRRRRRRRRRRRRRRRRRRRRRR
RRRRRRRRRRRRRRRRRRRRRRRRRRRRRRRRRRRRRRRR
RRRRRRRRRRRRRRRRRRRRRRRRRRRRRRRRRRRRRRRR
RRRRRRRRRRRRRRRRRRRRRRRRRRRRRRRRRRRRRRRR
RRRRRRRRRRRRRRRRRRRRRRRRRRRRRRRRRRRRRRRR
RRRRRRRRRRRRRRRRRRRRRRRRRRRRRRRRRRRRRRRR
RRRRRRRRRRRRRRRRRRRRRRRRRRRRRRRRRRRRRRRR
RRRRRRRRRRRRRRRRRRRRRRRRRRRRRRRRRRRRRRRR
RRRRRRRRRRRRRRRRRRRRRRRRRRRRRRRRRRRRRRRR
RRRRRRRRRRRRRRRRRRRRRRRRRRRRRRRRRRRRRRRR
RRRRRRRRRRRRRRRRRRRRRRRRRRRRRRRRRRRRRRRR
RRRRRRRRRRRRRRRRRRRRRRRRRRRRRRRRRRRRRRRR
RRRRRRRRRRRRRRRRRRRRRRRRRRRRRRRRRRRRRRRR
RRRRRRRRRRRRRRRRRRRRRRRRRRRRRRRRRRRRRRRR
RRRRRRRRRRRRRRRRRRRRRRRRRRRRRRRRRRRRRRRR
RRRRRRRRRRRRRRRRRRRRRRRRRRRRRRRRRRRRRRRR
RRRRRRRRRRRRRRRRRRRRRRRRRRRRRRRRRRRRRRRR
RRRRRRRRRRRRRRRRRRRRRRRRRRRRRRRRRRRRRRRR
RRRRRRRRRRRRRRRRRRRRRRRRRRRRRRRRRRRRRRRR
RRRRRRRRRRRRRRRRRRRRRRRRRRRRRRRRRRRRRRRR
RRRRRRRRRRRRRRRRRRRRRRRRRRRRRRRRRRRRRRRR

RRRRRRRRRRRRRRRRRRRRRRRRRRRRRRRRRRRRRRRRRRRRRRRRRRR
RRRRRRRRRRRRRRRRRRRRRRRRRRRRRRRRRRRRRRRRRRRRRRRRRRR
RRRRRRRRRRRRRRRRRRRRRRRRRRRRRRRRRRRRRRRRRRRRRRRRRRR
RRRRRRRRRRRRRRRRRRRRRRRRRRRRRRRRRRRRRRRRRRRRRRRRRRR
RRRRRRRRRRRRRRRRRRRRRRRRRRRRRRRRRRRRRRRRRRRRRRRRRRR
RRRRRRRRRRRRRRRRRRRRRRRRRRRRRRRRRRRRRRRRRRRRRRRRRRR
RRRRRRRRRRRRRRRRRRRRRRRRRRRRRRRRRRRRRRRRRRRRRRRRRRR
RRRRRRRRRRRRRRRRRRRRRRRRRRRRRRRRRRRRRRRRRRRRRRRRRRR
RRRRRRRRRRRRRRRRRRRRRRRRRRRRRRRRRRRRRRRRRRRRRRRRRRR
RRRRRRRRRRRRRRRRRRRRRRRRRRRRRRRRRRRRRRRRRRRRRRRRRRR
RRRRRRRRRRRRRRRRRRRRRRRRRRRRRRRRRRRRRRRRRRRRRRRRRRR
RRRRRRRRRRRRRRRRRRRRRRRRRRRRRRRRRRRRRRRRRRRRRRRRRRR
RRRRRRRRRRRRRRRRRRRRRRRRRRRRRRRRRRRRRRRRRRRRRRRRRRR
RRRRRRRRRRRRRRRRRRRRRRRRRRRRRRRRRRRRRRRRRRRRRRRRRRR
RRRRRRRRRRRRRRRRRRRRRRRRRRRRRRRRRRRRRRRRRRRRRRRRRRR
RRRRRRRRRRRRRRRRRRRRRRRRRRRRRRRRRRRRRRRRRRRRRRRRRRR
RRRRRRRRRRRRRRRRRRRRRRRRRRRRRRRRRRRRRRRRRRRRRRRRRRR
RRRRRRRRRRRRRRRRRRRRRRRRRRRRRRRRRRRRRRRRRRRRRRRRRRR
RRRRRRRRRRRRRRRRRRRRRRRRRRRRRRRRRRRRRRRRRRRRRRRRRRR
RRRRRRRRRRRRRRRRRRRRRRRRRRRRRRRRRRRRRRRRRRRRRRRRRRR
RRRRRRRRRRRRRRRRRRRRRRRRRRRRRRRRRRRRRRRRRRRRRRRRRRR
RRRRRRRRRRRRRRRRRRRRRRRRRRRRRRRRRRRRRRRRRRRRRRRRRRR
RRRRRRRRRRRRRRRRRRRRRRRRRRRRRRRRRRRRRRRRRRRRRRRRRRR
RRRRRRRRRRRRRRRRRRRRRRRRRRRRRRRRRRRRRRRRRRRRRRRRRRR
RRRRRRRRRRRRRRRRRRRRRRRRRRRRRRRRRRRRRRRRRRRRRRRRRRR
RRRRRRRRRRRRRRRRRRRRRRRRRRRRRRRRRRRRRRRRRRRRRRRRRRR
RRRRRRRRRRRRRRRRRRRRRRRRRRRRRRRRRRRRRRRRRRRRRRRRRRR
RRRRRRRRRRRRRRRRRRRRRRRRRRRRRRRRRRRRRRRRRRRRRRRRRRR

RRRRRRRRRRRRRRRRRRRRRRRRRRRRRRRRRRRRRRRR
RRRRRRRRRRRRRRRRRRRRRRRRRRRRRRRRRRRRRRRR
RRRRRRRRRRRRRRRRRRRRRRRRRRRRRRRRRRRRRRRR
RRRRRRRRRRRRRRRRRRRRRRRRRRRRRRRRRRRRRRRR
RRRRRRRRRRRRRRRRRRRRRRRRRRRRRRRRRRRRRRRR
RRRRRRRRRRRRRRRRRRRRRRRRRRRRRRRRRRRRRRRR
RRRRRRRRRRRRRRRRRRRRRRRRRRRRRRRRRRRRRRRR
RRRRRRRRRRRRRRRRRRRRRRRRRRRRRRRRRRRRRRRR
RRRRRRRRRRRRRRRRRRRRRRRRRRRRRRRRRRRRRRRR
RRRRRRRRRRRRRRRRRRRRRRRRRRRRRRRRRRRRRRRR
RRRRRRRRRRRRRRRRRRRRRRRRRRRRRRRRRRRRRRRR
RRRRRRRRRRRRRRRRRRRRRRRRRRRRRRRRRRRRRRRR
RRRRRRRRRRRRRRRRRRRRRRRRRRRRRRRRRRRRRRRR
RRRRRRRRRRRRRRRRRRRRRRRRRRRRRRRRRRRRRRRR
RRRRRRRRRRRRRRRRRRRRRRRRRRRRRRRRRRRRRRRR
RRRRRRRRRRRRRRRRRRRRRRRRRRRRRRRRRRRRRRRR
RRRRRRRRRRRRRRRRRRRRRRRRRRRRRRRRRRRRRRRR
RRRRRRRRRRRRRRRRRRRRRRRRRRRRRRRRRRRRRRRR
RRRRRRRRRRRRRRRRRRRRRRRRRRRRRRRRRRRRRRRR
RRRRRRRRRRRRRRRRRRRRRRRRRRRRRRRRRRRRRRRR
RRRRRRRRRRRRRRRRRRRRRRRRRRRRRRRRRRRRRRRR
RRRRRRRRRRRRRRRRRRRRRRRRRRRRRRRRRRRRRRRR
RRRRRRRRRRRRRRRRRRRRRRRRRRRRRRRRRRRRRRRR
RRRRRRRRRRRRRRRRRRRRRRRRRRRRRRRRRRRRRRRR
RRRRRRRRRRRRRRRRRRRRRRRRRRRRRRRRRRRRRRRR
RRRRRRRRRRRRRRRRRRRRRRRRRRRRRRRRRRRRRRRR
RRRRRRRRRRRRRRRRRRRRRRRRRRRRRRRRRRRRRRRR
RRRRRRRRRRRRRRRRRRRRRRRRRRRRRRRRRRRRRRRR

RRRRRRRRRRRRRRRRRRRRRRRRRRRRRRRRRRRRRRRRRRRRRRRRRRRR
RRRRRRRRRRRRRRRRRRRRRRRRRRRRRRRRRRRRRRRRRRRRRRRRRRRR
RRRRRRRRRRRRRRRRRRRRRRRRRRRRRRRRRRRRRRRRRRRRRRRRRRRR
RRRRRRRRRRRRRRRRRRRRRRRRRRRRRRRRRRRRRRRRRRRRRRRRRRRR
RRRRRRRRRRRRRRRRRRRRRRRRRRRRRRRRRRRRRRRRRRRRRRRRRRRR
RRRRRRRRRRRRRRRRRRRRRRRRRRRRRRRRRRRRRRRRRRRRRRRRRRRR
RRRRRRRRRRRRRRRRRRRRRRRRRRRRRRRRRRRRRRRRRRRRRRRRRRRR
RRRRRRRRRRRRRRRRRRRRRRRRRRRRRRRRRRRRRRRRRRRRRRRRRRRR
RRRRRRRRRRRRRRRRRRRRRRRRRRRRRRRRRRRRRRRRRRRRRRRRRRRR
RRRRRRRRRRRRRRRRRRRRRRRRRRRRRRRRRRRRRRRRRRRRRRRRRRRR
RRRRRRRRRRRRRRRRRRRRRRRRRRRRRRRRRRRRRRRRRRRRRRRRRRRR
RRRRRRRRRRRRRRRRRRRRRRRRRRRRRRRRRRRRRRRRRRRRRRRRRRRR
RRRRRRRRRRRRRRRRRRRRRRRRRRRRRRRRRRRRRRRRRRRRRRRRRRRR
RRRRRRRRRRRRRRRRRRRRRRRRRRRRRRRRRRRRRRRRRRRRRRRRRRRR
RRRRRRRRRRRRRRRRRRRRRRRRRRRRRRRRRRRRRRRRRRRRRRRRRRRR
RRRRRRRRRRRRRRRRRRRRRRRRRRRRRRRRRRRRRRRRRRRRRRRRRRRR
RRRRRRRRRRRRRRRRRRRRRRRRRRRRRRRRRRRRRRRRRRRRRRRRRRRR
RRRRRRRRRRRRRRRRRRRRRRRRRRRRRRRRRRRRRRRRRRRRRRRRRRRR
RRRRRRRRRRRRRRRRRRRRRRRRRRRRRRRRRRRRRRRRRRRRRRRRRRRR
RRRRRRRRRRRRRRRRRRRRRRRRRRRRRRRRRRRRRRRRRRRRRRRRRRRR
RRRRRRRRRRRRRRRRRRRRRRRRRRRRRRRRRRRRRRRRRRRRRRRRRRRR
RRRRRRRRRRRRRRRRRRRRRRRRRRRRRRRRRRRRRRRRRRRRRRRRRRRR
RRRRRRRRRRRRRRRRRRRRRRRRRRRRRRRRRRRRRRRRRRRRRRRRRRRR
RRRRRRRRRRRRRRRRRRRRRRRRRRRRRRRRRRRRRRRRRRRRRRRRRRRR
RRRRRRRRRRRRRRRRRRRRRRRRRRRRRRRRRRRRRRRRRRRRRRRRRRRR
RRRRRRRRRRRRRRRRRRRRRRRRRRRRRRRRRRRRRRRRRRRRRRRRRRRR
RRRRRRRRRRRRRRRRRRRRRRRRRRRRRRRRRRRRRRRRRRRRRRRRRRRR
RRRRRRRRRRRRRRRRRRRRRRRRRRRRRRRRRRRRRRRRRRRRRRRRRRRR
RRRRRRRRRRRRRRRRRRRRRRRRRRRRRRRRRRRRRRRRRRRRRRRRRRRR
RRRRRRRRRRRRRRRRRRRRRRRRRRRRRRRRRRRRRRRRRRRRRRRRRRRR

RRRRRRRRRRRRRRRRRRRRRRRRRRRRRRRRRRRRRRRRRRRRRRRRR
RRRRRRRRRRRRRRRRRRRRRRRRRRRRRRRRRRRRRRRRRRRRRRRRR
RRRRRRRRRRRRRRRRRRRRRRRRRRRRRRRRRRRRRRRRRRRRRRRRR
RRRRRRRRRRRRRRRRRRRRRRRRRRRRRRRRRRRRRRRRRRRRRRRRR
RRRRRRRRRRRRRRRRRRRRRRRRRRRRRRRRRRRRRRRRRRRRRRRRR
RRRRRRRRRRRRRRRRRRRRRRRRRRRRRRRRRRRRRRRRRRRRRRRRR
RRRRRRRRRRRRRRRRRRRRRRRRRRRRRRRRRRRRRRRRRRRRRRRRR
RRRRRRRRRRRRRRRRRRRRRRRRRRRRRRRRRRRRRRRRRRRRRRRRR
RRRRRRRRRRRRRRRRRRRRRRRRRRRRRRRRRRRRRRRRRRRRRRRRR
RRRRRRRRRRRRRRRRRRRRRRRRRRRRRRRRRRRRRRRRRRRRRRRRR
RRRRRRRRRRRRRRRRRRRRRRRRRRRRRRRRRRRRRRRRRRRRRRRRR
RRRRRRRRRRRRRRRRRRRRRRRRRRRRRRRRRRRRRRRRRRRRRRRRR
RRRRRRRRRRRRRRRRRRRRRRRRRRRRRRRRRRRRRRRRRRRRRRRRR
RRRRRRRRRRRRRRRRRRRRRRRRRRRRRRRRRRRRRRRRRRRRRRRRR
RRRRRRRRRRRRRRRRRRRRRRRRRRRRRRRRRRRRRRRRRRRRRRRRR
RRRRRRRRRRRRRRRRRRRRRRRRRRRRRRRRRRRRRRRRRRRRRRRRR
RRRRRRRRRRRRRRRRRRRRRRRRRRRRRRRRRRRRRRRRRRRRRRRRR
RRRRRRRRRRRRRRRRRRRRRRRRRRRRRRRRRRRRRRRRRRRRRRRRR
RRRRRRRRRRRRRRRRRRRRRRRRRRRRRRRRRRRRRRRRRRRRRRRRR
RRRRRRRRRRRRRRRRRRRRRRRRRRRRRRRRRRRRRRRRRRRRRRRRR
RRRRRRRRRRRRRRRRRRRRRRRRRRRRRRRRRRRRRRRRRRRRRRRRR
RRRRRRRRRRRRRRRRRRRRRRRRRRRRRRRRRRRRRRRRRRRRRRRRR
RRRRRRRRRRRRRRRRRRRRRRRRRRRRRRRRRRRRRRRRRRRRRRRRR
RRRRRRRRRRRRRRRRRRRRRRRRRRRRRRRRRRRRRRRRRRRRRRRRR
RRRRRRRRRRRRRRRRRRRRRRRRRRRRRRRRRRRRRRRRRRRRRRRRR
RRRRRRRRRRRRRRRRRRRRRRRRRRRRRRRRRRRRRRRRRRRRRRRRR
RRRRRRRRRRRRRRRRRRRRRRRRRRRRRRRRRRRRRRRRRRRRRRRRR

RRRRRRRRRRRRRRRRRRRRRRRRRRRRRRRRRRRRRRRRRRR
RRRRRRRRRRRRRRRRRRRRRRRRRRRRRRRRRRRRRRRRRRR
RRRRRRRRRRRRRRRRRRRRRRRRRRRRRRRRRRRRRRRRRRR
RRRRRRRRRRRRRRRRRRRRRRRRRRRRRRRRRRRRRRRRRRR
RRRRRRRRRRRRRRRRRRRRRRRRRRRRRRRRRRRRRRRRRRR
RRRRRRRRRRRRRRRRRRRRRRRRRRRRRRRRRRRRRRRRRRR
RRRRRRRRRRRRRRRRRRRRRRRRRRRRRRRRRRRRRRRRRRR
RRRRRRRRRRRRRRRRRRRRRRRRRRRRRRRRRRRRRRRRRRR
RRRRRRRRRRRRRRRRRRRRRRRRRRRRRRRRRRRRRRRRRRR
RRRRRRRRRRRRRRRRRRRRRRRRRRRRRRRRRRRRRRRRRRR
RRRRRRRRRRRRRRRRRRRRRRRRRRRRRRRRRRRRRRRRRRR
RRRRRRRRRRRRRRRRRRRRRRRRRRRRRRRRRRRRRRRRRRR
RRRRRRRRRRRRRRRRRRRRRRRRRRRRRRRRRRRRRRRRRRR
RRRRRRRRRRRRRRRRRRRRRRRRRRRRRRRRRRRRRRRRRRR
RRRRRRRRRRRRRRRRRRRRRRRRRRRRRRRRRRRRRRRRRRR
RRRRRRRRRRRRRRRRRRRRRRRRRRRRRRRRRRRRRRRRRRR
RRRRRRRRRRRRRRRRRRRRRRRRRRRRRRRRRRRRRRRRRRR
RRRRRRRRRRRRRRRRRRRRRRRRRRRRRRRRRRRRRRRRRRR
RRRRRRRRRRRRRRRRRRRRRRRRRRRRRRRRRRRRRRRRRRR
RRRRRRRRRRRRRRRRRRRRRRRRRRRRRRRRRRRRRRRRRRR
RRRRRRRRRRRRRRRRRRRRRRRRRRRRRRRRRRRRRRRRRRR
RRRRRRRRRRRRRRRRRRRRRRRRRRRRRRRRRRRRRRRRRRR
RRRRRRRRRRRRRRRRRRRRRRRRRRRRRRRRRRRRRRRRRRR
RRRRRRRRRRRRRRRRRRRRRRRRRRRRRRRRRRRRRRRRRRR
RRRRRRRRRRRRRRRRRRRRRRRRRRRRRRRRRRRRRRRRRRR
RRRRRRRRRRRRRRRRRRRRRRRRRRRRRRRRRRRRRRRRRRR
RRRRRRRRRRRRRRRRRRRRRRRRRRRRRRRRRRRRRRRRRRR
RRRRRRRRRRRRRRRRRRRRRRRRRRRRRRRRRRRRRRRRRRR
RRRRRRRRRRRRRRRRRRRRRRRRRRRRRRRRRRRRRRRRRRR
RRRRRRRRRRRRRRRRRRRRRRRRRRRRRRRRRRRRRRRRRRR

RRRRRRRRRRRRRRRRRRRRRRRRRRRRRRRRRRRRRRRRRRRRRRR
RRRRRRRRRRRRRRRRRRRRRRRRRRRRRRRRRRRRRRRRRRRRRRR
RRRRRRRRRRRRRRRRRRRRRRRRRRRRRRRRRRRRRRRRRRRRRRR
RRRRRRRRRRRRRRRRRRRRRRRRRRRRRRRRRRRRRRRRRRRRRRR
RRRRRRRRRRRRRRRRRRRRRRRRRRRRRRRRRRRRRRRRRRRRRRR
RRRRRRRRRRRRRRRRRRRRRRRRRRRRRRRRRRRRRRRRRRRRRRR
RRRRRRRRRRRRRRRRRRRRRRRRRRRRRRRRRRRRRRRRRRRRRRR
RRRRRRRRRRRRRRRRRRRRRRRRRRRRRRRRRRRRRRRRRRRRRRR
RRRRRRRRRRRRRRRRRRRRRRRRRRRRRRRRRRRRRRRRRRRRRRR
RRRRRRRRRRRRRRRRRRRRRRRRRRRRRRRRRRRRRRRRRRRRRRR
RRRRRRRRRRRRRRRRRRRRRRRRRRRRRRRRRRRRRRRRRRRRRRR
RRRRRRRRRRRRRRRRRRRRRRRRRRRRRRRRRRRRRRRRRRRRRRR
RRRRRRRRRRRRRRRRRRRRRRRRRRRRRRRRRRRRRRRRRRRRRRR
RRRRRRRRRRRRRRRRRRRRRRRRRRRRRRRRRRRRRRRRRRRRRRR
RRRRRRRRRRRRRRRRRRRRRRRRRRRRRRRRRRRRRRRRRRRRRRR
RRRRRRRRRRRRRRRRRRRRRRRRRRRRRRRRRRRRRRRRRRRRRRR
RRRRRRRRRRRRRRRRRRRRRRRRRRRRRRRRRRRRRRRRRRRRRRR
RRRRRRRRRRRRRRRRRRRRRRRRRRRRRRRRRRRRRRRRRRRRRRR
RRRRRRRRRRRRRRRRRRRRRRRRRRRRRRRRRRRRRRRRRRRRRRR
RRRRRRRRRRRRRRRRRRRRRRRRRRRRRRRRRRRRRRRRRRRRRRR
RRRRRRRRRRRRRRRRRRRRRRRRRRRRRRRRRRRRRRRRRRRRRRR
RRRRRRRRRRRRRRRRRRRRRRRRRRRRRRRRRRRRRRRRRRRRRRR
RRRRRRRRRRRRRRRRRRRRRRRRRRRRRRRRRRRRRRRRRRRRRRR
RRRRRRRRRRRRRRRRRRRRRRRRRRRRRRRRRRRRRRRRRRRRRRR
RRRRRRRRRRRRRRRRRRRRRRRRRRRRRRRRRRRRRRRRRRRRRRR
RRRRRRRRRRRRRRRRRRRRRRRRRRRRRRRRRRRRRRRRRRRRRRR
RRRRRRRRRRRRRRRRRRRRRRRRRRRRRRRRRRRRRRRRRRRRRRR
RRRRRRRRRRRRRRRRRRRRRRRRRRRRRRRRRRRRRRRRRRRRRRR

RRRRRRRRRRRRRRRRRRRRRRRRRRRRRRRRRRRRRRRRRRRR
RRRRRRRRRRRRRRRRRRRRRRRRRRRRRRRRRRRRRRRRRRRR
RRRRRRRRRRRRRRRRRRRRRRRRRRRRRRRRRRRRRRRRRRRR
RRRRRRRRRRRRRRRRRRRRRRRRRRRRRRRRRRRRRRRRRRRR
RRRRRRRRRRRRRRRRRRRRRRRRRRRRRRRRRRRRRRRRRRRR
RRRRRRRRRRRRRRRRRRRRRRRRRRRRRRRRRRRRRRRRRRRR
RRRRRRRRRRRRRRRRRRRRRRRRRRRRRRRRRRRRRRRRRRRR
RRRRRRRRRRRRRRRRRRRRRRRRRRRRRRRRRRRRRRRRRRRR
RRRRRRRRRRRRRRRRRRRRRRRRRRRRRRRRRRRRRRRRRRRR
RRRRRRRRRRRRRRRRRRRRRRRRRRRRRRRRRRRRRRRRRRRR
RRRRRRRRRRRRRRRRRRRRRRRRRRRRRRRRRRRRRRRRRRRR
RRRRRRRRRRRRRRRRRRRRRRRRRRRRRRRRRRRRRRRRRRRR
RRRRRRRRRRRRRRRRRRRRRRRRRRRRRRRRRRRRRRRRRRRR
RRRRRRRRRRRRRRRRRRRRRRRRRRRRRRRRRRRRRRRRRRRR
RRRRRRRRRRRRRRRRRRRRRRRRRRRRRRRRRRRRRRRRRRRR
RRRRRRRRRRRRRRRRRRRRRRRRRRRRRRRRRRRRRRRRRRRR
RRRRRRRRRRRRRRRRRRRRRRRRRRRRRRRRRRRRRRRRRRRR
RRRRRRRRRRRRRRRRRRRRRRRRRRRRRRRRRRRRRRRRRRRR
RRRRRRRRRRRRRRRRRRRRRRRRRRRRRRRRRRRRRRRRRRRR
RRRRRRRRRRRRRRRRRRRRRRRRRRRRRRRRRRRRRRRRRRRR
RRRRRRRRRRRRRRRRRRRRRRRRRRRRRRRRRRRRRRRRRRRR
RRRRRRRRRRRRRRRRRRRRRRRRRRRRRRRRRRRRRRRRRRRR
RRRRRRRRRRRRRRRRRRRRRRRRRRRRRRRRRRRRRRRRRRRR
RRRRRRRRRRRRRRRRRRRRRRRRRRRRRRRRRRRRRRRRRRRR
RRRRRRRRRRRRRRRRRRRRRRRRRRRRRRRRRRRRRRRRRRRR
RRRRRRRRRRRRRRRRRRRRRRRRRRRRRRRRRRRRRRRRRRRR
RRRRRRRRRRRRRRRRRRRRRRRRRRRRRRRRRRRRRRRRRRRR
RRRRRRRRRRRRRRRRRRRRRRRRRRRRRRRRRRRRRRRRRRRR

RRRRRRRRRRRRRRRRRRRRRRRRRRRRRRRRRRRRRRRRRRRRR
RRRRRRRRRRRRRRRRRRRRRRRRRRRRRRRRRRRRRRRRRRRRR
RRRRRRRRRRRRRRRRRRRRRRRRRRRRRRRRRRRRRRRRRRRRR
RRRRRRRRRRRRRRRRRRRRRRRRRRRRRRRRRRRRRRRRRRRRR
RRRRRRRRRRRRRRRRRRRRRRRRRRRRRRRRRRRRRRRRRRRRR
RRRRRRRRRRRRRRRRRRRRRRRRRRRRRRRRRRRRRRRRRRRRR
RRRRRRRRRRRRRRRRRRRRRRRRRRRRRRRRRRRRRRRRRRRRR
RRRRRRRRRRRRRRRRRRRRRRRRRRRRRRRRRRRRRRRRRRRRR
RRRRRRRRRRRRRRRRRRRRRRRRRRRRRRRRRRRRRRRRRRRRR
RRRRRRRRRRRRRRRRRRRRRRRRRRRRRRRRRRRRRRRRRRRRR
RRRRRRRRRRRRRRRRRRRRRRRRRRRRRRRRRRRRRRRRRRRRR
RRRRRRRRRRRRRRRRRRRRRRRRRRRRRRRRRRRRRRRRRRRRR
RRRRRRRRRRRRRRRRRRRRRRRRRRRRRRRRRRRRRRRRRRRRR
RRRRRRRRRRRRRRRRRRRRRRRRRRRRRRRRRRRRRRRRRRRRR
RRRRRRRRRRRRRRRRRRRRRRRRRRRRRRRRRRRRRRRRRRRRR
RRRRRRRRRRRRRRRRRRRRRRRRRRRRRRRRRRRRRRRRRRRRR
RRRRRRRRRRRRRRRRRRRRRRRRRRRRRRRRRRRRRRRRRRRRR
RRRRRRRRRRRRRRRRRRRRRRRRRRRRRRRRRRRRRRRRRRRRR
RRRRRRRRRRRRRRRRRRRRRRRRRRRRRRRRRRRRRRRRRRRRR
RRRRRRRRRRRRRRRRRRRRRRRRRRRRRRRRRRRRRRRRRRRRR
RRRRRRRRRRRRRRRRRRRRRRRRRRRRRRRRRRRRRRRRRRRRR
RRRRRRRRRRRRRRRRRRRRRRRRRRRRRRRRRRRRRRRRRRRRR
RRRRRRRRRRRRRRRRRRRRRRRRRRRRRRRRRRRRRRRRRRRRR
RRRRRRRRRRRRRRRRRRRRRRRRRRRRRRRRRRRRRRRRRRRRR
RRRRRRRRRRRRRRRRRRRRRRRRRRRRRRRRRRRRRRRRRRRRR
RRRRRRRRRRRRRRRRRRRRRRRRRRRRRRRRRRRRRRRRRRRRR
RRRRRRRRRRRRRRRRRRRRRRRRRRRRRRRRRRRRRRRRRRRRR
RRRRRRRRRRRRRRRRRRRRRRRRRRRRRRRRRRRRRRRRRRRRR

RRRRRRRRRRRRRRRRRRRRRRRRRRRRRRRRRRRRRRRRRRRRRR
RRRRRRRRRRRRRRRRRRRRRRRRRRRRRRRRRRRRRRRRRRRRRR
RRRRRRRRRRRRRRRRRRRRRRRRRRRRRRRRRRRRRRRRRRRRRR
RRRRRRRRRRRRRRRRRRRRRRRRRRRRRRRRRRRRRRRRRRRRRR
RRRRRRRRRRRRRRRRRRRRRRRRRRRRRRRRRRRRRRRRRRRRRR
RRRRRRRRRRRRRRRRRRRRRRRRRRRRRRRRRRRRRRRRRRRRRR
RRRRRRRRRRRRRRRRRRRRRRRRRRRRRRRRRRRRRRRRRRRRRR
RRRRRRRRRRRRRRRRRRRRRRRRRRRRRRRRRRRRRRRRRRRRRR
RRRRRRRRRRRRRRRRRRRRRRRRRRRRRRRRRRRRRRRRRRRRRR
RRRRRRRRRRRRRRRRRRRRRRRRRRRRRRRRRRRRRRRRRRRRRR
RRRRRRRRRRRRRRRRRRRRRRRRRRRRRRRRRRRRRRRRRRRRRR
RRRRRRRRRRRRRRRRRRRRRRRRRRRRRRRRRRRRRRRRRRRRRR
RRRRRRRRRRRRRRRRRRRRRRRRRRRRRRRRRRRRRRRRRRRRRR
RRRRRRRRRRRRRRRRRRRRRRRRRRRRRRRRRRRRRRRRRRRRRR
RRRRRRRRRRRRRRRRRRRRRRRRRRRRRRRRRRRRRRRRRRRRRR
RRRRRRRRRRRRRRRRRRRRRRRRRRRRRRRRRRRRRRRRRRRRRR
RRRRRRRRRRRRRRRRRRRRRRRRRRRRRRRRRRRRRRRRRRRRRR
RRRRRRRRRRRRRRRRRRRRRRRRRRRRRRRRRRRRRRRRRRRRRR
RRRRRRRRRRRRRRRRRRRRRRRRRRRRRRRRRRRRRRRRRRRRRR
RRRRRRRRRRRRRRRRRRRRRRRRRRRRRRRRRRRRRRRRRRRRRR
RRRRRRRRRRRRRRRRRRRRRRRRRRRRRRRRRRRRRRRRRRRRRR
RRRRRRRRRRRRRRRRRRRRRRRRRRRRRRRRRRRRRRRRRRRRRR
RRRRRRRRRRRRRRRRRRRRRRRRRRRRRRRRRRRRRRRRRRRRRR
RRRRRRRRRRRRRRRRRRRRRRRRRRRRRRRRRRRRRRRRRRRRRR

RRRRRRRRRRRRRRRRRRRRRRRRRRRRRRRRRRRRRRRRRRRRRRRR
RRRRRRRRRRRRRRRRRRRRRRRRRRRRRRRRRRRRRRRRRRRRRRRR
RRRRRRRRRRRRRRRRRRRRRRRRRRRRRRRRRRRRRRRRRRRRRRRR
RRRRRRRRRRRRRRRRRRRRRRRRRRRRRRRRRRRRRRRRRRRRRRRR
RRRRRRRRRRRRRRRRRRRRRRRRRRRRRRRRRRRRRRRRRRRRRRRR
RRRRRRRRRRRRRRRRRRRRRRRRRRRRRRRRRRRRRRRRRRRRRRRR
RRRRRRRRRRRRRRRRRRRRRRRRRRRRRRRRRRRRRRRRRRRRRRRR
RRRRRRRRRRRRRRRRRRRRRRRRRRRRRRRRRRRRRRRRRRRRRRRR
RRRRRRRRRRRRRRRRRRRRRRRRRRRRRRRRRRRRRRRRRRRRRRRR
RRRRRRRRRRRRRRRRRRRRRRRRRRRRRRRRRRRRRRRRRRRRRRRR
RRRRRRRRRRRRRRRRRRRRRRRRRRRRRRRRRRRRRRRRRRRRRRRR
RRRRRRRRRRRRRRRRRRRRRRRRRRRRRRRRRRRRRRRRRRRRRRRR
RRRRRRRRRRRRRRRRRRRRRRRRRRRRRRRRRRRRRRRRRRRRRRRR
RRRRRRRRRRRRRRRRRRRRRRRRRRRRRRRRRRRRRRRRRRRRRRRR
RRRRRRRRRRRRRRRRRRRRRRRRRRRRRRRRRRRRRRRRRRRRRRRR
RRRRRRRRRRRRRRRRRRRRRRRRRRRRRRRRRRRRRRRRRRRRRRRR
RRRRRRRRRRRRRRRRRRRRRRRRRRRRRRRRRRRRRRRRRRRRRRRR
RRRRRRRRRRRRRRRRRRRRRRRRRRRRRRRRRRRRRRRRRRRRRRRR
RRRRRRRRRRRRRRRRRRRRRRRRRRRRRRRRRRRRRRRRRRRRRRRR
RRRRRRRRRRRRRRRRRRRRRRRRRRRRRRRRRRRRRRRRRRRRRRRR
RRRRRRRRRRRRRRRRRRRRRRRRRRRRRRRRRRRRRRRRRRRRRRRR
RRRRRRRRRRRRRRRRRRRRRRRRRRRRRRRRRRRRRRRRRRRRRRRR
RRRRRRRRRRRRRRRRRRRRRRRRRRRRRRRRRRRRRRRRRRRRRRRR
RRRRRRRRRRRRRRRRRRRRRRRRRRRRRRRRRRRRRRRRRRRRRRRR

RRRRRRRRRRRRRRRRRRRRRRRRRRRRRRRRRRRRRRRRRRRRRRRR
RRRRRRRRRRRRRRRRRRRRRRRRRRRRRRRRRRRRRRRRRRRRRRRR
RRRRRRRRRRRRRRRRRRRRRRRRRRRRRRRRRRRRRRRRRRRRRRRR
RRRRRRRRRRRRRRRRRRRRRRRRRRRRRRRRRRRRRRRRRRRRRRRR
RRRRRRRRRRRRRRRRRRRRRRRRRRRRRRRRRRRRRRRRRRRRRRRR
RRRRRRRRRRRRRRRRRRRRRRRRRRRRRRRRRRRRRRRRRRRRRRRR
RRRRRRRRRRRRRRRRRRRRRRRRRRRRRRRRRRRRRRRRRRRRRRRR
RRRRRRRRRRRRRRRRRRRRRRRRRRRRRRRRRRRRRRRRRRRRRRRR
RRRRRRRRRRRRRRRRRRRRRRRRRRRRRRRRRRRRRRRRRRRRRRRR
RRRRRRRRRRRRRRRRRRRRRRRRRRRRRRRRRRRRRRRRRRRRRRRR
RRRRRRRRRRRRRRRRRRRRRRRRRRRRRRRRRRRRRRRRRRRRRRRR
RRRRRRRRRRRRRRRRRRRRRRRRRRRRRRRRRRRRRRRRRRRRRRRR
RRRRRRRRRRRRRRRRRRRRRRRRRRRRRRRRRRRRRRRRRRRRRRRR
RRRRRRRRRRRRRRRRRRRRRRRRRRRRRRRRRRRRRRRRRRRRRRRR
RRRRRRRRRRRRRRRRRRRRRRRRRRRRRRRRRRRRRRRRRRRRRRRR
RRRRRRRRRRRRRRRRRRRRRRRRRRRRRRRRRRRRRRRRRRRRRRRR
RRRRRRRRRRRRRRRRRRRRRRRRRRRRRRRRRRRRRRRRRRRRRRRR
RRRRRRRRRRRRRRRRRRRRRRRRRRRRRRRRRRRRRRRRRRRRRRRR
RRRRRRRRRRRRRRRRRRRRRRRRRRRRRRRRRRRRRRRRRRRRRRRR
RRRRRRRRRRRRRRRRRRRRRRRRRRRRRRRRRRRRRRRRRRRRRRRR
RRRRRRRRRRRRRRRRRRRRRRRRRRRRRRRRRRRRRRRRRRRRRRRR
RRRRRRRRRRRRRRRRRRRRRRRRRRRRRRRRRRRRRRRRRRRRRRRR
RRRRRRRRRRRRRRRRRRRRRRRRRRRRRRRRRRRRRRRRRRRRRRRR
RRRRRRRRRRRRRRRRRRRRRRRRRRRRRRRRRRRRRRRRRRRRRRRR
RRRRRRRRRRRRRRRRRRRRRRRRRRRRRRRRRRRRRRRRRRRRRRRR
RRRRRRRRRRRRRRRRRRRRRRRRRRRRRRRRRRRRRRRRRRRRRRRR

RRRRRRRRRRRRRRRRRRRRRRRRRRRRRRRRRRRRRRRRRRRRRRR
RRRRRRRRRRRRRRRRRRRRRRRRRRRRRRRRRRRRRRRRRRRRRRR
RRRRRRRRRRRRRRRRRRRRRRRRRRRRRRRRRRRRRRRRRRRRRRR
RRRRRRRRRRRRRRRRRRRRRRRRRRRRRRRRRRRRRRRRRRRRRRR
RRRRRRRRRRRRRRRRRRRRRRRRRRRRRRRRRRRRRRRRRRRRRRR
RRRRRRRRRRRRRRRRRRRRRRRRRRRRRRRRRRRRRRRRRRRRRRR
RRRRRRRRRRRRRRRRRRRRRRRRRRRRRRRRRRRRRRRRRRRRRRR
RRRRRRRRRRRRRRRRRRRRRRRRRRRRRRRRRRRRRRRRRRRRRRR
RRRRRRRRRRRRRRRRRRRRRRRRRRRRRRRRRRRRRRRRRRRRRRR
RRRRRRRRRRRRRRRRRRRRRRRRRRRRRRRRRRRRRRRRRRRRRRR
RRRRRRRRRRRRRRRRRRRRRRRRRRRRRRRRRRRRRRRRRRRRRRR
RRRRRRRRRRRRRRRRRRRRRRRRRRRRRRRRRRRRRRRRRRRRRRR
RRRRRRRRRRRRRRRRRRRRRRRRRRRRRRRRRRRRRRRRRRRRRRR
RRRRRRRRRRRRRRRRRRRRRRRRRRRRRRRRRRRRRRRRRRRRRRR
RRRRRRRRRRRRRRRRRRRRRRRRRRRRRRRRRRRRRRRRRRRRRRR
RRRRRRRRRRRRRRRRRRRRRRRRRRRRRRRRRRRRRRRRRRRRRRR
RRRRRRRRRRRRRRRRRRRRRRRRRRRRRRRRRRRRRRRRRRRRRRR
RRRRRRRRRRRRRRRRRRRRRRRRRRRRRRRRRRRRRRRRRRRRRRR
RRRRRRRRRRRRRRRRRRRRRRRRRRRRRRRRRRRRRRRRRRRRRRR
RRRRRRRRRRRRRRRRRRRRRRRRRRRRRRRRRRRRRRRRRRRRRRR
RRRRRRRRRRRRRRRRRRRRRRRRRRRRRRRRRRRRRRRRRRRRRRR
RRRRRRRRRRRRRRRRRRRRRRRRRRRRRRRRRRRRRRRRRRRRRRR
RRRRRRRRRRRRRRRRRRRRRRRRRRRRRRRRRRRRRRRRRRRRRRR
RRRRRRRRRRRRRRRRRRRRRRRRRRRRRRRRRRRRRRRRRRRRRRR
RRRRRRRRRRRRRRRRRRRRRRRRRRRRRRRRRRRRRRRRRRRRRRR
RRRRRRRRRRRRRRRRRRRRRRRRRRRRRRRRRRRRRRRRRRRRRRR

RRRRRRRRRRRRRRRRRRRRRRRRRRRRRRRRRRRRRRRRRRRRRR
RRRRRRRRRRRRRRRRRRRRRRRRRRRRRRRRRRRRRRRRRRRRRR
RRRRRRRRRRRRRRRRRRRRRRRRRRRRRRRRRRRRRRRRRRRRRR
RRRRRRRRRRRRRRRRRRRRRRRRRRRRRRRRRRRRRRRRRRRRRR
RRRRRRRRRRRRRRRRRRRRRRRRRRRRRRRRRRRRRRRRRRRRRR
RRRRRRRRRRRRRRRRRRRRRRRRRRRRRRRRRRRRRRRRRRRRRR
RRRRRRRRRRRRRRRRRRRRRRRRRRRRRRRRRRRRRRRRRRRRRR
RRRRRRRRRRRRRRRRRRRRRRRRRRRRRRRRRRRRRRRRRRRRRR
RRRRRRRRRRRRRRRRRRRRRRRRRRRRRRRRRRRRRRRRRRRRRR
RRRRRRRRRRRRRRRRRRRRRRRRRRRRRRRRRRRRRRRRRRRRRR
RRRRRRRRRRRRRRRRRRRRRRRRRRRRRRRRRRRRRRRRRRRRRR
RRRRRRRRRRRRRRRRRRRRRRRRRRRRRRRRRRRRRRRRRRRRRR
RRRRRRRRRRRRRRRRRRRRRRRRRRRRRRRRRRRRRRRRRRRRRR
RRRRRRRRRRRRRRRRRRRRRRRRRRRRRRRRRRRRRRRRRRRRRR
RRRRRRRRRRRRRRRRRRRRRRRRRRRRRRRRRRRRRRRRRRRRRR
RRRRRRRRRRRRRRRRRRRRRRRRRRRRRRRRRRRRRRRRRRRRRR
RRRRRRRRRRRRRRRRRRRRRRRRRRRRRRRRRRRRRRRRRRRRRR
RRRRRRRRRRRRRRRRRRRRRRRRRRRRRRRRRRRRRRRRRRRRRR
RRRRRRRRRRRRRRRRRRRRRRRRRRRRRRRRRRRRRRRRRRRRRR
RRRRRRRRRRRRRRRRRRRRRRRRRRRRRRRRRRRRRRRRRRRRRR
RRRRRRRRRRRRRRRRRRRRRRRRRRRRRRRRRRRRRRRRRRRRRR
RRRRRRRRRRRRRRRRRRRRRRRRRRRRRRRRRRRRRRRRRRRRRR
RRRRRRRRRRRRRRRRRRRRRRRRRRRRRRRRRRRRRRRRRRRRRR
RRRRRRRRRRRRRRRRRRRRRRRRRRRRRRRRRRRRRRRRRRRRRR
RRRRRRRRRRRRRRRRRRRRRRRRRRRRRRRRRRRRRRRRRRRRRR
RRRRRRRRRRRRRRRRRRRRRRRRRRRRRRRRRRRRRRRRRRRRRR
RRRRRRRRRRRRRRRRRRRRRRRRRRRRRRRRRRRRRRRRRRRRRR
RRRRRRRRRRRRRRRRRRRRRRRRRRRRRRRRRRRRRRRRRRRRRR

RRRRRRRRRRRRRRRRRRRRRRRRRRRRRRRRR
RRRRRRRRRRRRRRRRRRRRRRRRRRRRRRRRR
RRRRRRRRRRRRRRRRRRRRRRRRRRRRRRRRR
RRRRRRRRRRRRRRRRRRRRRRRRRRRRRRRRR
RRRRRRRRRRRRRRRRRRRRRRRRRRRRRRRRR
RRRRRRRRRRRRRRRRRRRRRRRRRRRRRRRRR
RRRRRRRRRRRRRRRRRRRRRRRRRRRRRRRRR
RRRRRRRRRRRRRRRRRRRRRRRRRRRRRRRRR
RRRRRRRRRRRRRRRRRRRRRRRRRRRRRRRRR
RRRRRRRRRRRRRRRRRRRRRRRRRRRRRRRRR
RRRRRRRRRRRRRRRRRRRRRRRRRRRRRRRRR
RRRRRRRRRRRRRRRRRRRRRRRRRRRRRRRRR
RRRRRRRRRRRRRRRRRRRRRRRRRRRRRRRRR
RRRRRRRRRRRRRRRRRRRRRRRRRRRRRRRRR
RRRRRRRRRRRRRRRRRRRRRRRRRRRRRRRRR
RRRRRRRRRRRRRRRRRRRRRRRRRRRRRRRRR
RRRRRRRRRRRRRRRRRRRRRRRRRRRRRRRRR
RRRRRRRRRRRRRRRRRRRRRRRRRRRRRRRRR
RRRRRRRRRRRRRRRRRRRRRRRRRRRRRRRRR
RRRRRRRRRRRRRRRRRRRRRRRRRRRRRRRRR
RRRRRRRRRRRRRRRRRRRRRRRRRRRRRRRRR
RRRRRRRRRRRRRRRRRRRRRRRRRRRRRRRRR
RRRRRRRRRRRRRRRRRRRRRRRRRRRRRRRRR
RRRRRRRRRRRRRRRRRRRRRRRRRRRRRRRRR

RRRRRRRRRRRRRRRRRRRRRRRRRRRRRRRRRRRRRRRRRRRRRRRR
RRRRRRRRRRRRRRRRRRRRRRRRRRRRRRRRRRRRRRRRRRRRRRRR
RRRRRRRRRRRRRRRRRRRRRRRRRRRRRRRRRRRRRRRRRRRRRRRR
RRRRRRRRRRRRRRRRRRRRRRRRRRRRRRRRRRRRRRRRRRRRRRRR
RRRRRRRRRRRRRRRRRRRRRRRRRRRRRRRRRRRRRRRRRRRRRRRR
RRRRRRRRRRRRRRRRRRRRRRRRRRRRRRRRRRRRRRRRRRRRRRRR
RRRRRRRRRRRRRRRRRRRRRRRRRRRRRRRRRRRRRRRRRRRRRRRR
RRRRRRRRRRRRRRRRRRRRRRRRRRRRRRRRRRRRRRRRRRRRRRRR
RRRRRRRRRRRRRRRRRRRRRRRRRRRRRRRRRRRRRRRRRRRRRRRR
RRRRRRRRRRRRRRRRRRRRRRRRRRRRRRRRRRRRRRRRRRRRRRRR
RRRRRRRRRRRRRRRRRRRRRRRRRRRRRRRRRRRRRRRRRRRRRRRR
RRRRRRRRRRRRRRRRRRRRRRRRRRRRRRRRRRRRRRRRRRRRRRRR
RRRRRRRRRRRRRRRRRRRRRRRRRRRRRRRRRRRRRRRRRRRRRRRR
RRRRRRRRRRRRRRRRRRRRRRRRRRRRRRRRRRRRRRRRRRRRRRRR
RRRRRRRRRRRRRRRRRRRRRRRRRRRRRRRRRRRRRRRRRRRRRRRR
RRRRRRRRRRRRRRRRRRRRRRRRRRRRRRRRRRRRRRRRRRRRRRRR
RRRRRRRRRRRRRRRRRRRRRRRRRRRRRRRRRRRRRRRRRRRRRRRR
RRRRRRRRRRRRRRRRRRRRRRRRRRRRRRRRRRRRRRRRRRRRRRRR
RRRRRRRRRRRRRRRRRRRRRRRRRRRRRRRRRRRRRRRRRRRRRRRR
RRRRRRRRRRRRRRRRRRRRRRRRRRRRRRRRRRRRRRRRRRRRRRRR
RRRRRRRRRRRRRRRRRRRRRRRRRRRRRRRRRRRRRRRRRRRRRRRR
RRRRRRRRRRRRRRRRRRRRRRRRRRRRRRRRRRRRRRRRRRRRRRRR
RRRRRRRRRRRRRRRRRRRRRRRRRRRRRRRRRRRRRRRRRRRRRRRR
RRRRRRRRRRRRRRRRRRRRRRRRRRRRRRRRRRRRRRRRRRRRRRRR
RRRRRRRRRRRRRRRRRRRRRRRRRRRRRRRRRRRRRRRRRRRRRRRR
RRRRRRRRRRRRRRRRRRRRRRRRRRRRRRRRRRRRRRRRRRRRRRRR
RRRRRRRRRRRRRRRRRRRRRRRRRRRRRRRRRRRRRRRRRRRRRRRR
RRRRRRRRRRRRRRRRRRRRRRRRRRRRRRRRRRRRRRRRRRRRRRRR

RRRRRRRRRRRRRRRRRRRRRRRRRRRRRRRRRRRRRRRRRRRRR
RRRRRRRRRRRRRRRRRRRRRRRRRRRRRRRRRRRRRRRRRRRRR
RRRRRRRRRRRRRRRRRRRRRRRRRRRRRRRRRRRRRRRRRRRRR
RRRRRRRRRRRRRRRRRRRRRRRRRRRRRRRRRRRRRRRRRRRRR
RRRRRRRRRRRRRRRRRRRRRRRRRRRRRRRRRRRRRRRRRRRRR
RRRRRRRRRRRRRRRRRRRRRRRRRRRRRRRRRRRRRRRRRRRRR
RRRRRRRRRRRRRRRRRRRRRRRRRRRRRRRRRRRRRRRRRRRRR
RRRRRRRRRRRRRRRRRRRRRRRRRRRRRRRRRRRRRRRRRRRRR
RRRRRRRRRRRRRRRRRRRRRRRRRRRRRRRRRRRRRRRRRRRRR
RRRRRRRRRRRRRRRRRRRRRRRRRRRRRRRRRRRRRRRRRRRRR
RRRRRRRRRRRRRRRRRRRRRRRRRRRRRRRRRRRRRRRRRRRRR
RRRRRRRRRRRRRRRRRRRRRRRRRRRRRRRRRRRRRRRRRRRRR
RRRRRRRRRRRRRRRRRRRRRRRRRRRRRRRRRRRRRRRRRRRRR
RRRRRRRRRRRRRRRRRRRRRRRRRRRRRRRRRRRRRRRRRRRRR
RRRRRRRRRRRRRRRRRRRRRRRRRRRRRRRRRRRRRRRRRRRRR
RRRRRRRRRRRRRRRRRRRRRRRRRRRRRRRRRRRRRRRRRRRRR
RRRRRRRRRRRRRRRRRRRRRRRRRRRRRRRRRRRRRRRRRRRRR
RRRRRRRRRRRRRRRRRRRRRRRRRRRRRRRRRRRRRRRRRRRRR
RRRRRRRRRRRRRRRRRRRRRRRRRRRRRRRRRRRRRRRRRRRRR
RRRRRRRRRRRRRRRRRRRRRRRRRRRRRRRRRRRRRRRRRRRRR
RRRRRRRRRRRRRRRRRRRRRRRRRRRRRRRRRRRRRRRRRRRRR
RRRRRRRRRRRRRRRRRRRRRRRRRRRRRRRRRRRRRRRRRRRRR
RRRRRRRRRRRRRRRRRRRRRRRRRRRRRRRRRRRRRRRRRRRRR
RRRRRRRRRRRRRRRRRRRRRRRRRRRRRRRRRRRRRRRRRRRRR
RRRRRRRRRRRRRRRRRRRRRRRRRRRRRRRRRRRRRRRRRRRRR

RRRRRRRRRRRRRRRRRRRRRRRRRRRRRRRRRRRRRRRRRRRR
RRRRRRRRRRRRRRRRRRRRRRRRRRRRRRRRRRRRRRRRRRRR
RRRRRRRRRRRRRRRRRRRRRRRRRRRRRRRRRRRRRRRRRRRR
RRRRRRRRRRRRRRRRRRRRRRRRRRRRRRRRRRRRRRRRRRRR
RRRRRRRRRRRRRRRRRRRRRRRRRRRRRRRRRRRRRRRRRRRR
RRRRRRRRRRRRRRRRRRRRRRRRRRRRRRRRRRRRRRRRRRRR
RRRRRRRRRRRRRRRRRRRRRRRRRRRRRRRRRRRRRRRRRRRR
RRRRRRRRRRRRRRRRRRRRRRRRRRRRRRRRRRRRRRRRRRRR
RRRRRRRRRRRRRRRRRRRRRRRRRRRRRRRRRRRRRRRRRRRR
RRRRRRRRRRRRRRRRRRRRRRRRRRRRRRRRRRRRRRRRRRRR
RRRRRRRRRRRRRRRRRRRRRRRRRRRRRRRRRRRRRRRRRRRR
RRRRRRRRRRRRRRRRRRRRRRRRRRRRRRRRRRRRRRRRRRRR
RRRRRRRRRRRRRRRRRRRRRRRRRRRRRRRRRRRRRRRRRRRR
RRRRRRRRRRRRRRRRRRRRRRRRRRRRRRRRRRRRRRRRRRRR
RRRRRRRRRRRRRRRRRRRRRRRRRRRRRRRRRRRRRRRRRRRR
RRRRRRRRRRRRRRRRRRRRRRRRRRRRRRRRRRRRRRRRRRRR
RRRRRRRRRRRRRRRRRRRRRRRRRRRRRRRRRRRRRRRRRRRR
RRRRRRRRRRRRRRRRRRRRRRRRRRRRRRRRRRRRRRRRRRRR
RRRRRRRRRRRRRRRRRRRRRRRRRRRRRRRRRRRRRRRRRRRR
RRRRRRRRRRRRRRRRRRRRRRRRRRRRRRRRRRRRRRRRRRRR
RRRRRRRRRRRRRRRRRRRRRRRRRRRRRRRRRRRRRRRRRRRR
RRRRRRRRRRRRRRRRRRRRRRRRRRRRRRRRRRRRRRRRRRRR
RRRRRRRRRRRRRRRRRRRRRRRRRRRRRRRRRRRRRRRRRRRR
RRRRRRRRRRRRRRRRRRRRRRRRRRRRRRRRRRRRRRRRRRRR
RRRRRRRRRRRRRRRRRRRRRRRRRRRRRRRRRRRRRRRRRRRR
RRRRRRRRRRRRRRRRRRRRRRRRRRRRRRRRRRRRRRRRRRRR
RRRRRRRRRRRRRRRRRRRRRRRRRRRRRRRRRRRRRRRRRRRR
RRRRRRRRRRRRRRRRRRRRRRRRRRRRRRRRRRRRRRRRRRRR

RRRRRRRRRRRRRRRRRRRRRRRRRRRRRRRRRRRRRRRRRRR
RRRRRRRRRRRRRRRRRRRRRRRRRRRRRRRRRRRRRRRRRRR
RRRRRRRRRRRRRRRRRRRRRRRRRRRRRRRRRRRRRRRRRRR
RRRRRRRRRRRRRRRRRRRRRRRRRRRRRRRRRRRRRRRRRRR
RRRRRRRRRRRRRRRRRRRRRRRRRRRRRRRRRRRRRRRRRRR
RRRRRRRRRRRRRRRRRRRRRRRRRRRRRRRRRRRRRRRRRRR
RRRRRRRRRRRRRRRRRRRRRRRRRRRRRRRRRRRRRRRRRRR
RRRRRRRRRRRRRRRRRRRRRRRRRRRRRRRRRRRRRRRRRRR
RRRRRRRRRRRRRRRRRRRRRRRRRRRRRRRRRRRRRRRRRRR
RRRRRRRRRRRRRRRRRRRRRRRRRRRRRRRRRRRRRRRRRRR
RRRRRRRRRRRRRRRRRRRRRRRRRRRRRRRRRRRRRRRRRRR
RRRRRRRRRRRRRRRRRRRRRRRRRRRRRRRRRRRRRRRRRRR
RRRRRRRRRRRRRRRRRRRRRRRRRRRRRRRRRRRRRRRRRRR
RRRRRRRRRRRRRRRRRRRRRRRRRRRRRRRRRRRRRRRRRRR
RRRRRRRRRRRRRRRRRRRRRRRRRRRRRRRRRRRRRRRRRRR
RRRRRRRRRRRRRRRRRRRRRRRRRRRRRRRRRRRRRRRRRRR
RRRRRRRRRRRRRRRRRRRRRRRRRRRRRRRRRRRRRRRRRRR
RRRRRRRRRRRRRRRRRRRRRRRRRRRRRRRRRRRRRRRRRRR
RRRRRRRRRRRRRRRRRRRRRRRRRRRRRRRRRRRRRRRRRRR
RRRRRRRRRRRRRRRRRRRRRRRRRRRRRRRRRRRRRRRRRRR
RRRRRRRRRRRRRRRRRRRRRRRRRRRRRRRRRRRRRRRRRRR
RRRRRRRRRRRRRRRRRRRRRRRRRRRRRRRRRRRRRRRRRRR
RRRRRRRRRRRRRRRRRRRRRRRRRRRRRRRRRRRRRRRRRRR
RRRRRRRRRRRRRRRRRRRRRRRRRRRRRRRRRRRRRRRRRRR
RRRRRRRRRRRRRRRRRRRRRRRRRRRRRRRRRRRRRRRRRRR
RRRRRRRRRRRRRRRRRRRRRRRRRRRRRRRRRRRRRRRRRRR
RRRRRRRRRRRRRRRRRRRRRRRRRRRRRRRRRRRRRRRRRRR
RRRRRRRRRRRRRRRRRRRRRRRRRRRRRRRRRRRRRRRRRRR
RRRRRRRRRRRRRRRRRRRRRRRRRRRRRRRRRRRRRRRRRRR

RRRRRRRRRRRRRRRRRRRRRRRRRRRRRRRRRRRRRRRRRRRRRRRR
RRRRRRRRRRRRRRRRRRRRRRRRRRRRRRRRRRRRRRRRRRRRRRRR
RRRRRRRRRRRRRRRRRRRRRRRRRRRRRRRRRRRRRRRRRRRRRRRR
RRRRRRRRRRRRRRRRRRRRRRRRRRRRRRRRRRRRRRRRRRRRRRRR
RRRRRRRRRRRRRRRRRRRRRRRRRRRRRRRRRRRRRRRRRRRRRRRR
RRRRRRRRRRRRRRRRRRRRRRRRRRRRRRRRRRRRRRRRRRRRRRRR
RRRRRRRRRRRRRRRRRRRRRRRRRRRRRRRRRRRRRRRRRRRRRRRR
RRRRRRRRRRRRRRRRRRRRRRRRRRRRRRRRRRRRRRRRRRRRRRRR
RRRRRRRRRRRRRRRRRRRRRRRRRRRRRRRRRRRRRRRRRRRRRRRR
RRRRRRRRRRRRRRRRRRRRRRRRRRRRRRRRRRRRRRRRRRRRRRRR
RRRRRRRRRRRRRRRRRRRRRRRRRRRRRRRRRRRRRRRRRRRRRRRR
RRRRRRRRRRRRRRRRRRRRRRRRRRRRRRRRRRRRRRRRRRRRRRRR
RRRRRRRRRRRRRRRRRRRRRRRRRRRRRRRRRRRRRRRRRRRRRRRR
RRRRRRRRRRRRRRRRRRRRRRRRRRRRRRRRRRRRRRRRRRRRRRRR
RRRRRRRRRRRRRRRRRRRRRRRRRRRRRRRRRRRRRRRRRRRRRRRR
RRRRRRRRRRRRRRRRRRRRRRRRRRRRRRRRRRRRRRRRRRRRRRRR
RRRRRRRRRRRRRRRRRRRRRRRRRRRRRRRRRRRRRRRRRRRRRRRR
RRRRRRRRRRRRRRRRRRRRRRRRRRRRRRRRRRRRRRRRRRRRRRRR
RRRRRRRRRRRRRRRRRRRRRRRRRRRRRRRRRRRRRRRRRRRRRRRR
RRRRRRRRRRRRRRRRRRRRRRRRRRRRRRRRRRRRRRRRRRRRRRRR
RRRRRRRRRRRRRRRRRRRRRRRRRRRRRRRRRRRRRRRRRRRRRRRR
RRRRRRRRRRRRRRRRRRRRRRRRRRRRRRRRRRRRRRRRRRRRRRRR
RRRRRRRRRRRRRRRRRRRRRRRRRRRRRRRRRRRRRRRRRRRRRRRR
RRRRRRRRRRRRRRRRRRRRRRRRRRRRRRRRRRRRRRRRRRRRRRRR
RRRRRRRRRRRRRRRRRRRRRRRRRRRRRRRRRRRRRRRRRRRRRRRR
RRRRRRRRRRRRRRRRRRRRRRRRRRRRRRRRRRRRRRRRRRRRRRRR

RRRRRRRRRRRRRRRRRRRRRRRRRRRRRRRRRRRRRRRR
RRRRRRRRRRRRRRRRRRRRRRRRRRRRRRRRRRRRRRRR
RRRRRRRRRRRRRRRRRRRRRRRRRRRRRRRRRRRRRRRR
RRRRRRRRRRRRRRRRRRRRRRRRRRRRRRRRRRRRRRRR
RRRRRRRRRRRRRRRRRRRRRRRRRRRRRRRRRRRRRRRR
RRRRRRRRRRRRRRRRRRRRRRRRRRRRRRRRRRRRRRRR
RRRRRRRRRRRRRRRRRRRRRRRRRRRRRRRRRRRRRRRR
RRRRRRRRRRRRRRRRRRRRRRRRRRRRRRRRRRRRRRRR
RRRRRRRRRRRRRRRRRRRRRRRRRRRRRRRRRRRRRRRR
RRRRRRRRRRRRRRRRRRRRRRRRRRRRRRRRRRRRRRRR
RRRRRRRRRRRRRRRRRRRRRRRRRRRRRRRRRRRRRRRR
RRRRRRRRRRRRRRRRRRRRRRRRRRRRRRRRRRRRRRRR
RRRRRRRRRRRRRRRRRRRRRRRRRRRRRRRRRRRRRRRR
RRRRRRRRRRRRRRRRRRRRRRRRRRRRRRRRRRRRRRRR
RRRRRRRRRRRRRRRRRRRRRRRRRRRRRRRRRRRRRRRR
RRRRRRRRRRRRRRRRRRRRRRRRRRRRRRRRRRRRRRRR
RRRRRRRRRRRRRRRRRRRRRRRRRRRRRRRRRRRRRRRR
RRRRRRRRRRRRRRRRRRRRRRRRRRRRRRRRRRRRRRRR
RRRRRRRRRRRRRRRRRRRRRRRRRRRRRRRRRRRRRRRR
RRRRRRRRRRRRRRRRRRRRRRRRRRRRRRRRRRRRRRRR
RRRRRRRRRRRRRRRRRRRRRRRRRRRRRRRRRRRRRRRR
RRRRRRRRRRRRRRRRRRRRRRRRRRRRRRRRRRRRRRRR
RRRRRRRRRRRRRRRRRRRRRRRRRRRRRRRRRRRRRRRR
RRRRRRRRRRRRRRRRRRRRRRRRRRRRRRRRRRRRRRRR
RRRRRRRRRRRRRRRRRRRRRRRRRRRRRRRRRRRRRRRR
RRRRRRRRRRRRRRRRRRRRRRRRRRRRRRRRRRRRRRRR
RRRRRRRRRRRRRRRRRRRRRRRRRRRRRRRRRRRRRRRR
RRRRRRRRRRRRRRRRRRRRRRRRRRRRRRRRRRRRRRRR

RRRRRRRRRRRRRRRRRRRRRRRRRRRRRRRRRRRRRRRRRRRRRRRR
RRRRRRRRRRRRRRRRRRRRRRRRRRRRRRRRRRRRRRRRRRRRRRRR
RRRRRRRRRRRRRRRRRRRRRRRRRRRRRRRRRRRRRRRRRRRRRRRR
RRRRRRRRRRRRRRRRRRRRRRRRRRRRRRRRRRRRRRRRRRRRRRRR
RRRRRRRRRRRRRRRRRRRRRRRRRRRRRRRRRRRRRRRRRRRRRRRR
RRRRRRRRRRRRRRRRRRRRRRRRRRRRRRRRRRRRRRRRRRRRRRRR
RRRRRRRRRRRRRRRRRRRRRRRRRRRRRRRRRRRRRRRRRRRRRRRR
RRRRRRRRRRRRRRRRRRRRRRRRRRRRRRRRRRRRRRRRRRRRRRRR
RRRRRRRRRRRRRRRRRRRRRRRRRRRRRRRRRRRRRRRRRRRRRRRR
RRRRRRRRRRRRRRRRRRRRRRRRRRRRRRRRRRRRRRRRRRRRRRRR
RRRRRRRRRRRRRRRRRRRRRRRRRRRRRRRRRRRRRRRRRRRRRRRR
RRRRRRRRRRRRRRRRRRRRRRRRRRRRRRRRRRRRRRRRRRRRRRRR
RRRRRRRRRRRRRRRRRRRRRRRRRRRRRRRRRRRRRRRRRRRRRRRR
RRRRRRRRRRRRRRRRRRRRRRRRRRRRRRRRRRRRRRRRRRRRRRRR
RRRRRRRRRRRRRRRRRRRRRRRRRRRRRRRRRRRRRRRRRRRRRRRR
RRRRRRRRRRRRRRRRRRRRRRRRRRRRRRRRRRRRRRRRRRRRRRRR
RRRRRRRRRRRRRRRRRRRRRRRRRRRRRRRRRRRRRRRRRRRRRRRR
RRRRRRRRRRRRRRRRRRRRRRRRRRRRRRRRRRRRRRRRRRRRRRRR
RRRRRRRRRRRRRRRRRRRRRRRRRRRRRRRRRRRRRRRRRRRRRRRR
RRRRRRRRRRRRRRRRRRRRRRRRRRRRRRRRRRRRRRRRRRRRRRRR
RRRRRRRRRRRRRRRRRRRRRRRRRRRRRRRRRRRRRRRRRRRRRRRR
RRRRRRRRRRRRRRRRRRRRRRRRRRRRRRRRRRRRRRRRRRRRRRRR
RRRRRRRRRRRRRRRRRRRRRRRRRRRRRRRRRRRRRRRRRRRRRRRR
RRRRRRRRRRRRRRRRRRRRRRRRRRRRRRRRRRRRRRRRRRRRRRRR
RRRRRRRRRRRRRRRRRRRRRRRRRRRRRRRRRRRRRRRRRRRRRRRR
RRRRRRRRRRRRRRRRRRRRRRRRRRRRRRRRRRRRRRRRRRRRRRRR

RRRRRRRRRRRRRRRRRRRRRRRRRRRRRRRRRRRRRRRRRRRR
RRRRRRRRRRRRRRRRRRRRRRRRRRRRRRRRRRRRRRRRRRRR
RRRRRRRRRRRRRRRRRRRRRRRRRRRRRRRRRRRRRRRRRRRR
RRRRRRRRRRRRRRRRRRRRRRRRRRRRRRRRRRRRRRRRRRRR
RRRRRRRRRRRRRRRRRRRRRRRRRRRRRRRRRRRRRRRRRRRR
RRRRRRRRRRRRRRRRRRRRRRRRRRRRRRRRRRRRRRRRRRRR
RRRRRRRRRRRRRRRRRRRRRRRRRRRRRRRRRRRRRRRRRRRR
RRRRRRRRRRRRRRRRRRRRRRRRRRRRRRRRRRRRRRRRRRRR
RRRRRRRRRRRRRRRRRRRRRRRRRRRRRRRRRRRRRRRRRRRR
RRRRRRRRRRRRRRRRRRRRRRRRRRRRRRRRRRRRRRRRRRRR
RRRRRRRRRRRRRRRRRRRRRRRRRRRRRRRRRRRRRRRRRRRR
RRRRRRRRRRRRRRRRRRRRRRRRRRRRRRRRRRRRRRRRRRRR
RRRRRRRRRRRRRRRRRRRRRRRRRRRRRRRRRRRRRRRRRRRR
RRRRRRRRRRRRRRRRRRRRRRRRRRRRRRRRRRRRRRRRRRRR
RRRRRRRRRRRRRRRRRRRRRRRRRRRRRRRRRRRRRRRRRRRR
RRRRRRRRRRRRRRRRRRRRRRRRRRRRRRRRRRRRRRRRRRRR
RRRRRRRRRRRRRRRRRRRRRRRRRRRRRRRRRRRRRRRRRRRR
RRRRRRRRRRRRRRRRRRRRRRRRRRRRRRRRRRRRRRRRRRRR
RRRRRRRRRRRRRRRRRRRRRRRRRRRRRRRRRRRRRRRRRRRR
RRRRRRRRRRRRRRRRRRRRRRRRRRRRRRRRRRRRRRRRRRRR
RRRRRRRRRRRRRRRRRRRRRRRRRRRRRRRRRRRRRRRRRRRR
RRRRRRRRRRRRRRRRRRRRRRRRRRRRRRRRRRRRRRRRRRRR
RRRRRRRRRRRRRRRRRRRRRRRRRRRRRRRRRRRRRRRRRRRR
RRRRRRRRRRRRRRRRRRRRRRRRRRRRRRRRRRRRRRRRRRRR
RRRRRRRRRRRRRRRRRRRRRRRRRRRRRRRRRRRRRRRRRRRR

RRRRRRRRRRRRRRRRRRRRRRRRRRRRRRRRRRRRRRRRRRRRRRR
RRRRRRRRRRRRRRRRRRRRRRRRRRRRRRRRRRRRRRRRRRRRRRR
RRRRRRRRRRRRRRRRRRRRRRRRRRRRRRRRRRRRRRRRRRRRRRR
RRRRRRRRRRRRRRRRRRRRRRRRRRRRRRRRRRRRRRRRRRRRRRR
RRRRRRRRRRRRRRRRRRRRRRRRRRRRRRRRRRRRRRRRRRRRRRR
RRRRRRRRRRRRRRRRRRRRRRRRRRRRRRRRRRRRRRRRRRRRRRR
RRRRRRRRRRRRRRRRRRRRRRRRRRRRRRRRRRRRRRRRRRRRRRR
RRRRRRRRRRRRRRRRRRRRRRRRRRRRRRRRRRRRRRRRRRRRRRR
RRRRRRRRRRRRRRRRRRRRRRRRRRRRRRRRRRRRRRRRRRRRRRR
RRRRRRRRRRRRRRRRRRRRRRRRRRRRRRRRRRRRRRRRRRRRRRR
RRRRRRRRRRRRRRRRRRRRRRRRRRRRRRRRRRRRRRRRRRRRRRR
RRRRRRRRRRRRRRRRRRRRRRRRRRRRRRRRRRRRRRRRRRRRRRR
RRRRRRRRRRRRRRRRRRRRRRRRRRRRRRRRRRRRRRRRRRRRRRR
RRRRRRRRRRRRRRRRRRRRRRRRRRRRRRRRRRRRRRRRRRRRRRR
RRRRRRRRRRRRRRRRRRRRRRRRRRRRRRRRRRRRRRRRRRRRRRR
RRRRRRRRRRRRRRRRRRRRRRRRRRRRRRRRRRRRRRRRRRRRRRR
RRRRRRRRRRRRRRRRRRRRRRRRRRRRRRRRRRRRRRRRRRRRRRR
RRRRRRRRRRRRRRRRRRRRRRRRRRRRRRRRRRRRRRRRRRRRRRR
RRRRRRRRRRRRRRRRRRRRRRRRRRRRRRRRRRRRRRRRRRRRRRR
RRRRRRRRRRRRRRRRRRRRRRRRRRRRRRRRRRRRRRRRRRRRRRR
RRRRRRRRRRRRRRRRRRRRRRRRRRRRRRRRRRRRRRRRRRRRRRR
RRRRRRRRRRRRRRRRRRRRRRRRRRRRRRRRRRRRRRRRRRRRRRR
RRRRRRRRRRRRRRRRRRRRRRRRRRRRRRRRRRRRRRRRRRRRRRR
RRRRRRRRRRRRRRRRRRRRRRRRRRRRRRRRRRRRRRRRRRRRRRR
RRRRRRRRRRRRRRRRRRRRRRRRRRRRRRRRRRRRRRRRRRRRRRR
RRRRRRRRRRRRRRRRRRRRRRRRRRRRRRRRRRRRRRRRRRRRRRR
RRRRRRRRRRRRRRRRRRRRRRRRRRRRRRRRRRRRRRRRRRRRRRR
RRRRRRRRRRRRRRRRRRRRRRRRRRRRRRRRRRRRRRRRRRRRRRR

RRRRRRRRRRRRRRRRRRRRRRRRRRRRRRRRRRRRRRRRRRRRRRRRR
RRRRRRRRRRRRRRRRRRRRRRRRRRRRRRRRRRRRRRRRRRRRRRRRR
RRRRRRRRRRRRRRRRRRRRRRRRRRRRRRRRRRRRRRRRRRRRRRRRR
RRRRRRRRRRRRRRRRRRRRRRRRRRRRRRRRRRRRRRRRRRRRRRRRR
RRRRRRRRRRRRRRRRRRRRRRRRRRRRRRRRRRRRRRRRRRRRRRRRR
RRRRRRRRRRRRRRRRRRRRRRRRRRRRRRRRRRRRRRRRRRRRRRRRR
RRRRRRRRRRRRRRRRRRRRRRRRRRRRRRRRRRRRRRRRRRRRRRRRR
RRRRRRRRRRRRRRRRRRRRRRRRRRRRRRRRRRRRRRRRRRRRRRRRR
RRRRRRRRRRRRRRRRRRRRRRRRRRRRRRRRRRRRRRRRRRRRRRRRR
RRRRRRRRRRRRRRRRRRRRRRRRRRRRRRRRRRRRRRRRRRRRRRRRR
RRRRRRRRRRRRRRRRRRRRRRRRRRRRRRRRRRRRRRRRRRRRRRRRR
RRRRRRRRRRRRRRRRRRRRRRRRRRRRRRRRRRRRRRRRRRRRRRRRR
RRRRRRRRRRRRRRRRRRRRRRRRRRRRRRRRRRRRRRRRRRRRRRRRR
RRRRRRRRRRRRRRRRRRRRRRRRRRRRRRRRRRRRRRRRRRRRRRRRR
RRRRRRRRRRRRRRRRRRRRRRRRRRRRRRRRRRRRRRRRRRRRRRRRR
RRRRRRRRRRRRRRRRRRRRRRRRRRRRRRRRRRRRRRRRRRRRRRRRR
RRRRRRRRRRRRRRRRRRRRRRRRRRRRRRRRRRRRRRRRRRRRRRRRR
RRRRRRRRRRRRRRRRRRRRRRRRRRRRRRRRRRRRRRRRRRRRRRRRR
RRRRRRRRRRRRRRRRRRRRRRRRRRRRRRRRRRRRRRRRRRRRRRRRR
RRRRRRRRRRRRRRRRRRRRRRRRRRRRRRRRRRRRRRRRRRRRRRRRR
RRRRRRRRRRRRRRRRRRRRRRRRRRRRRRRRRRRRRRRRRRRRRRRRR
RRRRRRRRRRRRRRRRRRRRRRRRRRRRRRRRRRRRRRRRRRRRRRRRR
RRRRRRRRRRRRRRRRRRRRRRRRRRRRRRRRRRRRRRRRRRRRRRRRR
RRRRRRRRRRRRRRRRRRRRRRRRRRRRRRRRRRRRRRRRRRRRRRRRR
RRRRRRRRRRRRRRRRRRRRRRRRRRRRRRRRRRRRRRRRRRRRRRRRR
RRRRRRRRRRRRRRRRRRRRRRRRRRRRRRRRRRRRRRRRRRRRRRRRR
RRRRRRRRRRRRRRRRRRRRRRRRRRRRRRRRRRRRRRRRRRRRRRRRR
RRRRRRRRRRRRRRRRRRRRRRRRRRRRRRRRRRRRRRRRRRRRRRRRR

RRRRRRRRRRRRRRRRRRRRRRRRRRRRRRRRRRRRRRRRRRR
RRRRRRRRRRRRRRRRRRRRRRRRRRRRRRRRRRRRRRRRRRR
RRRRRRRRRRRRRRRRRRRRRRRRRRRRRRRRRRRRRRRRRRR
RRRRRRRRRRRRRRRRRRRRRRRRRRRRRRRRRRRRRRRRRRR
RRRRRRRRRRRRRRRRRRRRRRRRRRRRRRRRRRRRRRRRRRR
RRRRRRRRRRRRRRRRRRRRRRRRRRRRRRRRRRRRRRRRRRR
RRRRRRRRRRRRRRRRRRRRRRRRRRRRRRRRRRRRRRRRRRR
RRRRRRRRRRRRRRRRRRRRRRRRRRRRRRRRRRRRRRRRRRR
RRRRRRRRRRRRRRRRRRRRRRRRRRRRRRRRRRRRRRRRRRR
RRRRRRRRRRRRRRRRRRRRRRRRRRRRRRRRRRRRRRRRRRR
RRRRRRRRRRRRRRRRRRRRRRRRRRRRRRRRRRRRRRRRRRR
RRRRRRRRRRRRRRRRRRRRRRRRRRRRRRRRRRRRRRRRRRR
RRRRRRRRRRRRRRRRRRRRRRRRRRRRRRRRRRRRRRRRRRR
RRRRRRRRRRRRRRRRRRRRRRRRRRRRRRRRRRRRRRRRRRR
RRRRRRRRRRRRRRRRRRRRRRRRRRRRRRRRRRRRRRRRRRR
RRRRRRRRRRRRRRRRRRRRRRRRRRRRRRRRRRRRRRRRRRR
RRRRRRRRRRRRRRRRRRRRRRRRRRRRRRRRRRRRRRRRRRR
RRRRRRRRRRRRRRRRRRRRRRRRRRRRRRRRRRRRRRRRRRR
RRRRRRRRRRRRRRRRRRRRRRRRRRRRRRRRRRRRRRRRRRR
RRRRRRRRRRRRRRRRRRRRRRRRRRRRRRRRRRRRRRRRRRR
RRRRRRRRRRRRRRRRRRRRRRRRRRRRRRRRRRRRRRRRRRR
RRRRRRRRRRRRRRRRRRRRRRRRRRRRRRRRRRRRRRRRRRR
RRRRRRRRRRRRRRRRRRRRRRRRRRRRRRRRRRRRRRRRRRR
RRRRRRRRRRRRRRRRRRRRRRRRRRRRRRRRRRRRRRRRRRR
RRRRRRRRRRRRRRRRRRRRRRRRRRRRRRRRRRRRRRRRRRR
RRRRRRRRRRRRRRRRRRRRRRRRRRRRRRRRRRRRRRRRRRR
RRRRRRRRRRRRRRRRRRRRRRRRRRRRRRRRRRRRRRRRRRR
RRRRRRRRRRRRRRRRRRRRRRRRRRRRRRRRRRRRRRRRRRR

RRRRRRRRRRRRRRRRRRRRRRRRRRRRRRRRRRRRRRRRRRRR
RRRRRRRRRRRRRRRRRRRRRRRRRRRRRRRRRRRRRRRRRRRR
RRRRRRRRRRRRRRRRRRRRRRRRRRRRRRRRRRRRRRRRRRRR
RRRRRRRRRRRRRRRRRRRRRRRRRRRRRRRRRRRRRRRRRRRR
RRRRRRRRRRRRRRRRRRRRRRRRRRRRRRRRRRRRRRRRRRRR
RRRRRRRRRRRRRRRRRRRRRRRRRRRRRRRRRRRRRRRRRRRR
RRRRRRRRRRRRRRRRRRRRRRRRRRRRRRRRRRRRRRRRRRRR
RRRRRRRRRRRRRRRRRRRRRRRRRRRRRRRRRRRRRRRRRRRR
RRRRRRRRRRRRRRRRRRRRRRRRRRRRRRRRRRRRRRRRRRRR
RRRRRRRRRRRRRRRRRRRRRRRRRRRRRRRRRRRRRRRRRRRR
RRRRRRRRRRRRRRRRRRRRRRRRRRRRRRRRRRRRRRRRRRRR
RRRRRRRRRRRRRRRRRRRRRRRRRRRRRRRRRRRRRRRRRRRR
RRRRRRRRRRRRRRRRRRRRRRRRRRRRRRRRRRRRRRRRRRRR
RRRRRRRRRRRRRRRRRRRRRRRRRRRRRRRRRRRRRRRRRRRR
RRRRRRRRRRRRRRRRRRRRRRRRRRRRRRRRRRRRRRRRRRRR
RRRRRRRRRRRRRRRRRRRRRRRRRRRRRRRRRRRRRRRRRRRR
RRRRRRRRRRRRRRRRRRRRRRRRRRRRRRRRRRRRRRRRRRRR
RRRRRRRRRRRRRRRRRRRRRRRRRRRRRRRRRRRRRRRRRRRR
RRRRRRRRRRRRRRRRRRRRRRRRRRRRRRRRRRRRRRRRRRRR
RRRRRRRRRRRRRRRRRRRRRRRRRRRRRRRRRRRRRRRRRRRR
RRRRRRRRRRRRRRRRRRRRRRRRRRRRRRRRRRRRRRRRRRRR
RRRRRRRRRRRRRRRRRRRRRRRRRRRRRRRRRRRRRRRRRRRR
RRRRRRRRRRRRRRRRRRRRRRRRRRRRRRRRRRRRRRRRRRRR
RRRRRRRRRRRRRRRRRRRRRRRRRRRRRRRRRRRRRRRRRRRR
RRRRRRRRRRRRRRRRRRRRRRRRRRRRRRRRRRRRRRRRRRRR
RRRRRRRRRRRRRRRRRRRRRRRRRRRRRRRRRRRRRRRRRRRR
RRRRRRRRRRRRRRRRRRRRRRRRRRRRRRRRRRRRRRRRRRRR
RRRRRRRRRRRRRRRRRRRRRRRRRRRRRRRRRRRRRRRRRRRR
RRRRRRRRRRRRRRRRRRRRRRRRRRRRRRRRRRRRRRRRRRRR
RRRRRRRRRRRRRRRRRRRRRRRRRRRRRRRRRRRRRRRRRRRR

RRRRRRRRRRRRRRRRRRRRRRRRRRRRRRRRRRRRRRRRRRRRRRR
RRRRRRRRRRRRRRRRRRRRRRRRRRRRRRRRRRRRRRRRRRRRRRR
RRRRRRRRRRRRRRRRRRRRRRRRRRRRRRRRRRRRRRRRRRRRRRR
RRRRRRRRRRRRRRRRRRRRRRRRRRRRRRRRRRRRRRRRRRRRRRR
RRRRRRRRRRRRRRRRRRRRRRRRRRRRRRRRRRRRRRRRRRRRRRR
RRRRRRRRRRRRRRRRRRRRRRRRRRRRRRRRRRRRRRRRRRRRRRR
RRRRRRRRRRRRRRRRRRRRRRRRRRRRRRRRRRRRRRRRRRRRRRR
RRRRRRRRRRRRRRRRRRRRRRRRRRRRRRRRRRRRRRRRRRRRRRR
RRRRRRRRRRRRRRRRRRRRRRRRRRRRRRRRRRRRRRRRRRRRRRR
RRRRRRRRRRRRRRRRRRRRRRRRRRRRRRRRRRRRRRRRRRRRRRR
RRRRRRRRRRRRRRRRRRRRRRRRRRRRRRRRRRRRRRRRRRRRRRR
RRRRRRRRRRRRRRRRRRRRRRRRRRRRRRRRRRRRRRRRRRRRRRR
RRRRRRRRRRRRRRRRRRRRRRRRRRRRRRRRRRRRRRRRRRRRRRR
RRRRRRRRRRRRRRRRRRRRRRRRRRRRRRRRRRRRRRRRRRRRRRR
RRRRRRRRRRRRRRRRRRRRRRRRRRRRRRRRRRRRRRRRRRRRRRR
RRRRRRRRRRRRRRRRRRRRRRRRRRRRRRRRRRRRRRRRRRRRRRR
RRRRRRRRRRRRRRRRRRRRRRRRRRRRRRRRRRRRRRRRRRRRRRR
RRRRRRRRRRRRRRRRRRRRRRRRRRRRRRRRRRRRRRRRRRRRRRR
RRRRRRRRRRRRRRRRRRRRRRRRRRRRRRRRRRRRRRRRRRRRRRR
RRRRRRRRRRRRRRRRRRRRRRRRRRRRRRRRRRRRRRRRRRRRRRR
RRRRRRRRRRRRRRRRRRRRRRRRRRRRRRRRRRRRRRRRRRRRRRR
RRRRRRRRRRRRRRRRRRRRRRRRRRRRRRRRRRRRRRRRRRRRRRR
RRRRRRRRRRRRRRRRRRRRRRRRRRRRRRRRRRRRRRRRRRRRRRR
RRRRRRRRRRRRRRRRRRRRRRRRRRRRRRRRRRRRRRRRRRRRRRR
RRRRRRRRRRRRRRRRRRRRRRRRRRRRRRRRRRRRRRRRRRRRRRR
RRRRRRRRRRRRRRRRRRRRRRRRRRRRRRRRRRRRRRRRRRRRRRR
RRRRRRRRRRRRRRRRRRRRRRRRRRRRRRRRRRRRRRRRRRRRRRR
RRRRRRRRRRRRRRRRRRRRRRRRRRRRRRRRRRRRRRRRRRRRRRR
RRRRRRRRRRRRRRRRRRRRRRRRRRRRRRRRRRRRRRRRRRRRRRR

RRRRRRRRRRRRRRRRRRRRRRRRRRRRRRRRRRRRRRRRRRR
RRRRRRRRRRRRRRRRRRRRRRRRRRRRRRRRRRRRRRRRRRR
RRRRRRRRRRRRRRRRRRRRRRRRRRRRRRRRRRRRRRRRRRR
RRRRRRRRRRRRRRRRRRRRRRRRRRRRRRRRRRRRRRRRRRR
RRRRRRRRRRRRRRRRRRRRRRRRRRRRRRRRRRRRRRRRRRR
RRRRRRRRRRRRRRRRRRRRRRRRRRRRRRRRRRRRRRRRRRR
RRRRRRRRRRRRRRRRRRRRRRRRRRRRRRRRRRRRRRRRRRR
RRRRRRRRRRRRRRRRRRRRRRRRRRRRRRRRRRRRRRRRRRR
RRRRRRRRRRRRRRRRRRRRRRRRRRRRRRRRRRRRRRRRRRR
RRRRRRRRRRRRRRRRRRRRRRRRRRRRRRRRRRRRRRRRRRR
RRRRRRRRRRRRRRRRRRRRRRRRRRRRRRRRRRRRRRRRRRR
RRRRRRRRRRRRRRRRRRRRRRRRRRRRRRRRRRRRRRRRRRR
RRRRRRRRRRRRRRRRRRRRRRRRRRRRRRRRRRRRRRRRRRR
RRRRRRRRRRRRRRRRRRRRRRRRRRRRRRRRRRRRRRRRRRR
RRRRRRRRRRRRRRRRRRRRRRRRRRRRRRRRRRRRRRRRRRR
RRRRRRRRRRRRRRRRRRRRRRRRRRRRRRRRRRRRRRRRRRR
RRRRRRRRRRRRRRRRRRRRRRRRRRRRRRRRRRRRRRRRRRR
RRRRRRRRRRRRRRRRRRRRRRRRRRRRRRRRRRRRRRRRRRR
RRRRRRRRRRRRRRRRRRRRRRRRRRRRRRRRRRRRRRRRRRR
RRRRRRRRRRRRRRRRRRRRRRRRRRRRRRRRRRRRRRRRRRR
RRRRRRRRRRRRRRRRRRRRRRRRRRRRRRRRRRRRRRRRRRR
RRRRRRRRRRRRRRRRRRRRRRRRRRRRRRRRRRRRRRRRRRR
RRRRRRRRRRRRRRRRRRRRRRRRRRRRRRRRRRRRRRRRRRR
RRRRRRRRRRRRRRRRRRRRRRRRRRRRRRRRRRRRRRRRRRR
RRRRRRRRRRRRRRRRRRRRRRRRRRRRRRRRRRRRRRRRRRR
RRRRRRRRRRRRRRRRRRRRRRRRRRRRRRRRRRRRRRRRRRR

RRRRRRRRRRRRRRRRRRRRRRRRRRRRRRRRRRRRRRRR
RRRRRRRRRRRRRRRRRRRRRRRRRRRRRRRRRRRRRRRR
RRRRRRRRRRRRRRRRRRRRRRRRRRRRRRRRRRRRRRRR
RRRRRRRRRRRRRRRRRRRRRRRRRRRRRRRRRRRRRRRR
RRRRRRRRRRRRRRRRRRRRRRRRRRRRRRRRRRRRRRRR
RRRRRRRRRRRRRRRRRRRRRRRRRRRRRRRRRRRRRRRR
RRRRRRRRRRRRRRRRRRRRRRRRRRRRRRRRRRRRRRRR
RRRRRRRRRRRRRRRRRRRRRRRRRRRRRRRRRRRRRRRR
RRRRRRRRRRRRRRRRRRRRRRRRRRRRRRRRRRRRRRRR
RRRRRRRRRRRRRRRRRRRRRRRRRRRRRRRRRRRRRRRR
RRRRRRRRRRRRRRRRRRRRRRRRRRRRRRRRRRRRRRRR
RRRRRRRRRRRRRRRRRRRRRRRRRRRRRRRRRRRRRRRR
RRRRRRRRRRRRRRRRRRRRRRRRRRRRRRRRRRRRRRRR
RRRRRRRRRRRRRRRRRRRRRRRRRRRRRRRRRRRRRRRR
RRRRRRRRRRRRRRRRRRRRRRRRRRRRRRRRRRRRRRRR
RRRRRRRRRRRRRRRRRRRRRRRRRRRRRRRRRRRRRRRR
RRRRRRRRRRRRRRRRRRRRRRRRRRRRRRRRRRRRRRRR
RRRRRRRRRRRRRRRRRRRRRRRRRRRRRRRRRRRRRRRR
RRRRRRRRRRRRRRRRRRRRRRRRRRRRRRRRRRRRRRRR
RRRRRRRRRRRRRRRRRRRRRRRRRRRRRRRRRRRRRRRR
RRRRRRRRRRRRRRRRRRRRRRRRRRRRRRRRRRRRRRRR
RRRRRRRRRRRRRRRRRRRRRRRRRRRRRRRRRRRRRRRR
RRRRRRRRRRRRRRRRRRRRRRRRRRRRRRRRRRRRRRRR
RRRRRRRRRRRRRRRRRRRRRRRRRRRRRRRRRRRRRRRR
RRRRRRRRRRRRRRRRRRRRRRRRRRRRRRRRRRRRRRRR
RRRRRRRRRRRRRRRRRRRRRRRRRRRRRRRRRRRRRRRR

RRRRRRRRRRRRRRRRRRRRRRRRRRRRRRRRRRRRRRRRRRR
RRRRRRRRRRRRRRRRRRRRRRRRRRRRRRRRRRRRRRRRRRR
RRRRRRRRRRRRRRRRRRRRRRRRRRRRRRRRRRRRRRRRRRR
RRRRRRRRRRRRRRRRRRRRRRRRRRRRRRRRRRRRRRRRRRR
RRRRRRRRRRRRRRRRRRRRRRRRRRRRRRRRRRRRRRRRRRR
RRRRRRRRRRRRRRRRRRRRRRRRRRRRRRRRRRRRRRRRRRR
RRRRRRRRRRRRRRRRRRRRRRRRRRRRRRRRRRRRRRRRRRR
RRRRRRRRRRRRRRRRRRRRRRRRRRRRRRRRRRRRRRRRRRR
RRRRRRRRRRRRRRRRRRRRRRRRRRRRRRRRRRRRRRRRRRR
RRRRRRRRRRRRRRRRRRRRRRRRRRRRRRRRRRRRRRRRRRR
RRRRRRRRRRRRRRRRRRRRRRRRRRRRRRRRRRRRRRRRRRR
RRRRRRRRRRRRRRRRRRRRRRRRRRRRRRRRRRRRRRRRRRR
RRRRRRRRRRRRRRRRRRRRRRRRRRRRRRRRRRRRRRRRRRR
RRRRRRRRRRRRRRRRRRRRRRRRRRRRRRRRRRRRRRRRRRR
RRRRRRRRRRRRRRRRRRRRRRRRRRRRRRRRRRRRRRRRRRR
RRRRRRRRRRRRRRRRRRRRRRRRRRRRRRRRRRRRRRRRRRR
RRRRRRRRRRRRRRRRRRRRRRRRRRRRRRRRRRRRRRRRRRR
RRRRRRRRRRRRRRRRRRRRRRRRRRRRRRRRRRRRRRRRRRR
RRRRRRRRRRRRRRRRRRRRRRRRRRRRRRRRRRRRRRRRRRR
RRRRRRRRRRRRRRRRRRRRRRRRRRRRRRRRRRRRRRRRRRR
RRRRRRRRRRRRRRRRRRRRRRRRRRRRRRRRRRRRRRRRRRR
RRRRRRRRRRRRRRRRRRRRRRRRRRRRRRRRRRRRRRRRRRR
RRRRRRRRRRRRRRRRRRRRRRRRRRRRRRRRRRRRRRRRRRR
RRRRRRRRRRRRRRRRRRRRRRRRRRRRRRRRRRRRRRRRRRR
RRRRRRRRRRRRRRRRRRRRRRRRRRRRRRRRRRRRRRRRRRR
RRRRRRRRRRRRRRRRRRRRRRRRRRRRRRRRRRRRRRRRRRR

RRRRRRRRRRRRRRRRRRRRRRRRRRRRRRRRRRRRRRRRRRRRR
RRRRRRRRRRRRRRRRRRRRRRRRRRRRRRRRRRRRRRRRRRRRR
RRRRRRRRRRRRRRRRRRRRRRRRRRRRRRRRRRRRRRRRRRRRR
RRRRRRRRRRRRRRRRRRRRRRRRRRRRRRRRRRRRRRRRRRRRR
RRRRRRRRRRRRRRRRRRRRRRRRRRRRRRRRRRRRRRRRRRRRR
RRRRRRRRRRRRRRRRRRRRRRRRRRRRRRRRRRRRRRRRRRRRR
RRRRRRRRRRRRRRRRRRRRRRRRRRRRRRRRRRRRRRRRRRRRR
RRRRRRRRRRRRRRRRRRRRRRRRRRRRRRRRRRRRRRRRRRRRR
RRRRRRRRRRRRRRRRRRRRRRRRRRRRRRRRRRRRRRRRRRRRR
RRRRRRRRRRRRRRRRRRRRRRRRRRRRRRRRRRRRRRRRRRRRR
RRRRRRRRRRRRRRRRRRRRRRRRRRRRRRRRRRRRRRRRRRRRR
RRRRRRRRRRRRRRRRRRRRRRRRRRRRRRRRRRRRRRRRRRRRR
RRRRRRRRRRRRRRRRRRRRRRRRRRRRRRRRRRRRRRRRRRRRR
RRRRRRRRRRRRRRRRRRRRRRRRRRRRRRRRRRRRRRRRRRRRR
RRRRRRRRRRRRRRRRRRRRRRRRRRRRRRRRRRRRRRRRRRRRR
RRRRRRRRRRRRRRRRRRRRRRRRRRRRRRRRRRRRRRRRRRRRR
RRRRRRRRRRRRRRRRRRRRRRRRRRRRRRRRRRRRRRRRRRRRR
RRRRRRRRRRRRRRRRRRRRRRRRRRRRRRRRRRRRRRRRRRRRR
RRRRRRRRRRRRRRRRRRRRRRRRRRRRRRRRRRRRRRRRRRRRR
RRRRRRRRRRRRRRRRRRRRRRRRRRRRRRRRRRRRRRRRRRRRR
RRRRRRRRRRRRRRRRRRRRRRRRRRRRRRRRRRRRRRRRRRRRR
RRRRRRRRRRRRRRRRRRRRRRRRRRRRRRRRRRRRRRRRRRRRR
RRRRRRRRRRRRRRRRRRRRRRRRRRRRRRRRRRRRRRRRRRRRR
RRRRRRRRRRRRRRRRRRRRRRRRRRRRRRRRRRRRRRRRRRRRR
RRRRRRRRRRRRRRRRRRRRRRRRRRRRRRRRRRRRRRRRRRRRR
RRRRRRRRRRRRRRRRRRRRRRRRRRRRRRRRRRRRRRRRRRRRR
RRRRRRRRRRRRRRRRRRRRRRRRRRRRRRRRRRRRRRRRRRRRR

RRRRRRRRRRRRRRRRRRRRRRRRRRRRRRRRRRRRRRRRRRRRRR
RRRRRRRRRRRRRRRRRRRRRRRRRRRRRRRRRRRRRRRRRRRRRR
RRRRRRRRRRRRRRRRRRRRRRRRRRRRRRRRRRRRRRRRRRRRRR
RRRRRRRRRRRRRRRRRRRRRRRRRRRRRRRRRRRRRRRRRRRRRR
RRRRRRRRRRRRRRRRRRRRRRRRRRRRRRRRRRRRRRRRRRRRRR
RRRRRRRRRRRRRRRRRRRRRRRRRRRRRRRRRRRRRRRRRRRRRR
RRRRRRRRRRRRRRRRRRRRRRRRRRRRRRRRRRRRRRRRRRRRRR
RRRRRRRRRRRRRRRRRRRRRRRRRRRRRRRRRRRRRRRRRRRRRR
RRRRRRRRRRRRRRRRRRRRRRRRRRRRRRRRRRRRRRRRRRRRRR
RRRRRRRRRRRRRRRRRRRRRRRRRRRRRRRRRRRRRRRRRRRRRR
RRRRRRRRRRRRRRRRRRRRRRRRRRRRRRRRRRRRRRRRRRRRRR
RRRRRRRRRRRRRRRRRRRRRRRRRRRRRRRRRRRRRRRRRRRRRR
RRRRRRRRRRRRRRRRRRRRRRRRRRRRRRRRRRRRRRRRRRRRRR
RRRRRRRRRRRRRRRRRRRRRRRRRRRRRRRRRRRRRRRRRRRRRR
RRRRRRRRRRRRRRRRRRRRRRRRRRRRRRRRRRRRRRRRRRRRRR
RRRRRRRRRRRRRRRRRRRRRRRRRRRRRRRRRRRRRRRRRRRRRR
RRRRRRRRRRRRRRRRRRRRRRRRRRRRRRRRRRRRRRRRRRRRRR
RRRRRRRRRRRRRRRRRRRRRRRRRRRRRRRRRRRRRRRRRRRRRR
RRRRRRRRRRRRRRRRRRRRRRRRRRRRRRRRRRRRRRRRRRRRRR
RRRRRRRRRRRRRRRRRRRRRRRRRRRRRRRRRRRRRRRRRRRRRR
RRRRRRRRRRRRRRRRRRRRRRRRRRRRRRRRRRRRRRRRRRRRRR
RRRRRRRRRRRRRRRRRRRRRRRRRRRRRRRRRRRRRRRRRRRRRR
RRRRRRRRRRRRRRRRRRRRRRRRRRRRRRRRRRRRRRRRRRRRRR
RRRRRRRRRRRRRRRRRRRRRRRRRRRRRRRRRRRRRRRRRRRRRR
RRRRRRRRRRRRRRRRRRRRRRRRRRRRRRRRRRRRRRRRRRRRRR
RRRRRRRRRRRRRRRRRRRRRRRRRRRRRRRRRRRRRRRRRRRRRR

RRRRRRRRRRRRRRRRRRRRRRRRRRRRRRRRRRRRRRRRRRRRRRRRRRRRR
RRRRRRRRRRRRRRRRRRRRRRRRRRRRRRRRRRRRRRRRRRRRRRRRRRRRR
RRRRRRRRRRRRRRRRRRRRRRRRRRRRRRRRRRRRRRRRRRRRRRRRRRRRR
RRRRRRRRRRRRRRRRRRRRRRRRRRRRRRRRRRRRRRRRRRRRRRRRRRRRR
RRRRRRRRRRRRRRRRRRRRRRRRRRRRRRRRRRRRRRRRRRRRRRRRRRRRR
RRRRRRRRRRRRRRRRRRRRRRRRRRRRRRRRRRRRRRRRRRRRRRRRRRRRR
RRRRRRRRRRRRRRRRRRRRRRRRRRRRRRRRRRRRRRRRRRRRRRRRRRRRR
RRRRRRRRRRRRRRRRRRRRRRRRRRRRRRRRRRRRRRRRRRRRRRRRRRRRR
RRRRRRRRRRRRRRRRRRRRRRRRRRRRRRRRRRRRRRRRRRRRRRRRRRRRR
RRRRRRRRRRRRRRRRRRRRRRRRRRRRRRRRRRRRRRRRRRRRRRRRRRRRR
RRRRRRRRRRRRRRRRRRRRRRRRRRRRRRRRRRRRRRRRRRRRRRRRRRRRR
RRRRRRRRRRRRRRRRRRRRRRRRRRRRRRRRRRRRRRRRRRRRRRRRRRRRR
RRRRRRRRRRRRRRRRRRRRRRRRRRRRRRRRRRRRRRRRRRRRRRRRRRRRR
RRRRRRRRRRRRRRRRRRRRRRRRRRRRRRRRRRRRRRRRRRRRRRRRRRRRR
RRRRRRRRRRRRRRRRRRRRRRRRRRRRRRRRRRRRRRRRRRRRRRRRRRRRR
RRRRRRRRRRRRRRRRRRRRRRRRRRRRRRRRRRRRRRRRRRRRRRRRRRRRR
RRRRRRRRRRRRRRRRRRRRRRRRRRRRRRRRRRRRRRRRRRRRRRRRRRRRR
RRRRRRRRRRRRRRRRRRRRRRRRRRRRRRRRRRRRRRRRRRRRRRRRRRRRR
RRRRRRRRRRRRRRRRRRRRRRRRRRRRRRRRRRRRRRRRRRRRRRRRRRRRR
RRRRRRRRRRRRRRRRRRRRRRRRRRRRRRRRRRRRRRRRRRRRRRRRRRRRR
RRRRRRRRRRRRRRRRRRRRRRRRRRRRRRRRRRRRRRRRRRRRRRRRRRRRR
RRRRRRRRRRRRRRRRRRRRRRRRRRRRRRRRRRRRRRRRRRRRRRRRRRRRR
RRRRRRRRRRRRRRRRRRRRRRRRRRRRRRRRRRRRRRRRRRRRRRRRRRRRR
RRRRRRRRRRRRRRRRRRRRRRRRRRRRRRRRRRRRRRRRRRRRRRRRRRRRR
RRRRRRRRRRRRRRRRRRRRRRRRRRRRRRRRRRRRRRRRRRRRRRRRRRRRR
RRRRRRRRRRRRRRRRRRRRRRRRRRRRRRRRRRRRRRRRRRRRRRRRRRRRR

RRRRRRRRRRRRRRRRRRRRRRRRRRRRRRRRRRRRRRRRRRRR
RRRRRRRRRRRRRRRRRRRRRRRRRRRRRRRRRRRRRRRRRRRR
RRRRRRRRRRRRRRRRRRRRRRRRRRRRRRRRRRRRRRRRRRRR
RRRRRRRRRRRRRRRRRRRRRRRRRRRRRRRRRRRRRRRRRRRR
RRRRRRRRRRRRRRRRRRRRRRRRRRRRRRRRRRRRRRRRRRRR
RRRRRRRRRRRRRRRRRRRRRRRRRRRRRRRRRRRRRRRRRRRR
RRRRRRRRRRRRRRRRRRRRRRRRRRRRRRRRRRRRRRRRRRRR
RRRRRRRRRRRRRRRRRRRRRRRRRRRRRRRRRRRRRRRRRRRR
RRRRRRRRRRRRRRRRRRRRRRRRRRRRRRRRRRRRRRRRRRRR
RRRRRRRRRRRRRRRRRRRRRRRRRRRRRRRRRRRRRRRRRRRR
RRRRRRRRRRRRRRRRRRRRRRRRRRRRRRRRRRRRRRRRRRRR
RRRRRRRRRRRRRRRRRRRRRRRRRRRRRRRRRRRRRRRRRRRR
RRRRRRRRRRRRRRRRRRRRRRRRRRRRRRRRRRRRRRRRRRRR
RRRRRRRRRRRRRRRRRRRRRRRRRRRRRRRRRRRRRRRRRRRR
RRRRRRRRRRRRRRRRRRRRRRRRRRRRRRRRRRRRRRRRRRRR
RRRRRRRRRRRRRRRRRRRRRRRRRRRRRRRRRRRRRRRRRRRR
RRRRRRRRRRRRRRRRRRRRRRRRRRRRRRRRRRRRRRRRRRRR
RRRRRRRRRRRRRRRRRRRRRRRRRRRRRRRRRRRRRRRRRRRR
RRRRRRRRRRRRRRRRRRRRRRRRRRRRRRRRRRRRRRRRRRRR
RRRRRRRRRRRRRRRRRRRRRRRRRRRRRRRRRRRRRRRRRRRR
RRRRRRRRRRRRRRRRRRRRRRRRRRRRRRRRRRRRRRRRRRRR
RRRRRRRRRRRRRRRRRRRRRRRRRRRRRRRRRRRRRRRRRRRR
RRRRRRRRRRRRRRRRRRRRRRRRRRRRRRRRRRRRRRRRRRRR
RRRRRRRRRRRRRRRRRRRRRRRRRRRRRRRRRRRRRRRRRRRR
RRRRRRRRRRRRRRRRRRRRRRRRRRRRRRRRRRRRRRRRRRRR
RRRRRRRRRRRRRRRRRRRRRRRRRRRRRRRRRRRRRRRRRRRR
RRRRRRRRRRRRRRRRRRRRRRRRRRRRRRRRRRRRRRRRRRRR
RRRRRRRRRRRRRRRRRRRRRRRRRRRRRRRRRRRRRRRRRRRR
RRRRRRRRRRRRRRRRRRRRRRRRRRRRRRRRRRRRRRRRRRRR
RRRRRRRRRRRRRRRRRRRRRRRRRRRRRRRRRRRRRRRRRRRR

RRRRRRRRRRRRRRRRRRRRRRRRRRRRRRRRRRRRRRRRRRRRRRRR
RRRRRRRRRRRRRRRRRRRRRRRRRRRRRRRRRRRRRRRRRRRRRRRR
RRRRRRRRRRRRRRRRRRRRRRRRRRRRRRRRRRRRRRRRRRRRRRRR
RRRRRRRRRRRRRRRRRRRRRRRRRRRRRRRRRRRRRRRRRRRRRRRR
RRRRRRRRRRRRRRRRRRRRRRRRRRRRRRRRRRRRRRRRRRRRRRRR
RRRRRRRRRRRRRRRRRRRRRRRRRRRRRRRRRRRRRRRRRRRRRRRR
RRRRRRRRRRRRRRRRRRRRRRRRRRRRRRRRRRRRRRRRRRRRRRRR
RRRRRRRRRRRRRRRRRRRRRRRRRRRRRRRRRRRRRRRRRRRRRRRR
RRRRRRRRRRRRRRRRRRRRRRRRRRRRRRRRRRRRRRRRRRRRRRRR
RRRRRRRRRRRRRRRRRRRRRRRRRRRRRRRRRRRRRRRRRRRRRRRR
RRRRRRRRRRRRRRRRRRRRRRRRRRRRRRRRRRRRRRRRRRRRRRRR
RRRRRRRRRRRRRRRRRRRRRRRRRRRRRRRRRRRRRRRRRRRRRRRR
RRRRRRRRRRRRRRRRRRRRRRRRRRRRRRRRRRRRRRRRRRRRRRRR
RRRRRRRRRRRRRRRRRRRRRRRRRRRRRRRRRRRRRRRRRRRRRRRR
RRRRRRRRRRRRRRRRRRRRRRRRRRRRRRRRRRRRRRRRRRRRRRRR
RRRRRRRRRRRRRRRRRRRRRRRRRRRRRRRRRRRRRRRRRRRRRRRR
RRRRRRRRRRRRRRRRRRRRRRRRRRRRRRRRRRRRRRRRRRRRRRRR
RRRRRRRRRRRRRRRRRRRRRRRRRRRRRRRRRRRRRRRRRRRRRRRR
RRRRRRRRRRRRRRRRRRRRRRRRRRRRRRRRRRRRRRRRRRRRRRRR
RRRRRRRRRRRRRRRRRRRRRRRRRRRRRRRRRRRRRRRRRRRRRRRR
RRRRRRRRRRRRRRRRRRRRRRRRRRRRRRRRRRRRRRRRRRRRRRRR
RRRRRRRRRRRRRRRRRRRRRRRRRRRRRRRRRRRRRRRRRRRRRRRR
RRRRRRRRRRRRRRRRRRRRRRRRRRRRRRRRRRRRRRRRRRRRRRRR
RRRRRRRRRRRRRRRRRRRRRRRRRRRRRRRRRRRRRRRRRRRRRRRR
RRRRRRRRRRRRRRRRRRRRRRRRRRRRRRRRRRRRRRRRRRRRRRRR
RRRRRRRRRRRRRRRRRRRRRRRRRRRRRRRRRRRRRRRRRRRRRRRR

RRRRRRRRRRRRRRRRRRRRRRRRRRRRRRRRRRRRRRRRRRRRRR
RRRRRRRRRRRRRRRRRRRRRRRRRRRRRRRRRRRRRRRRRRRRRR
RRRRRRRRRRRRRRRRRRRRRRRRRRRRRRRRRRRRRRRRRRRRRR
RRRRRRRRRRRRRRRRRRRRRRRRRRRRRRRRRRRRRRRRRRRRRR
RRRRRRRRRRRRRRRRRRRRRRRRRRRRRRRRRRRRRRRRRRRRRR
RRRRRRRRRRRRRRRRRRRRRRRRRRRRRRRRRRRRRRRRRRRRRR
RRRRRRRRRRRRRRRRRRRRRRRRRRRRRRRRRRRRRRRRRRRRRR
RRRRRRRRRRRRRRRRRRRRRRRRRRRRRRRRRRRRRRRRRRRRRR
RRRRRRRRRRRRRRRRRRRRRRRRRRRRRRRRRRRRRRRRRRRRRR
RRRRRRRRRRRRRRRRRRRRRRRRRRRRRRRRRRRRRRRRRRRRRR
RRRRRRRRRRRRRRRRRRRRRRRRRRRRRRRRRRRRRRRRRRRRRR
RRRRRRRRRRRRRRRRRRRRRRRRRRRRRRRRRRRRRRRRRRRRRR
RRRRRRRRRRRRRRRRRRRRRRRRRRRRRRRRRRRRRRRRRRRRRR
RRRRRRRRRRRRRRRRRRRRRRRRRRRRRRRRRRRRRRRRRRRRRR
RRRRRRRRRRRRRRRRRRRRRRRRRRRRRRRRRRRRRRRRRRRRRR
RRRRRRRRRRRRRRRRRRRRRRRRRRRRRRRRRRRRRRRRRRRRRR
RRRRRRRRRRRRRRRRRRRRRRRRRRRRRRRRRRRRRRRRRRRRRR
RRRRRRRRRRRRRRRRRRRRRRRRRRRRRRRRRRRRRRRRRRRRRR
RRRRRRRRRRRRRRRRRRRRRRRRRRRRRRRRRRRRRRRRRRRRRR
RRRRRRRRRRRRRRRRRRRRRRRRRRRRRRRRRRRRRRRRRRRRRR
RRRRRRRRRRRRRRRRRRRRRRRRRRRRRRRRRRRRRRRRRRRRRR
RRRRRRRRRRRRRRRRRRRRRRRRRRRRRRRRRRRRRRRRRRRRRR
RRRRRRRRRRRRRRRRRRRRRRRRRRRRRRRRRRRRRRRRRRRRRR
RRRRRRRRRRRRRRRRRRRRRRRRRRRRRRRRRRRRRRRRRRRRRR
RRRRRRRRRRRRRRRRRRRRRRRRRRRRRRRRRRRRRRRRRRRRRR
RRRRRRRRRRRRRRRRRRRRRRRRRRRRRRRRRRRRRRRRRRRRRR
RRRRRRRRRRRRRRRRRRRRRRRRRRRRRRRRRRRRRRRRRRRRRR
RRRRRRRRRRRRRRRRRRRRRRRRRRRRRRRRRRRRRRRRRRRRRR

RRRRRRRRRRRRRRRRRRRRRRRRRRRRRRRRRRRRRRRRRRRRRRR
RRRRRRRRRRRRRRRRRRRRRRRRRRRRRRRRRRRRRRRRRRRRRRR
RRRRRRRRRRRRRRRRRRRRRRRRRRRRRRRRRRRRRRRRRRRRRRR
RRRRRRRRRRRRRRRRRRRRRRRRRRRRRRRRRRRRRRRRRRRRRRR
RRRRRRRRRRRRRRRRRRRRRRRRRRRRRRRRRRRRRRRRRRRRRRR
RRRRRRRRRRRRRRRRRRRRRRRRRRRRRRRRRRRRRRRRRRRRRRR
RRRRRRRRRRRRRRRRRRRRRRRRRRRRRRRRRRRRRRRRRRRRRRR
RRRRRRRRRRRRRRRRRRRRRRRRRRRRRRRRRRRRRRRRRRRRRRR
RRRRRRRRRRRRRRRRRRRRRRRRRRRRRRRRRRRRRRRRRRRRRRR
RRRRRRRRRRRRRRRRRRRRRRRRRRRRRRRRRRRRRRRRRRRRRRR
RRRRRRRRRRRRRRRRRRRRRRRRRRRRRRRRRRRRRRRRRRRRRRR
RRRRRRRRRRRRRRRRRRRRRRRRRRRRRRRRRRRRRRRRRRRRRRR
RRRRRRRRRRRRRRRRRRRRRRRRRRRRRRRRRRRRRRRRRRRRRRR
RRRRRRRRRRRRRRRRRRRRRRRRRRRRRRRRRRRRRRRRRRRRRRR
RRRRRRRRRRRRRRRRRRRRRRRRRRRRRRRRRRRRRRRRRRRRRRR
RRRRRRRRRRRRRRRRRRRRRRRRRRRRRRRRRRRRRRRRRRRRRRR
RRRRRRRRRRRRRRRRRRRRRRRRRRRRRRRRRRRRRRRRRRRRRRR
RRRRRRRRRRRRRRRRRRRRRRRRRRRRRRRRRRRRRRRRRRRRRRR
RRRRRRRRRRRRRRRRRRRRRRRRRRRRRRRRRRRRRRRRRRRRRRR
RRRRRRRRRRRRRRRRRRRRRRRRRRRRRRRRRRRRRRRRRRRRRRR
RRRRRRRRRRRRRRRRRRRRRRRRRRRRRRRRRRRRRRRRRRRRRRR
RRRRRRRRRRRRRRRRRRRRRRRRRRRRRRRRRRRRRRRRRRRRRRR
RRRRRRRRRRRRRRRRRRRRRRRRRRRRRRRRRRRRRRRRRRRRRRR
RRRRRRRRRRRRRRRRRRRRRRRRRRRRRRRRRRRRRRRRRRRRRRR
RRRRRRRRRRRRRRRRRRRRRRRRRRRRRRRRRRRRRRRRRRRRRRR
RRRRRRRRRRRRRRRRRRRRRRRRRRRRRRRRRRRRRRRRRRRRRRR

RRRRRRRRRRRRRRRRRRRRRRRRRRRRRRRRRRRRRRRRRRRRR
RRRRRRRRRRRRRRRRRRRRRRRRRRRRRRRRRRRRRRRRRRRRR
RRRRRRRRRRRRRRRRRRRRRRRRRRRRRRRRRRRRRRRRRRRRR
RRRRRRRRRRRRRRRRRRRRRRRRRRRRRRRRRRRRRRRRRRRRR
RRRRRRRRRRRRRRRRRRRRRRRRRRRRRRRRRRRRRRRRRRRRR
RRRRRRRRRRRRRRRRRRRRRRRRRRRRRRRRRRRRRRRRRRRRR
RRRRRRRRRRRRRRRRRRRRRRRRRRRRRRRRRRRRRRRRRRRRR
RRRRRRRRRRRRRRRRRRRRRRRRRRRRRRRRRRRRRRRRRRRRR
RRRRRRRRRRRRRRRRRRRRRRRRRRRRRRRRRRRRRRRRRRRRR
RRRRRRRRRRRRRRRRRRRRRRRRRRRRRRRRRRRRRRRRRRRRR
RRRRRRRRRRRRRRRRRRRRRRRRRRRRRRRRRRRRRRRRRRRRR
RRRRRRRRRRRRRRRRRRRRRRRRRRRRRRRRRRRRRRRRRRRRR
RRRRRRRRRRRRRRRRRRRRRRRRRRRRRRRRRRRRRRRRRRRRR
RRRRRRRRRRRRRRRRRRRRRRRRRRRRRRRRRRRRRRRRRRRRR
RRRRRRRRRRRRRRRRRRRRRRRRRRRRRRRRRRRRRRRRRRRRR
RRRRRRRRRRRRRRRRRRRRRRRRRRRRRRRRRRRRRRRRRRRRR
RRRRRRRRRRRRRRRRRRRRRRRRRRRRRRRRRRRRRRRRRRRRR
RRRRRRRRRRRRRRRRRRRRRRRRRRRRRRRRRRRRRRRRRRRRR
RRRRRRRRRRRRRRRRRRRRRRRRRRRRRRRRRRRRRRRRRRRRR
RRRRRRRRRRRRRRRRRRRRRRRRRRRRRRRRRRRRRRRRRRRRR
RRRRRRRRRRRRRRRRRRRRRRRRRRRRRRRRRRRRRRRRRRRRR
RRRRRRRRRRRRRRRRRRRRRRRRRRRRRRRRRRRRRRRRRRRRR
RRRRRRRRRRRRRRRRRRRRRRRRRRRRRRRRRRRRRRRRRRRRR
RRRRRRRRRRRRRRRRRRRRRRRRRRRRRRRRRRRRRRRRRRRRR
RRRRRRRRRRRRRRRRRRRRRRRRRRRRRRRRRRRRRRRRRRRRR
RRRRRRRRRRRRRRRRRRRRRRRRRRRRRRRRRRRRRRRRRRRRR

RRRRRRRRRRRRRRRRRRRRRRRRRRRRRRRRRRRRRRRRRRRRRRR
RRRRRRRRRRRRRRRRRRRRRRRRRRRRRRRRRRRRRRRRRRRRRRR
RRRRRRRRRRRRRRRRRRRRRRRRRRRRRRRRRRRRRRRRRRRRRRR
RRRRRRRRRRRRRRRRRRRRRRRRRRRRRRRRRRRRRRRRRRRRRRR
RRRRRRRRRRRRRRRRRRRRRRRRRRRRRRRRRRRRRRRRRRRRRRR
RRRRRRRRRRRRRRRRRRRRRRRRRRRRRRRRRRRRRRRRRRRRRRR
RRRRRRRRRRRRRRRRRRRRRRRRRRRRRRRRRRRRRRRRRRRRRRR
RRRRRRRRRRRRRRRRRRRRRRRRRRRRRRRRRRRRRRRRRRRRRRR
RRRRRRRRRRRRRRRRRRRRRRRRRRRRRRRRRRRRRRRRRRRRRRR
RRRRRRRRRRRRRRRRRRRRRRRRRRRRRRRRRRRRRRRRRRRRRRR
RRRRRRRRRRRRRRRRRRRRRRRRRRRRRRRRRRRRRRRRRRRRRRR
RRRRRRRRRRRRRRRRRRRRRRRRRRRRRRRRRRRRRRRRRRRRRRR
RRRRRRRRRRRRRRRRRRRRRRRRRRRRRRRRRRRRRRRRRRRRRRR
RRRRRRRRRRRRRRRRRRRRRRRRRRRRRRRRRRRRRRRRRRRRRRR
RRRRRRRRRRRRRRRRRRRRRRRRRRRRRRRRRRRRRRRRRRRRRRR
RRRRRRRRRRRRRRRRRRRRRRRRRRRRRRRRRRRRRRRRRRRRRRR
RRRRRRRRRRRRRRRRRRRRRRRRRRRRRRRRRRRRRRRRRRRRRRR
RRRRRRRRRRRRRRRRRRRRRRRRRRRRRRRRRRRRRRRRRRRRRRR
RRRRRRRRRRRRRRRRRRRRRRRRRRRRRRRRRRRRRRRRRRRRRRR
RRRRRRRRRRRRRRRRRRRRRRRRRRRRRRRRRRRRRRRRRRRRRRR
RRRRRRRRRRRRRRRRRRRRRRRRRRRRRRRRRRRRRRRRRRRRRRR
RRRRRRRRRRRRRRRRRRRRRRRRRRRRRRRRRRRRRRRRRRRRRRR
RRRRRRRRRRRRRRRRRRRRRRRRRRRRRRRRRRRRRRRRRRRRRRR
RRRRRRRRRRRRRRRRRRRRRRRRRRRRRRRRRRRRRRRRRRRRRRR
RRRRRRRRRRRRRRRRRRRRRRRRRRRRRRRRRRRRRRRRRRRRRRR
RRRRRRRRRRRRRRRRRRRRRRRRRRRRRRRRRRRRRRRRRRRRRRR

RRRRRRRRRRRRRRRRRRRRRRRRRRRRRRRRRRRRRRRRR
RRRRRRRRRRRRRRRRRRRRRRRRRRRRRRRRRRRRRRRRR
RRRRRRRRRRRRRRRRRRRRRRRRRRRRRRRRRRRRRRRRR
RRRRRRRRRRRRRRRRRRRRRRRRRRRRRRRRRRRRRRRRR
RRRRRRRRRRRRRRRRRRRRRRRRRRRRRRRRRRRRRRRRR
RRRRRRRRRRRRRRRRRRRRRRRRRRRRRRRRRRRRRRRRR
RRRRRRRRRRRRRRRRRRRRRRRRRRRRRRRRRRRRRRRRR
RRRRRRRRRRRRRRRRRRRRRRRRRRRRRRRRRRRRRRRRR
RRRRRRRRRRRRRRRRRRRRRRRRRRRRRRRRRRRRRRRRR
RRRRRRRRRRRRRRRRRRRRRRRRRRRRRRRRRRRRRRRRR
RRRRRRRRRRRRRRRRRRRRRRRRRRRRRRRRRRRRRRRRR
RRRRRRRRRRRRRRRRRRRRRRRRRRRRRRRRRRRRRRRRR
RRRRRRRRRRRRRRRRRRRRRRRRRRRRRRRRRRRRRRRRR
RRRRRRRRRRRRRRRRRRRRRRRRRRRRRRRRRRRRRRRRR
RRRRRRRRRRRRRRRRRRRRRRRRRRRRRRRRRRRRRRRRR
RRRRRRRRRRRRRRRRRRRRRRRRRRRRRRRRRRRRRRRRR
RRRRRRRRRRRRRRRRRRRRRRRRRRRRRRRRRRRRRRRRR
RRRRRRRRRRRRRRRRRRRRRRRRRRRRRRRRRRRRRRRRR
RRRRRRRRRRRRRRRRRRRRRRRRRRRRRRRRRRRRRRRRR
RRRRRRRRRRRRRRRRRRRRRRRRRRRRRRRRRRRRRRRRR
RRRRRRRRRRRRRRRRRRRRRRRRRRRRRRRRRRRRRRRRR
RRRRRRRRRRRRRRRRRRRRRRRRRRRRRRRRRRRRRRRRR
RRRRRRRRRRRRRRRRRRRRRRRRRRRRRRRRRRRRRRRRR
RRRRRRRRRRRRRRRRRRRRRRRRRRRRRRRRRRRRRRRRR
RRRRRRRRRRRRRRRRRRRRRRRRRRRRRRRRRRRRRRRRR
RRRRRRRRRRRRRRRRRRRRRRRRRRRRRRRRRRRRRRRRR

RRRRRRRRRRRRRRRRRRRRRRRRRRRRRRRRRRRRRRRRRRRRRR
RRRRRRRRRRRRRRRRRRRRRRRRRRRRRRRRRRRRRRRRRRRRRR
RRRRRRRRRRRRRRRRRRRRRRRRRRRRRRRRRRRRRRRRRRRRRR
RRRRRRRRRRRRRRRRRRRRRRRRRRRRRRRRRRRRRRRRRRRRRR
RRRRRRRRRRRRRRRRRRRRRRRRRRRRRRRRRRRRRRRRRRRRRR
RRRRRRRRRRRRRRRRRRRRRRRRRRRRRRRRRRRRRRRRRRRRRR
RRRRRRRRRRRRRRRRRRRRRRRRRRRRRRRRRRRRRRRRRRRRRR
RRRRRRRRRRRRRRRRRRRRRRRRRRRRRRRRRRRRRRRRRRRRRR
RRRRRRRRRRRRRRRRRRRRRRRRRRRRRRRRRRRRRRRRRRRRRR
RRRRRRRRRRRRRRRRRRRRRRRRRRRRRRRRRRRRRRRRRRRRRR
RRRRRRRRRRRRRRRRRRRRRRRRRRRRRRRRRRRRRRRRRRRRRR
RRRRRRRRRRRRRRRRRRRRRRRRRRRRRRRRRRRRRRRRRRRRRR
RRRRRRRRRRRRRRRRRRRRRRRRRRRRRRRRRRRRRRRRRRRRRR
RRRRRRRRRRRRRRRRRRRRRRRRRRRRRRRRRRRRRRRRRRRRRR
RRRRRRRRRRRRRRRRRRRRRRRRRRRRRRRRRRRRRRRRRRRRRR
RRRRRRRRRRRRRRRRRRRRRRRRRRRRRRRRRRRRRRRRRRRRRR
RRRRRRRRRRRRRRRRRRRRRRRRRRRRRRRRRRRRRRRRRRRRRR
RRRRRRRRRRRRRRRRRRRRRRRRRRRRRRRRRRRRRRRRRRRRRR
RRRRRRRRRRRRRRRRRRRRRRRRRRRRRRRRRRRRRRRRRRRRRR
RRRRRRRRRRRRRRRRRRRRRRRRRRRRRRRRRRRRRRRRRRRRRR
RRRRRRRRRRRRRRRRRRRRRRRRRRRRRRRRRRRRRRRRRRRRRR
RRRRRRRRRRRRRRRRRRRRRRRRRRRRRRRRRRRRRRRRRRRRRR
RRRRRRRRRRRRRRRRRRRRRRRRRRRRRRRRRRRRRRRRRRRRRR
RRRRRRRRRRRRRRRRRRRRRRRRRRRRRRRRRRRRRRRRRRRRRR
RRRRRRRRRRRRRRRRRRRRRRRRRRRRRRRRRRRRRRRRRRRRRR
RRRRRRRRRRRRRRRRRRRRRRRRRRRRRRRRRRRRRRRRRRRRRR
RRRRRRRRRRRRRRRRRRRRRRRRRRRRRRRRRRRRRRRRRRRRRR

RRRRRRRRRRRRRRRRRRRRRRRRRRRRRRRRRRRRRRRRRRRRR
RRRRRRRRRRRRRRRRRRRRRRRRRRRRRRRRRRRRRRRRRRRRR
RRRRRRRRRRRRRRRRRRRRRRRRRRRRRRRRRRRRRRRRRRRRR
RRRRRRRRRRRRRRRRRRRRRRRRRRRRRRRRRRRRRRRRRRRRR
RRRRRRRRRRRRRRRRRRRRRRRRRRRRRRRRRRRRRRRRRRRRR
RRRRRRRRRRRRRRRRRRRRRRRRRRRRRRRRRRRRRRRRRRRRR
RRRRRRRRRRRRRRRRRRRRRRRRRRRRRRRRRRRRRRRRRRRRR
RRRRRRRRRRRRRRRRRRRRRRRRRRRRRRRRRRRRRRRRRRRRR
RRRRRRRRRRRRRRRRRRRRRRRRRRRRRRRRRRRRRRRRRRRRR
RRRRRRRRRRRRRRRRRRRRRRRRRRRRRRRRRRRRRRRRRRRRR
RRRRRRRRRRRRRRRRRRRRRRRRRRRRRRRRRRRRRRRRRRRRR
RRRRRRRRRRRRRRRRRRRRRRRRRRRRRRRRRRRRRRRRRRRRR
RRRRRRRRRRRRRRRRRRRRRRRRRRRRRRRRRRRRRRRRRRRRR
RRRRRRRRRRRRRRRRRRRRRRRRRRRRRRRRRRRRRRRRRRRRR
RRRRRRRRRRRRRRRRRRRRRRRRRRRRRRRRRRRRRRRRRRRRR
RRRRRRRRRRRRRRRRRRRRRRRRRRRRRRRRRRRRRRRRRRRRR
RRRRRRRRRRRRRRRRRRRRRRRRRRRRRRRRRRRRRRRRRRRRR
RRRRRRRRRRRRRRRRRRRRRRRRRRRRRRRRRRRRRRRRRRRRR
RRRRRRRRRRRRRRRRRRRRRRRRRRRRRRRRRRRRRRRRRRRRR
RRRRRRRRRRRRRRRRRRRRRRRRRRRRRRRRRRRRRRRRRRRRR
RRRRRRRRRRRRRRRRRRRRRRRRRRRRRRRRRRRRRRRRRRRRR
RRRRRRRRRRRRRRRRRRRRRRRRRRRRRRRRRRRRRRRRRRRRR
RRRRRRRRRRRRRRRRRRRRRRRRRRRRRRRRRRRRRRRRRRRRR
RRRRRRRRRRRRRRRRRRRRRRRRRRRRRRRRRRRRRRRRRRRRR
RRRRRRRRRRRRRRRRRRRRRRRRRRRRRRRRRRRRRRRRRRRRR
RRRRRRRRRRRRRRRRRRRRRRRRRRRRRRRRRRRRRRRRRRRRR
RRRRRRRRRRRRRRRRRRRRRRRRRRRRRRRRRRRRRRRRRRRRR

RRRRRRRRRRRRRRRRRRRRRRRRRRRRRRRRRRRRRRRRRRRRRRRR
RRRRRRRRRRRRRRRRRRRRRRRRRRRRRRRRRRRRRRRRRRRRRRRR
RRRRRRRRRRRRRRRRRRRRRRRRRRRRRRRRRRRRRRRRRRRRRRRR
RRRRRRRRRRRRRRRRRRRRRRRRRRRRRRRRRRRRRRRRRRRRRRRR
RRRRRRRRRRRRRRRRRRRRRRRRRRRRRRRRRRRRRRRRRRRRRRRR
RRRRRRRRRRRRRRRRRRRRRRRRRRRRRRRRRRRRRRRRRRRRRRRR
RRRRRRRRRRRRRRRRRRRRRRRRRRRRRRRRRRRRRRRRRRRRRRRR
RRRRRRRRRRRRRRRRRRRRRRRRRRRRRRRRRRRRRRRRRRRRRRRR
RRRRRRRRRRRRRRRRRRRRRRRRRRRRRRRRRRRRRRRRRRRRRRRR
RRRRRRRRRRRRRRRRRRRRRRRRRRRRRRRRRRRRRRRRRRRRRRRR
RRRRRRRRRRRRRRRRRRRRRRRRRRRRRRRRRRRRRRRRRRRRRRRR
RRRRRRRRRRRRRRRRRRRRRRRRRRRRRRRRRRRRRRRRRRRRRRRR
RRRRRRRRRRRRRRRRRRRRRRRRRRRRRRRRRRRRRRRRRRRRRRRR
RRRRRRRRRRRRRRRRRRRRRRRRRRRRRRRRRRRRRRRRRRRRRRRR
RRRRRRRRRRRRRRRRRRRRRRRRRRRRRRRRRRRRRRRRRRRRRRRR
RRRRRRRRRRRRRRRRRRRRRRRRRRRRRRRRRRRRRRRRRRRRRRRR
RRRRRRRRRRRRRRRRRRRRRRRRRRRRRRRRRRRRRRRRRRRRRRRR
RRRRRRRRRRRRRRRRRRRRRRRRRRRRRRRRRRRRRRRRRRRRRRRR
RRRRRRRRRRRRRRRRRRRRRRRRRRRRRRRRRRRRRRRRRRRRRRRR
RRRRRRRRRRRRRRRRRRRRRRRRRRRRRRRRRRRRRRRRRRRRRRRR
RRRRRRRRRRRRRRRRRRRRRRRRRRRRRRRRRRRRRRRRRRRRRRRR
RRRRRRRRRRRRRRRRRRRRRRRRRRRRRRRRRRRRRRRRRRRRRRRR
RRRRRRRRRRRRRRRRRRRRRRRRRRRRRRRRRRRRRRRRRRRRRRRR
RRRRRRRRRRRRRRRRRRRRRRRRRRRRRRRRRRRRRRRRRRRRRRRR
RRRRRRRRRRRRRRRRRRRRRRRRRRRRRRRRRRRRRRRRRRRRRRRR
RRRRRRRRRRRRRRRRRRRRRRRRRRRRRRRRRRRRRRRRRRRRRRRR
RRRRRRRRRRRRRRRRRRRRRRRRRRRRRRRRRRRRRRRRRRRRRRRR

RRRRRRRRRRRRRRRRRRRRRRRRRRRRRRRRRRRRRRRRRRRRRR
RRRRRRRRRRRRRRRRRRRRRRRRRRRRRRRRRRRRRRRRRRRRRR
RRRRRRRRRRRRRRRRRRRRRRRRRRRRRRRRRRRRRRRRRRRRRR
RRRRRRRRRRRRRRRRRRRRRRRRRRRRRRRRRRRRRRRRRRRRRR
RRRRRRRRRRRRRRRRRRRRRRRRRRRRRRRRRRRRRRRRRRRRRR
RRRRRRRRRRRRRRRRRRRRRRRRRRRRRRRRRRRRRRRRRRRRRR
RRRRRRRRRRRRRRRRRRRRRRRRRRRRRRRRRRRRRRRRRRRRRR
RRRRRRRRRRRRRRRRRRRRRRRRRRRRRRRRRRRRRRRRRRRRRR
RRRRRRRRRRRRRRRRRRRRRRRRRRRRRRRRRRRRRRRRRRRRRR
RRRRRRRRRRRRRRRRRRRRRRRRRRRRRRRRRRRRRRRRRRRRRR
RRRRRRRRRRRRRRRRRRRRRRRRRRRRRRRRRRRRRRRRRRRRRR
RRRRRRRRRRRRRRRRRRRRRRRRRRRRRRRRRRRRRRRRRRRRRR
RRRRRRRRRRRRRRRRRRRRRRRRRRRRRRRRRRRRRRRRRRRRRR
RRRRRRRRRRRRRRRRRRRRRRRRRRRRRRRRRRRRRRRRRRRRRR
RRRRRRRRRRRRRRRRRRRRRRRRRRRRRRRRRRRRRRRRRRRRRR
RRRRRRRRRRRRRRRRRRRRRRRRRRRRRRRRRRRRRRRRRRRRRR
RRRRRRRRRRRRRRRRRRRRRRRRRRRRRRRRRRRRRRRRRRRRRR
RRRRRRRRRRRRRRRRRRRRRRRRRRRRRRRRRRRRRRRRRRRRRR
RRRRRRRRRRRRRRRRRRRRRRRRRRRRRRRRRRRRRRRRRRRRRR
RRRRRRRRRRRRRRRRRRRRRRRRRRRRRRRRRRRRRRRRRRRRRR
RRRRRRRRRRRRRRRRRRRRRRRRRRRRRRRRRRRRRRRRRRRRRR
RRRRRRRRRRRRRRRRRRRRRRRRRRRRRRRRRRRRRRRRRRRRRR
RRRRRRRRRRRRRRRRRRRRRRRRRRRRRRRRRRRRRRRRRRRRRR
RRRRRRRRRRRRRRRRRRRRRRRRRRRRRRRRRRRRRRRRRRRRRR
RRRRRRRRRRRRRRRRRRRRRRRRRRRRRRRRRRRRRRRRRRRRRR
RRRRRRRRRRRRRRRRRRRRRRRRRRRRRRRRRRRRRRRRRRRRRR
RRRRRRRRRRRRRRRRRRRRRRRRRRRRRRRRRRRRRRRRRRRRRR
RRRRRRRRRRRRRRRRRRRRRRRRRRRRRRRRRRRRRRRRRRRRRR

RRRRRRRRRRRRRRRRRRRRRRRRRRRRRRRRRRRRRRRRR
RRRRRRRRRRRRRRRRRRRRRRRRRRRRRRRRRRRRRRRRR
RRRRRRRRRRRRRRRRRRRRRRRRRRRRRRRRRRRRRRRRR
RRRRRRRRRRRRRRRRRRRRRRRRRRRRRRRRRRRRRRRRR
RRRRRRRRRRRRRRRRRRRRRRRRRRRRRRRRRRRRRRRRR
RRRRRRRRRRRRRRRRRRRRRRRRRRRRRRRRRRRRRRRRR
RRRRRRRRRRRRRRRRRRRRRRRRRRRRRRRRRRRRRRRRR
RRRRRRRRRRRRRRRRRRRRRRRRRRRRRRRRRRRRRRRRR
RRRRRRRRRRRRRRRRRRRRRRRRRRRRRRRRRRRRRRRRR
RRRRRRRRRRRRRRRRRRRRRRRRRRRRRRRRRRRRRRRRR
RRRRRRRRRRRRRRRRRRRRRRRRRRRRRRRRRRRRRRRRR
RRRRRRRRRRRRRRRRRRRRRRRRRRRRRRRRRRRRRRRRR
RRRRRRRRRRRRRRRRRRRRRRRRRRRRRRRRRRRRRRRRR
RRRRRRRRRRRRRRRRRRRRRRRRRRRRRRRRRRRRRRRRR
RRRRRRRRRRRRRRRRRRRRRRRRRRRRRRRRRRRRRRRRR
RRRRRRRRRRRRRRRRRRRRRRRRRRRRRRRRRRRRRRRRR
RRRRRRRRRRRRRRRRRRRRRRRRRRRRRRRRRRRRRRRRR
RRRRRRRRRRRRRRRRRRRRRRRRRRRRRRRRRRRRRRRRR
RRRRRRRRRRRRRRRRRRRRRRRRRRRRRRRRRRRRRRRRR
RRRRRRRRRRRRRRRRRRRRRRRRRRRRRRRRRRRRRRRRR
RRRRRRRRRRRRRRRRRRRRRRRRRRRRRRRRRRRRRRRRR
RRRRRRRRRRRRRRRRRRRRRRRRRRRRRRRRRRRRRRRRR
RRRRRRRRRRRRRRRRRRRRRRRRRRRRRRRRRRRRRRRRR
RRRRRRRRRRRRRRRRRRRRRRRRRRRRRRRRRRRRRRRRR
RRRRRRRRRRRRRRRRRRRRRRRRRRRRRRRRRRRRRRRRR
RRRRRRRRRRRRRRRRRRRRRRRRRRRRRRRRRRRRRRRRR
RRRRRRRRRRRRRRRRRRRRRRRRRRRRRRRRRRRRRRRRR
RRRRRRRRRRRRRRRRRRRRRRRRRRRRRRRRRRRRRRRRR
RRRRRRRRRRRRRRRRRRRRRRRRRRRRRRRRRRRRRRRRR

RRRRRRRRRRRRRRRRRRRRRRRRRRRRRRRRRRRRRRRRRRRRRR
RRRRRRRRRRRRRRRRRRRRRRRRRRRRRRRRRRRRRRRRRRRRRR
RRRRRRRRRRRRRRRRRRRRRRRRRRRRRRRRRRRRRRRRRRRRRR
RRRRRRRRRRRRRRRRRRRRRRRRRRRRRRRRRRRRRRRRRRRRRR
RRRRRRRRRRRRRRRRRRRRRRRRRRRRRRRRRRRRRRRRRRRRRR
RRRRRRRRRRRRRRRRRRRRRRRRRRRRRRRRRRRRRRRRRRRRRR
RRRRRRRRRRRRRRRRRRRRRRRRRRRRRRRRRRRRRRRRRRRRRR
RRRRRRRRRRRRRRRRRRRRRRRRRRRRRRRRRRRRRRRRRRRRRR
RRRRRRRRRRRRRRRRRRRRRRRRRRRRRRRRRRRRRRRRRRRRRR
RRRRRRRRRRRRRRRRRRRRRRRRRRRRRRRRRRRRRRRRRRRRRR
RRRRRRRRRRRRRRRRRRRRRRRRRRRRRRRRRRRRRRRRRRRRRR
RRRRRRRRRRRRRRRRRRRRRRRRRRRRRRRRRRRRRRRRRRRRRR
RRRRRRRRRRRRRRRRRRRRRRRRRRRRRRRRRRRRRRRRRRRRRR
RRRRRRRRRRRRRRRRRRRRRRRRRRRRRRRRRRRRRRRRRRRRRR
RRRRRRRRRRRRRRRRRRRRRRRRRRRRRRRRRRRRRRRRRRRRRR
RRRRRRRRRRRRRRRRRRRRRRRRRRRRRRRRRRRRRRRRRRRRRR
RRRRRRRRRRRRRRRRRRRRRRRRRRRRRRRRRRRRRRRRRRRRRR
RRRRRRRRRRRRRRRRRRRRRRRRRRRRRRRRRRRRRRRRRRRRRR
RRRRRRRRRRRRRRRRRRRRRRRRRRRRRRRRRRRRRRRRRRRRRR
RRRRRRRRRRRRRRRRRRRRRRRRRRRRRRRRRRRRRRRRRRRRRR
RRRRRRRRRRRRRRRRRRRRRRRRRRRRRRRRRRRRRRRRRRRRRR
RRRRRRRRRRRRRRRRRRRRRRRRRRRRRRRRRRRRRRRRRRRRRR
RRRRRRRRRRRRRRRRRRRRRRRRRRRRRRRRRRRRRRRRRRRRRR
RRRRRRRRRRRRRRRRRRRRRRRRRRRRRRRRRRRRRRRRRRRRRR
RRRRRRRRRRRRRRRRRRRRRRRRRRRRRRRRRRRRRRRRRRRRRR
RRRRRRRRRRRRRRRRRRRRRRRRRRRRRRRRRRRRRRRRRRRRRR
RRRRRRRRRRRRRRRRRRRRRRRRRRRRRRRRRRRRRRRRRRRRRR

RRRRRRRRRRRRRRRRRRRRRRRRRRRRRRRRRRRRRRRRRRRRRR
RRRRRRRRRRRRRRRRRRRRRRRRRRRRRRRRRRRRRRRRRRRRRR
RRRRRRRRRRRRRRRRRRRRRRRRRRRRRRRRRRRRRRRRRRRRRR
RRRRRRRRRRRRRRRRRRRRRRRRRRRRRRRRRRRRRRRRRRRRRR
RRRRRRRRRRRRRRRRRRRRRRRRRRRRRRRRRRRRRRRRRRRRRR
RRRRRRRRRRRRRRRRRRRRRRRRRRRRRRRRRRRRRRRRRRRRRR
RRRRRRRRRRRRRRRRRRRRRRRRRRRRRRRRRRRRRRRRRRRRRR
RRRRRRRRRRRRRRRRRRRRRRRRRRRRRRRRRRRRRRRRRRRRRR
RRRRRRRRRRRRRRRRRRRRRRRRRRRRRRRRRRRRRRRRRRRRRR
RRRRRRRRRRRRRRRRRRRRRRRRRRRRRRRRRRRRRRRRRRRRRR
RRRRRRRRRRRRRRRRRRRRRRRRRRRRRRRRRRRRRRRRRRRRRR
RRRRRRRRRRRRRRRRRRRRRRRRRRRRRRRRRRRRRRRRRRRRRR
RRRRRRRRRRRRRRRRRRRRRRRRRRRRRRRRRRRRRRRRRRRRRR
RRRRRRRRRRRRRRRRRRRRRRRRRRRRRRRRRRRRRRRRRRRRRR
RRRRRRRRRRRRRRRRRRRRRRRRRRRRRRRRRRRRRRRRRRRRRR
RRRRRRRRRRRRRRRRRRRRRRRRRRRRRRRRRRRRRRRRRRRRRR
RRRRRRRRRRRRRRRRRRRRRRRRRRRRRRRRRRRRRRRRRRRRRR
RRRRRRRRRRRRRRRRRRRRRRRRRRRRRRRRRRRRRRRRRRRRRR
RRRRRRRRRRRRRRRRRRRRRRRRRRRRRRRRRRRRRRRRRRRRRR
RRRRRRRRRRRRRRRRRRRRRRRRRRRRRRRRRRRRRRRRRRRRRR
RRRRRRRRRRRRRRRRRRRRRRRRRRRRRRRRRRRRRRRRRRRRRR
RRRRRRRRRRRRRRRRRRRRRRRRRRRRRRRRRRRRRRRRRRRRRR
RRRRRRRRRRRRRRRRRRRRRRRRRRRRRRRRRRRRRRRRRRRRRR
RRRRRRRRRRRRRRRRRRRRRRRRRRRRRRRRRRRRRRRRRRRRRR
RRRRRRRRRRRRRRRRRRRRRRRRRRRRRRRRRRRRRRRRRRRRRR
RRRRRRRRRRRRRRRRRRRRRRRRRRRRRRRRRRRRRRRRRRRRRR
RRRRRRRRRRRRRRRRRRRRRRRRRRRRRRRRRRRRRRRRRRRRRR

RRRRRRRRRRRRRRRRRRRRRRRRRRRRRRRRRRRRRRRRRRRRR
RRRRRRRRRRRRRRRRRRRRRRRRRRRRRRRRRRRRRRRRRRRRR
RRRRRRRRRRRRRRRRRRRRRRRRRRRRRRRRRRRRRRRRRRRRR
RRRRRRRRRRRRRRRRRRRRRRRRRRRRRRRRRRRRRRRRRRRRR
RRRRRRRRRRRRRRRRRRRRRRRRRRRRRRRRRRRRRRRRRRRRR
RRRRRRRRRRRRRRRRRRRRRRRRRRRRRRRRRRRRRRRRRRRRR
RRRRRRRRRRRRRRRRRRRRRRRRRRRRRRRRRRRRRRRRRRRRR
RRRRRRRRRRRRRRRRRRRRRRRRRRRRRRRRRRRRRRRRRRRRR
RRRRRRRRRRRRRRRRRRRRRRRRRRRRRRRRRRRRRRRRRRRRR
RRRRRRRRRRRRRRRRRRRRRRRRRRRRRRRRRRRRRRRRRRRRR
RRRRRRRRRRRRRRRRRRRRRRRRRRRRRRRRRRRRRRRRRRRRR
RRRRRRRRRRRRRRRRRRRRRRRRRRRRRRRRRRRRRRRRRRRRR
RRRRRRRRRRRRRRRRRRRRRRRRRRRRRRRRRRRRRRRRRRRRR
RRRRRRRRRRRRRRRRRRRRRRRRRRRRRRRRRRRRRRRRRRRRR
RRRRRRRRRRRRRRRRRRRRRRRRRRRRRRRRRRRRRRRRRRRRR
RRRRRRRRRRRRRRRRRRRRRRRRRRRRRRRRRRRRRRRRRRRRR
RRRRRRRRRRRRRRRRRRRRRRRRRRRRRRRRRRRRRRRRRRRRR
RRRRRRRRRRRRRRRRRRRRRRRRRRRRRRRRRRRRRRRRRRRRR
RRRRRRRRRRRRRRRRRRRRRRRRRRRRRRRRRRRRRRRRRRRRR
RRRRRRRRRRRRRRRRRRRRRRRRRRRRRRRRRRRRRRRRRRRRR
RRRRRRRRRRRRRRRRRRRRRRRRRRRRRRRRRRRRRRRRRRRRR
RRRRRRRRRRRRRRRRRRRRRRRRRRRRRRRRRRRRRRRRRRRRR
RRRRRRRRRRRRRRRRRRRRRRRRRRRRRRRRRRRRRRRRRRRRR
RRRRRRRRRRRRRRRRRRRRRRRRRRRRRRRRRRRRRRRRRRRRR
RRRRRRRRRRRRRRRRRRRRRRRRRRRRRRRRRRRRRRRRRRRRR
RRRRRRRRRRRRRRRRRRRRRRRRRRRRRRRRRRRRRRRRRRRRR
RRRRRRRRRRRRRRRRRRRRRRRRRRRRRRRRRRRRRRRRRRRRR

RRRRRRRRRRRRRRRRRRRRRRRRRRRRRRRRRRRRRRRRRRRRR
RRRRRRRRRRRRRRRRRRRRRRRRRRRRRRRRRRRRRRRRRRRRR
RRRRRRRRRRRRRRRRRRRRRRRRRRRRRRRRRRRRRRRRRRRRR
RRRRRRRRRRRRRRRRRRRRRRRRRRRRRRRRRRRRRRRRRRRRR
RRRRRRRRRRRRRRRRRRRRRRRRRRRRRRRRRRRRRRRRRRRRR
RRRRRRRRRRRRRRRRRRRRRRRRRRRRRRRRRRRRRRRRRRRRR
RRRRRRRRRRRRRRRRRRRRRRRRRRRRRRRRRRRRRRRRRRRRR
RRRRRRRRRRRRRRRRRRRRRRRRRRRRRRRRRRRRRRRRRRRRR
RRRRRRRRRRRRRRRRRRRRRRRRRRRRRRRRRRRRRRRRRRRRR
RRRRRRRRRRRRRRRRRRRRRRRRRRRRRRRRRRRRRRRRRRRRR
RRRRRRRRRRRRRRRRRRRRRRRRRRRRRRRRRRRRRRRRRRRRR
RRRRRRRRRRRRRRRRRRRRRRRRRRRRRRRRRRRRRRRRRRRRR
RRRRRRRRRRRRRRRRRRRRRRRRRRRRRRRRRRRRRRRRRRRRR
RRRRRRRRRRRRRRRRRRRRRRRRRRRRRRRRRRRRRRRRRRRRR
RRRRRRRRRRRRRRRRRRRRRRRRRRRRRRRRRRRRRRRRRRRRR
RRRRRRRRRRRRRRRRRRRRRRRRRRRRRRRRRRRRRRRRRRRRR
RRRRRRRRRRRRRRRRRRRRRRRRRRRRRRRRRRRRRRRRRRRRR
RRRRRRRRRRRRRRRRRRRRRRRRRRRRRRRRRRRRRRRRRRRRR
RRRRRRRRRRRRRRRRRRRRRRRRRRRRRRRRRRRRRRRRRRRRR
RRRRRRRRRRRRRRRRRRRRRRRRRRRRRRRRRRRRRRRRRRRRR
RRRRRRRRRRRRRRRRRRRRRRRRRRRRRRRRRRRRRRRRRRRRR
RRRRRRRRRRRRRRRRRRRRRRRRRRRRRRRRRRRRRRRRRRRRR
RRRRRRRRRRRRRRRRRRRRRRRRRRRRRRRRRRRRRRRRRRRRR
RRRRRRRRRRRRRRRRRRRRRRRRRRRRRRRRRRRRRRRRRRRRR
RRRRRRRRRRRRRRRRRRRRRRRRRRRRRRRRRRRRRRRRRRRRR
RRRRRRRRRRRRRRRRRRRRRRRRRRRRRRRRRRRRRRRRRRRRR
RRRRRRRRRRRRRRRRRRRRRRRRRRRRRRRRRRRRRRRRRRRRR
RRRRRRRRRRRRRRRRRRRRRRRRRRRRRRRRRRRRRRRRRRRRR

RRRRRRRRRRRRRRRRRRRRRRRRRRRRRRRRRRRRRRRR
RRRRRRRRRRRRRRRRRRRRRRRRRRRRRRRRRRRRRRRR
RRRRRRRRRRRRRRRRRRRRRRRRRRRRRRRRRRRRRRRR
RRRRRRRRRRRRRRRRRRRRRRRRRRRRRRRRRRRRRRRR
RRRRRRRRRRRRRRRRRRRRRRRRRRRRRRRRRRRRRRRR
RRRRRRRRRRRRRRRRRRRRRRRRRRRRRRRRRRRRRRRR
RRRRRRRRRRRRRRRRRRRRRRRRRRRRRRRRRRRRRRRR
RRRRRRRRRRRRRRRRRRRRRRRRRRRRRRRRRRRRRRRR
RRRRRRRRRRRRRRRRRRRRRRRRRRRRRRRRRRRRRRRR
RRRRRRRRRRRRRRRRRRRRRRRRRRRRRRRRRRRRRRRR
RRRRRRRRRRRRRRRRRRRRRRRRRRRRRRRRRRRRRRRR
RRRRRRRRRRRRRRRRRRRRRRRRRRRRRRRRRRRRRRRR
RRRRRRRRRRRRRRRRRRRRRRRRRRRRRRRRRRRRRRRR
RRRRRRRRRRRRRRRRRRRRRRRRRRRRRRRRRRRRRRRR
RRRRRRRRRRRRRRRRRRRRRRRRRRRRRRRRRRRRRRRR
RRRRRRRRRRRRRRRRRRRRRRRRRRRRRRRRRRRRRRRR
RRRRRRRRRRRRRRRRRRRRRRRRRRRRRRRRRRRRRRRR
RRRRRRRRRRRRRRRRRRRRRRRRRRRRRRRRRRRRRRRR
RRRRRRRRRRRRRRRRRRRRRRRRRRRRRRRRRRRRRRRR
RRRRRRRRRRRRRRRRRRRRRRRRRRRRRRRRRRRRRRRR
RRRRRRRRRRRRRRRRRRRRRRRRRRRRRRRRRRRRRRRR
RRRRRRRRRRRRRRRRRRRRRRRRRRRRRRRRRRRRRRRR
RRRRRRRRRRRRRRRRRRRRRRRRRRRRRRRRRRRRRRRR
RRRRRRRRRRRRRRRRRRRRRRRRRRRRRRRRRRRRRRRR
RRRRRRRRRRRRRRRRRRRRRRRRRRRRRRRRRRRRRRRR

RRRRRRRRRRRRRRRRRRRRRRRRRRRRRRRRRRRRRRRRRRRRR
RRRRRRRRRRRRRRRRRRRRRRRRRRRRRRRRRRRRRRRRRRRRR
RRRRRRRRRRRRRRRRRRRRRRRRRRRRRRRRRRRRRRRRRRRRR
RRRRRRRRRRRRRRRRRRRRRRRRRRRRRRRRRRRRRRRRRRRRR
RRRRRRRRRRRRRRRRRRRRRRRRRRRRRRRRRRRRRRRRRRRRR
RRRRRRRRRRRRRRRRRRRRRRRRRRRRRRRRRRRRRRRRRRRRR
RRRRRRRRRRRRRRRRRRRRRRRRRRRRRRRRRRRRRRRRRRRRR
RRRRRRRRRRRRRRRRRRRRRRRRRRRRRRRRRRRRRRRRRRRRR
RRRRRRRRRRRRRRRRRRRRRRRRRRRRRRRRRRRRRRRRRRRRR
RRRRRRRRRRRRRRRRRRRRRRRRRRRRRRRRRRRRRRRRRRRRR
RRRRRRRRRRRRRRRRRRRRRRRRRRRRRRRRRRRRRRRRRRRRR
RRRRRRRRRRRRRRRRRRRRRRRRRRRRRRRRRRRRRRRRRRRRR
RRRRRRRRRRRRRRRRRRRRRRRRRRRRRRRRRRRRRRRRRRRRR
RRRRRRRRRRRRRRRRRRRRRRRRRRRRRRRRRRRRRRRRRRRRR
RRRRRRRRRRRRRRRRRRRRRRRRRRRRRRRRRRRRRRRRRRRRR
RRRRRRRRRRRRRRRRRRRRRRRRRRRRRRRRRRRRRRRRRRRRR
RRRRRRRRRRRRRRRRRRRRRRRRRRRRRRRRRRRRRRRRRRRRR
RRRRRRRRRRRRRRRRRRRRRRRRRRRRRRRRRRRRRRRRRRRRR
RRRRRRRRRRRRRRRRRRRRRRRRRRRRRRRRRRRRRRRRRRRRR
RRRRRRRRRRRRRRRRRRRRRRRRRRRRRRRRRRRRRRRRRRRRR
RRRRRRRRRRRRRRRRRRRRRRRRRRRRRRRRRRRRRRRRRRRRR
RRRRRRRRRRRRRRRRRRRRRRRRRRRRRRRRRRRRRRRRRRRRR
RRRRRRRRRRRRRRRRRRRRRRRRRRRRRRRRRRRRRRRRRRRRR
RRRRRRRRRRRRRRRRRRRRRRRRRRRRRRRRRRRRRRRRRRRRR
RRRRRRRRRRRRRRRRRRRRRRRRRRRRRRRRRRRRRRRRRRRRR
RRRRRRRRRRRRRRRRRRRRRRRRRRRRRRRRRRRRRRRRRRRRR
RRRRRRRRRRRRRRRRRRRRRRRRRRRRRRRRRRRRRRRRRRRRR
RRRRRRRRRRRRRRRRRRRRRRRRRRRRRRRRRRRRRRRRRRRRR

RRRRRRRRRRRRRRRRRRRRRRRRRRRRRRRRRRRRRRRR
RRRRRRRRRRRRRRRRRRRRRRRRRRRRRRRRRRRRRRRR
RRRRRRRRRRRRRRRRRRRRRRRRRRRRRRRRRRRRRRRR
RRRRRRRRRRRRRRRRRRRRRRRRRRRRRRRRRRRRRRRR
RRRRRRRRRRRRRRRRRRRRRRRRRRRRRRRRRRRRRRRR
RRRRRRRRRRRRRRRRRRRRRRRRRRRRRRRRRRRRRRRR
RRRRRRRRRRRRRRRRRRRRRRRRRRRRRRRRRRRRRRRR
RRRRRRRRRRRRRRRRRRRRRRRRRRRRRRRRRRRRRRRR
RRRRRRRRRRRRRRRRRRRRRRRRRRRRRRRRRRRRRRRR
RRRRRRRRRRRRRRRRRRRRRRRRRRRRRRRRRRRRRRRR
RRRRRRRRRRRRRRRRRRRRRRRRRRRRRRRRRRRRRRRR
RRRRRRRRRRRRRRRRRRRRRRRRRRRRRRRRRRRRRRRR
RRRRRRRRRRRRRRRRRRRRRRRRRRRRRRRRRRRRRRRR
RRRRRRRRRRRRRRRRRRRRRRRRRRRRRRRRRRRRRRRR
RRRRRRRRRRRRRRRRRRRRRRRRRRRRRRRRRRRRRRRR
RRRRRRRRRRRRRRRRRRRRRRRRRRRRRRRRRRRRRRRR
RRRRRRRRRRRRRRRRRRRRRRRRRRRRRRRRRRRRRRRR
RRRRRRRRRRRRRRRRRRRRRRRRRRRRRRRRRRRRRRRR
RRRRRRRRRRRRRRRRRRRRRRRRRRRRRRRRRRRRRRRR
RRRRRRRRRRRRRRRRRRRRRRRRRRRRRRRRRRRRRRRR
RRRRRRRRRRRRRRRRRRRRRRRRRRRRRRRRRRRRRRRR
RRRRRRRRRRRRRRRRRRRRRRRRRRRRRRRRRRRRRRRR
RRRRRRRRRRRRRRRRRRRRRRRRRRRRRRRRRRRRRRRR
RRRRRRRRRRRRRRRRRRRRRRRRRRRRRRRRRRRRRRRR
RRRRRRRRRRRRRRRRRRRRRRRRRRRRRRRRRRRRRRRR
RRRRRRRRRRRRRRRRRRRRRRRRRRRRRRRRRRRRRRRR
RRRRRRRRRRRRRRRRRRRRRRRRRRRRRRRRRRRRRRRR
RRRRRRRRRRRRRRRRRRRRRRRRRRRRRRRRRRRRRRRR

RRRRRRRRRRRRRRRRRRRRRRRRRRRRRRRRRRRRRRRRRRRRRRRR
RRRRRRRRRRRRRRRRRRRRRRRRRRRRRRRRRRRRRRRRRRRRRRRR
RRRRRRRRRRRRRRRRRRRRRRRRRRRRRRRRRRRRRRRRRRRRRRRR
RRRRRRRRRRRRRRRRRRRRRRRRRRRRRRRRRRRRRRRRRRRRRRRR
RRRRRRRRRRRRRRRRRRRRRRRRRRRRRRRRRRRRRRRRRRRRRRRR
RRRRRRRRRRRRRRRRRRRRRRRRRRRRRRRRRRRRRRRRRRRRRRRR
RRRRRRRRRRRRRRRRRRRRRRRRRRRRRRRRRRRRRRRRRRRRRRRR
RRRRRRRRRRRRRRRRRRRRRRRRRRRRRRRRRRRRRRRRRRRRRRRR
RRRRRRRRRRRRRRRRRRRRRRRRRRRRRRRRRRRRRRRRRRRRRRRR
RRRRRRRRRRRRRRRRRRRRRRRRRRRRRRRRRRRRRRRRRRRRRRRR
RRRRRRRRRRRRRRRRRRRRRRRRRRRRRRRRRRRRRRRRRRRRRRRR
RRRRRRRRRRRRRRRRRRRRRRRRRRRRRRRRRRRRRRRRRRRRRRRR
RRRRRRRRRRRRRRRRRRRRRRRRRRRRRRRRRRRRRRRRRRRRRRRR
RRRRRRRRRRRRRRRRRRRRRRRRRRRRRRRRRRRRRRRRRRRRRRRR
RRRRRRRRRRRRRRRRRRRRRRRRRRRRRRRRRRRRRRRRRRRRRRRR
RRRRRRRRRRRRRRRRRRRRRRRRRRRRRRRRRRRRRRRRRRRRRRRR
RRRRRRRRRRRRRRRRRRRRRRRRRRRRRRRRRRRRRRRRRRRRRRRR
RRRRRRRRRRRRRRRRRRRRRRRRRRRRRRRRRRRRRRRRRRRRRRRR
RRRRRRRRRRRRRRRRRRRRRRRRRRRRRRRRRRRRRRRRRRRRRRRR
RRRRRRRRRRRRRRRRRRRRRRRRRRRRRRRRRRRRRRRRRRRRRRRR
RRRRRRRRRRRRRRRRRRRRRRRRRRRRRRRRRRRRRRRRRRRRRRRR
RRRRRRRRRRRRRRRRRRRRRRRRRRRRRRRRRRRRRRRRRRRRRRRR
RRRRRRRRRRRRRRRRRRRRRRRRRRRRRRRRRRRRRRRRRRRRRRRR
RRRRRRRRRRRRRRRRRRRRRRRRRRRRRRRRRRRRRRRRRRRRRRRR
RRRRRRRRRRRRRRRRRRRRRRRRRRRRRRRRRRRRRRRRRRRRRRRR
RRRRRRRRRRRRRRRRRRRRRRRRRRRRRRRRRRRRRRRRRRRRRRRR
RRRRRRRRRRRRRRRRRRRRRRRRRRRRRRRRRRRRRRRRRRRRRRRR
RRRRRRRRRRRRRRRRRRRRRRRRRRRRRRRRRRRRRRRRRRRRRRRR
RRRRRRRRRRRRRRRRRRRRRRRRRRRRRRRRRRRRRRRRRRRRRRRR

RRRRRRRRRRRRRRRRRRRRRRRRRRRRRRRRRRRRRRRRRRR
RRRRRRRRRRRRRRRRRRRRRRRRRRRRRRRRRRRRRRRRRRR
RRRRRRRRRRRRRRRRRRRRRRRRRRRRRRRRRRRRRRRRRRR
RRRRRRRRRRRRRRRRRRRRRRRRRRRRRRRRRRRRRRRRRRR
RRRRRRRRRRRRRRRRRRRRRRRRRRRRRRRRRRRRRRRRRRR
RRRRRRRRRRRRRRRRRRRRRRRRRRRRRRRRRRRRRRRRRRR
RRRRRRRRRRRRRRRRRRRRRRRRRRRRRRRRRRRRRRRRRRR
RRRRRRRRRRRRRRRRRRRRRRRRRRRRRRRRRRRRRRRRRRR
RRRRRRRRRRRRRRRRRRRRRRRRRRRRRRRRRRRRRRRRRRR
RRRRRRRRRRRRRRRRRRRRRRRRRRRRRRRRRRRRRRRRRRR
RRRRRRRRRRRRRRRRRRRRRRRRRRRRRRRRRRRRRRRRRRR
RRRRRRRRRRRRRRRRRRRRRRRRRRRRRRRRRRRRRRRRRRR
RRRRRRRRRRRRRRRRRRRRRRRRRRRRRRRRRRRRRRRRRRR
RRRRRRRRRRRRRRRRRRRRRRRRRRRRRRRRRRRRRRRRRRR
RRRRRRRRRRRRRRRRRRRRRRRRRRRRRRRRRRRRRRRRRRR
RRRRRRRRRRRRRRRRRRRRRRRRRRRRRRRRRRRRRRRRRRR
RRRRRRRRRRRRRRRRRRRRRRRRRRRRRRRRRRRRRRRRRRR
RRRRRRRRRRRRRRRRRRRRRRRRRRRRRRRRRRRRRRRRRRR
RRRRRRRRRRRRRRRRRRRRRRRRRRRRRRRRRRRRRRRRRRR
RRRRRRRRRRRRRRRRRRRRRRRRRRRRRRRRRRRRRRRRRRR
RRRRRRRRRRRRRRRRRRRRRRRRRRRRRRRRRRRRRRRRRRR
RRRRRRRRRRRRRRRRRRRRRRRRRRRRRRRRRRRRRRRRRRR
RRRRRRRRRRRRRRRRRRRRRRRRRRRRRRRRRRRRRRRRRRR
RRRRRRRRRRRRRRRRRRRRRRRRRRRRRRRRRRRRRRRRRRR
RRRRRRRRRRRRRRRRRRRRRRRRRRRRRRRRRRRRRRRRRRR
RRRRRRRRRRRRRRRRRRRRRRRRRRRRRRRRRRRRRRRRRRR
RRRRRRRRRRRRRRRRRRRRRRRRRRRRRRRRRRRRRRRRRRR
RRRRRRRRRRRRRRRRRRRRRRRRRRRRRRRRRRRRRRRRRRR

RRRRRRRRRRRRRRRRRRRRRRRRRRRRRRRRRRRRRRRRRRRRRRR
RRRRRRRRRRRRRRRRRRRRRRRRRRRRRRRRRRRRRRRRRRRRRRR
RRRRRRRRRRRRRRRRRRRRRRRRRRRRRRRRRRRRRRRRRRRRRRR
RRRRRRRRRRRRRRRRRRRRRRRRRRRRRRRRRRRRRRRRRRRRRRR
RRRRRRRRRRRRRRRRRRRRRRRRRRRRRRRRRRRRRRRRRRRRRRR
RRRRRRRRRRRRRRRRRRRRRRRRRRRRRRRRRRRRRRRRRRRRRRR
RRRRRRRRRRRRRRRRRRRRRRRRRRRRRRRRRRRRRRRRRRRRRRR
RRRRRRRRRRRRRRRRRRRRRRRRRRRRRRRRRRRRRRRRRRRRRRR
RRRRRRRRRRRRRRRRRRRRRRRRRRRRRRRRRRRRRRRRRRRRRRR
RRRRRRRRRRRRRRRRRRRRRRRRRRRRRRRRRRRRRRRRRRRRRRR
RRRRRRRRRRRRRRRRRRRRRRRRRRRRRRRRRRRRRRRRRRRRRRR
RRRRRRRRRRRRRRRRRRRRRRRRRRRRRRRRRRRRRRRRRRRRRRR
RRRRRRRRRRRRRRRRRRRRRRRRRRRRRRRRRRRRRRRRRRRRRRR
RRRRRRRRRRRRRRRRRRRRRRRRRRRRRRRRRRRRRRRRRRRRRRR
RRRRRRRRRRRRRRRRRRRRRRRRRRRRRRRRRRRRRRRRRRRRRRR
RRRRRRRRRRRRRRRRRRRRRRRRRRRRRRRRRRRRRRRRRRRRRRR
RRRRRRRRRRRRRRRRRRRRRRRRRRRRRRRRRRRRRRRRRRRRRRR
RRRRRRRRRRRRRRRRRRRRRRRRRRRRRRRRRRRRRRRRRRRRRRR
RRRRRRRRRRRRRRRRRRRRRRRRRRRRRRRRRRRRRRRRRRRRRRR
RRRRRRRRRRRRRRRRRRRRRRRRRRRRRRRRRRRRRRRRRRRRRRR
RRRRRRRRRRRRRRRRRRRRRRRRRRRRRRRRRRRRRRRRRRRRRRR
RRRRRRRRRRRRRRRRRRRRRRRRRRRRRRRRRRRRRRRRRRRRRRR
RRRRRRRRRRRRRRRRRRRRRRRRRRRRRRRRRRRRRRRRRRRRRRR
RRRRRRRRRRRRRRRRRRRRRRRRRRRRRRRRRRRRRRRRRRRRRRR
RRRRRRRRRRRRRRRRRRRRRRRRRRRRRRRRRRRRRRRRRRRRRRR
RRRRRRRRRRRRRRRRRRRRRRRRRRRRRRRRRRRRRRRRRRRRRRR

RRRRRRRRRRRRRRRRRRRRRRRRRRRRRRRRRRRRRRRRRRRRRRRR
RRRRRRRRRRRRRRRRRRRRRRRRRRRRRRRRRRRRRRRRRRRRRRRR
RRRRRRRRRRRRRRRRRRRRRRRRRRRRRRRRRRRRRRRRRRRRRRRR
RRRRRRRRRRRRRRRRRRRRRRRRRRRRRRRRRRRRRRRRRRRRRRRR
RRRRRRRRRRRRRRRRRRRRRRRRRRRRRRRRRRRRRRRRRRRRRRRR
RRRRRRRRRRRRRRRRRRRRRRRRRRRRRRRRRRRRRRRRRRRRRRRR
RRRRRRRRRRRRRRRRRRRRRRRRRRRRRRRRRRRRRRRRRRRRRRRR
RRRRRRRRRRRRRRRRRRRRRRRRRRRRRRRRRRRRRRRRRRRRRRRR
RRRRRRRRRRRRRRRRRRRRRRRRRRRRRRRRRRRRRRRRRRRRRRRR
RRRRRRRRRRRRRRRRRRRRRRRRRRRRRRRRRRRRRRRRRRRRRRRR
RRRRRRRRRRRRRRRRRRRRRRRRRRRRRRRRRRRRRRRRRRRRRRRR
RRRRRRRRRRRRRRRRRRRRRRRRRRRRRRRRRRRRRRRRRRRRRRRR
RRRRRRRRRRRRRRRRRRRRRRRRRRRRRRRRRRRRRRRRRRRRRRRR
RRRRRRRRRRRRRRRRRRRRRRRRRRRRRRRRRRRRRRRRRRRRRRRR
RRRRRRRRRRRRRRRRRRRRRRRRRRRRRRRRRRRRRRRRRRRRRRRR
RRRRRRRRRRRRRRRRRRRRRRRRRRRRRRRRRRRRRRRRRRRRRRRR
RRRRRRRRRRRRRRRRRRRRRRRRRRRRRRRRRRRRRRRRRRRRRRRR
RRRRRRRRRRRRRRRRRRRRRRRRRRRRRRRRRRRRRRRRRRRRRRRR
RRRRRRRRRRRRRRRRRRRRRRRRRRRRRRRRRRRRRRRRRRRRRRRR
RRRRRRRRRRRRRRRRRRRRRRRRRRRRRRRRRRRRRRRRRRRRRRRR
RRRRRRRRRRRRRRRRRRRRRRRRRRRRRRRRRRRRRRRRRRRRRRRR
RRRRRRRRRRRRRRRRRRRRRRRRRRRRRRRRRRRRRRRRRRRRRRRR
RRRRRRRRRRRRRRRRRRRRRRRRRRRRRRRRRRRRRRRRRRRRRRRR
RRRRRRRRRRRRRRRRRRRRRRRRRRRRRRRRRRRRRRRRRRRRRRRR
RRRRRRRRRRRRRRRRRRRRRRRRRRRRRRRRRRRRRRRRRRRRRRRR
RRRRRRRRRRRRRRRRRRRRRRRRRRRRRRRRRRRRRRRRRRRRRRRR

RRRRRRRRRRRRRRRRRRRRRRRRRRRRRRRRRRRRRRRRRRRRRR
RRRRRRRRRRRRRRRRRRRRRRRRRRRRRRRRRRRRRRRRRRRRRR
RRRRRRRRRRRRRRRRRRRRRRRRRRRRRRRRRRRRRRRRRRRRRR
RRRRRRRRRRRRRRRRRRRRRRRRRRRRRRRRRRRRRRRRRRRRRR
RRRRRRRRRRRRRRRRRRRRRRRRRRRRRRRRRRRRRRRRRRRRRR
RRRRRRRRRRRRRRRRRRRRRRRRRRRRRRRRRRRRRRRRRRRRRR
RRRRRRRRRRRRRRRRRRRRRRRRRRRRRRRRRRRRRRRRRRRRRR
RRRRRRRRRRRRRRRRRRRRRRRRRRRRRRRRRRRRRRRRRRRRRR
RRRRRRRRRRRRRRRRRRRRRRRRRRRRRRRRRRRRRRRRRRRRRR
RRRRRRRRRRRRRRRRRRRRRRRRRRRRRRRRRRRRRRRRRRRRRR
RRRRRRRRRRRRRRRRRRRRRRRRRRRRRRRRRRRRRRRRRRRRRR
RRRRRRRRRRRRRRRRRRRRRRRRRRRRRRRRRRRRRRRRRRRRRR
RRRRRRRRRRRRRRRRRRRRRRRRRRRRRRRRRRRRRRRRRRRRRR
RRRRRRRRRRRRRRRRRRRRRRRRRRRRRRRRRRRRRRRRRRRRRR
RRRRRRRRRRRRRRRRRRRRRRRRRRRRRRRRRRRRRRRRRRRRRR
RRRRRRRRRRRRRRRRRRRRRRRRRRRRRRRRRRRRRRRRRRRRRR
RRRRRRRRRRRRRRRRRRRRRRRRRRRRRRRRRRRRRRRRRRRRRR
RRRRRRRRRRRRRRRRRRRRRRRRRRRRRRRRRRRRRRRRRRRRRR
RRRRRRRRRRRRRRRRRRRRRRRRRRRRRRRRRRRRRRRRRRRRRR
RRRRRRRRRRRRRRRRRRRRRRRRRRRRRRRRRRRRRRRRRRRRRR
RRRRRRRRRRRRRRRRRRRRRRRRRRRRRRRRRRRRRRRRRRRRRR
RRRRRRRRRRRRRRRRRRRRRRRRRRRRRRRRRRRRRRRRRRRRRR
RRRRRRRRRRRRRRRRRRRRRRRRRRRRRRRRRRRRRRRRRRRRRR
RRRRRRRRRRRRRRRRRRRRRRRRRRRRRRRRRRRRRRRRRRRRRR
RRRRRRRRRRRRRRRRRRRRRRRRRRRRRRRRRRRRRRRRRRRRRR
RRRRRRRRRRRRRRRRRRRRRRRRRRRRRRRRRRRRRRRRRRRRRR
RRRRRRRRRRRRRRRRRRRRRRRRRRRRRRRRRRRRRRRRRRRRRR

RRRRRRRRRRRRRRRRRRRRRRRRRRRRRRRRRRRRRRRRRRRRRR
RRRRRRRRRRRRRRRRRRRRRRRRRRRRRRRRRRRRRRRRRRRRRR
RRRRRRRRRRRRRRRRRRRRRRRRRRRRRRRRRRRRRRRRRRRRRR
RRRRRRRRRRRRRRRRRRRRRRRRRRRRRRRRRRRRRRRRRRRRRR
RRRRRRRRRRRRRRRRRRRRRRRRRRRRRRRRRRRRRRRRRRRRRR
RRRRRRRRRRRRRRRRRRRRRRRRRRRRRRRRRRRRRRRRRRRRRR
RRRRRRRRRRRRRRRRRRRRRRRRRRRRRRRRRRRRRRRRRRRRRR
RRRRRRRRRRRRRRRRRRRRRRRRRRRRRRRRRRRRRRRRRRRRRR
RRRRRRRRRRRRRRRRRRRRRRRRRRRRRRRRRRRRRRRRRRRRRR
RRRRRRRRRRRRRRRRRRRRRRRRRRRRRRRRRRRRRRRRRRRRRR
RRRRRRRRRRRRRRRRRRRRRRRRRRRRRRRRRRRRRRRRRRRRRR
RRRRRRRRRRRRRRRRRRRRRRRRRRRRRRRRRRRRRRRRRRRRRR
RRRRRRRRRRRRRRRRRRRRRRRRRRRRRRRRRRRRRRRRRRRRRR
RRRRRRRRRRRRRRRRRRRRRRRRRRRRRRRRRRRRRRRRRRRRRR
RRRRRRRRRRRRRRRRRRRRRRRRRRRRRRRRRRRRRRRRRRRRRR
RRRRRRRRRRRRRRRRRRRRRRRRRRRRRRRRRRRRRRRRRRRRRR
RRRRRRRRRRRRRRRRRRRRRRRRRRRRRRRRRRRRRRRRRRRRRR
RRRRRRRRRRRRRRRRRRRRRRRRRRRRRRRRRRRRRRRRRRRRRR
RRRRRRRRRRRRRRRRRRRRRRRRRRRRRRRRRRRRRRRRRRRRRR
RRRRRRRRRRRRRRRRRRRRRRRRRRRRRRRRRRRRRRRRRRRRRR
RRRRRRRRRRRRRRRRRRRRRRRRRRRRRRRRRRRRRRRRRRRRRR
RRRRRRRRRRRRRRRRRRRRRRRRRRRRRRRRRRRRRRRRRRRRRR
RRRRRRRRRRRRRRRRRRRRRRRRRRRRRRRRRRRRRRRRRRRRRR
RRRRRRRRRRRRRRRRRRRRRRRRRRRRRRRRRRRRRRRRRRRRRR

RRRRRRRRRRRRRRRRRRRRRRRRRRRRRRRRRRRRRRRRRRRRRR
RRRRRRRRRRRRRRRRRRRRRRRRRRRRRRRRRRRRRRRRRRRRRR
RRRRRRRRRRRRRRRRRRRRRRRRRRRRRRRRRRRRRRRRRRRRRR
RRRRRRRRRRRRRRRRRRRRRRRRRRRRRRRRRRRRRRRRRRRRRR
RRRRRRRRRRRRRRRRRRRRRRRRRRRRRRRRRRRRRRRRRRRRRR
RRRRRRRRRRRRRRRRRRRRRRRRRRRRRRRRRRRRRRRRRRRRRR
RRRRRRRRRRRRRRRRRRRRRRRRRRRRRRRRRRRRRRRRRRRRRR
RRRRRRRRRRRRRRRRRRRRRRRRRRRRRRRRRRRRRRRRRRRRRR
RRRRRRRRRRRRRRRRRRRRRRRRRRRRRRRRRRRRRRRRRRRRRR
RRRRRRRRRRRRRRRRRRRRRRRRRRRRRRRRRRRRRRRRRRRRRR
RRRRRRRRRRRRRRRRRRRRRRRRRRRRRRRRRRRRRRRRRRRRRR
RRRRRRRRRRRRRRRRRRRRRRRRRRRRRRRRRRRRRRRRRRRRRR
RRRRRRRRRRRRRRRRRRRRRRRRRRRRRRRRRRRRRRRRRRRRRR
RRRRRRRRRRRRRRRRRRRRRRRRRRRRRRRRRRRRRRRRRRRRRR
RRRRRRRRRRRRRRRRRRRRRRRRRRRRRRRRRRRRRRRRRRRRRR
RRRRRRRRRRRRRRRRRRRRRRRRRRRRRRRRRRRRRRRRRRRRRR
RRRRRRRRRRRRRRRRRRRRRRRRRRRRRRRRRRRRRRRRRRRRRR
RRRRRRRRRRRRRRRRRRRRRRRRRRRRRRRRRRRRRRRRRRRRRR
RRRRRRRRRRRRRRRRRRRRRRRRRRRRRRRRRRRRRRRRRRRRRR
RRRRRRRRRRRRRRRRRRRRRRRRRRRRRRRRRRRRRRRRRRRRRR
RRRRRRRRRRRRRRRRRRRRRRRRRRRRRRRRRRRRRRRRRRRRRR
RRRRRRRRRRRRRRRRRRRRRRRRRRRRRRRRRRRRRRRRRRRRRR
RRRRRRRRRRRRRRRRRRRRRRRRRRRRRRRRRRRRRRRRRRRRRR
RRRRRRRRRRRRRRRRRRRRRRRRRRRRRRRRRRRRRRRRRRRRRR
RRRRRRRRRRRRRRRRRRRRRRRRRRRRRRRRRRRRRRRRRRRRRR
RRRRRRRRRRRRRRRRRRRRRRRRRRRRRRRRRRRRRRRRRRRRRR
RRRRRRRRRRRRRRRRRRRRRRRRRRRRRRRRRRRRRRRRRRRRRR

RRRRRRRRRRRRRRRRRRRRRRRRRRRRRRRRRRRRRRRRRRRRRRRRR
RRRRRRRRRRRRRRRRRRRRRRRRRRRRRRRRRRRRRRRRRRRRRRRRR
RRRRRRRRRRRRRRRRRRRRRRRRRRRRRRRRRRRRRRRRRRRRRRRRR
RRRRRRRRRRRRRRRRRRRRRRRRRRRRRRRRRRRRRRRRRRRRRRRRR
RRRRRRRRRRRRRRRRRRRRRRRRRRRRRRRRRRRRRRRRRRRRRRRRR
RRRRRRRRRRRRRRRRRRRRRRRRRRRRRRRRRRRRRRRRRRRRRRRRR
RRRRRRRRRRRRRRRRRRRRRRRRRRRRRRRRRRRRRRRRRRRRRRRRR
RRRRRRRRRRRRRRRRRRRRRRRRRRRRRRRRRRRRRRRRRRRRRRRRR
RRRRRRRRRRRRRRRRRRRRRRRRRRRRRRRRRRRRRRRRRRRRRRRRR
RRRRRRRRRRRRRRRRRRRRRRRRRRRRRRRRRRRRRRRRRRRRRRRRR
RRRRRRRRRRRRRRRRRRRRRRRRRRRRRRRRRRRRRRRRRRRRRRRRR
RRRRRRRRRRRRRRRRRRRRRRRRRRRRRRRRRRRRRRRRRRRRRRRRR
RRRRRRRRRRRRRRRRRRRRRRRRRRRRRRRRRRRRRRRRRRRRRRRRR
RRRRRRRRRRRRRRRRRRRRRRRRRRRRRRRRRRRRRRRRRRRRRRRRR
RRRRRRRRRRRRRRRRRRRRRRRRRRRRRRRRRRRRRRRRRRRRRRRRR
RRRRRRRRRRRRRRRRRRRRRRRRRRRRRRRRRRRRRRRRRRRRRRRRR
RRRRRRRRRRRRRRRRRRRRRRRRRRRRRRRRRRRRRRRRRRRRRRRRR
RRRRRRRRRRRRRRRRRRRRRRRRRRRRRRRRRRRRRRRRRRRRRRRRR
RRRRRRRRRRRRRRRRRRRRRRRRRRRRRRRRRRRRRRRRRRRRRRRRR
RRRRRRRRRRRRRRRRRRRRRRRRRRRRRRRRRRRRRRRRRRRRRRRRR
RRRRRRRRRRRRRRRRRRRRRRRRRRRRRRRRRRRRRRRRRRRRRRRRR
RRRRRRRRRRRRRRRRRRRRRRRRRRRRRRRRRRRRRRRRRRRRRRRRR
RRRRRRRRRRRRRRRRRRRRRRRRRRRRRRRRRRRRRRRRRRRRRRRRR
RRRRRRRRRRRRRRRRRRRRRRRRRRRRRRRRRRRRRRRRRRRRRRRRR
RRRRRRRRRRRRRRRRRRRRRRRRRRRRRRRRRRRRRRRRRRRRRRRRR
RRRRRRRRRRRRRRRRRRRRRRRRRRRRRRRRRRRRRRRRRRRRRRRRR
RRRRRRRRRRRRRRRRRRRRRRRRRRRRRRRRRRRRRRRRRRRRRRRRR

RRRRRRRRRRRRRRRRRRRRRRRRRRRRRRRRRRRRRRRRRRRRR
RRRRRRRRRRRRRRRRRRRRRRRRRRRRRRRRRRRRRRRRRRRRR
RRRRRRRRRRRRRRRRRRRRRRRRRRRRRRRRRRRRRRRRRRRRR
RRRRRRRRRRRRRRRRRRRRRRRRRRRRRRRRRRRRRRRRRRRRR
RRRRRRRRRRRRRRRRRRRRRRRRRRRRRRRRRRRRRRRRRRRRR
RRRRRRRRRRRRRRRRRRRRRRRRRRRRRRRRRRRRRRRRRRRRR
RRRRRRRRRRRRRRRRRRRRRRRRRRRRRRRRRRRRRRRRRRRRR
RRRRRRRRRRRRRRRRRRRRRRRRRRRRRRRRRRRRRRRRRRRRR
RRRRRRRRRRRRRRRRRRRRRRRRRRRRRRRRRRRRRRRRRRRRR
RRRRRRRRRRRRRRRRRRRRRRRRRRRRRRRRRRRRRRRRRRRRR
RRRRRRRRRRRRRRRRRRRRRRRRRRRRRRRRRRRRRRRRRRRRR
RRRRRRRRRRRRRRRRRRRRRRRRRRRRRRRRRRRRRRRRRRRRR
RRRRRRRRRRRRRRRRRRRRRRRRRRRRRRRRRRRRRRRRRRRRR
RRRRRRRRRRRRRRRRRRRRRRRRRRRRRRRRRRRRRRRRRRRRR
RRRRRRRRRRRRRRRRRRRRRRRRRRRRRRRRRRRRRRRRRRRRR
RRRRRRRRRRRRRRRRRRRRRRRRRRRRRRRRRRRRRRRRRRRRR
RRRRRRRRRRRRRRRRRRRRRRRRRRRRRRRRRRRRRRRRRRRRR
RRRRRRRRRRRRRRRRRRRRRRRRRRRRRRRRRRRRRRRRRRRRR
RRRRRRRRRRRRRRRRRRRRRRRRRRRRRRRRRRRRRRRRRRRRR
RRRRRRRRRRRRRRRRRRRRRRRRRRRRRRRRRRRRRRRRRRRRR
RRRRRRRRRRRRRRRRRRRRRRRRRRRRRRRRRRRRRRRRRRRRR
RRRRRRRRRRRRRRRRRRRRRRRRRRRRRRRRRRRRRRRRRRRRR
RRRRRRRRRRRRRRRRRRRRRRRRRRRRRRRRRRRRRRRRRRRRR
RRRRRRRRRRRRRRRRRRRRRRRRRRRRRRRRRRRRRRRRRRRRR
RRRRRRRRRRRRRRRRRRRRRRRRRRRRRRRRRRRRRRRRRRRRR

RRRRRRRRRRRRRRRRRRRRRRRRRRRRRRRRRRRRRRRRRRRR
RRRRRRRRRRRRRRRRRRRRRRRRRRRRRRRRRRRRRRRRRRRR
RRRRRRRRRRRRRRRRRRRRRRRRRRRRRRRRRRRRRRRRRRRR
RRRRRRRRRRRRRRRRRRRRRRRRRRRRRRRRRRRRRRRRRRRR
RRRRRRRRRRRRRRRRRRRRRRRRRRRRRRRRRRRRRRRRRRRR
RRRRRRRRRRRRRRRRRRRRRRRRRRRRRRRRRRRRRRRRRRRR
RRRRRRRRRRRRRRRRRRRRRRRRRRRRRRRRRRRRRRRRRRRR
RRRRRRRRRRRRRRRRRRRRRRRRRRRRRRRRRRRRRRRRRRRR
RRRRRRRRRRRRRRRRRRRRRRRRRRRRRRRRRRRRRRRRRRRR
RRRRRRRRRRRRRRRRRRRRRRRRRRRRRRRRRRRRRRRRRRRR
RRRRRRRRRRRRRRRRRRRRRRRRRRRRRRRRRRRRRRRRRRRR
RRRRRRRRRRRRRRRRRRRRRRRRRRRRRRRRRRRRRRRRRRRR
RRRRRRRRRRRRRRRRRRRRRRRRRRRRRRRRRRRRRRRRRRRR
RRRRRRRRRRRRRRRRRRRRRRRRRRRRRRRRRRRRRRRRRRRR
RRRRRRRRRRRRRRRRRRRRRRRRRRRRRRRRRRRRRRRRRRRR
RRRRRRRRRRRRRRRRRRRRRRRRRRRRRRRRRRRRRRRRRRRR
RRRRRRRRRRRRRRRRRRRRRRRRRRRRRRRRRRRRRRRRRRRR
RRRRRRRRRRRRRRRRRRRRRRRRRRRRRRRRRRRRRRRRRRRR
RRRRRRRRRRRRRRRRRRRRRRRRRRRRRRRRRRRRRRRRRRRR
RRRRRRRRRRRRRRRRRRRRRRRRRRRRRRRRRRRRRRRRRRRR
RRRRRRRRRRRRRRRRRRRRRRRRRRRRRRRRRRRRRRRRRRRR
RRRRRRRRRRRRRRRRRRRRRRRRRRRRRRRRRRRRRRRRRRRR
RRRRRRRRRRRRRRRRRRRRRRRRRRRRRRRRRRRRRRRRRRRR
RRRRRRRRRRRRRRRRRRRRRRRRRRRRRRRRRRRRRRRRRRRR
RRRRRRRRRRRRRRRRRRRRRRRRRRRRRRRRRRRRRRRRRRRR
RRRRRRRRRRRRRRRRRRRRRRRRRRRRRRRRRRRRRRRRRRRR
RRRRRRRRRRRRRRRRRRRRRRRRRRRRRRRRRRRRRRRRRRRR
RRRRRRRRRRRRRRRRRRRRRRRRRRRRRRRRRRRRRRRRRRRR
RRRRRRRRRRRRRRRRRRRRRRRRRRRRRRRRRRRRRRRRRRRR

RRRRRRRRRRRRRRRRRRRRRRRRRRRRRRRRRRRRRRRRRRRRR
RRRRRRRRRRRRRRRRRRRRRRRRRRRRRRRRRRRRRRRRRRRRR
RRRRRRRRRRRRRRRRRRRRRRRRRRRRRRRRRRRRRRRRRRRRR
RRRRRRRRRRRRRRRRRRRRRRRRRRRRRRRRRRRRRRRRRRRRR
RRRRRRRRRRRRRRRRRRRRRRRRRRRRRRRRRRRRRRRRRRRRR
RRRRRRRRRRRRRRRRRRRRRRRRRRRRRRRRRRRRRRRRRRRRR
RRRRRRRRRRRRRRRRRRRRRRRRRRRRRRRRRRRRRRRRRRRRR
RRRRRRRRRRRRRRRRRRRRRRRRRRRRRRRRRRRRRRRRRRRRR
RRRRRRRRRRRRRRRRRRRRRRRRRRRRRRRRRRRRRRRRRRRRR
RRRRRRRRRRRRRRRRRRRRRRRRRRRRRRRRRRRRRRRRRRRRR
RRRRRRRRRRRRRRRRRRRRRRRRRRRRRRRRRRRRRRRRRRRRR
RRRRRRRRRRRRRRRRRRRRRRRRRRRRRRRRRRRRRRRRRRRRR
RRRRRRRRRRRRRRRRRRRRRRRRRRRRRRRRRRRRRRRRRRRRR
RRRRRRRRRRRRRRRRRRRRRRRRRRRRRRRRRRRRRRRRRRRRR
RRRRRRRRRRRRRRRRRRRRRRRRRRRRRRRRRRRRRRRRRRRRR
RRRRRRRRRRRRRRRRRRRRRRRRRRRRRRRRRRRRRRRRRRRRR
RRRRRRRRRRRRRRRRRRRRRRRRRRRRRRRRRRRRRRRRRRRRR
RRRRRRRRRRRRRRRRRRRRRRRRRRRRRRRRRRRRRRRRRRRRR
RRRRRRRRRRRRRRRRRRRRRRRRRRRRRRRRRRRRRRRRRRRRR
RRRRRRRRRRRRRRRRRRRRRRRRRRRRRRRRRRRRRRRRRRRRR
RRRRRRRRRRRRRRRRRRRRRRRRRRRRRRRRRRRRRRRRRRRRR
RRRRRRRRRRRRRRRRRRRRRRRRRRRRRRRRRRRRRRRRRRRRR
RRRRRRRRRRRRRRRRRRRRRRRRRRRRRRRRRRRRRRRRRRRRR
RRRRRRRRRRRRRRRRRRRRRRRRRRRRRRRRRRRRRRRRRRRRR
RRRRRRRRRRRRRRRRRRRRRRRRRRRRRRRRRRRRRRRRRRRRR
RRRRRRRRRRRRRRRRRRRRRRRRRRRRRRRRRRRRRRRRRRRRR
RRRRRRRRRRRRRRRRRRRRRRRRRRRRRRRRRRRRRRRRRRRRR
RRRRRRRRRRRRRRRRRRRRRRRRRRRRRRRRRRRRRRRRRRRRR.

You did it. Not only do you have diamond hands, but you read a book that was 150 pages of GME GO BRRR. You most certainly do not have paper hands.  You are a legend, even if you are like me and only have 1 GME stonk! We will hodl the line together!

www.ingramcontent.com/pod-product-compliance
Lightning Source LLC
Chambersburg PA
CBHW080715120726

48001CB00010B/3023